BLACKPOOL LASS

A gritty, emotional tale of 1930s Blackpool from bestselling saga author Mary Wood, writing as Maggie Mason

Blackpool, 1932. When Grace's Ma passes away and her Da's ship sinks with all hands, Grace is utterly alone in the world. She's sent to an orphanage in Blackpool, but the master has an eye for a pretty young lass. Grace won't be his victim, so she runs, destitute, into the night. In Blackpool, she finds a home with the kindly Sheila and Peggy – and meets a lovely airman. But it's 1938, and war is on the horizon. Will Grace ever find the happiness and home she deserves?

BLACKPOOL LASS

BLACKPOOL LASS

by

Maggie Mason

Magna Large Print Books
Gargrave, North Yorkshire,
BD23 3SE, England.

British Library Cataloguing in Publication Data.

A catalogue record of this book is
available from the British Library

ISBN   978-0-7505-4731-4

First published in Great Britain in 2018 by Sphere

Published in Large Print 2019 by arrangement with
Little, Brown Book Group

Magna Large Print is an imprint of Library Magna Books Ltd.

Printed and bound in Great Britain by
T.J. (International) Ltd., Cornwall, PL28 8RW

To the memory of my dear brother Frank Olley, brother-in-law Frank Brough, and sister-in-law Marjorie Wood.

You all gave me your love, support and encouragement. Thank you – I was privileged to have you in my life.

PROLOGUE

1924–1932

Ma looked beautiful. Her shining red hair hung in ringlets. Grace, known by everyone as Gracie, put up her hand and gently pulled one, then giggled as it sprung back into a coil.

'Button up your coat, lass, the wind will fair cut through you.' Ma's smile twinkled with excitement and lit her deep blue eyes. 'Da's coming home, Gracie. The skipper's radioed the harbour master to say they'll be in by noon. And aye, word is they have a good catch, so it'll be fish and chips for supper, lass.'

Gracie hugged her body as a surge of happy feelings zinged through her. *Me da's coming, me da's coming!*

As they stepped out of their cottage on Fisherman's Way, in Mount Road, Fleetwood, just eight miles from the seaside resort of Blackpool, the wind that whipped off the Irish Sea caught Gracie's breath and lifted her bonnet. Her ma patted it back down, then squatted on her haunches and tied the ribbons tighter.

'It's strangling me now, Ma.'

'Well, it's that or lose your bonnet and have your lugs frozen off. Which do you want?'

The thought of her ears dropping off made Gracie's mind up. She'd stick with the bonnet.

11

The street suddenly filled with neighbours as the doors of all the other cottages opened, and women and children came out, dressed in their Sunday best, calling out to one another. 'It's a good catch they have.' 'Aye, we're in clover again.' 'I'm in for a new coat this time.' 'About time, Maud, that one's only just clinging to you, lass.'

Everyone laughed as Mrs Barton did a twirl. 'Nowt wrong with this. I mean, it's that old, it's back in fashion. You're only jealous, Polly. I'll tell you what. I'll pass it on to you, it has a good few years left in it.'

The sound of the women's laughter enhanced the feeling in five-year-old Gracie. Everyone was happy, and that happiness made her want to skip with the joy of it.

Aunt Massie popped her head out of her door. Her cottage was next to theirs. She wouldn't be coming down to the dock to greet the trawlers as her man worked in the fish shed, near to the railway, where they gutted and packed the fish. 'They're coming in, then, Brenda?' she called out to Ma.

'Aye.'

'You watch yourself, lass, you'll have your belly up again.'

Gracie wished Aunt Massie hadn't said this, as she knew there was always a sadness around her ma having her belly up. She'd see her ma bending over the bucket, throwing up, and her ma's belly would begin to swell, but then Ma would take to her bed and after a few days, Gracie would know that there wasn't going to be a babby, and she'd to look after her ma.

'Eeh, I didn't mean to dampen things, Brenda. I – I–'

'Naw. Don't worry about it. I hope it does happen, and that this time I manage to carry it full time. It's funny, but I had no trouble carrying our Gracie.'

'Aye, and no trouble since, she's a little darling, and if you have no more, you've been blessed. Me and Percy don't want another.' She laughed and nudged Ma. 'Our Reggie's enough for any mother to cope with. Anyroad, hang on a mo, I'll walk a ways with you. I've nowt spoiling. Let me get me shawl.'

When Aunt Massie came out again, she had Reggie with her. She linked arms with Ma and they giggled together. Reggie fell into step with Gracie. 'Can I come to the dock with you, Gracie? I like the boats.'

'Naw, you'll be in the way. Only those greeting their man go to the docks.'

Reggie kicked a stone. 'Well, you can't stop me from sitting on the rocks and watching.'

'Please yourself.'

On the quayside, everyone scanned the horizon. A silence that held friendship and a feeling of being all in this together settled around Gracie. Even Mrs Tonge, whom everyone called Mrs Wagging-Tongue, was quiet for once as she held her hand above her brow and looked out to sea.

'There! Look. I can see the first trawler!'

A cheer went up. Gracie did a little dance and clapped her hands.

Happiness filled her as she watched the tiny specks that looked as though they were on the

13

edge of the world, where the sky met the sea, gradually become bigger and bigger.

The women began to wave and call out the names of their husbands. Gracie copied them, calling out, 'Da, Da!' and knew such joy as the boat docked and her da waved.

Impatiently, she waited while the fish were unloaded, listening to the banter of the women and their husbands and sons as they called out to one another.

And then he was there. A giant of a man. The most handsome of all the men.

Dropping his rucksack, he ran to Ma, picked her up and twirled her around, holding her tiny waist in his big strong hands. 'Me Brenda, me lass. Your man's home, lass.'

After giving Ma a kiss on her lips, that made Gracie blush and had her looking around to see what everyone thought, only to find that all the men and women were doing the same, her da spotted her. 'Me Gracie, me little Gracie. Come here, little one.' Her da's huge hands wrapped around her and took her to soar in the air above his head. 'You're the prettiest lass in Fleetwood, me little Gracie.' With this he lowered her and tickled her tummy with the top of his head, before he swung her onto his shoulders.

Her joy released from her in squeals as this was the best place in the world for Gracie. She clung on to her da, wrapping her arms around his neck. But once her da had hold of her ankles, she knew that she was safe, and let go, to run her fingers through her da's black curly hair.

He smelt of tobacco, and fish, and sweat, smells

that should have had her wrinkling her nose, but instead filled her with the knowledge that her da was home and this was how love smelt.

Eight years had passed since that happy day and the time had wrought change. Many babbies had left her ma's womb without ever breathing life and each had taken its toll on her ma.

Gracie stood at the window of their cottage and watched the happy wives running to the shore, while her own ma lay in her bed, her life ebbing from her.

No happiness entered Gracie at the thought of her da coming home, only dread. The trusting little child that she'd been was long gone. For she had found out that there were many kinds of love and ways that love can be used, and that a love that had once sustained you could destroy you, too.

Now, her da wasn't someone to welcome home, but someone to fear.

PART ONE

1932–1933

AT THE MERCY OF OTHERS

CHAPTER ONE

The creak of the floorboards had Gracie stiffening. Outside, though mid-August, the wind howled, and the sound of the crashing waves drowned out most noises. But Gracie had her ear tuned in to any sign that her da was coming to her attic bedroom.

Sitting up in bed and staring at the trap door that she had to climb through to get to her bed, she prayed to a God who rarely listened to her to not let it open. But the iron ring-handle began to turn.

A tear ran down Gracie's cheek. At thirteen years old, she had more than her share to cope with. This tiny, one up, one down cottage, with space made in the attic for her bed, housed her misery. Money was short as her da didn't often get taken on the trawlers these days.

Her ma's sickness had ravaged her body and had her coughing up blood and gunge. She never left her bed. Gracie cared for her and did all the chores around the home. And though a clever child, she rarely attended school, only doing so when her granny came to stay. Granny lived in Blackpool and would come to care for her daughter and granddaughter, but Da hated her, and wouldn't have her in the house when he was at home.

'Gracie, me little Gracie. Aren't you me darlin'

girl, eh?'

'Naw, Da. Go away. Please don't touch me, I'll scream for me ma!'

'Ha, your ma's on cloud nine, me lovely Gracie. I gave her the night medicine, and she is in a world of peace. Now, give your da a kiss.'

Beery breath wafted over Gracie, and she tasted the stale smoke that mingled with the smell of the drink. Her da's large hand cupped her tiny breast.

'Naw, Da. It ain't right, you doing this to me.' With all the strength that she could muster she pushed him away, but though he lost his balance for a moment, he swayed back towards her.

'I don't hurt you, do I, me Gracie? I just like to fondle you. You like to please your da, don't you? It's nice what I do, ain't it?'

'You're drunk, Da. And I'm warning you, I'll tell me granny this time. I will.'

'That sour puss. I'd sooner drown her as look at her. She won't come near me, she's scared of me. But you ain't, are you, Gracie? You're me little girl. Move up, let me lay beside you.'

The bed creaked under his weight. His bulk shoved Gracie to the edge of the mattress. Her body stiffened. She daren't scream; although she'd tried to frighten her da away by saying she would, she'd never want to wake her ma. When she was awake her ma was in constant pain.

Silently, she endured her da squeezing her breasts, then running his hand down to her leg and pulling up her nightie, while he moaned her name in a funny way.

Holding her legs tightly together, Gracie found her voice and begged him to stop. Something in

20

what she said, and her sobs, finally got through to him. He rolled off the bed.

'Don't be telling your ma, or your granny, will you, our Gracie? This is our little secret. Your da didn't mean it. It were the drink. I forgot meself. I didn't hurt you, did I?'

'Naw, Da, you didn't hurt me, now go away, I'm tired.'

She wanted to scream that though he hadn't hurt her body, he had hurt her heart. But despite it all, Gracie loved her da.

And, the next morning, as she stood on the door-step of the pub with an enamel jug, her eyes swollen from crying, her stomach rumbling for the want of food, she tried to hold on to the memories she visited often, of the days before her ma's illness changed everything – happy, carefree days.

Reluctantly, she handed over the shilling that would have bought some tatties and a few meaty bones to make a stew, but instead would pay for the jug to be filled with ale.

Within an hour, with the jug empty, her da left the house. Gracie heard the door click shut as she tucked the clean sheet she'd put on the bed around her ma.

'Bill?'

'Me da's gone out, Ma. Rest now.'

Gracie's heart ached to see her ma so ill. Her beauty was gone, her hair lay lank on the pillow, and the freckles that had once dotted her face had joined together and left her skin yellow. Her eyes didn't twinkle any more, but drooped with pain.

Gracie knew that she took after her ma in looks. At least how Ma had used to look. Now it was Gracie's hair that was a vibrant red and hung in ringlets, and her eyes that were as blue as the sky. She shuddered as her da's words came to her. 'You've the beauty and passion in you that your ma once had, me Gracie.'

Gracie didn't want to understand what he meant.

As her ma closed her eyes, Gracie scooped up the pile of soiled bed linen, took it down the stone stairs to the kitchen-cum-living room and then through the door to the yard. Outside she dragged the tin bath nearer to the well that stood in the centre of the yard, and pumped buckets and buckets of water to fill the bath with, enjoying the sound of the water hitting the metal, till the work became harder.

Dunking the sheets into the water, she'd leave them to soak for an hour, while she filled the copper that stood in the corner of the kitchen and set a fire underneath it. While it came to the boil, she'd grate some soap, then she'd drop that and the sheets into the copper for ten minutes. She'd have them rinsed, mangled and blowing on the line by midday.

In this warm breeze, they'd dry enough to air off in front of the fire, ready to change her ma's bed once more. A job that she had to do twice a day, and sometimes in the night, too.

Once she had the bits of flotsam burning under the copper, Gracie stretched her aching limbs. She'd have to make another trip to the beach to collect whatever was burnable out of what was washed up there. There was no money to pay the coalman, and he'd said last time that he'd not leave any more until her da paid him for at least one of the hundredweight bags he owed him for.

As the sun shone down on her, the child that Gracie was surfaced and her empty belly took all her thoughts. Maybe if her ma was peaceful she could get Aunt Massie to sit with her while she went to her granny's. Aunt Massie wasn't her real aunt, but her and Ma had been friends since they were babbies and she looked out for Gracie, and loved her like a real aunt would.

Gracie knew that if she could get to her granny, she would give her a threepence and she could buy some fish and chips and sit on Blackpool promenade and eat them. She could collect flotsam from the beach on her way home.

'Reggie, are you there?'

Reggie often bunked off school. Gracie could hear him kicking a ball in the next yard. There was a scrambling sound and she saw his head pop up above the wall that divided their yards. 'What's up, Gracie?'

'Will you ask your ma to look out for me ma while I visit me granny, Reggie?'

'Aye, just a mo. I'll come with you if you like.'

'Naw, I don't want no school board man on me back. They'll be looking for you.'

'And not you, then?'

'I'm exempt, on account of me ma needing me. They knaw I can only attend when me granny comes to stay. They never knaw when me da's in dock, so they don't take into account that he could sit with me ma.'

Gracie hoped this dissuaded Reggie. She liked him well enough, but she didn't want him tagging along. He was all right most of the time, but she always had to do what he wanted her to, or he'd sulk, and she liked to be free of shackles at times.

As soon as she had the sheets on the line, a task Aunt Massie helped her with, Gracie had grabbed her bonnet and set out for her granny's. She'd made good time as she hadn't gone far when the rumbling of the tram could be heard in the distance. When it slowed near to her, Gracie knew Joe Pike, who lived in a cottage a few up from hers, would be driving it. He always gave her a free ride into Blackpool.

From a family of eight lads, Joe was the only son who hadn't become a fisherman, instead training to be a tram driver. He'd surprised everyone, as he was what you'd term a penny short of a shilling. Gracie loved Joe's simple outlook on life.

'You going to your granny's, Gracie?'

Joe always stated the obvious – there would be no other reason for her to go to Blackpool – but she nodded and smiled.

On the tram, she stood in the space left for pushchairs – she daren't take a seat, for she'd have a few moaning at Joe if she did. The regulars didn't mind Gracie having a free ride, as long as she knew her place. Though today, being a Tuesday, there were a lot of strangers packing the tram. Holidaymakers loaded with bags of bargains they'd bought from Fleetwood Market, a favourite haunt that brought trippers to Fleetwood.

Gracie watched as the houses seemed to float

by, and then the posh Rossall School came into view and disappeared as they entered Cleveleys. Soon she could see the coastline. The Irish Sea was calm now. Often it was so after a night of storms. Today it looked a lovely blue. Usually it was choppy, grey and murky.

Gracie loved Blackpool and a familiar tingle started up in her stomach as they trundled along. Queens Parade, North Shore and the Gynn Inn came into view. Hotels and boarding houses lined the Promenade, and an ice-cream van stood on a beach dotted with deckchairs.

This was the quiet end. Soon they would reach the North Pier and travel the Golden Mile, a part of Blackpool where an aroma of fish and chips and hot doughnuts vied with the smell of the salty sea. Noise whipped up excitement as music rang out from a mechanical organ. No one played it – a man just fed the organ with cards punched through with a thousand holes. It was like magic! And then there were the penny arcades that shone with bright lights and emitted jingling noises as the handles of the many machines were pulled by a punter hoping for the jackpot. And the stall-holders shouted their wares, or called out, 'A penny a go! Hit a coconut and win a prize!'

Amidst it all, the wonderful Blackpool Tower rose up and stood majestic. Once Gracie's teacher had shown her a picture of the Eiffel Tower, and as she looked up now, she thought that their tower looked as though it had walked from Paris and plonked itself down on top of a building. Gracie loved it all.

'Better get off at the next stop, Gracie, I can't

take you any further in case the inspector gets on. Say hello to your granny for me.'

The tram had stopped just past the tower. Gracie thanked Joe as she alighted, and then ran all the way to Central Pier, before taking a breather. Her granny lived a good mile from there and Gracie was already feeling weary. Slowing her pace, she eventually saw South Pier come into view. Rawcliffe Road, where her granny's cottage was, jutted off the Prom, almost opposite the pier.

As she neared the turning and was about to cross the road, a break in the crowds milling around on the Prom gave her sight of the rock stall.

'Hey, want to buy some rock? Lovely Blackpool rock!'

Gracie was surprised to see a girl manning the stall. Usually an old man stood on the stall near to the pier selling the sticks of pink and gaily striped rock, which, no matter how many times you broke pieces off it, magically had the name of Blackpool showing through its centre. The girl had long dark hair tied in bunches that stuck out from each side of her head. These were wrapped with bows of pink ribbon. She wore a bright pink checked dress, covered by a white pinny, of the sort that went over your head and tied under each of your arms. She smiled at Gracie. 'Buy some rock, love, me trade's slow today.'

'Do I look as though I can afford rock? Eeh, I'd love some, but I've nowt to me name.'

'Here, I have some chippings, you can have them if you like. Sometimes, I have to cut the long sticks as the punters won't buy them, and I have these bits that I pack into bags. I sell them for a farthing, but you can have them for free. Me name's Sheila, what's yourn?'

'Ta, ever so much. Me name's Grace. Most folk call me Gracie.'

'Why ain't you in school, Gracie?'

Between sucking and chewing the delicious, sticky rock pieces, Gracie told Sheila a bit about her life.

'Eeh, that's sad. I've just started to run me ma's rock stall. Me grandda used to do it, but he's not strong enough now. School let me leave. Well, I ain't very clever, and anyroad once you have a job, they're happy to let you go.'

'But you only look the same age as me – just on thirteen.'

'I'm thirteen and a half. And once you're that close to leaving, they can't wait to get rid of you. I hated school anyroad.'

Gracie smiled. She liked Sheila. She envied her her job, selling the colourful rock, and seeming to be clear of troubles, only worrying if she sold enough to keep her ma going.

She learned that Sheila's ma made the rock in her back kitchen. Her da worked as a clown in the Tower Circus, but only brought in what he could collect in his bucket after his performance.

'That ain't never much, despite him being the funniest clown ever. I'll get tickets for the circus for you if you like. They're free to me. I go to most evening performances. I'd love to be a clown, but it's man's work.'

The thought of going to the Tower Circus thrilled Gracie. 'Really? Eeh, Sheila, I'd love that.'

27

'Well, you come here on the day that you can go to the circus, and I'll make arrangements to meet you there.'

When she left Sheila, Gracie skipped along, thinking that this was the best day ever. She'd made a friend. And one who would take her to the circus! Dreams did come true.

If only, by the time she got home, her da could say that he had a trip on a trawler, and her ma could feel better, then everything in her world would be wonderful.

Granny was sat on her doorstep. The front door of her terraced house led straight onto the street and stood wide open behind her. As Gracie walked towards her, her granny looked at her, but didn't seem to register it was her.

'Granny?'

Still the vacant look. Granny was getting forgetful, and this worried Gracie. A few weeks back, a man had brought her to their door, saying he'd found her wandering and that she'd given their address as the place she was trying to make for. Luckily, Da had been out at the pub, and after seeing that her daughter was still there, Granny had let Gracie take her back home. That time, Granny had enough money in her purse for Gracie to pay for them both on the tram, but she'd had to walk back as she couldn't get Granny to understand that she needed her fare, and she wouldn't take it from her purse.

For a moment Granny's vacant look frightened Gracie, but then Granny suddenly smiled and said, 'Eeh, me Brenda, it's you. I thought I recognised you. Come here, me darling.'

'No, it's me, Granny. Gracie.' Gracie's fear deepened. Was her granny losing her marbles? But no. Old people did get forgetful, it was to be expected.

Confusion crossed Granny's face. 'Gracie?'

'Yes. Your Brenda's daughter. Me ... Gracie.'

'Eeh, Gracie, me little love. I thought as you were your ma there for a mo. By, you get more like her. Come in, I've some lemonade, and no doubt, you need a bite to eat?'

Going into her granny's arms shocked Gracie, as Granny no longer felt plump and squidgy. 'Are you eating, Granny? You're losing weight, you feel like a bag of bones.'

Granny laughed at her, showing her one tooth hanging down in the front of her mouth. Her face lit up, giving a hint of the beauty that she must have been. Her hair, still thick, had turned wiry, and was what was termed salt and pepper in colour as her grey didn't completely cover the red that it had once been. Her eyes shone the same blue as Ma's and Gracie's did.

'Course, I am. I made a stew, and there's some left for you an' all.'

When Gracie entered the little kitchen that lay at the back of the house, a smell met her that had her wrinkling her nose. The source was a saucepan on the stove. In it was the remains of a stew that must have stood a week as it had a growth of mould on the top of it. 'Eeh, Granny, you haven't been eating that have you? It's reeking.'

'I don't knaw.' A tear trickled from Granny's eyes.

The fear that Gracie had banished shot back

into her. 'Are you all right, Granny?'

'Aye, I am. I'm just tired. And when I get like this, I don't know what day it is. I'll be reet. Eeh, now you've mentioned food, me belly's dropping out.'

'I'll clean this up, and then I'll run along to the chippy, how would that be, eh?'

'Just the ticket, lass. Just the ticket. I'll fetch me purse.'

With Granny sat on the step once more with the newspaper containing her fish and chips on her lap and a trail of vinegar running down her chin, she looked her old self again. The food seemed to put her mind back in order, too, as she chatted normally and asked after her daughter, and when Gracie thought her da might get a trip on a trawler so that she could come and visit.

Gracie's concern for her granny lightened. 'I'll eat me fish and chips on the way, Granny. Only I can't leave Aunt Massie too long, she's good to me, but I don't want to take advantage. Promise me that you'll eat regular, Granny. Promise me.'

'I will, lass. I just forget when I last ate some-times, that's all. Here, take enough money from me purse for your fare, you can't walk all that way, it'll take you hours.'

Gracie dug out the penny that she'd need. 'Ta, Granny, I'm grateful for it. Me legs don't feel as though they'll carry me to Fleetwood.'

'Give me a kiss, then, lass, and get on your way.'

'Wipe your chin first. Ha, you'll cover me in grease!'

Granny laughed again, and Gracie's heart

warmed with love for her.

Walking along the Prom eating her fish and chips, a good feeling, like she hadn't known for a long time, came into Gracie. She wouldn't let her mind visit her worries over her granny, her ma and her da. Life was good at this moment. She was filling her belly with the delicious fish and chips, the breeze was blowing her hair, waves were lapping at the beach and her step was light.

Her new friend had called out to her as she'd passed, and she'd shared a couple of chips with her and then had promised that she'd see her soon, before walking on.

She could see the Blackpool Tower ahead as she stopped and leant on the railings and looked out to sea. She'd have to finish her chips before catching a tram as eating food on the tram was forbidden.

Clutching the fish that she'd saved till last close to her chest, Gracie kept a wary eye on the seagulls as they swooped above her. Their noise was deafening. They knew there was food in the offing. *Well, you ain't having any of mine, you've plenty in the sea, you lazy so and sos.* As she thought this, one of them stretched itself in an elegant dive and plunged into the water, a sight Gracie never grew tired of. For all their noise and their stealing of folk's food, she admired the huge birds. They went hand-in-glove with all that she'd ever known – the sea, the fishing boats and magical Blackpool.

Paying her fare and taking a seat some ten minutes later, Gracie remembered she'd to collect some flotsam for the fires. She knew that she wouldn't have a problem doing so: after the roughness of the sea the night before, there'd be plenty of it on the nearest beach to her home, even if others had been out before her. And with the conditions how they were now, surely her da would get a boat to take him on tonight? She hoped so. With all her heart, she hoped so.

CHAPTER TWO

'So, what did the old bag have to say, then? I'm warning you, our Gracie, I'll do that wizened old hag in if you've said owt to her.'

'I ain't, Da. I went 'cause I were hungry and there was nowt here to eat.'

'Aye, well, I'm sorry. I didn't realise, and I'm sorry if I scared you last night. It were the drink. I'd never hurt you, me little Gracie. I just look for comfort, that's all. Look, I've left a couple of bob on the table. That'll get you some food and pay the doctor. I'm going to the dock to see if I can get set on. Make sure you get the doctor to your ma, she seems worse this evening.'

Not letting him off by acknowledging his apology, Gracie picked up the coins and pocketed them in case her da changed his mind. 'See you later, Da.'

She didn't hear if her da replied as she ran upstairs to her ma.

The change in her ma since this morning shocked Gracie, as did seeing Aunt Massie still sat with her. 'Eeh, Aunt Massie, I didn't expect to see you here with me da being back. How's me ma?'

'I couldn't leave her with him, Gracie. He were that drunk when he came in. He's slept all afternoon. Anyroad, your ma hasn't had a good day, but she's sleeping now. I'm worried about her though, lass, she's not had a drop of water pass her lips.'

'I'll run for the doctor, if you can stay a few minutes more.'

'I can't, lass. Your uncle Percy'll be in from the fish sheds soon, and'll want his supper. I'll send our Reggie for the doctor. You try to get your ma to drink. She might take it from you. Poor love.'

'Ta, Aunt Massie. I don't knaw what I'd do without your help.' As she said this, Gracie doubled over as a gripping pain clenched her stomach. At the same time, a wetness came from her and dampened her knickers.

'Are you all right, love? You've gone very pale.'

'Eeh, Aunt Massie, I think I've wet me knickers, and yet I didn't feel as if I wanted a pee.'

'That'll be your monthly starting, I shouldn't wonder. Have you had them before?'

'Naw.' A fear shook Gracie as she realised what was happening. The last time she was at school, Betty Makham was boasting that she'd started her monthlies and had all the girls in awe as she explained what they were. Gracie hadn't liked the sound of them at all, and had wondered about the mess they would make, but Betty had said that you just pinned some rag into your knickers and that saw to catching the blood.

'Don't look so scared, lass, you must have known they would come. Have you got owt to protect

33

yourself with? An old sheet that you can rip up, maybe? Eeh, you're a woman now, lass. And you're to watch what you do. Don't be letting no lads touch you, as you'll cop for a babby.'

Gracie's fear deepened. She wanted to scream out that her da touched her, and that she didn't want a babby.

'Look, I'll wait here a mo while you see to yourself. Now stop worrying, it's a natural process. I'll come back later to have a little talk with you. One that your ma would have if she could. Well, I'll do it for her. Come here and have a hug, love. You've a lot on your plate for a young un.'

Going into Aunt Massie's arms gave Gracie a good feeling. As did the gentle stroking of her hair.

'Eeh, I allus wanted a daughter, Gracie, and look on you as that. I'm allus here for you, you knaw that.'

A tear plopped onto Gracie's cheek.

'Now, none of that. Like I say, lass you're to get on with it. Go on, get yourself sorted.'

As Gracie found some odd bits of sheeting and some pins in her ma's old sewing basket, she remembered her ma saying: 'These bits will come in handy for dusters, or I might just start that quilting I've allus wanted to do. I can practise with these before buying some good bits of material from the market. Just to see if I'm any good at it.'

How long ago was that? Gracie couldn't remember, but long enough for her ma not to have even considered the use that Gracie was going to put them to now.

Once she was comfortable again, she went back

to her ma and Aunt Massie.

'There, are you all right now? Good. But I can see you don't feel well, me darling. Don't worry, that usually only lasts for the first day. If your tummy gets really bad, sit with a hot water bottle pressed against it. Well, I'm away back home. You concentrate on your ma, and think no more of what's happening to you.'

As she passed Gracie, Aunt Massie hugged her to her once more. 'You'll be fine, lass.'

Gracie had listened many times to tales of what Aunt Massie and her ma got up to, from when they were kids until they grew to be young women. She'd seen pictures of them laughing together. They'd had such fun and had always looked out for one another. Gracie had often thought that she would like a friend like that, but with not going to school often and not able to play out, the girls in the row had formed alliances that didn't include her. They weren't nasty to her, but she just didn't feel like one of them.

The photos had shown that Aunt Massie hadn't been the beauty her ma had been. Her dark hair had always been frizzy rather than having the soft ringlet curls that her ma had, and her face had a sort of flat appearance, with small eyes and nose, and yet her mouth was wide and always ready with a smile, which changed her and gave her a loveliness of a different kind. Her heart was of gold, and everyone loved her. Most felt sorry for her as she was ruled by her husband who was much older than her, and by her son who copied his da's attitude, to the point that Aunt Massie could hardly move without their say so. But they never objected to her looking out for Gracie's ma, which was a blessing.

'Ta ever so much, Aunt Massie. I'm sorry I were so long away. But I'm glad as you were here, I feel better for your help. I'll let you knaw what the doctor says.'

'Eeh, lass. Me heart goes out to you.'

Gracie couldn't answer this as the tears threatened again, and she'd to be strong for her ma.

When the doctor arrived, he took one look at Ma and shook his head.

'Now, Gracie, it is that you have to prepare yourself, your ma isn't long for this world. I'm sorry, wee one, but I think that she will go to heaven in the next couple of days. She'll probably be hanging on till your pappy comes home, though. And, it is that I'm powerful sorry for your lot, wee one.'

Gracie knew an acceptance over this news from the doctor. A lovely Irish man, he'd looked after everyone in Fleetwood for as long as she could remember, often refusing payment and being content with anything they could manage – a jar of jam, or a dish they'd made from the fish their men had brought home.

'It's glad that I am that you are taking it like this, but we have to take care of you, too. The reality will hit you and it is then that you will feel the pain. Come to see me when that happens. Now, it is pasty you look, are you feeling all right?'

'I am, Doctor, I've just got me monthly for the first time, that's all.' She could talk to the doctor like that, he understood, and she didn't feel embarrassed.

'Aye, well, I expect you'll be having some questions, then?'

'Naw. Aunt Massie is going to have a chat with me later. I think she will stay most of the night, as it looks like me da got set on the trawler, as he hasn't come back home, though he could be in the pub.'

'I wasn't for seeing him. I dropped me flask off for the landlord to fill with a drop of whisky for me. I like a tipple afore I take to me bed at night. His pub was empty and he told me that a good few trawlers had gone out and that all the men had been set on. So that'll be good news for you. Now, I'll be on me way, your dear ma will sleep for a good few hours with that medicine I managed to get into her.'

'I have a shilling for you, Doctor, here you go.'

'No, you keep it, little one. Your need is for being greater than mine.'

'Ta, Doctor. I do need it for food, we've nowt in the cupboard, and me da only gave me this just afore he went out.'

'Is it nothing at all that you have, and all the shops closed now? That's a wicked shame, so it is.'

'I can go around the back of Mr Winter's store, he'll serve me with some tatties and flour and stuff. He might even have a hock that I can boil, and I can mix some bread dough once I have the flour and leave it to prove and then cook it off in the morning, I'll be fine.'

'You're a good girl, Gracie. Now, you listen carefully to what Aunt Massie will tell you, and be doing as she says. You have a look that will drive the boys wild, so you have, and temptation will cross your path. It is that you will be having a hard time turning the young men away, but it is important that you do.'

Gracie blushed.

The doctor didn't say any more as he left.

Aunt Massie sat on the doorstep with Gracie. The moon was up and the air was warm. They sipped their tea.

'I'm glad Mr Winter served you, lass. He's a good-un. What did you get?'

'He let me have all that I needed – tatties, flour, eggs, margarine and a hock, and it only cost me one and a tanner, so I've a bit left over. I'll catch the milkman in the morning and get a couple of pints, then I'll be set.'

'Right, afore you have to go back up to your ma, I'll tell you what you need to know, lass. Then I'll go home for a while, and come back at midnight, so you can go to your bed. I can stay till about four, then I'll get you up, is that okay?

'Aye, that's grand, ta, Aunt Massie.'

Gracie listened to what Aunt Massie termed *the birds and the bees*, though what she said didn't seem to have anything to do with these creatures and a lot to do with what Gracie's da did to her. She hoped with all her heart that he never did what Aunt Massie said that a man would have to do to her to give her a babby; she couldn't bear that. Not her own da, she couldn't.

'So, do you understand what I'm saying, then, lass?'

'Aye, I do.'

'Good, we'll say no more about it. Now, I forgot to tell you, I sent Reggie to tell your granny that your da's away. The lad should be back soon and no doubt with your granny in tow, bless her. Having her here will ease your mind and be a comfort. And if she does come, you can maybe get a bit more sleep than you're in for as things stand.'

When the door closed on Aunt Massie, loneliness engulfed Gracie. She sat in the chair next to her ma's bed, and took her ma's small cold hand in hers. With all her heart, she wanted to share with her ma what was happening to her, and to receive her comfort and help. Suddenly, the knot inside her burst and she bent her head and sobbed.

'I'm here, Brenda, me darling.'

Granny! Oh, Granny!

Taking the steps, two at a time, Gracie went into her granny's arms.

'Eeh, lass. I've not seen you this good while. Where have you been?'

'I came to see you this afternoon, remember, Granny?'

A vacant look crossed her granny's face.

'We had fish and chips. You loved them and had grease all down your chin.'

Granny's cackling didn't lift the heaviness that pressed on Gracie's chest. *Poor Granny, I can tell as she don't remember. She's just laughing to cover her confusion.*

This thought was borne out as Granny changed the subject: 'Well, him as thinks he's the big-I-am has gone, then? Good. Hope he never comes back. Now, get kettle on, lass, your granny feels like she's spitting feathers. I'll go up and see our Brenda.'

Though Granny's mind seemed to be failing her, her body was strong. She climbed the stairs like a youngster.

When Gracie arrived in the bedroom, she found her gran bending over Ma, talking to her and not seeming to notice that Ma wasn't answering her.

'Here's your tea, Granny. Sit down in the comfy armchair, I'll sit on the floor.'

The bedroom, like the whole of the cottage, was sparsely furnished. The big double bed took up most of the room, and beside that stood an arm-chair with horsehair poking through the many holes in its grey upholstery. It had long wooden arms, which were almost back to the natural wood they were made of as very little varnish remained on them. A threadbare rug covered the floor-boards. Under the window, the chest of drawers showed its age, as its drawers had lost their handles and had to be opened by pulling the screws that were still in place. Ma had bought it from a second-hand shop a few years back.

'Mmm, you make a nice cuppa, lass. How old are you now? I've not seen you since you were a nipper.'

Gracie ignored this. When Granny was con-fused, arguing with her only made her frustrated. 'I'm thirteen, Granny, and I started me monthly today!'

Somehow, the fact had gone from being fright-ening to something to be proud of, and Gracie wanted everyone to know.

'Umph! You keep your legs closed then, lass. Them lads'll be sniffing around you now. You'll be like a dog on heat to them.'

'Granny!'

'It's true. And you come to see your granny more often as well. I won't be here for ever, and then you'll be sorry.'

A pain cut through Gracie's heart. She didn't want her granny to have thoughts like this.

A moan from her ma took her attention. 'Ma? What is it, does you want something?'

'G – Gracie?'

'I'm here, Ma.'

'I – I love you, m – me Gracie.'

'I knaws as you do, Ma. Don't try to talk. Granny's here.'

'M – Ma?'

'I'm here, me darling Brenda. You'll be all right, lass, I'm going to make you better.'

A small smile crossed Ma's face. 'A – and Bill?'

'What d'yer want to ask after that oaf for?'

'Shush, Granny. Da's got taken on, Ma. He'll most likely be gone a few days.'

Ma's eyes closed. A feeling settled in Gracie that what the doctor had said was true. Ma wouldn't go to her rest until Da came home. Gracie wished that she'd never go, and yet, she wanted her out of pain.

'I'll lay on the bed with you, Ma. Me and Granny won't leave you.'

Two days later the shattering news came that one of the trawlers that had gone out on the night her da had left had sent an SOS. It hadn't been heard of since. The reports were of a freak storm that had raged off the coast of Ireland where they had been fishing.

Gracie knew a pain of a different kind enter her as she heard the rumours. The pain surprised her as there had been times that she'd prayed that her da wouldn't come home. Now she prayed with all her heart that he would. *Please don't let it be his boat, please God.*

CHAPTER THREE

Crowds of anguished women lined the quayside. All stared out to sea. The boat that had sunk had been named as the *Herald,* but none of the women knew which boat their man was on.

Gracie stood among them. Their sobs and whispered chatter vied with the waves of the sea. Waves that lapped rather than crashed, as if they were innocent of any wrongdoing, and it was hard to imagine one of the huge trawlers being smashed to pieces by them. But then Gracie had seen them at their angriest, and knew the destruction they were capable of.

The harbour master walked up to them holding a paper in his hand. All eyes turned towards him, fearful of what he might tell them.

'Ladies, I regret to inform you that the men lost with the *Herald* are as follows: Captain Mike Anderson...'

The names droned on. Gracie held her breath, counting them off. They were men she knew well. Around her there were gasps of pain as each lost man's wife registered her grief. Then it came: 'Bill Rimmer...'

'Naw... Naw, not me da... Naw!'

An arm came around her. She looked up into Aunt Massie's face. 'Eeh, lass, me little lass. I'm sorry.'

'Naw, Aunt Massie, naw.'

'Come on. It'll take a while to sink in. Let's go home.'

'But me ma's waiting for him, she...' Gracie couldn't say that she was waiting to see him before she let go and went to heaven.

'I knaw. We will have to tell her so that she can get her release. I'm sorry, me darling. If I could make your lot better, I would.'

Gracie's mind seemed to twirl with all that went through it. *I'll be an orphan! I'll have no one but me granny, and she can't take care of me!*

'W – what will happen to me, Aunt Massie? They won't take me into care, will they?'

Aunt Massie didn't answer, didn't say what Gracie hoped she would – that she would take her in. But then, that was a decision that she'd not be able to make. Gracie knew her heart would want her to, but Uncle Percy would have sommat to say and Gracie couldn't see him saying yes.

Granny clapped her hands in glee at the news.

'Naw, Mrs Peirce, that ain't no way to behave. You have to think of Gracie. Bill were her dad and for all his faults she loved him.'

At this from Aunt Massie, Granny's arms enclosed Gracie. 'I knaw you loved him, lass, but he weren't worthy of that love. Anyroad, that don't matter at a time like this, and Granny's sorry. I'm here for you, me little darling. I'm here for you.'

To find Granny lucid was a relief and a comfort to Gracie and the thought came to her that she and her granny would take care of each other.

'We have to tell your Brenda, Mrs Peirce, and you know what that will mean, don't you?'

'Aye. I do. But I can't bear it. I can't.'

'You're to be strong for Gracie.'

'We'll be strong together, for Ma, Granny. We can do it for her.' With this a strength came into Gracie. She didn't know where it came from, but something told her that she was needed more than ever now. Her ma needed her to help her to pass over, and her granny needed her to take care of her and to help her to bear it all.

'Come on. I'll be the one to tell me ma.'

'Are you sure, Gracie?'

'I am. I want to do it for me da.'

On hearing the news, a terrible gasp came from her ma. It cut into Gracie's heart. The sound undid Granny; she'd been stroking Ma's hair, but now she let go and buried her face in her hands as if to hide from what was happening.

'Brenda, lass, he's waiting for you. He went first so that he could be there for you.'

Aunt Massie's words helped Gracie. *Yes, me da will greet me ma, and she won't feel alone. I allus worried about that, and now I don't have to.*

Ma became still. Climbing on to the bed next

44

to her, Gracie put her arm around her. 'I love you, Ma. Don't worry about me. Me Granny will take care of me.'

Granny lifted her head from her hands. 'Aye, I will, me Brenda. I'll look out for Gracie. She can come and live with me. She can have your old bed.'

Ma's face changed. A smile formed on her dry, cracked lips. Then, her body gave a deep sigh and became stiller than Gracie had ever known a body to be. 'Ma ... oh, Ma!'

Pain like she'd never felt entered Gracie. It took all of her into its depth and though she didn't think it possible, it increased with the anguished cry of her granny, 'Brenda, me Brenda, me little girl ... naw, naw.'

Gracie turned away. Wanting to be released from all the hurt and fear, she pulled her knees up till they were under her chin. *Help me... Please help me!*

A hand touched her. 'Come on, lass. We need to send for the doctor. Give your ma a kiss. Say your goodbyes. She's happy now and out of pain. And I bet she's already in your da's arms, and they're like the lovebirds they used be before your ma took ill.'

The picture was a nice one but it was tainted with bad memories for Gracie. She wanted things to be how her Aunt Massie said, but her mind gave her the feel of her da's hands pawing her and she opened her mouth and screamed. The scream rasped her throat, making her retch.

'Quick, Mrs Peirce, bring the goes-under over here. Poor mite's going to be sick.'

45

After the doctor had been, giving his condolences and a piece of paper that said her ma had died of cancer, and the date and the time, Granny said, 'We need to lay her out, Massie.'

'Yes, we do. I'd be honoured to help. Would you like to help, Gracie?'

'What is it? What do we do?'

'We give your ma a nice wash down, and dress her in her finery. I'll go and get Uncle Percy to fetch the undertaker, then they will take your ma, and fix up a burial time.'

Gracie nodded. Something in her wanted to do this for her ma.

A kind of peace came over her as Gracie looked at her ma. Dressed in her Sunday best – a grey frock with a lace edged bodice, she looked grand. Her face still had the small smile, but now it looked as though it was made of wax, all pain lines gone. And her hair spread out on the pillow, a bright red once more as the shampoo Aunt Massie had brought round had washed out all the grease and sweat that had marred it.

Though the pain of her loss was deep, this gave Gracie a nice feeling. Her ma was happy, and that's all that mattered. She would remember this picture of her ma for ever. She'd forget all others, the sunken pain-filled expressions, the crying in agony. This picture of her beautiful ma would re-place them all.

Though her da's body wasn't recovered, the truth of his death came home to Gracie when the rest of the trawlers that had gone out on the same night came into dock and he wasn't on one of them. That day Gracie had seen women wailing as the truth hit them, too. And other women hugging their men, as both men and women cried. In Fleetwood, a fishing disaster hit all. All grieved, but all rallied around those who had suffered loss.

Lost and alone, Gracie looked around her. Mrs Pike, Joe's ma, came over to her. 'Eeh, Gracie, lass. I'm sorry.'

'Are your lads all safe, Mrs Pike?'

'Aye, they are, ta, love. Now, is there owt we can do for you? Me and a few as are not bereft are forming a committee and we'll make it our aim to support you all and give aid where needed. The first thing that I've done is to apply to the Fisherman's Guild for funeral costs for you. We all want your ma to have a good send off, and we're all going to chip in and do the wake for you. You've not to worry about a thing. When is the burial?'

'I don't knaw. The undertaker said he'd arrange a pauper's grave for me ma and that she'd be under afore I knew it.'

'That bugger! Right. I'll go and see him right now. That ain't going to happen. You're going to have a proper do for your ma, lass, a proper do. And a place in the cemetery where you can visit her. And your da an' all. 'Cause, though we don't have his body, we can have a double service, and have his name on the grave stone. How would that be, lass?'

The tears welled up in Gracie's eyes. 'It'd be grand, ta, Mrs Pike.'

Before Gracie realised what was happening, Mrs

Pike pulled her into her fat bosom and squeezed her till she thought she'd lose her breath. 'Me heart's sore for you, me little lass. But, you don't have to suffer alone. We'll be here for you. All the townsfolk'll lighten your load for you.'

It crossed Gracie's mind to ask where they'd been this last while, but she understood why she'd had little help. Her da hadn't been the easiest and would have shunned their charity, so she didn't say anything. She just put her arms around Mrs Pike's bulk as best as she could and held on to her as if doing so would stop her falling. Because that's how she felt lately – as if she were falling into a deep hole.

During the funeral service, Gracie had a feeling on her that she wasn't there, not the real her. She did what was expected of her and held herself together for her granny. Granny sobbed her heart out, but still managed a humph every time Gracie's dad was mentioned.

The whole town turned out, and it was announced that a plaque would eventually be placed in the church with all the names of the lost fishermen inscribed on it. This made Gracie feel sad, but that sadness was mixed with pride, too. To think her dad would have his name up on the church wall for ever – it was something she never thought to see.

At the wake, Gracie found herself enjoying the antics of the folk as they washed down jug after jug of beer, and got into a festive mood. At first, she'd thought it all strange, but was glad when she saw her granny doing a jig.

'Eeh, Granny, you're drunk.'

'I am that, and me Brenda would be proud of me. She loved a tipple herself when she was well, and we often danced in the pub when old Harry Bentwhistle played the piano... Ha, I don't know how he got that name, as I never saw him with a whistle, nor his da afore him. Maybe it was the one they had in their trousers!'

Granny crackled with laughter at this, and Gracie couldn't help joining in with her.

'That's the spirit, you two. Good to see you laughing together. You'll go along nicely together.'

'Oh, Aunt Massie, you should have heard what me granny said.'

'I can guess. She was allus one for near-to-the-mark sayings, and allus had us all in stitches. Now, Gracie...' Aunt Massie pulled her to one side. 'Your Granny is in high spirits at the moment, but we are all worried about her. Have you noticed that she has episodes?'

'Aye, I have. She has times when she can't re-member who I am, or when she last saw me.'

'Well, that's her age, but it could be a little more than that. I've seen it before. Some completely lose touch with reality. If that happens you're to let me know, and we'll see that you're taken care of. I wish your Uncle Percy would let me have you with me, but he won't. It's nowt to do with you, lass, just that he thinks that we'd be too squashed. Our Reggie sleeps in the attic and it wouldn't be right for you to sleep there, too. I've asked about a shake-me-down in the living room, but no. He says he'd never feel as though his house is his own, and would feel that he has to go to bed early on account of you wanting to settle down. So, there's nowt as I can do, lass. But that don't mean that I'm not there for you. I am. You only have to come knocking if you need me.'

'I knaw all that you're saying, Aunt Massie. I'll be right with me granny. I can cope with her episodes.'

'Well, now the funeral is done, you'll have to shift your things up to Blackpool to be with her. The Fisheries will want their cottage back. They'll be a few put out, poor sods. Anyroad, the Pike lads have all got bikes as you know, and they say that if you bundle your stuff up, they'll take them to your granny's for you. Is there owt big that you want to keep, as a keepsake, like?'

'Naw. I'm taking me ma's rings and her locket with a picture of her and me da in, and the few photos that she had – they're all in a box – but I don't knaw what to do with the furniture.'

'If you're sure you don't need it, then I'll get second-hand Molly to take a look. She'll shift it all, and might give you a little bit for it. There's nowt much by way of furniture, but your ma's china and cooking stuff should fetch you a little bit. I'll come around tomorrow and we'll get it all sorted and get you off to your gran's.'

The thought of her home being sold off to all and sundry nudged the sadness that had formed a tight knot inside Gracie, but still she didn't feel like releasing it all. It was as if she was a book that had closed, and no one could open it. But at least she had her Aunt Massie to look out for her, and her lovely granny. She just hoped that Granny didn't have too many of her episodes.

50

CHAPTER FOUR

Going back to school felt strange. Gracie didn't feel that she fitted in, and all the others of her age seemed so young compared to how she felt. The girls were silly and giggly, and the boys took pleasure in teasing and pulling hair as if they were still toddlers. It all irritated Gracie. And although fearful that she'd find it difficult to catch up, when tested by her teacher to assess how far behind she'd fallen she was found to be more advanced than the rest of her class.

On the third day, the head teacher called her into his office. His portly body swayed back and forth and his hand constantly brushed his floppy hair out of his eyes. These nervous actions increased the trepidation that made Gracie feel as though a swarm of flies had invaded her stomach.

'Gracie. It goes without saying how sorry we all were to hear of your troubles.'

Gracie could only nod her head.

'I have called you in because your teacher feels that they cannot take you much further than the standard you are at. Well done, Gracie. You must have spent some of your time studying?'

'Naw, sir. It just comes natural to me. Though I do love reading books if I can get them.'

'Of course. That's good. Well, your teacher has suggested that you sit the school certificate now. I understand you will be eligible to leave school in a few months, anyway, and we would be looking at releasing you sooner. You can start to apply for employment, as once you have a job, then that will be the end of your school days.'

'I'd like that, sir.'

'Well, we'll arrange for you to take your certificate, and you look around to see what's going. I think that many an employer would be willing to take you on. You're a very bright girl. You needn't attend until we send for you to take your exam. But use your time to find employment.'

'I will, sir.'

It was a relief to get out of the gates, even though she had a long way to get home, as she'd had to attend her school in Fleetwood, and hadn't transferred to one near to her granny. But as luck would have it, Joe was driving the next tram to come along, and she jumped on for a free ride.

Getting off just past the tower as she always did, Gracie ran most of the way to the South Pier. Her heart swelled to see that Sheila was still there touting her rock. 'Sheila! Sheila!'

'Eeh, it's you, Gracie. Where have you been? I've looked out for you most days.'

Gracie told her what had happened, and as she did, she once more felt the shifting of the hard knot of pain, but she kept it under control.

'By, Gracie, I've never known the like. I did think about you when I heard of the disaster, and I prayed yer da weren't a victim. But to lose him and your ma. I feel right sorry for you. Here, have a bag of rock bits, sommat sweet allus makes you feel better.'

'Ta, Sheila.'

The rock tasted delicious, though Gracie had put a bit in her mouth that was more than she could chew and caused her to slobber.

'Ha! You dirty mare. Here, I've some clean cloths. Wipe yourself, then take that big piece out, your eyes are bigger than your mouth.'

They both laughed, and it felt good.

'How about you come to the circus tonight, Gracie? I've told me da about you and he said he'd love to see you in the audience.'

'I'd love that, but I worry about leaving me granny too long. Thank goodness, I haven't to go to school any more, but I've to find work, which will still mean that she's on her own during the day.'

'She managed before, didn't she? Sure, she'll be right. And it's good news that you can leave school. You'll get set on easy. I can ask around if you like.'

Gracie told Sheila about her granny's loss of memory.

'Eeh, I knaws what you mean, me grandda's about the same. He gives me ma the run around. He even forgets to dress sometimes – not a pretty sight, I can tell you.'

They laughed again at this, and Gracie had a warm feeling enter her. It was good to have a friend, a real friend of her own age, as she felt that's what Sheila was, even though she hadn't known her long.

'Look, I'll tell you what. Bring your granny with you. She'll love it. I'll wait around the back of the tower until a quarter to six, as the show starts at six and I have another job now. I take the

53

popcorn around the audience. Me ma makes it in a machine in the back of the arena. She's clever, me ma. She puts it into little bags and I sell it for a farthing a bag. I make a good bit if the house is full.'

'Me granny would love that, she allus said she'd take me to the circus one of these days, but it never happened.'

'Right, see you there. Mind, I can't wait no longer than a quarter-to, so if you're not there then, I'll have to take it that you're not coming.'

Gracie skipped away, dodging the people, the landaus and a tram as she crossed the road. But the joy she felt turned to worry as soon as she turned into Rawcliffe Road. Standing on her granny's step were two men dressed in black. One of them knocked on the door as if he would break it down. Granny wasn't answering and her curtains were closed, which was an unusual sight.

'What do you want with me granny, mister?'

'Are you related to Mrs Peirce?'

'Aye, I just said, she's me granny.'

'Right, get her to open this door, we know she's in there. She closed the curtains when we knocked. We've come to evict her.'

Fear tightened Gracie's throat. 'Kick her out? Why, what's she done?'

'She hasn't paid her rent for six weeks; she owes us eighteen shillings. My family's not a charity. She'll have to go into the poor house if she can't pay her way.'

A relief entered Gracie. Though this was an enormous sum, she knew her granny had it. She kept a tin box under her bed and every now and again she emptied it and counted it. Gracie had wondered how she was accumulating such a sum. Well, now she knew some of it was because she was withholding her rent. 'Me granny's not well in her head at the mo. She can't remember what she's paid and hasn't paid.'

'She's no need to remember, she just needs to answer her door and pay up.'

'I can't explain, but she thinks the likes of you are out to get her and make her poor. If I get the money for you, will you let us stay?'

'Yes. If the rent's paid, that'll be the end of the matter, but you have to make sure she keeps straight from now on.'

How she was going to do that, Gracie didn't know, but she lifted the letter box and shouted for her granny.

'Have them men gone, Gracie?'

'No, Granny, and they won't go without the rent. You have to pay, or we lose the house. Let me in, Granny, I'll help you. No one will hurt you.'

The sound of the bolt being pulled back had Gracie sighing with relief. She turned to the men. 'You won't try to come in, will you? That will scare her. I'll sort it. I'll be out in a minute.'

The one who'd spoken before nodded his head.

'Eeh, Granny, you've got to pay them, or they'll put us in the poor house.'

'All right. But they need to come and mend the gutter. If you pay them, they'll never put it right.'

'I'll talk to them. Eeh, Granny, you're shaking, what's to do?'

Her granny sat down on the chair. 'I'll be all

right, our Brenda. You fetch the box and we'll sort this out.'

Not attempting to correct her granny, Gracie ran up the stairs and retrieved the box. 'Where's the key, Granny?'

'I've got it here. How much do they want?'

'Eighteen shillings, but why not give them a couple of weeks in advance besides what you owe, then that will give me a chance to sort out how we're going to pay them in the future, as I might not always be in when they call.'

Granny counted out the twenty-four shillings.

Taking the money to the door, Gracie made sure the men gave her a written receipt, listing all the dates that the money covered. 'Can I have an address, please, as I might have to come to your house to pay each week? Only Granny is getting afraid to open the door these days.'

The men agreed and went on their way.

'There, Granny, all done.'

'Eeh, our Brenda, how're we going to manage? I've you to care for now, and I don't have much coming in. I only have the bonuses of me penny insurance, and me widow's war pension, on account of your da being killed in the war.'

'Don't worry, Granny, I will be earning soon. I've been told that I can apply for a job.'

Her granny looked at her with a comical look, then grabbed her and held her. 'Eeh, me little Gracie. You're a good girl.'

Happy that her granny was back once more, Gracie told her about the circus and was rewarded with a smile that lit Granny's face.

The performance was magical. The elephants were Gracie's favourite. They danced and circled the ring holding each other's tails. And the Indian lady, who danced on their backs, was amazing too, as she jumped through hoops hanging from the ceiling and landed on the back of each elephant. And oh, the colours, the shimmering ribbons, the beautiful costumes of the girls with feather plumes on their heads – Gracie had never seen anything like it. She and Granny clapped and clapped.

Then came a boy with a monkey. He was so funny. The monkey made him tea and poured it into cups. Gracie assumed the monkey was a she as it was dressed in a pink, frilly frock and had frilly knickers on. Suddenly the monkey leaned on one arm and held a cup in the other. She looked around and then, as if choosing who she liked the look of, ambled over to Granny and handed her the cup. Granny laughed her head off as she saw the murky water in the cup, but she took it and pretended to drink it. The monkey clapped her hands, then shook Granny's hand before scrambling back to the boy. The boy bowed towards them, and then to the audience. When he took the monkey's hand, the monkey made a squealing noise, pulled away, and ran to Granny putting her arms out to her. Granny took her onto her knee and cuddled her. This made the monkey happy and she ran back to the boy. The crowd went mad, calling, laughing and clapping.

There was a break after that, and Sheila came up to them. Granny looked at her as if she'd never seen her before. 'This is me friend, Granny. Her name's Sheila. You remember, she met us outside.'

'Pleased to meet you, me dear. What a lovely surprise this was for us. Ta very much. I knaw about your da, and when he comes on, I'll put plenty in his bucket. Now, we'll take two bags of your popcorn, please.'

Gracie felt so proud of Granny.

'There you go, missus. You enjoy that. Me ma made it, and everything she makes is delicious.'

'I'm sure.'

To Gracie it was the best time she'd had in her whole life, made extra special as her granny was behaving herself.

Sheila's da came on after that, and his antics had the whole audience in uproar. Gracie couldn't stop giggling. A huge man, he pranced around in gigantic trousers that swung around his body, and he had a hooter that he kept bleeping every time he made a joke. Most of his jokes were near the mark, but it didn't matter.

When he passed his bucket around, Granny stood up and shouted, 'Dig deep everyone, this man has brought us all pleasure tonight, and he has his wife and kids to feed.'

Gracie could have died, she was that embarrassed. Someone shouted: 'Are you a plant, then, missus? Looks to me like you work for them.'

'No, I don't, this is me first time here, but I just knaw of his circumstances.'

'Fair enough. I'll give a tanner.'

The bucket jingled its way around the audience, and Popsi the clown, did a little jig as he got handfuls of coins and let them drop back into the bucket. His bows were low, and as he left, he threw kisses towards Granny.

Sheila met them at the door. The boy with the monkey act was with her. 'Eeh, Sheila, I'm sorry. I didn't knaw as me granny'd do that.'

'Don't be sorry; it's the most me da's ever taken, he's jumping through hoops. He says you can come to every performance, and bring your granny, and he'll give you a cut.'

'Aye, and she can help me with me act an' all. I've never had such a reaction and Suzy, me monkey, has never took to anyone like she took to your granny. Me name's Rory, pleased to meet you.'

Gracie judged Rory to be the same age as herself. His hair was dark and curly, his skin tanned and he had an earring in one ear. His smile showed lovely white teeth. Gracie liked him and felt as if she'd known him a long time. 'Pleased to meet you, Rory.'

'I've seen you talking to Sheila. I work on the pier, in the daytime, getting the holidaymakers to have a photo taken with Suzy. You won't have seen me, I was leaning on the railings.'

Granny tugged on Gracie's arm. 'Tell them that we had a good time, Brenda.'

'It's Gracie, Granny.' The look that Gracie knew only too well crossed Granny's face. 'She's tired. I'll get her home. But it has been wonderful, thanks, Sheila. I'll never forget it.'

'Come to me stall whenever you can, Gracie. And maybe we can all go on the pier one day. I know all the stallholders. We can have some fun as they'll all give us a free go.'

Without thinking, Gracie hugged Sheila. Sheila hugged her back. And it settled in Gracie that she'd found a good friend, a friend like her ma had had in Aunt Massie. And with the thought, the cold knot inside her eased a little.

CHAPTER FIVE

A door banged, catapulting Gracie from being in a deep sleep, to sitting upright. Fear gripped her. She listened. Nothing. Her feet felt the cold of the linoleum as she jumped from her bed and crept towards her bedroom door.

Opening it, a draught blew towards her. 'Granny?'

No answer came, but a light shone onto the dark landing from her granny's bedroom. Making her way there, Gracie found that her granny had lit a candle by her bed, but her bed was empty. 'Granny? Granny?'

Running downstairs, her fear for herself forgotten, wind rushed at Gracie through the open front door. 'Oh, Granny! Granny!'

The silence and the darkness of the living room held a terror for her. Closing the front door, she made her way to the mantelpiece. Reaching for the matches, she was glad to feel the heat from the fire and see that a few embers still glowed. After holding a lighted match to the gas mantle, it jumped into life. The light eased her fear, but as she saw the time, a deep worry replaced it. Twenty past two!

What should I do? What can I do? Feeling sick,

Gracie put a shovel of coal on the fire and sat on the chair that stood opposite her granny's rocking chair.

A knock on the window woke her, though she hadn't remembered falling asleep. Her heart banged against her chest as she went to the window, pulled the curtain back and peeped out. A man stood there with her granny.

Running to the door, she opened it. 'Granny, oh Granny, where have you been?'

'I went to see me Brenda, but I didn't find her.'

'Come on in, Granny. Come and sit down and I'll make you a cuppa. Thanks, mister ... Joe? Eeh, Joe, I didn't see that it was you. Me granny didn't get all the way to Fleetwood, did she?'

'Naw. I were out for a walk. I found her wandering along the Prom.'

This puzzled Gracie. She glanced at the clock and saw that it was now four in the morning. 'Come on in, Joe. I'll put the kettle on.'

'Ta, Gracie. I could do with a cuppa. I've been walking a while. All the way from Fleetwood, in fact.'

'At this time? That's a strange thing to do.'

'Not for me it ain't. I don't sleep well. I have nightmares. I'd rather walk the streets than face them. And I'm starting me early run in Blackpool. So, I'm in good time.'

Unsure about this, as she didn't know what time the first tram left Blackpool, Gracie didn't comment. Taking her granny to her chair, she sat her down and wrapped her in a blanket before moving the kettle onto the hob.

'She needs help, Gracie. She'll get hurt wandering the streets at night.'

'She's never done that before. I don't knaw, Joe, it's getting difficult to look after her.'

Joe looked blank for a moment – the same look she often saw on her granny's face.

'I understand her, Gracie. Me mind wanders like hers. It gives you a feeling of being lost, and not sure where you want to be.'

Gracie felt too tired to deal with this. Granny hadn't spoken; she sat looking just as Joe had said – lost.

The whistling of the kettle sounded alien in the strange atmosphere of Joe and Granny staring into space and Gracie was glad to be able to busy herself making the tea. As Granny sipped hers, she began to sob.

It was then that Gracie understood the lost feeling, as she now had it weighing on her own shoulders. She sank down at the table. Her arms rested on the velvet cloth and her head sank down on to them.

'Come on, old girl. Crying don't help none. I know. I've cried buckets of lonely tears.'

Gracie listened to Joe talking to her granny and felt that she knew him for the first time ever. 'Poor Joe, I'm sorry for you. To have this feeling all your life, I can't imagine what that must that be like?'

'I think of sommat good. Like the sun shining, and me driving me tram. That's good, Mrs Peirce, you should try it.'

Gracie burst out laughing at the thought. Her granny lifted her head. A grin came over her face. Gracie doubled over. 'Oh, Joe, Joe...'

'What? What did I say?'

Granny, as if by a miracle, was back to being herself. She put out her hands as if holding levers, and made a noise like a tram rumbling along. It was when she went 'beep, beep' that Joe finally saw the joke.

Gracie thought that she would die with the pain of her laughing, but it felt good.

'Well, enough of this. I don't know about you two, but I'm off to bed.' This from Granny made everything seem normal again.

'Give me a kiss, Gracie, and get yourself to bed. I don't knaw what you're going to do, Joe, but you can kip on the floor if you like. I'll send a blanket down with Gracie.'

'Ta, Mrs Peirce. I will. But I have to wake at six.'

'I'll set the alarm for you, Joe.'

Walking up the stairs, Gracie had a feeling descend on her that gave her the unreality of it all. *Has all of this really happened, or am I dreaming?* Whichever it was, she knew one thing – there was never a dull moment with her gran.

Three nights later, Gracie was once more woken in the early hours of the morning, this time by a knock on the door. Calling to her granny, she got no reply. The door knocker banged again. A voice came through the letterbox. 'Police. Anyone at home?'

Gracie gasped her fear as she ran down the stairs. 'What d'yer want? What's happened?'

'Open the door, love.'

The policeman had to bend over to enter the house.

Gracie held her breath. Her body began to tremble. The police calling meant that there was trouble. *Oh Granny, what have you done. Where are you?*

'Does a Mrs Peirce live here, love?'

'Aye, she's me granny.'

'Have you anyone here with you?'

'Naw, just me and me granny live here. Have you found her, did she go walking again?'

'Yes, she has been found, love. Is there anyone we can call to be with you?'

'Not in Blackpool. Only in Fleetwood. I have me Aunt Massie there.'

'Well, get your clothes on and I'll take you to her.'

'Why? Where's me granny?'

'Come on, love. Just go and get your clothes on. I'll tell you when you're with your aunt.'

The ride in the car was Gracie's first ever, but she didn't really register what it felt like as her fear of what might have happened held her in a cocoon of distress.

At her Aunt Massie's home it took a while for the policeman to get an answer. When he did, it was Uncle Percy who came to the door. 'What the bloody hell? Is that you, Gracie? What you been up to?'

Gracie couldn't speak.

'It's not her that I'm here about, it's her granny. I need to speak to you, sir. Will you let us in so that this young lady has someone with her while I tell her what's happened?'

'Aye, come in.'

'What is it, Percy...? Gracie! Oh, Gracie!' Aunt

Massie came down the stairs. If it wasn't for the dread in her, Gracie would have giggled as Aunt Massie looked a sight with her hair tied in many rag bows.

'She's not in trouble, missus. At least, not the kind you are thinking of, but I have sad news for her.'

Gracie held her breath.

'Eeh, come here, lass. Whatever's happened?'

Gracie couldn't move, but Aunt Massie came over to her and cradled her in her arms, all the while stroking her hair and looking at the policeman.

He cleared his throat. Gracie wanted to scream, *Don't … don't speak. Don't tell me!*

'I'm afraid that a member of the public called in to the station about two and a half hours ago to tell us that he'd seen an old lady he knew walk into the sea. He said that he ran after her, but the waves took her. He said that it was Mrs Peirce...'

'Naw. Naw. Not me granny!' Gracie felt her body crumble.

'Hold on, lass. Let's hear the policeman out. Have you found her? Are you sure it was Mrs Peirce?'

'Yes. By the time we got to the beach, her body had been washed back onto the shore. The man was Joe Pike, the tram driver. We all know him. He's a bit short up top, but a nice bloke.'

'Joe? What was he doing up in Blackpool at this time of night?'

'We often see him. He walks the Prom. He doesn't do any harm, and in this instance, he tried to save Mrs Peirce. He identified her, and then we

65

found her handbag. It had a folded post office book in it with her name printed inside. Joe's in a bit of a state. He wanted to come with us to Mrs Peirce's house. He kept saying, "Gracie, poor Gracie."'

These words undid Gracie. Her legs gave way. Screams came rasping through her throat. 'Help me, Aunt Massie. Help me.'

Aunt Massie didn't speak. She just clung on to Gracie, stroking her, holding her. Uncle Percy sat down shaking his head. The policeman took his helmet off and scratched his head. All of this Gracie saw as if it wasn't really happening, yet she registered every detail.

'Can you take care of her tonight? She says that you are all she has.'

'Yes. We'll see to her.'

Still seeing every little movement, Gracie didn't miss Uncle Percy's head jerk upwards as he gave a look to Aunt Massie that said he didn't agree. She looked up at Aunt Massie, saw her hesitate. Then she heard the words she'd heard before, but never thought would be uttered when she so needed her aunt.

'Well, I mean ... well, I – I, we can't. We've no room. I'm sorry, Gracie, I'm sorry.'

Tears rolled down her Aunt Massie's face. Gracie understood, but at this moment she hated her Uncle Percy.

Hugging her Aunt Massie, she tried to tell her that she knew. She did know, but oh, she wanted to beg them to change their minds. She wanted to beg and beg...

'Right. Well, I'll take her to the police station,

and they'll sort her. I'll say goodnight.'

Gracie could hear the anger in the policeman's voice. She didn't want him to be angry with Aunt Massie. She wanted to tell him that it wasn't Aunt Massie's fault, but nothing would come out of her mouth.

CHAPTER SIX

The lamp outside the police station lit up the street. Inside, the brick walls were painted cream. A long counter divided the room.

'Sit on that bench, love.'

The policeman disappeared after saying this. He came back a few minutes later with a hot drink and a blanket. 'I've only got this bench, love, as though we have beds in the cells, I'll not put you in one of them. Have your drink of cocoa and then lie down. Try to get some rest.' He stood a moment looking down at her. 'I'm sorry for all you've been through, love. Don't worry, now. You'll be warm and safe here. And I'll get someone to see to you.'

The someone woke her the next morning. It was a stout woman in a green uniform. 'You're to come with me, miss. We're going to Manchester. You'll be fine. There's a home there for you. You'll be with other girls of your age. Don't worry.'

Wiping her swollen eyes, Gracie lifted her heavy body off the bench. Her legs still felt shaky and she needed a pee. But she went with the woman without protesting.

Outside, the early October air had a chill to it and rain drizzled down. Gracie pulled her coat around her. Her urge to pee became stronger, but she couldn't seem to find her voice, nor stop her body from trembling.

A taxi pulled up. 'Where to, missus?'

'The station.'

Nothing about the journey to Blackpool North Station registered with Gracie, except the clock when she arrived. She couldn't believe that it was already nine o'clock.

'Right. You visit the toilet, as you must need to go, and I'll purchase our tickets. Wash your face and hands while you're there, and try to do something with your hair. Run along, they're just over there.'

The relief after having a pee eased Gracie, and she'd thought she'd never stop. Washing her hands and face, she looked into the mirror. A stranger looked back at her. A pale, swollen-eyed stranger. Trying to calm her curly red hair, she dampened it and patted it. But she didn't really care that it looked unruly; it was as if the world had shut down for her, and she could only feel the trembling of her legs. Her mind wouldn't let in what had happened, or what was happening now.

'Is that the best you could do? Here, I've a hairbrush with me, as I knew the police wouldn't have anything. Come here.'

Gracie's eyes filled with water as the woman tried to untangle her hair, but somehow she welcomed the pain and didn't protest.

'They'll cut this lot off when you get there.

You've likely got nits as it is. Right, sit on that bench and I'll get us a cup of tea, and a bun if they've got any.'

The woman came back with a steaming mug of strong tea and a stale raspberry bun. Gracie shook her head at the bun, but welcomed the hot drink. It tasted stewed, to use her granny's term. For a moment she wondered who would get her granny a cup of tea, but the thought gave her a pain, so she shut it out.

Not having registered much of the journey on the train, or the ride through the busy streets of Manchester, nerves clenched Gracie's stomach as the taxi pulled up outside a huge building that stood in its own grounds. Above the door was a sign which said, 'Hallford House, Children's Refuge'. In smaller letters Gracie read, 'Christian Fellows'.

'Come along, girl. Out you get.'

As they entered the vast, overheated and stuffy hall, an overwhelming smell of polish hit Gracie. It turned her stomach, but she swallowed hard.

A man came out of a door that led off the left-hand side of the hall, his shoes squeaking as he walked towards them. 'Ahh, another waif and stray. Who do we have here, then, Miss Browne?'

'Orphaned. No relative to care for her. From Blackpool. Name, Grace Rimmer. Age thirteen. Quiet, given no trouble at all. I have a report of her circumstances here, given to me by the Blackpool Police. She has been beset by three consecutive tragedies that have brought her to this point.'

'Hum, pretty young thing.'

Miss Browne tutted in a disapproving way.

The man ignored her. 'Now, Grace Rimmer, my name is Mr Graves, but you will call me Master, understand?'

Gracie nodded.

'Look at me, when I speak to you!'

Gracie jumped at the harshness of his tone. When she looked up, she saw a thin, weedy-looking man with piercing, dark eyes. His black hair was parted in the middle and plastered down with oil. His moustache seemed to be stuck onto his face. As she stared at him, his eyes changed. In them she saw an expression that made her skin crawl.

'Leave her details with me, and take her along to the nurse. With that hair, she will be full of lice. And no doubt needs a bath – I can smell her from here.'

'This way, girl.'

Gracie's blood ran cold as they walked towards a wide staircase that snaked upwards. Its banister shone and brown carpet covered the steps. To her it seemed like a stairway to her doom. But they passed them by and walked ahead to where several highly polished doors led off the hall. All had brass plaques on them – 'Administration', 'Register' and 'Nurse'.

Miss Browne knocked on the one that said 'Nurse' and opened the door. 'New intake for examination.' With this, she turned and left Gracie standing just inside the room.

'Name?'

'Grace Rimmer.'

'Date of birth?'

Questions like these, asked by the nurse in a cold, indifferent voice, went on and on – her last known address, any known relatives, any recent illnesses.

'Right. Go behind that curtain and strip.'

Shivering, a naked Gracie came from behind the curtain and stood in front of the nurse. A big woman with warts on her face, the nurse looked her up and down with her small eyes that seemed encased in fat layers of flesh. What Gracie could see of her hair was tightly permed and bleached blonde. 'Hum, pubic hair and breasts that are sprouting nicely. Have you begun to menstruate yet?'

Gracie had never heard the word.

'Monthly bleeding! Do you have monthly bleeding, girl?'

'Yes.'

'When was your last?'

'Two weeks ago.'

'Ever had a relationship with a man?'

Gracie couldn't answer. The shivering of her body increased.

'I'll take that as a no. Good. But no doubt that will soon change. Now, lie on that bed, I am going to look at you between your legs to see if you are telling the truth and if you are clean.'

Gracie wanted the floor to open and swallow her. Never had anyone looked between her legs before. Not even the doctor.

When the nurse's cold hand touched her, Gracie recoiled from her.

'None of that. It will hurt more if you resist, and I'm a damn sight stronger than you, madam.'

Pain seared her as the nurse examined her. The examination went on and on. The soreness of it had Gracie crying out, 'Stop, please, stop.'

'Humph! A virgin. Well, that's rare for a girl brought in here of your age. Get down off the bed and sit on that chair.'

As Gracie did as she was asked, the nurse went behind her. Her gnarled hands came around Gracie and cupped her breasts.

'Nice. Developing well.' Her body leaned into Gracie's. Gracie felt sick and couldn't control the retching that shook her body. The nurse jumped away. 'Get through there to the bathroom, you dirty tyke!'

Gracie ran through the door the nurse had pointed to, her hand over her mouth trying to stop the vomit from escaping. She just reached the bowl in time.

'Swill that clean, then get back in here.'

Feeling empty and afraid, Gracie went back to the nurse. 'Sit down and open your mouth.'

A torch was shone into her mouth and eyes. 'Now, one more examination. Your hair.'

As if the nurse needed to punish her, she pulled clumps of hair, while shoving Gracie's head, this way and that. 'Just as I thought – lice!'

This shocked Gracie. She'd always kept free of head lice, even when it had been rife in school.

Grabbing a pair of huge scissors, the nurse came towards her.

'No. No, don't cut my hair, please.'

'Sit still and do as you're told. Dirty tykes like you can't run around with a head of hair like that! You'll infect everybody. This is a clean home, and you will learn to keep yourself clean. Do you hear me?'

Gracie nodded. She wanted to scream and scream, but her fear held her like a cold statue.

On and on, snip, snip, snip. Large chunks of her beautiful hair fell on to her shoulders, her arms and her lap.

'There! Now you won't pass on your vermin, and nor will you be attractive to the boys. Get back into the bathroom and under the shower.'

The water ran cold, freezing Gracie's body, but she didn't care. It numbed her, and that was what she wanted – not to be able to feel anything. Tentatively, she touched between her legs. The soreness was unbearable and made her catch her breath. She directed the water there hoping it would soothe the burning feeling.

'Hurry up. Dry yourself off.'

As Gracie dried herself, she looked in the mirror above the sink and gasped in horror. The girl looking back was unrecognisable. Her hair. Her lovely, curly, red hair was chopped in uneven strands, the longest only an inch in length. She looked hideous.

Going back into the nurse's room, a feeling took Gracie that she wanted to punch and kick this vile woman. But she dutifully stood in front of her.

'Put these on.'

Taking the pile of clothes and putting them on the chair, Gracie donned the vest, then the liberty bodice and navy knickers. As she did, her body began to tingle as it warmed up once more. The grey frock was plain, with long sleeves and a white collar. It flowed to her ankles, and there was a pinafore to cover it all. Lastly, she found a pair of socks and black pumps. These were a little too big for her, but she put them on and said nothing. The nurse watched her every move with her eyes half-closed and her head resting on her elbows.

'Now you look presentable.'

The sound of her ringing a bell that stood on the desk made Gracie jump. The door opened and an old woman entered. 'Take her to D section,' said the nurse.

Gracie followed the woman. Despite what had happened to her at the hands of the nurse, nothing really touched her. Still, everything inside her was shut down. She couldn't let thoughts in, and didn't want to. She had questions, but she suppressed them. Nothing mattered anymore. Nothing.

They walked along corridor after corridor. A dizziness came over Gracie as they turned a corner. Her shoes squeaked on the polished linoleum.

'Walk on the carpet at all times!'

Steadying herself, Gracie stepped back onto the carpet strip. Beige in colour, it ran the length of the corridors, leaving bare a polished edging of flooring to the skirting boards. The further they walked, the more the soreness between Gracie's legs smarted.

Stopping at last, and opening a door, the old woman indicated she pass through it. Once she had, the door closed behind her.

The silence that met her enclosed her in fear. The room was a classroom with rows and rows of wooden desks. Silent faces looked up and stared at her. All were girls and all wore the same grey frock and pinafore as the one she had on. Their expressions showed an interest, but Gracie thought she'd never seen or felt such unhappiness. This room was full of the atmosphere she'd only ever felt at the church on the day of her ma and da's funeral.

'Name?'

The voice came from the side of her. Turning in that direction, she saw it had come from the most peculiar-looking woman. Everything about her was pointed. Her nose, her chin, the way her fringe jutted out from her tightly drawn-back brown hair, and the bun that it was fixed into. Even her bosom was pointed, sticking out way in front of her but with no roundness to it.

'Grace Rimmer.'

'Speak up, girl!'

Gracie repeated her name more clearly.

'I know nothing about you! I wasn't expecting you. This place gets worse! Sit down in row four, girl. You'll find an embroidery cloth and bracket in the desk. Fix the cloth to the bracket and start to stitch.'

Gracie had no idea what the woman was talking about. She'd read in books that ladies embroidered, but never thought to do it herself.

Taking a seat next to a girl who wore thick glasses and whose teeth protruded, Gracie lifted the lid of the desk. The girl did the same. In a low whisper, she said, 'Hello, Grace. Me name's Jeannie, I'll help you. Just put the frame and cloth on the desk, then you take mine, and I'll get yours ready.'

'Ta, Jeannie.'

When Jeannie handed the cloth back it was stretched and secured tightly onto a frame. Jeannie nudged her, then took a length of yellow silk and threaded a needle with it. Gracie sat fascinated as she watched Jeannie stick her needle through her cloth, then back in nearly the same place, leaving a loop. Then she brought the needle through the top of the loop and back over it and through the cloth again. The result was a petal-like shape that fitted the petal of one of the flowers printed on the cloth.

Gracie took the frame and tried it. She was thrilled to see the same result, and for a while completely lost herself in filling in as many petals as she could. A peace came over her. If this is what you did in a refuge for children then she could be happy here. At least, she could if she never let her memories in. No, she was to keep them locked up tightly, or she'd be lost.

CHAPTER SEVEN

They were in the dining room when Jeannie spoke to her again. 'We can talk quietly, but we have to keep an eye out for Foggie.'

'Foggie?'

'Aye, he's a bastard!'

This shocked Gracie. She hadn't heard a girl swear before.

'He's deputy to the master, and'll have you in front of the master as soon as look at you.'

Trepidation crept over Gracie.

'Don't look so scared, Grace, you just have to learn the tricks that get you by, though naw tricks will get you out of the master's clutches, if he takes a shine to you.'

'Everyone calls me Gracie, I like it better. And what does the master do then?'

'You'll find out, Gracie. Did you get the finger treatment from Nurse?'

'Aye, I did, it really hurt me.'

'You've not had nowt like that before, then?'

'Naw.'

'Eeh, I feel sorry for you. Once the master knows you're a virgin, he'll be after you. Nurse checks for him, and enjoys herself while she's at it.'

Shocked, Gracie didn't know what to say. She had a sick feeling in her stomach, and then a picture tried to come to her of her da, but she refused it entry into her mind.

'Look, he's got a favourite at the moment. That blonde girl on the end. Her name's Lizzie, and she's all right, but very quiet, on account of what she has to go through every night.'

Hardy able to speak, Gracie asked, 'Does he do that thing that makes you have babbies?'

'Aye, and more.'

Gracie swallowed hard. 'Has he done it to you, then?'

'Aye, he has, Gracie. He said he needed to break me in, but that was all. He said that he wouldn't want me regular on account of me looks. But the once was enough and I've never been grateful before for being an ugly duckling, but I am now.'

Gracie couldn't eat the slop that had been put

in front of her, a bowl of thin soup-like liquid, brown in colour with a dumpling that looked like a stone, and a few carrots floating in it. She pushed it away.

'Here, if you're not going to eat that, I'll have it. That's another thing that you'll learn, eat whatever they give you, as there'll be nowt else. And hunger's a constant anyway, without leaving your food.'

'You're welcome to it.'

Gracie couldn't take her eyes off Lizzie. She'd never seen a girl more beautiful, and yet more sad. She spoke to no one, and kept her head down, slurping her soup as if every mouthful was making her feel sick. Her hair hadn't been cut, like most of the girls' had. It hung in ringlets, and her face had a cherub look to it. She seemed to sense that someone was looking at her, and looked back at Gracie. It was then that Gracie saw how lovely Lizzie's eyes were. A deep blue, they had lashes framing them that looked as though they would brush her eyebrows, they were that long.

Gracie managed a small smile, something she never thought she'd do again. Lizzie smiled back.

Outside, in what the girls called the exercise yard, Lizzie joined Gracie and Jeannie. Jeannie put her arm around her as she came up to them. 'This new girl's all right, Lizzie. She's called Gracie.'

Lizzie nodded. It was as if she was dead inside. Gracie wanted to hold her as Jeannie was doing.

'Are you feeling ill, Lizzie?'

'I were sick this morning, Jeannie. And I haven't

had me monthly. I'm scared they'll send me to the correction convent. I reckon as they'll say it were Barry Greenwood, as last night they took me to a room and he was in there, but he didn't touch me. He only cried, as Foggie had been at him.'

'Naw! Awe, Lizzie, I'm sorry, lass. And, I'm sorry for Barry as well, as the boys say as Foggie really hurts them when he does it to them.'

Gracie didn't know what to make of this; her stomach was tied in knots as it was. But she calmed when Lizzie looked up at her. 'Nice to meet you, Gracie, only I don't think as I'll knaw you for long.'

Gracie knew what Lizzie had meant by the correction convent, and she felt a horror fill her. The convent was for unmarried mothers. She couldn't take in what these girls seemed to accept as normal.

'I'm sorry to say this, Gracie, but you could be next.' The tone of Lizzie's voice deepened the fear in Gracie, and her next words compounded that fear. 'The master will send for you. He's had most girls, but left them alone while I were his favourite. But for them to put me in with Barry means that the nurse has told the master that I have me belly up, so he'll not want to touch me again.'

Gracie found her voice. 'Naw! Naw, I'll not do it! I won't!'

'Gracie, you'll have no choice. And I'll tell you, what I was told, and every girl passes on to the next. Just do as he asks. Don't object, don't fight. That way, it ain't too bad and is soon done. If you play him up you can be put on starvation rations and kept in a room on your own for hours and hours, but he don't give up. He has a go at you every night, until he breaks your will. Then if you're lucky, he'll go on to someone else. That is if he don't take you as his favourite, like he did me.'

'I were telling her, you're better off looking like me, he only had me the once. I couldn't have taken it again, like you have, Lizzie. I'm sorry for you.'

'Don't be, Jeannie, it's over now. I'm more sorry for Gracie here.'

Gracie couldn't imagine what it must be like to have the master paw you. This time her mind let in the horror of her da, and her legs gave way.

'Gracie, Gracie. Awe, love. Come on. It'll be all right.'

The voice of Lizzie seemed a long way away. A darkness descended on Gracie. It held all her fears and her pain, and she screamed out against it. But before long her screams turned to sobs, and her body collapsed under the weight of her grief. She wailed for her ma, and her granny, but she didn't let her da in. His memory gave her his hands, clawing at her. 'I can't bear it, I can't ... help me ... help me!'

A hand grabbing her arm and a sharp slap across her face shocked Gracie into silence. 'We have none of that here, girl!'

She looked up into the nurse's beady eyes. The spittle gathered in her mouth. All the fear and pain she had in her erupted as she spat in the nurse's face.

'You little tyke! You dirty scum!' Another blow smashed her head. 'Get up! Get up now!'

Gracie kicked out at the nurse and caught her

in her stomach. The girls began to gather around and turned into a mob as they screamed at her, 'Kill Nursey, kill her!'

Getting up, Gracie hit out with all her might at the bent-over figure of the nurse, flaying her with her fists, the while screaming abuse at her. 'You touched me, you vile, vile woman! You touched me with your filthy hands! Well, you'll never do that again!'

Grabbing the nurse's hair, she pulled her over and began to kick her as if to release every bad thing she'd gone through onto the cowering, crying woman. Other girls joined in. Jeannie, and Lizzie, and those that Gracie didn't know.

It was the shrill, piercing whistle that stopped them.

A silence fell. Into it came the moans of the nurse. Gracie began to shake as she looked at the bloodied heap on the floor. The crowd parted. Through them strode the master. In his hand he held a long thin stick.

The first slice of the stick caught Gracie on her arm. The stinging pain had her catching her breath and gasping with the intensity; but before she let her breath out another thwack caught her across her waist. As she bent against it, another cut across her back. Her body sank onto her knees. Then the sharpest and most painful of all landed on her buttocks. Gasping and slobbering, Gracie begged him to stop. But the onslaught went on. 'You'll learn a lesson if it kills me! You never, never, attack one of the staff.'

Each 'never' was accompanied by a strike with the stick that was harder than the last one. Gracie felt her skin tearing, as the onslaught went on and on, reducing her to a heap of moaning wretchedness.

Around her girls were crying. One screamed, 'Stop, stop!' Others joined in, their voices reaching fever pitch.

But it wasn't until she heard the voice of the pointed lady that mercy was shown. 'For pity's sake, stop! You'll kill her.'

The master threw the stick down. Gracie looked up at him from her position of lying on the concrete in a pool of her own blood, and saw him trying to catch his breath. Then his arm lifted and with his finger pointed, he indicated the crowd of girls as his voice boomed out, 'Everyone here won't see the light of day for a week, and they are to be on rations of bread and water only! Get them all into the classroom, close the shutters and lock the door. Get nurse to sick bay. And this ... this lump of dirt ... get her cleaned up, then lock her in the broom cupboard until I say she can come out!'

With this he stormed off.

Cries of 'No! No, I weren't involved, I did nothing!' set up around her but faded as the girls were herded away from her. Two men arrived with a stretcher and lifted the nurse onto it. Then Gracie was alone. Every part of her body smarted. Her eyes leaked salty tears that stung the cuts on her face. She didn't try to stop them. The knot that had tied her insides was broken. Her sobs were painful but her cries of 'Ma ... Ma', and 'Granny... Oh, Granny!' went unheard. Despair clothed her. But then, the blessed relief of sinking into a black,

black place came to her, and she knew no more.

Scrunched up, unable to move or penetrate the darkness, the smell around her of dusters, polish and a dirty mop gave Gracie the realisation that she was in the threatened broom cupboard. How long she'd been there she didn't know. Her mouth was so dry that she couldn't swallow or form any words. Her eyes so swollen, she couldn't open them enough to try to pierce the darkness. Something dug into her back. When she felt it, she knew it to be a bucket. The pain of that was worse than all the smarting of her cuts, but she couldn't shift herself off it.

In her mind, she begged God, her ma and her granny to help her, but no help came. Time was something she couldn't measure, but dragged out until it felt as though she would die in this cupboard. Something scurried over her foot. A furry feeling brushed her leg. The sensation released her voice, and though it hurt her throat to do so, she screamed and screamed until she was exhausted. Nobody came.

Eventually, the pain took her back into the blackness. There she knew relief as she swirled around and around. But it was as if her soul was lost, and a deep loneliness shrouded her.

CHAPTER EIGHT

'Look, Master, she's been in there two days now, without water. She'll dehydrate and will die if you don't let us get her out. Not to mention that her wounds may be infected and the chance of pneumonia!'

'Very well, but if you value your job, you will stick to the report that this was done by the other inmates attacking her.'

'Yes, Master. I understand. Now, please give me the key.'

These voices drifted into Gracie's semi-consciousness. *It's over. Oh God, it's over.*

She cried out with the agony of them pulling her through the door, and cringed against the light in the hall.

'You're all right now, lass. We're going to get you to sick bay.'

As her eyes adjusted, Gracie saw the back of the master walking away. A hate settled in her like nothing she'd ever felt before. She tried to form the only words that meant anything to her.

'I – I want me ma.'

'Don't we all, lass. Now quieten down, and lie still.'

When Gracie next woke, she was in a world of white. White walls, white ceiling and white bedding. A man stood next to her bed. 'About time, lass. You've been out for the count for hours. We need you to drink this.'

A sip of the cool water soothed her dry cracked lips and sore throat. She tried to take another, but it was held back. 'A little at a time. If you drink it too fast you'll only throw it up again. That's right. Are you cold, lass?'

She wanted to say that she was boiling hot, but knew that her limbs were shaking and so she must look cold.

'Look at that sweat on her forehead, John. I reckon as she's coming down with a fever.'

A thermometer was put under her tongue. Gracie found it difficult to keep it there, and was glad when they took it away.

'You're in trouble, lass. We're going to have to cool you down.'

For the next few hours, Gracie drifted in and out of sleep. When awake she was conscious of them washing her down with cold water. She moaned at the pain of this, but they encouraged her, telling her that they had to get her fever down.

When she surfaced above the fog that seemed to be her constant companion, she heard the hateful voice of the master.

'Well, how's she doing?'

'She should be in hospital. We're struggling to keep her alive. She has infections all over her. You should have let us treat her earlier.'

'She's not going to hospital. Now, get her sorted. This has gone on long enough.'

'She needs penicillin and we can't get it. She at least needs to see a doctor.'

'I'll ring Parker. He'll do anything for a bob or two so that he can buy another bottle of whisky.'

'Is he still practising?'

'He was a few weeks back when I had a mishap with that Patsy. Stitched her up nicely, he did, and wrote a report that one of the boys had tried to rape her, but she wouldn't say which one. Then he sectioned her, so we'll hear no more of her foul mouth around the place.'

'Well, he's better than nothing, I suppose. As long as he can get us penicillin. We don't want a death on our hands – that would mean an investigation, and there's plenty of mud to churn up around here.'

'Ha! They can't prove anything. And they won't listen to a load of kids whose only motive is to get out of here. Besides, it wouldn't pay them to as they've no other place to put them. So stop worrying.'

For Gracie, it was as if she was living on a cloud. Her body drifted along. Every now and then she heard snippets of conversation about herself, or the two men who were taking care of her talking about the boys that they'd taken to their bedroom. All of it seemed like a nightmare. In amongst the nightmare would be nice moments, when her ma floated by and smiled at her, but then a pain would slice her heart as she couldn't take hold of her ma, as she faded away again. Granny, too, came to visit. She never lost her memory now, and knew Gracie, and talked of the good times they'd had. Once her da had come, but she'd screamed at him that he was no better than the men here, and he went away. That time she'd felt a weight holding her down. Through the haze that was always around her, she saw one of the men who were

86

looking after her. He was soothing her, telling her to lie still and not to call out.

Somehow, she knew these were nurses, but couldn't understand why they were male. Nurses were always women, weren't they?

A voice calling her brought her to the surface of the haze. 'Gracie, Gracie.'

Opening her eyes, she saw a man she hadn't seen before. 'There, she's fine, she responds to her name. Start to get her out of bed and moving around. It's time she came around properly, as there's no physical reason for her to be in a comatose state. It's her mind keeping her there. She's been through a lot of trauma, I understand. And this attack didn't help matters. Withdraw the penicillin now too. She doesn't need it. And get her eating, even if you have to force feed her. She should be up and about in a week.'

'If you say so, Doctor.'

'I do. And I want you to carry out my orders. I'll call again next week, and I expect to see her up and about. Good day.'

A few days later, Gracie took a few tentative steps. The two men clapped their hands and looked as if they were about to dance. She giggled at their exaggerated, feminine movements. She couldn't make them out at all.

At last, the sick feeling left her and she enjoyed the bowl of porridge they gave her. It was as if every step forward she took was a mountain of joy for them.

While the one called John was changing the dressings on her wounds, she asked him if he knew how all the girls were. 'Are they free? And getting food?'

'Oh, aye. They're all back to normal. They were only kept in for two days in the end. Anyway, most of them will have forgotten it all by now – it was three weeks ago, you know.'

'Three weeks! I can't believe it, I thought it was yesterday!'

They both laughed at this.

'John, do you think they'll let Lizzie and Jeannie come and see me?'

'No, lass, and don't even ask. Anyway, Lizzie left here last week. Got herself into trouble canoodling with one of the boys, now she has her belly up and is where she belongs, in a correction convent. Those nuns will sort her out, little hussy.'

'But she didn't–'

'Shut your mouth. Hear nothing, see nothing is the motto around here, and you'd better remember it, lass.'

At that moment, the loneliness that Gracie had let go of, thinking these nurses were her friends, crowded in on her again, as did conversations she'd heard but not registered about the fun times they had with the boys. And she knew there was no escaping what went on in this house. All the staff were in on it. There was no one to turn to.

It was a week later that Gracie left sick bay and rejoined the rest of the girls. Instead of them being hostile to her as she feared, they looked on her as a hero and cheered when she walked into the dormitory. Crowding around her, they praised her and told her how they all felt revenged by landing a kick on the nurse. 'She's gone by the way. Pensioned off, we think, and good riddance. Though the nancy boys are almost as bad, at least they don't bother with us girls.'

'Nancy boys?'

'Them as been looking after you. Queer as owt, they are. They like boys, not girls.'

Gracie felt lost. None of this was anything that she understood, or had ever heard talked about. An arm came around her. She turned and found it was Jeannie. 'Come and sit on me bed, Gracie. Go back to your own beds, everyone, you're frightening Gracie, and after all she's been through an' all.'

The others didn't protest. They all seemed to like Jeannie, even though she was the typical type that most kids bullied. Gracie was glad that they didn't.

'I'm glad you're all right, Gracie. I've said prayers for you every night, as have all the girls.'

'Ta, love. Have you heard from Lizzie? I heard that she'd left.'

'Naw, and we won't either. None of the girls that go to the correction convent ever come back. It's not easy to get out of them places.'

'Poor Lizzie. At least she'll have her babby.'

'She won't, they'll take it the minute it's born and sell it to a childless couple. Naw, she'll never see her babby. But then, she said she didn't want to. She didn't want a reminder of how she got it. I think she'll fare well in the convent. She's a quiet type, and it was her who taught us all to pray. She were religious, was Lizzie. She used to say that God will only send her what she can

89

cope with. Well, he nearly broke her, but she went out of here with her head held high. And as she got to the door, she yelled that she would pray for us all and for the master and all the evil staff. Shocked them, that did. She'll be all right will Lizzie. Now, how about you? Have you got many scars?'

'Naw, I don't think so. And that John said that as I were young, any that I do have would fade with time.'

'That's good. Eeh, it's good to have you back. I knaw I only had you for a little while, well hours really, but I felt that we were friends from the start.'

'I did an' all, Jeannie.'

The door opening stopped their conversation. The master stood there. 'All of you, off with your nightshirts.'

A hush settled on the room.

'Now!'

This bellow from the master had them all jumping. Gracie looked amazed as they all discarded their nightshirts and stood straight.

'You!... Ahh, the vixen. So, you're back with us, then. And all mended. Take off your nightshirt, vixen!'

Gracie wanted to scream that she wouldn't, but all the girls were looking fearfully at her, and she didn't want to bring down on them what she had before. Slowly, with her cheeks burning, she took off her nightie.

The master walked over to her. 'Hum, nice, but still a bit marked. No, I'll leave you for next week.' Turning, he pointed at a girl with dark curly hair.

'You! Come with me.' The girl whimpered, but went without protest.

Gracie trembled. 'Eeh, Jeannie. We have to get away from here. We have to go to the police.'

'That won't help you. The master'll get you sectioned. Anyroad, the police won't believe you above him and all the rest of them. Just do as Lizzie said, and go along with it. It's the only way.'

Gracie crept into bed and pulled the covers over her head. Within minutes her pillow was wet from her silent tears.

But these stopped when the girl who'd been chosen came back to the room. Her crying drowned out that of the others. Gracie went over, and lay on her bed with her. She stayed until the girl fell into a fitful sleep.

CHAPTER NINE

Over the last ten days, the ritual of the master telling them to strip had happened three times. Every night, Gracie had dreaded the door opening.

She had been sitting on her bed chatting to Jeannie the next time it did. She'd learned that Jeannie didn't know who her parents were, and had been abandoned on a doorstep. She'd been in care all her life, always hoping that someone would adopt her, but now she'd given up and only longed for her sixteenth birthday, when the gates would open and they would let her out. She had no idea where she'd go.

Gracie told her that if she ever did get free and that Gracie herself was free by then, to make her way to Blackpool and to find Sheila near to the south pier or Rory at the circus. Either one would know where Jeannie could find Gracie.

Later, Gracie had pondered on why she hadn't mentioned her Aunt Massie's as well, but then she wondered if she would ever see her Aunt Massie again. She didn't blame her for not taking her in – she knew the reason why she hadn't – but neither did she long to see her, or any of them. She did long to see Sheila, though. And she often thought about Rory. She'd never known anyone like those two. It made her feel good just remembering them.

Those memories shot from her mind as the door burst open. The master looked straight at Gracie. 'You! Come with me.'

Shock held the room silent. Some had already got off their beds ready to take their shirts off. All looked towards her.

'Naw... Naw.'

'Oh, yes. And none of your antics.' The master lifted his arm. In his hand was the long stick.

Gracie cringed away.

'I said, come with me. Now, madam!'

He stood to the side and indicated that she should go through the open door. Trembling, she walked towards him.

'You just try it, madam, you just try it.'

Walking past him, she waited outside the door.

'Right, lights out, you lot.'

With this he strode past Gracie, telling her to follow him.

It took a while to reach the room he finally stopped at and entered. As Gracie followed, she saw that she was in a bedroom with a double bed. The gas mantle, turned low, gave a shadowy feel that increased the fear in her. The master closed and locked the door. Gracie watched as if hypnotised as he undressed. His bony body had a thick mass of hair on the chest. Gracie dare not look further down than his waist.

'Now, come here. I'll have the pleasure of taking your nightshirt off, thank you very much.'

Just do everything he says... Don't fight. It's worse if you struggle. Lizzie's voice in Gracie's head was as if she was standing next to her. Gracie walked forward. She allowed her shirt to be removed. 'Good girl. Mmm. You *are* a good girl.'

Gracie retched.

'Don't! I'm warning you!'

She swallowed hard.

'Take a drink of that water. And don't spoil the moment again, or you'll get another beating, but it'll be worse than what you had before!'

Gulping the water, Gracie tried to blank out everything that was happening to her. It wasn't until he lay her down and got on top of her that she tried to protest. 'Naw, please, don't. Please, Master.'

Ignoring her, he bore down on her. A stretching pain wrung a scream of protest from deep inside her.

His hand came over her mouth. His threatening 'Shut up!' came out as a growl as his body shuddered and he began to move.

She wanted to bite his hand, to stop him any

93

way that she could, but was afraid of what he'd do, so lay still beneath him. At last, he stiffened and cried out. The sound was akin to that of an injured animal. His body flopped down on her, crushing the breath from her. Pushing hard with her hands on his chest, Gracie instinctively knew that she had the advantage over him now. He rolled off her offering no resistance, and coiled up with his back towards her.

Disgust entered Gracie. In that moment, she left all childhood behind her. She lifted herself, and swiped out at him, landing a resounding slap on his bare buttocks. 'You pig. You dirty, filthy pig!'

The master lay trembling, his mumbles indistinguishable. Bile rose up into Gracie's throat. Just making it to the sink, in the adjoining bathroom, she heaved her heart up.

After swilling the sink, Gracie stood holding on to it. Her body shook. Her tears and snot mingled as loneliness engulfed her. She had the idea to wash every part of her body, but when she went to fill the sink, the noise from the taps made her too afraid that she would anger the master.

Waiting in terror, she expected him to call out to her, but all she could hear were snorting noises.

Creeping back into the bedroom, she saw that the master was asleep with his thumb in his mouth. Gracie donned her nightshirt as fast as she could. As she pulled it over her head she saw something glint. A key had escaped being pushed into the confines of the master's jacket that hung on the side of the wardrobe. Going to it she pulled it, and then froze as the whole bunch came loose with a jangling sound that echoed around the room. Looking at the master, she breathed a sigh of relief as he hadn't moved, or woken.

Emboldened and with an idea that she could escape this awful place, she plunged her hand into all the pockets and found his wallet. Grabbing the three one-pound notes tucked inside, she ran towards the door, freezing as a noise behind her terrified her. Looking back, she saw the master had turned onto his back, making the bed creak as he did, but he was still asleep. In a flash she was at the other side of the door. Fumbling with the keys, she found the one that fitted his door and locked him in.

Back in the dormitory, she felt strangely empowered. Jeannie was awake and came over to her, whispering so as not to wake the others. 'Eeh, Gracie, you weren't long. Are you all right?'

Gracie whispered, too. She had an idea to save herself and Jeannie, but couldn't if the others woke. They would all want to come and would cause a commotion. 'Aye, I am. Get dressed, Jeannie, we're leaving.'

'What? Naw, you can't get out of here.'

'I can, I've got the keys. Hurry.'

'Naw. I can't. Please don't go, Gracie.'

Gracie already had her vest on from the pile of her clothes that she'd folded neatly in the way they were all instructed to do. In no time she'd donned the rest of her clothes, leaving the pinny behind. 'I'm going, Jeannie. Don't stop me. Where can I get a coat? It was freezing earlier.'

'They're in the cloakroom. I'll show you. They only take us there when it snows, or there's a frost.

The rest of the time, we have to take our chances.'

The cloakroom was up a flight of stairs. It took a moment to identify the key to it. But within minutes of donning the first one that fitted her, and slipping her feet into some outdoor shoes, Gracie was making for the door through which she'd entered this awful place.

Jeannie had hugged her and gone back to the dormitory. Gracie had waited a moment for her to get there, her heart thudding her fear around her body as she did.

Now she had to find the key. She guessed it might be the largest one, but found that it wasn't. Fumbling now, she tried the next in size. But no.

Sweat stood out on her forehead and her hands felt clammy. At last, she heard the click of the lock releasing. It resounded around her.

Moving on fear alone, she was through the door, closing it behind her, and scampering across the yard.

This time it was the largest key that opened the gate.

Gracie held her breath as the creak it made would surely alert the whole house. She froze, but nothing happened.

Leaving the gate open she began to run along the road. The darkness hindered her. The cold bit at her cheeks. She hadn't gone far when she folded with a stitch in her side. Bending, she felt almost crippled. Gradually, the pain eased. But she knew that she hadn't the strength to run. In the distance, she could see lights, and remembered that when the taxi had brought her here there had been mainly built-up areas from the station, and then they'd seemed to go into the countryside, but only for a little way.

Soon she felt safer as there were houses each side of the road. The gas street lamps were lit and gave comfort. She tried to walk as if she hadn't a care in the world so as not to attract attention.

A dog gave her a scare. It came running out of a garden and snapped at her heels. The owners of the house pulled their curtains back and looked out of the window. Gracie tried to pet the dog, but he was having none of it. Then, to her relief the window opened and a man yelled at the dog. At last he left her.

Trembling from all she'd been through, Gracie walked on. When she came to an alleyway, she walked up it, afraid to stay on the main road. After walking through several alleyways, she came to another main road, only this one was busy with traffic. She prayed that a taxi would come along. It did, and it stopped when she flagged it down. In her most grown up voice, she said, 'Please take me to the station, driver.'

He didn't question her.

At the station, she ran inside. The ticket office was closed. A porter was putting shutters down. 'Excuse me, what time is the train to Blackpool tomorrow?'

'There's one first thing. Eight o'clock. The ticket office opens at seven.'

'Thank you.'

Still no suspicion of her. But her mind raced. Where would she go for the night? She had to get out of Manchester. If they put the police on her the station would be the first place they looked.

As she went back outside, the taxi was still there. The driver wound the window down. 'I thought you'd be lucky to get a train, love. What're you doing out at this time of night, anyroad?'

Swallowing hard, Gracie looked at him. 'I – I...'

'Are you running away?'

Defeated, Gracie nodded. 'Please don't take me back. Please. I can't bear it, the master–'

'Say no more. I don't want to hear it. I know where you've come from. I were there not many years ago, meself. How did you get out? I've not known that happen before.'

'I – the master, well, I stole the keys and some money.'

'Good on yer. Jump in. Where d'yer want to go?'

Gracie couldn't believe what she was hearing. 'Blackpool.'

'Eeh, I've no petrol to take you that far. I'll take you to me mam's. She'll take care of you till morning, then I'll pick you up and take you to the station at six-thirty tomorrow.'

'I thought you said you were in Hallford House. How come you've got a ma?'

'I have now, but she were in prison at the time. Don't worry, she ain't no murderer, she just did a bit of thieving to get by. You've nowt to worry over. She'll welcome you. She welcomes all waifs and strays. What's your name? Mine's Gary.'

Gary asked few questions, after she told him her name. He seemed to know she just wanted to get somewhere where she felt safe.

Entering his ma's house she felt just that. Gary's ma was a jolly woman with a shock of red hair, like she'd had herself before the nurse had taken her scissors to it. Not very tall, Mo, as she told Gracie to call her, had a huge bosom that her bright blue blouse struggled to contain, and a tiny waist and hips that wriggled in the tight black skirt she wore. Her lips were painted bright red. Her brown eyes were outlined with black mascara. And her teeth, though crooked, were a lovely pearly white and seemed to sparkle when she smiled.

'Hello, love. What's this you've dragged in then? I don't know. Our Gary's allus landing someone on me. Well, you're welcome, darlin'. What's your name, then?'

'She's called Gracie. Now, don't overwhelm her, Mam.'

But Gary's warning was too late. The welcome and the relief were too much for Gracie. Tears gushed from her. Sobs racked her body.

'Now then, love. Eeh, don't take on. Tell Mo, what's the matter, eh?'

'She's come from Hallford House, Mam.'

'Aw. Poor sod. Here, you go on off out again, Gary, or you'll miss getting another fare. I'll see to her. I can see the signs. That bastard up there's been at her, I'd like to bet you.'

Cradled in Mo's arms, Gracie poured her heart out, telling of her ma, her da and finally of her granny.

'And has that bastard at the refuge been at you, love?'

Gracie nodded.

'Aw. Pool little soul. You've enough cares for a lifetime, and how old are you?'

'I turned fourteen in August, just gone.'

'Eeh, he makes me blood boil. And no one can touch him, he's got it all sewn up tight. He did the same to my Gary. It's took years to get him right, and still he has nightmares. Look, love, I ain't got much, but what I have you're welcome to. Then Gary will get you on your way to your friends in the morning. Are you sure they'll take you in, eh?'

'Yes. I'm sure as Sheila will help me. She's a good sort.' As she said this, Gracie wasn't at all sure, after all. She'd only known Sheila a short time before all of this had happened. But she'd have to try. As her granny used to say, you get nowt if you don't try.

'That's good then. Now, let's get a bowl of water for you to have a wash. I ain't got no bathroom, and I ain't dragging the tin bath in at this time of night, lass. We can wash you down and I've got some soothing creams that will make you feel better. Then you can get a night's sleep. How does that sound, eh?'

'Ta, Mo. I don't know what I would have done without you.'

'Think nowt of it. But, lass, I'll worry over you, so send me a card will you? One of them saucy Blackpool ones so as I know as your settled.'

While helping her to wash herself down, Mo chatted on. Relating tales of her visits to Blackpool and making Gracie laugh. Gracie began to feel human again. That man had been cleaned from her, and soothing Vaseline had helped her to feel less sore. She just had to get what happened out of her head, but would she ever be able to? As she snuggled down on the sofa in front of the fire, she prayed that Jeannie would be all right. One day they would meet again, she felt sure of it.

CHAPTER TEN

Gracie felt strange as she stepped off the train in Blackpool. Fear vied with the relief that she was so close to being safe. And though she'd slept well, tiredness made her body ache. The weight of her worries, and the fact that she'd had to stand all the way as the train was packed with holidaymakers going to Blackpool to do their Christmas shopping, had worn her out.

Gary's trousers, an old pair that he'd grown out of, were making her legs itch, and his shirt and jacket were alien clothes for her. As was the cloth cap she wore. To complete her disguise, Mo had trimmed her hair, as although it hadn't grown much, it had been longer than a boy would wear it. But worse were the shoes. They were at least two sizes too big, and were heavy to walk in. Mo had stuffed the toes with newspaper to stop them flopping about on her feet, but they were the most uncomfortable shoes she'd ever worn.

Gracie hadn't been sure about the disguise, or if she could carry it off, until Mo reminded her that it was possible that the police would be looking for her and they would think that the obvious place she would make for would be her home town.

This had shocked her, and then terrified her as Mo had said that she was now a criminal. Not only had she absconded from where she was a ward, but worse, she'd stolen money and keys.

'You leave them keys here, love, I'll take care of them. But you can't just waltz into Blackpool looking like yourself, lass. The police will more than likely have a description of you.'

These words came back to Gracie now as she made sure she was in the middle of the heaving, excited crowd who pushed and shoved their way towards the ticket collector.

Her heart was in her mouth as her ticket was punched and she looked up to see a policeman scrutinising each passenger. But she did as Mo had said and acted as naturally as she could, not looking at the policeman as she made her way past him. He didn't stop her.

Once outside the station she wanted to run like the wind, but remembered Mo's words. 'Don't do owt that will draw attention to yourself, Gracie. Walk at a normal pace as if you haven't got a care in the world, and act as if you are a stranger, not sure which way to go. Just follow the rest of the crowd, and keep close to a family if you can, so that you look part of them.'

All of this paid off as Gracie found herself walking down Talbot Road, still flanked by people, and having got this far without raising any suspicions.

Anticipation tightened her tummy muscles as the excitement of the crowd took her along with it. Blackpool buzzed at this time of the year. No other seaside town offered the extended season, even after the beautiful light show – free of charge if you managed to dodge the collection buckets along the route – was switched off. Crowds came at weekends and stalls stayed open to accommodate them.

When she eventually came to the Prom opposite the North Pier, Gracie relaxed. The Prom thronged with people, all huddled in long winter coats trying to protect themselves from the strong, bitter winds. Gracie did the opposite. She threw back her head, losing her cap in the process, and embraced the feel of the wind and the sea spray that tingled her cheeks.

Tears filled her eyes as familiar smells and sounds assailed her, but then she realised she was getting some funny looks and attracting attention to herself, so she huddled up against the wind, head down, and crossed the road to board the tram to take her to South Pier. She sighed with relief that the driver wasn't Joe. And then knew a joy to fill her as she alighted from the tram to the sound of a familiar voice:

'Blackpool rock – get your Blackpool rock here.'

Sheila!

'Sheila, Sheila. Oh, Sheila, it's good to see you, love.'

'Gracie! Where've you been, lass? I've been worried sick. I went to your gran's but there were a family living there and they told me what had happened to your gran. I was right sorry, and didn't knaw where else to look for you.'

Gracie couldn't stop her eyes welling up. She swallowed hard, but couldn't speak.

'Eeh, Gracie. Whatever happened to you wasn't good, I can see that. By, you look a sight an' all.

If you thought to disguise yourself, you've done a bad job, at least to them as knaws you. But, why have you had to...? Naw, don't try to tell me... Look, I'm running out of stock, I've been that busy, and it's nearly time for me snap. I've to go home to get more stock, so I'll shut up shop and I'll take you there with me.'

Gracie waited, the while trying to hold back the tears. Knowing they weren't far from her granny's house, and having it mentioned didn't help, nor did seeing the crashing waves at the spot that she understood her granny had walked into the sea. *Why? Why? Oh, Granny, why?* But then she had to remember that her granny hadn't been well in her mind, and might not have known which direction she was heading in. She maybe thought to walk along the beach to get to Ma's, having forgotten that Ma had passed on.

As these thoughts threatened to overwhelm her, Gracie brushed them aside.

'Right, I'm ready. Come on, Gracie.' Sheila unhooked her bike from the railings. With its huge basket attached to the front, it wasn't easy to manoeuvre. 'You'll be right, once you see me ma. She's a tonic for anyone. And she'll knaw what to do an' all.'

Sheila's house surprised Gracie. Hornby Road was full of boarding houses and Sheila's home was one of them.

'I forgot to say as me ma's taking in holiday-makers now an' all. We've lived here a while and she allus intended to open it up, but it's took her time to get all she needed in place. The beds and the linen and such.'

'How does she manage with making the rock an' all and then making popcorn in the evening?'

'Oh, she only does breakfast for the punters, and they bring the food themselves, she just cooks it. Then, me Aunt Aggie does the bedrooms and the laundry. Mind, that's a shame in itself, as she used to be a trapeze artiste, but fell and broke her leg, and is now afraid of heights. But she's a help to me ma, as once the dishes are done Ma doesn't have to worry about the rest of the household chores and can get on with making rock. Besides, if she gets behind she has a stock in the shed in the yard, where there are shelves full of rock.'

This world of Sheila's was so different to anything Gracie had ever known. Everyone was doing something special, and *was* special, and talented. Just hearing about them lifted Gracie's spirits, but when she was with them, as she had been on the night of the circus visit, she was raised above all her cares.

'Ma ... Ma?'

'Eeh, Sheila, lass, what's to do, you're home early... Oh, who's this young man ... I mean, girl... Or, er...'

'Ha, it's a girl, Ma. This is Gracie, who I told you about. I haven't pushed her as to why she's dressed as a boy 'cause she's upset, so I thought to bring her to you to sort out.'

'Ahh, Gracie. Yes, Sheila did tell me about you, and the tragedy you've faced, and then for your Granny to ... well, we won't talk about that, but Sheila's been very worried about you since you disappeared, lass.'

'I – I...' The pain and tension of all Gracie had

105

been through cracked at that moment as she looked into the kindly eyes of Sheila's ma. She reminded her of her own ma in her ways, and with her direct way of speaking. And she was about the same age too, but there the similarities ended. The curly hair that fell to her shoulders was very dark, like Sheila's. Her face was nice – rounded and dimply when she smiled.

When she took Gracie in her arms, she felt squidgy, like Gracie's granny had before she lost weight. And she smelled of cooking, and home, and love.

'Let it all out, lass. God knaws as you've a lot to cry over.'

'I'll put the kettle on, Ma. It's enough to freeze your lugs off out there, but there's plenty of punters about. I'm not home early just because Gracie turned up, but because I've had a cracking morning and I'm almost out of stock, so I thought I'd have an early snap and collect some more.'

Sheila's ma carried on stroking and soothing Gracie as she answered this. 'Ooh, that's good. And I have all the rooms full of guests an' all. I didn't expect that, not at this time of year. But folk are coming for the weekends now, and to do their Christmas shopping at all the cheap stalls. It's a knock-on effect. We're on the up and up, lass.'

'What is the commotion, is the fair come to the street? Oh, it is sorry that I am, I didn't know that you had a guest.'

The foreign voice belonged to a beautiful lady, who looked as though she were made of porcelain. Her tiny frame and the graceful way she had glided into the kitchen made Gracie think she wasn't real.

'I come back in a moment.' With this, she went out of the door.

'That was Aunt Aggie. Well, she's not really called Aggie, her real name is Agashka. She's Russian, and married to me Uncle Ron, me ma's brother. He sets up the trapezes and keeps them maintained and designs new ones. They met when she came to work at the tower. She's lovely, but a little shy and out of her depth with strangers.'

'You can meet her another time, Gracie. Now, are you feeling better, love? Can you tell us what's to do with you?' Sheila's ma had a lovely caring smile on her face as she said this, and Gracie felt herself being pulled into the warmth and love that came from her.

'We'll sit around the little table, Ma, I've set the cups there.'

Whilst sipping her tea, and between rebound sobs, Gracie told them what had happened to her since her granny had died. They both sat in silence as Gracie finished by begging of Sheila's ma: 'Please, missus, don't send me back, and please don't do owt like go to the police. They wouldn't believe me, and they'd make me go back.'

'My, I've never heard the like. And I'd never dream of sending you back to such a place. Me name's Peggy, and you can call me that – none of us are formal here. Now, we have to think what's to do.'

'Didn't you say you had an aunt, Gracie, won't she take you in?'

'Naw. Well, she would, but...' Gracie told them

107

how things were with her Aunt Massie, and how she came to call her Aunt, even though they weren't related. 'Me Aunt Massie were good to me ma, and I knaw that her heart will be breaking over me, but if I went there me Uncle Percy'd call the police sooner than have me under his roof.'

'You can stay here. But, you mustn't get caught, or we'll all be in trouble, so I reckon for a while you'll have to stay out of sight and the only fresh air you'll get is in the back yard, or sitting in the front garden in the evening. But you can help me, I've plenty of chores, and we'll look after you and keep you safe. In the meantime, we'll try to find out how you stand if you've found a home and someone willing to look after you, though the tricky bit is the thieving. I knaw as you had no choice, lass, but if, as you say, you won't be believed about what is happening at that place, then you will have a job to get away with taking that money and the keys.'

'Have you got much of it left, Gracie?'

'Aye, all but me train fare. Why what're yer thinking?'

Sheila didn't answer, but looked at her ma. 'Couldn't we make it up, and then Gracie just hand it in, Ma?'

'It might work. Especially if we say we're willing to take her in and take care of her. Given everything that she's been through, they might be lenient. But it's a risk. I'll get the ring master to sound out the copper that checks up on us at the circus, he has a good relationship with him, even though we all feel like criminals when he's around.'

Gracie didn't know what to say, she was too

grateful for thanks to cover it, and the relief that she hadn't to go back overwhelmed her, bringing on the tears once more.

'Aye, well, lass, you've a lot to cry about, so let it out.'

Sheila came around the back of her and put her arm around her. 'Eeh, I'm that glad to have you, Gracie. We'll be like sisters. And we'll think of sommat that'll allow you to get out sometimes, until we can make things right, you'll see.'

'That's settled then. Sheila, take Gracie to your room and find one of your frocks for her, we don't want her looking like a ... but, wait a mo ... that's it! There is a way you could go out and about, Gracie. You can do as you have done and dress as a boy! You're slight of figure, and we have the very best masters of costume in the business amongst our circle. They could make you look very convincing.'

'Ooh, that'd be great, Ma, then Gracie could come to the circus and help there too. There's a lot to do now that the season has finished, and we open up again soon after Christmas. Oh, it'll be grand to have you working with me, Gracie.' Sheila clapped her hands together.

Their excitement and enthusiasm infected Gracie and she went along with them. 'I could learn to lower me voice and walk like a lad, an' all.'

'What is all the excitement?' Aunt Aggie came through the door. 'Sorry to intrude, but it is that I must put away the mop and bucket and get the washing in the tub. And Granddad is walking around and needs you, Peggy. He is naked as the day he was born!'

Peggy laughed. 'You're not intruding, Aggie. This is Gracie, soon to be Garth.'

To Gracie's surprise Aunt Aggie didn't bat an eyelid. 'Oh, I see. I am pleased to meet you, Garth. You are fine-looking boy.'

Sheila laughed out loud. 'Don't look like that, Gracie, you're in a circus family now. Such things as turning a girl into a boy are natural to us.'

Gracie felt a smile creasing her face and with it, a happy feeling filled her. She was safe. She never had to do that thing with the master again, and if she could help it, she'd never do it with anyone ever, for as long as she lived.

CHAPTER ELEVEN

Gracie looked around the empty arena. Always when she came to the circus, she could see her granny sitting in the front row. The happiness of that night stayed with Gracie and lifted her when she felt down.

Two months had passed, Christmas had come and gone. For the most part, it had been a jolly and magical time, but a deep sadness had cloyed at Gracie, marring the festivities as she'd coped with this being her first Christmas without her family.

Not that they'd ever had anything like what Sheila's family had. Gracie remembered that their table had only been a fraction more laden than on a normal day. But before she got ill Ma would have baked some mince pies, and made paper chains to hang around the walls. Granny would have brought one of her old stockings for Gracie, filled with an orange and some nuts, and a spinning top and yoyo, something of that kind. But it had been a jolly time, with Da accepting Granny and them having a bit more than a scrag end to eat, as Granny always brought a chicken with her. It had been delicious and altogether a magical day for Gracie.

At Sheila's the table had been laden with a huge, roasted cockerel as the main dish, and more vegetables than Gracie had ever seen. They'd played games and drunk sherry; and then the most magical thing of all happened. Silence had fallen and into it had come the whistling and crackling of the wireless set as Bertram, Sheila's da, had fiddled with the knobs trying to tune into the very first King's Christmas Message ever to be broadcast. They'd all held their breaths, and then it happened. It was just as if the King was in their living room as his voice came from the little brown box with a golden lattice-grid at the front of it.

'Through one of the marvels of modern science, I am enabled, this Christmas Day, to speak to all my peoples throughout the Empire.'

Gracie didn't think she would ever forget that experience.

Now, here it was already the end of February in the year 1933 and the whole of Sheila's family was engaged in getting the circus ready to open at Easter. The circus family, as she knew they all looked on each other, was glad that this year

111

Easter was to be late – it wasn't until 16 April – giving them plenty of time to paint everything that could be painted, and mend apparatus and costumes, and to practise. Always they practised their routines and added new moves, dances or tricks to make the show fresh for returning visitors.

It was a magical world to Gracie. She loved every minute of her time there, and especially any time spent with Rory and Suzy his monkey. Rory's remit was to care for the animals, and his love for them shone from him. Even the lions welcomed him, becoming like friendly household cats when he was around them.

Today they were to take the elephants to the beach – a time they, and any members of the public who were around, loved.

Walking with Rory across the Promenade with a string of elephants following them felt surreal, and yet the most natural thing in the world to do.

'I could fancy you, you know, Gracie. You make a very attractive boy.'

'What? And you would fancy a boy?'

'Aye, I would. I'm not like other boys. I don't find girls attractive.'

This statement shocked Gracie. For a moment, she thought of the horrid Foggie Jeannie had told her about, and the two nurses she'd since come to hate for the misery she knew they had caused. Surely Rory wasn't like them? 'You're having me on. A handsome lad like you, you'll have your pick of the lasses.'

'Naw, I told you. I feel different to most lads. I have done since I were knee high to a donkey.'

Embarrassed by the turn of this conversation, Gracie sought to change the subject. 'What happened to your family, Rory? You never talk about them.'

At that moment, the elephants took Rory's attention as he guided them through the gap in the railings that wrapped around the edge of the beach and ushered them down the slope onto the sand. When they felt the sand under their feet they became restless and hard to handle.

'Hup, Hup!' The sea breeze took Rory's cry into the air, but the elephants responded and calmed a little. But their pace had quickened and Gracie and Rory had to run to keep them in check.

The breeze whipped around Gracie, flapping her shirt and lifting her cap. She clung on to it as sea spray wet her face, tingling an ice cold feeling through her.

Once in the water, the elephants were ecstatic, rolling around, and filling their trunks with the salty water before spraying it over themselves, at each other and at the laughing crowd.

Rory stood still, allowing them this playtime. At last, he answered her question. 'We all work at different circuses. It works better that way. Me ma is a trapeze artist, and me da's a lion tamer. But he – well, he's like me. He shouldn't have married.'

'I don't understand, Rory. I mean, I do knaw of such things, but to be honest, them as I knew, who liked boys, were horrible. I don't think that you're like that.'

'We're not all perverts. Me da's not. He lives with a man who is a strongman act who can lift the front of a bus up in the air, and in his act, he lifts a plank with his teeth, with two women sitting on it. And yet, he is the gentlest of men and he and me da love each other. And they're safe, as circus folk accept these things and protect them and treat them as normal.'

'Well, I think of you as normal, and knowing this about you hasn't changed that.'

'Ta, Gracie, that's put me mind at rest. I were afraid as you were looking on me as a possible boyfriend.'

'Naw, I don't want a boy, not ever. I – I, well, I expect Sheila's told you what I went through at that home.'

'Aye, she has, and I'm sorry.'

'Rory, can I tell you sommat? Sommat as is private, but is scaring me.'

'Aye, owt as yer like.'

'Well, you knaw as how we girls have our bleeding? Well, mine ain't happened since I left that place, and me Aunt Massie told me that they stopped when you were caught for a babby. I – I'm scared, Rory. I don't knaw what to do.'

Rory looked shocked. 'You mean, someone did that to you?'

This surprised Gracie. She'd assumed that Sheila and Peggy would have told everyone what had happened to her. She regretted confiding in Rory now, but he was so easy to talk to and even more so now that all thoughts were dispelled of his thinking of her in the same light as her da and the master had.

'Don't tell anyone, please Rory, but aye, I've had that done to me.' Explaining to Rory what

114

had happened was easier than she'd thought.

'Well, you must tell Peggy. She'll knaw what to do. She'll take care of you. Eeh, don't be afraid, and don't get upset. Lift your head, and face all you have to, that's the circus way, and you're one of us now. Come on, let's get these elephants back over the road. They've tired themselves out, so'll be compliant.'

Peggy's look of sympathy nearly undid Gracie, but she did as Rory said, and it felt good to feel the strength it gave to her.

'Eeh, me lass. I'm sorry. I hoped this wouldn't be the outcome, but have wondered as you've never asked for some rags, which would indicate that you'd come on with your monthly. But, it's early days. You say you think you've missed two? Well, we can't confirm that you're pregnant until you miss three, but we will have to sort sommat out so as to protect you. This could ruin your life, but we won't let it.'

Gracie couldn't speak. The fear in her was compounded now that Peggy had almost confirmed her suspicions, but something in her knew that she would be all right. Peggy would see to that.

'Let me think this through, lass. I've an idea, but I need to talk to my Bertram, he has to approve what I'm thinking, and don't worry, we'll protect you one way or another. But it may mean that you stay around here from now on. No one as knaws you must see you. We'll tell them that you have gone to your aunt's.'

All of this was reassuring, but frightening, too. And to have to give up going to help at the circus

115

was a big blow. But, at the same time, as Peggy took her into her arms, Gracie felt safe and wrapped in love.

The plan Peggy talked of, after speaking to Bertram, surprised Gracie. Peggy was to tell everyone that after all these years and her nearly going through the change, she'd copped for a babby again. The plans they made had them giggling as Peggy tried various things strapped around her stomach to make her look in the different stages of pregnancy.

Only the family and Rory were to know what was happening. Gracie was glad that Rory would be allowed to visit her. She had a bond with him that she couldn't explain but thought that it might be akin to having a brother.

Somehow, they all made it sound like an adventure they were going on, and instead of feeling afraid and upset, an excitement gripped Gracie.

'What do you want to happen when the babby's born, Gracie?'

'Oh, I hadn't thought of that, Sheila. I can't really think of it as being a proper babby, I don't knaw why.'

They were sitting on their beds, Gracie writing the promised card to Mo, months after she should have done. Though something stopped her telling too much. She just told Mo that she was safe and being looked after, and sent her thanks to her and to Gary. This eased her conscience a little, but not telling Mo her address made her feel a little ashamed. She just didn't want any ties with that part of her life. Though she often thought of Jeannie and hoped that she would seek her out once she was free. Signing her name and adding a kiss, she looked up. She loved this bedroom that she shared with Sheila with its pink walls and gaily coloured curtains in a butterfly print. The floor was covered with grey linoleum, and there was a rug between the beds which was also multi-coloured. Around the room were bits of Sheila's childhood – a teddy bear with only one glass eye, and a rag doll with an arm missing, a jack-in-the-box, only the jack would no longer stay in the box but flopped over the side of it.

Sometimes when she looked at these and other bits of memorabilia around the room, Gracie wondered what had happened to her own box of memories, and all of Granny's things for that matter, but it was too painful to dwell on the subject so she would brush it aside.

'Well, it is going to be a babby, so you had better get used to it, lass. I reckon as though Ma'll want to keep it, she's that excited. You'd think that she really were expecting a child.'

Gracie didn't know what to think of this. Part of her couldn't give any attention to it as it all seemed unreal.

'Anyroad, once the babby's born me and you can get back on with our lives. It'll be winter again, by then, but we can still have some fun.'

The talking and planning didn't match the reality, as day after day, Gracie had to rush to the bucket to empty her stomach, and clothes no longer fitted. Then there was the constant backache and the tiredness.

Her days were filled with helping Peggy, as they

listened to the wireless. Gracie thought she knew everything that was happening in the world. One of the most talked-about events was that someone called Hitler had become a dictator of Germany. She wasn't sure what this meant, but from the many reports over the months, she knew she didn't like him, or what he stood for.

But there were lighter moments, too, when music blared out from a foreign station they managed to pick up, or they listened to a short play on the BBC.

Of all the chores, she loved the rock making the best, and learned the correct temperature for the boiling of the sugar, and how to mould the blob that resulted, and the hard work of pulling it on the hooks on the wall until it turned into a white, sweet toffee. But the best part was helping to make the letters. This Gracie found fascinating.

Part of the toffee was dyed red and then left on an iron plate over the stove to keep it warm. Then strips of it were moulded around the white toffee to form the letters. Each of the strips of a letter were laid in the correct order to spell Blackpool, between strips of white toffee. The resulting large square was then rolled and pulled until it was long and thin, and then cut into rock-size lengths. Once she had mastered the process, Gracie loved every minute of the painstaking task, and felt a sense of pride when the finished product was good enough to be wrapped in wax paper ready for Sheila to sell on her stall.

'You're a dab hand at this work, Gracie love, but it is heavy going, and we'll have to put you onto just wrapping the rock as you get further into your time.'

That time dragged. With the circus up and running and Blackpool busier than ever, the sense of missing out on the excitement ground Gracie down. Not to mention the heat. For many an hour she would sit on the step of the back door, trying to cool off.

At last September arrived and the birth was on her. Pain like she never thought to experience wracked her body, and tore at her heart.

'Help me. Please help me, Peggy.'

'Try to relax, lass, it will be better for you. Take deep breaths when the pain comes.'

This was easier said than done, and Gracie found more relief in screaming the walls down.

'They'll hear you at the tower at this rate, quieten down, lass, you're not helping yourself.'

Gracie didn't care who heard her. Curses came from her that she never thought to utter as she clung to the bedstead and hollered at anyone and everyone.

Sheila tried to mop her brow. But, angry at her for her innocence, and at the world for what had befallen her, Gracie grabbed the flannel and whipped it around Sheila's face.

'Eeh, Gracie. That weren't nice.'

'Nice? What's nice about this, eh?'

'Eeh, there's a side to you, Gracie, that I've not seen afore. And I don't like it. We should leave her to stew, Ma.'

'Naw, don't, I'm sorry, I'm sorry, I love you both. Don't leave me.'

'We knaws as you do, lass, and we love you, but you're not making it any easier. You're fighting it and us, instead of using your energy to get babby into the world. Sheila was only trying to make you comfortable. Now come on, chin on your chest, and push hard with the next pain.'

After ten minutes of this, Gracie flopped back exhausted.

'I should go for the doctor, Ma.'

'Naw, lass. We have to keep this a secret. Gracie's life will be ruined if we don't. It'll be over with the next pain, I promise. You hold that leg, Sheila, and I'll hold this one, and when she pushes, push against her, that'll give her plenty of leverage.'

This did the trick. With the next pain, the babby slipped from her. As it did, she gasped in her breath as if the master's cane had sliced her. And with thinking of him, Gracie had a feeling on her that she wanted nothing to do with this babby. It was born of his rape of her, and she didn't need reminding of that.

Peggy told her that she was going to cut and tie the cord, and that in a few minutes the mass that had been feeding the babby would come away from her, and then it would all be over.

This done, Peggy took the child, instructing Sheila to clean Gracie up.

Gracie didn't object, and watched with horror as Peggy cradled the babby to her. The blood and gunge attached to the babby clung to Peggy's pinny. To Gracie this made the child a monster.

'I have a son. A son. Oh, Sheila, you have a brother, at last.'

'Ma, what are you saying? He's Gracie's son, not yours.'

120

'I don't want him. Your ma can have him. Take him, Peggy. I want nowt to do with him.'

'Gracie! That ain't natural. Give him to Gracie, Ma... Ma, please!'

Peggy came towards her. Gracie cringed away, but Sheila took the babby, now swaddled in a piece of sheeting and brought him so that she couldn't refuse him. 'Hold him, Gracie, for pity's sake, take hold of your little boy.'

Unable to refuse, Gracie put out her arms. When she looked into the face of her son, she saw her granny. His little features were as wizened as her granny's had been, and the hand he held out to her was just as wrinkly as she remembered her granny's being.

A wave of love for this little son of hers swept over Gracie. Tears formed in her eyes and spilled over, running down her cheeks. She looked up at Peggy, saw the fear in her eyes, and made a decision that was the hardest she'd ever made. 'You can have him, Peggy.'

Peggy leaned forward and took the babby. 'Thank you. We will take care of him together. It will be your milk that nurtures him, and you can do as much as you want to for him, but it is better that he is known as mine, then you can go forward and make a life for yourself, better than the one you could have if you were known as an unmarried mother. He will be our secret, and he will grow up with two mams.'

Gracie nodded.

'What shall we call him, then, Gracie?'

'I'd like to call him Bertram, after your da, Sheila. He has been so kind to me and more of a da to me than me own da ever was. Besides, he's willing to take my son on as his own and that's sommat, an' all.'

'Eeh, Gracie, me da'll be so honoured. And so we don't get mixed up we can call the babby Bertie.'

Peggy hadn't spoken, but Gracie saw her wipe a tear away as she smiled lovingly at Bertie, before looking up and covering her emotions with saying, 'Eeh, Sheila, take hold of your brother a mo. I have to get these cushions out of me pants, they're killing me. And me labour's over now.'

At this and Peggy's antics as she pushed down and removed one cushion after the other, they all burst into a fit of laughter.

It was a healing laughter and a laughter that promised that these three women of different generations would go forward together, watching each other's backs, and that of little Bertie's, who now gurgled as if to lend his approval.

PART TWO

1938–1939

HAPPINESS BEFORE A FALL

CHAPTER TWELVE

'Well, that's another batch done, Bertie. Now, give over pinching bits, you'll rot your teeth.'

'Ma said that I can have all I want of the rock pieces, and you can't stop me, Gracie.'

There had been so many times over the last four and half years when Gracie had wanted to scream that *she* was his ma, and he would do as she told him, but she bit her tongue.

Scooping up the rest of the bits that had chipped off as she cut the rock into lengths, Gracie smiled at him. 'I'll be glad when you're at school out of our way.'

Bertie wrinkled his nose. More and more, he was looking like her, with his shock of red hair and freckled face. 'Now, scamper as there's another boiling ready, and it is too dangerous for you in here.'

They were in the extended shed that stood at the back of the boarding house. Together, she and Peggy had built up their custom, and their operation was too big for the kitchen now. Times had been good in Blackpool and with the income from the boarding house and the increased sales of the rock, besides the little money left to Peggy from her da passing – a sad time, but a relief to all, especially Sheila, who was mortified to see the deterioration in her grandfather – they'd been able to purchase a comical looking machine which did the pulling for them, and to install a long bench so that they could make bigger batches to roll out. In one corner was a stove for the boiling.

Many rock factories had opened up in and around Blackpool over the last thirty years or so, and competition was fierce, but Peggy's rock had built a name for itself and they now sold as far as Rhyl in Wales. They would pack the rock into cases and take it to the station. There it was loaded onto the goods train to start its journey.

How there was a market for their small concern, Gracie couldn't fathom, but between them, she and Peggy made a good living. Although, mostly, Gracie worked on her own these days as Peggy's hands had become gnarled with arthritis and were too painful for her to help with the rolling.

Just as Gracie finished wrapping the last stick of the day, the door to the shed opened. 'Are you nearly finished, Gracie?'

'I am, Sheila, I'm just cleaning down.'

'I thought we'd go and see Stanley Holloway and Betty Driver in *All The Best* at the Opera House. I've been told it's really good.'

'You not working at the circus tonight then?'

'Naw, I've got a night off. The Prom's teeming with holidaymakers and loads of airmen are about. They always come in from Warton on a Friday night. Perhaps we'll meet someone to sweep us off our feet.'

'Ha! You say that every time you have a night off, but it ain't happened yet.'

'Tonight's the night, I can feel it in me bones.'

Gracie smiled. Since turning twenty, a birthday Gracie herself would be celebrating soon, Sheila had seemed intent on finding a husband. 'Will Rory join us later?'

'He will, he has his eye on someone too. You remember he was chatting to that chef from the Warton Air Base? Well, he's never stopped going on about him. He said he'll meet us after the show, as his last performance at the circus is at nine. We can go to the chippy on Talbot Road, the one that has seating inside. Then Rory will go on to a bar he knows where he is hoping to meet his chef.'

'Sounds good. Has your ma cooked us owt?'

'Naw, I told her not to. She's left us a butty, so that'll keep us going.'

'I worry about your ma, Sheila.'

'Don't, she's fine. Her joy is in having Bertie to look after, and him thinking that she is his ma. Aye, the rock business is a bit much for her these days, but she still puts the hours into the circus and her popcorn making, and still runs the boarding house. She's happy. I'd just let her go her own way. You can manage the rock making on your own, can't you?'

'Aye, I can, and I love doing it. It takes me out of meself, and I can be creative, too. I've a new line for you. I'll show you.'

Taking one of her last batch, Gracie unwrapped the lemon-coloured stick. 'There, see? I have a picture of a lemon going right through the centre.'

'Eeh, Gracie, that's amazing. I've seen a few who have fruit pictures going through, but one single one, I think you've hit on a winner there.'

'It's lemon flavoured, an' all, and I have some strawberry flavouring, so I'm going to have a go at that tomorrow. The options are endless. I was thinking that we need something a bit unique, and maybe I'll go into specialised rock. You knaw, small batches for parties that have the birthday child's name through it. I'm in a good position to do that stuff, as the large factories have to make such huge quantities that it wouldn't be profitable for them to take on commissions.'

'Well, who'd have thought it? You're a dark horse. I never knew you had such creativity in you. I reckon as that's a good idea. Now, come on, let's get our glad rags on and a bit of lippy and paint Blackpool red.'

'Ha, not much chance of that in the opera house. We should go to the Tower Ballroom – that's where you'll find your Romeo.'

'Yes, let's, I can call down at the circus and let Rory know.'

Donning her new cotton frock, which had a sheen on it that almost made it look like silk, Gracie revelled in the way it clung to her body to just below her hips and then flared out. The neckline was rounded, and the colour, a sea green, made her think that the whole effect made her look like a mermaid. Falling to her ankles, the frock went well with the silver pumps she'd bought from the Abingdon Street Market a couple of weeks back. Her hair hung in perfect ringlets after she'd washed it and let it dry without towelling it. A lengthy business, but they had plenty of time.

Sheila looked lovely, too. Her lilac frock was straight cut, and clung in all the right places. The neckline was a little low for Gracie's taste, but Sheila had a lovely creamy skin, not freckly like her own, and the cut suited her really well. She'd chosen a beige shoe with a tiny heel, which added an elegance to her outfit. She'd taken to wearing her hair in a similar style to Ginger Rogers after they had been to see the film *Swing Time*, which also starred Fred Astaire. Ginger had looked so pretty with her hair parted on the left side and swept back before falling into a mound of waves from behind her ears. The style suited Sheila so well.

The Prom was heaving. The warm July evening had the crowds out enjoying the stalls and all that Blackpool had to offer. The queue for the tower stretched five hundred yards along the Prom when Gracie and Sheila joined it. The air was filled with excited anticipation.

'Can we come in with you, ladies? Only we heard that men are not allowed in on their own.'

Gracie turned to see an airman looking down at her. Tall, and with the bluest eyes she'd ever seen, he smiled a smile that jolted her heart. Shaking herself, she reminded herself that she didn't want a boyfriend, not now, not ever. She didn't smile back.

'Hey, sorry, we thought you'd like some company.'

'No, we–'

'Yes, we do, nice to meet you, me name's Sheila and this is Gracie.'

'I'm Freddie and this is Bob. We're stationed at Warton. Bob is training to be a pilot, and I'm an aircraft technician, but if ... well, your friend doesn't seem too keen.'

'Don't mind her. Where you from? I mean, before Warton?'

'I'm from Nottingham, Bob's from Surrey.'

'Ain't you got a tongue then, Bob?'

Bob, shorter than Freddie, blushed at this remark from Sheila.

'He's shy; I do all the talking.'

'Well, he's no need to be shy with me. Though the silent type would suit me as I like to talk an' all. You queue with me, Bob. You can link in if you like.'

'Sheila!'

'What? Oh, Gracie, don't be a fuddy-duddy. It costs nowt to be friendly.'

Defeated, Gracie looked ahead, keeping herself as far away as she could from Freddie. She didn't like how his rakish looks and charm were affecting her. She'd long vowed that she would remain single, never wanting to experience again what she remembered the master doing to her, or to go through the birth of a child – not ever! And yet, she couldn't deny how she felt so aware of Freddie, to the point that she jumped when he stepped closer to her.

'Look, Gracie, there's no need to worry. Once we're inside I'll leave you alone. I'm sure there'll be plenty of girls for me to dance with, even though none will ever match your beauty. I fell for you the moment I spotted your glorious hair.'

'You can save your breath. I've heard it all afore, and I'm not interested, thank you.' The trouble was, she was interested, and had thrilled at him calling her beautiful. She hadn't heard things like that said to her before. Not even from Reggie, who had the misguided notion that he was her boyfriend.

It had been after her nineteenth birthday last year that she'd finally gone to see her Aunt Massie. Their reunion had been wonderful, and Aunt Massie had begged her forgiveness.

'There's no need for you to even ask that of me, Aunt Massie,' she'd told her. 'I knaws why you couldn't, but more than that, I knaws that if you could, you would have. I've been happy since I escaped.'

She'd told Aunt Massie then a bit of what had happened to her, leaving out the birth of her son and the details of all that went on at the home she'd been taken to. Gracie had found that after he'd listened to her tale, her Uncle Percy was sorry too. She'd found it easy to forgive him.

The best thing about the visit was to be given her box of treasures. It seemed that when her granny's house was cleared, Aunt Massie found out that Secondhand Molly had taken on the job and had been able to get one or two things to keep for if she ever saw Gracie again. There was her granny's lovely china tea set with a pattern of violets on the cups and saucers, and her granny's bible with all sorts of cuttings stored in its pages. Gracie had been so moved to have these things that she'd shed a tear, especially at having her treasure box again. Her ma's wedding ring, her da's cufflinks, a photo of them both and one of her da holding Gracie on his shoulders were all still safely inside it.

Now her hand went to her locket – the one with a picture of her ma and da inside of when they were very young. She never went anywhere without it these days and she remembered how she'd been gazing in wonderment at it, with her tears threatening to undo her, when Reggie walked into the room. He'd changed beyond all recognition. From a spotty, gangly lad, he was now a tall, muscly, handsome man, with the same dark, tight curly hair that his ma had. His eyes were browner than she remembered, and the skin around them crinkled when he smiled. 'Good to see you, Gracie. You look just like your ma.'

'I could say the same about you, Reggie. What're you doing now?'

'I'm a trawler man. Though not one who has to stand on the dock waiting for work. Naw, I'm an engineer, so me work's regular as I keep the boat afloat, and I go out on most trips. I work for Wellings and Co. It's a good number. What about yourself?'

They'd chatted and Reggie had accompanied her back to Sheila's. She'd felt obliged to ask him in, and she had been teased unmercifully about him ever since. But to her, Reggie had become a nuisance. He hadn't lost that 'wanting his own way' and could be petulant if she refused to go with him or do what he wanted to do. He called most weekends, and again, to save any aggravation, she'd often walked out with him. On occasions they'd had a laugh and enjoyed each other's company. That is until one day he'd tried to kiss her. She'd slapped his face. It had been a reaction that she couldn't explain to him, and she was sorry at how hurt he was, but she had not liked what he'd said then: 'You're me girl, I have a right to kiss you.'

'You can get that out of your head,' she'd told

him. 'I'm no one's girl and never will be.'

He'd gone off in a huff. That had been two weeks ago and she hadn't seen him since, and didn't care if she didn't see him again.

'You look very cross, Gracie.' Freddie brought her back to the present. 'I promise that once we are inside, I'll leave you alone.'

Gracie tensed, willing herself not to be friendly with this man who had sidled into her life, upsetting her resolve.

'At least we could have a friendly chat while we are queueing, couldn't we? There's no harm in that, surely? Tell me about yourself. Do you live locally?'

Against all her instincts, before they had reached the head of the queue, Gracie found herself chatting to Freddie as if she'd known him all her life. He was so direct that he was funny. She'd never spoken to anyone like him. There was an honesty about him that allowed him to say almost anything that he wanted to. She listened as he related tales about his family life. 'My mother is the best cook in the world, so I will be looking for that in a future wife. Can you cook?'

Though sounding forward, it didn't seem that way, it was just a truth – he loved food, his ma cooked well, and he'd like that to continue for the rest of his life.

'I do actually, and well. In fact, me business is cooking – well, making rock, which is a highly skilled occupation. I'm one of the very few female sugar boilers, as it happens.'

'You're just what I'm looking for. I'd like to stake my claim. I could ask you here and now to marry me on that talent alone, but I know you would refuse, so what about we do stay together in the ballroom, and have a few dances? I'm a good dancer.'

'Is there owt that you're not good at? Talking is a talent you have, and cheek, besides a way of getting on folk's nerves. And the answer's naw, I only dance with Sheila.'

Freddie's sigh was audible, and Gracie thought that at last the message had got through to him. *But do I want it, too? Oh, I'm not sure.* Fear vied with a longing to continue to get to know Freddie, and yes, being held by him on the dance floor, she knew would be heaven, but now she'd ruined every chance of that happening.

Although she'd seen it many times, the interior of the Tower Ballroom still filled Gracie with a sense of wonderment – from the beautiful parquet floor to the golden balconies and the paintings on the ceiling outlined by golden latticework, beautifully contrasted by the deep red velvet chairs, and flowing stage curtains.

The excitement in her increased, as the first chords of 'Oh, I Do Like to be Beside the Seaside' could be heard, and the curtains opened and Reginald Dixon, sitting playing his Wurlitzer organ, rose from a hole in the stage into full view.

Freddie clapped his hands. 'Wonderful, I can't believe I am here. I have always loved hearing Reginald Dixon on the radio; my mother knows exactly how to tune into him. I have danced around our front room many a time, and now I am here. Please do me the honour of dancing with me, Gracie.'

Before she knew what was happening Gracie found herself expertly guided into a quickstep in time to the music. It was exhilarating, if a little embarrassing, as not many had taken to the floor to Mr Dixon's signature tune. It was as if they were on show.

Everyone cheered and clapped as the music came to an end and, to Gracie's chagrin, they seemed to be directing a lot of their applause at her and Freddie. Freddie did as her short acquaintance with him had led her to expect, and bowed low to all parts of the room. For her part, she couldn't leave the floor quickly enough. 'What are you doing? You've made a fool of me!'

He didn't answer, as now Reginald was playing, 'Falling In Love Again', and she found herself once more being held in Freddie's strong arms and waltzed onto the dance floor.

All the practice that she and Sheila had done, when Sheila had taught her to dance, paid off as she glided effortlessly around. And though she fought the feelings assailing her, Gracie found herself enjoying the experience, the feel of being held, and even the roughness of Freddie's uniform against her skin.

When his arms held her closer to him, she didn't object. Her heart wouldn't let her. With a mind of its own, it beat faster, making her breathless. Its rhythm seemed to be saying, 'You are falling in love.'

This notion was rudely nipped in the bud as Gracie felt herself being roughly pulled out of Freddie's arms. 'What d'yer think you're doing, eh?'

'Reggie! I – I–'

'Excuse me, but please don't manhandle Gracie like that. Who are you?'

'Gracie, is it? I'll show you who I am.' With this, Reggie took a swing at Freddie.

Freddie ducked out of the way, but somehow managed to catch Reggie's arm and held it as if in a steel clamp. 'That is no way to behave in front of a lady. And I wouldn't advise it on account of me being a champion boxer. So, leave us alone, or you might find yourself sprawled across the dance floor, crying for your mother.'

Reggie looked shocked. Wrenching his arm free, he sneered at Gracie, 'I'll see you later', before turning and leaving them alone.

Gracie watched Reggie walk away and out of the room. Her whole body trembled, making her feel sick. Her cheeks burned with embarrassment.

'You didn't tell me that he was the reason that you didn't want to be with me. I'm sorry, I wouldn't have–'

'He's not. And he's not my boyfriend. He wants to be, but I don't want a boyfriend, so can we please go and sit down? Everyone is looking at us.'

When they sat down it was to find Sheila and Bob in deep conversation. The un-talkative Bob was explaining something about aeroplanes to a very attentive Sheila, who was hanging onto his every word.

Freddie pulled a chair out for Gracie. 'Perhaps it's as well that he's not your boyfriend, as he may have pursued the fight thing further, and I can't fight for toffee!'

This made Gracie laugh out loud, and caught

Sheila's attention. 'Share the joke, you two.'

'Didn't you see Reggie come over to us, Sheila? He was spoiling for a fight. I think he was drunk. Reckoned that I was his girl. Flipping cheek!'

'No, I didn't. I don't like him, Gracie. I knaw you've known him all your life, but he scares me.'

Gracie had to admit that she too felt afraid of Reggie at times. The look he'd given her was like a threat. She shuddered.

'I'll get you a drink. What would you like? A sherry?'

'Ta, Freddie, we'll both have a sherry.'

As Freddie walked away from them, Bob joined him.

'Eeh, Sheila, I wasn't going to have a sherry, you knaw how it goes to me head.'

'You'll be all right.' Sheila nudged her, 'What d'yer think of them, eh? I reckon as I'm falling in love. Bob's the quiet, smart, type, but he's ever so nice. He's a good listener, but so interesting when he talks. Oh, I don't know, there's sommat about him. Me hearts all a-flutter.'

'He does seem nice. But I'm not taking to Freddie, he's too sure of himself.' *Liar!* Where that thought came from, Gracie didn't know, but she did know that she was in denial. She was feeling something for Freddie, and it was a feeling that she couldn't deny.

CHAPTER THIRTEEN

Although Freddie had asked her to meet him again, and Gracie had refused, she hoped every day that today would be the day that he called.

A fortnight had gone by, and her only caller had been Reggie. He'd called round the boarding house at least five times, and stood with her now in the back garden.

'Reggie, I keep telling you, I don't want a boyfriend. I don't want any man, it's not just you. I don't want to tie myself to anyone.'

'Except that RAF bloke. You were canoodling with him all right.'

'I wasn't, I was dancing. Anyroad, it's none of your business. I can be with whoever I like.'

'Why him? He looked like a nancy boy to me.'

This was getting them nowhere, and Reggie didn't seem to want to leave. 'Look, Reggie, I'd like us to be friends, but nothing more. Why can't you understand that?'

'There's sommat fishy about all of this. We grew up together and have been friends all our lives. Even while you were away, I allus thought about you. Now you don't seem to want me near to you.'

Before she could answer, the door opened and Bertie came out. 'What you doing out here, Gracie? Are you courting?'

'Naw, Bertie. Go in and don't be so nosy.'

Reggie looked taken aback. 'Who did you say

he was? How come he looks so much like you?'

'He's Bertram and Peggy's lad. And that's just because he has the same colour hair as me, nowt more. Apparently, his grandfather had red hair.'

'Funny they didn't have him till you came along.'

'And just what are you implying with that statement?' Though she made her voice sound strong, inside Gracie felt herself wobble.

'Nowt. I just think it a coincidence. No kids for years, and then a redhead who looks exactly like you comes along.'

'Yes, it is a coincidence and nowt more. I've had enough of you now, Reggie. Just leave me alone. I'll see you when I visit me Aunt Massie, but that's all. Find yourself another girl.'

Reggie moved closer to her. His voice hardened. 'I don't want another girl. You're my girl, and you knaw it. Why're you being like this, eh?'

'I'm going in. You can either follow me and I'll see you to the door, or I'll leave you here and go to my bedroom. It's up to you.'

With this Gracie went to open the kitchen door. Reggie grabbed her arm. 'I'm warning you, Gracie.'

Gracie acted without thinking as she always did when under threat. Her hand came up and she swiped him across the face. 'No one warns me! D'yer hear? No one.'

With this she turned and opened the door and was through it before Reggie could regain his stance. He followed her in. His look sent a shiver through Gracie. She walked in front of him through the house to the front door. Opening it, she said, 'Goodbye, Reggie.'

139

Without uttering a word, Reggie walked through it. Slamming it after him, Gracie turned. A sob escaped her as she went to mount the stairs.

'Oh, my little one, what is wrong?'

'I – I didn't see you there, Aggie. I – I'm all right.'

'No, but something is troubling you. Come. I will make you some cocoa. Who was that?'

'Only Reggie. He seems to think that he owns me.'

Aggie didn't speak much as she glided around the kitchen. When the steaming cocoa was ready, she put the mug in front of Gracie and sat down on the opposite side of the table.

'Tell me, what is troubling you? I know little about you.'

This was true. Although they had lived in the same house for more than four years, they had rarely had a full conversation, and never on their own.

'I think that I know you have been abused, and now you cannot love. Oh, do not look surprised, I said that I knew little, but of course I knew that. I watched you pregnant with Bertie. I heard the screams of his birth, and I have seen that cold spot in you that is never to be touched. I understand. I do. I have experienced this same fear. I was the very best of trapeze artists, of famous Romonskov family. I fell, and my fear began.'

'I knaw, I'm sorry. And I do reckon as our fear is similar. Though, well, I've never known the good side, I – I mean, you do have good memories. I don't.'

'That does not mean that there is not good side. There is, my dear. Very beautiful side to loving a man. And not all men are bad. This is the thing. You have to find good man. Then you will be all right. I promise you.'

'Will you ever be all right, Aggie?' Never did a shortening of a name seem so unsuitable for a person as Aggie did for this beautiful lady.

'Yes, it is that I no longer want to walk the wires. I am happy. I love when I can go to circus and help, and I love training artists, but for me, no. The wire holds a fear I cannot surmount. For you, love can help you to conquer your fear.'

'Thank you, Aggie. I feel a lot better now.'

'Good. But, little one. Not that Reggie. No. Never give in to him. He is not the right one.' With this, Aggie got up and glided to the door. 'Goodnight, little one.'

Something seemed changed inside of Gracie. She couldn't have said what, but she did feel differently. Freddie came to her mind, and suddenly she longed for him to contact her.

Upstairs, she found Sheila sitting on her bed, with her sewing in front of her. She was making herself a new frock for her work, having declared that the pink ones she'd always worn were now too childish. She'd chosen two-tone colours, grey for the skirt and white for the bodice.

'How's it coming along?'

'Oh, fine, but you knaw, I don't want to be selling rock all me life, Gracie. It was all right when I was a youngster, but now I just feel that it is soul-destroying. And I hate being out in all weathers. I want to work in the circus more. I reckon as me da could disguise me. No one would knaw as I were a girl clown. I could work with him,

141

and we could make his act even better. There's talk of letting him go, for a more famous clown, Charlie Cairoli. I could maybe change that.'

Gracie sank down on the end of the bed. 'Oh, Sheila, that's just a dream. Being a clown isn't the right thing for you. Why don't we look at renting a shop, eh? If we find the right place, I could maybe move the making of the rock to the back of it, and we'd be together all the time then.'

'I never thought of that. Aye, I'd like that. And Rory can work just outside our shop. He can bring the punters in after they have a photo with Suzy.'

The idea began to take shape.

'Why don't we have a day out on Sunday? The three of us – you, me and Rory. It's ages since we went to the pleasure beach and the piers. We had such a giggle when we did it last time, and then we can talk it through while we're all together.'

'That'd be grand.'

'Settled, then.'

They were both in bed before Sheila spoke again. 'Are you all right, Gracie? I mean, really all right?'

'Aye. I am. I had a bad experience with Reggie earlier. He's a pest. But I talked with Aggie and I feel better about myself now.'

'Not better enough to consider Reggie as a boyfriend, I hope.'

'Naw. Never that, but ... well, I might consider someone else.'

'Freddie?'

'Aye, but he's given up on me. It's nigh on three weeks since we met them.'

'They've been on intense training. I had a note from Bob. They're free this weekend and Bob wondered if you would consider making a foursome?'

'Really? Oh, I would. I would, Sheila.'

With the weekend to look forward to, the rest of the week dragged, but at last Saturday night came and Gracie felt an excitement as she and Sheila got ready.

'Wear that frock with a flared skirt that falls to your calves, Gracie, the wide shoulders and the little capped sleeves make it glamorous enough for the tower, and the navy with a white collar really suits your skin.'

'Mmm, I think I will. I haven't worn it for ages.'

As Gracie pulled the belt of the frock around her waist, she caught a glimpse in the mirror, and loved the effect the outfit had on her figure. She rooted out a pair of silk stockings and once again donned her silver pumps. But she still felt that something about her appearance was missing. 'I wish that I could do sommat different with me hair. I get fed up with just wearing it down.'

'Come here and sit at the dressing table. I'll try sommat as I saw in a magazine.'

With a little trepidation, Gracie sat. Sheila began to plait sections of her hair from above her ears. She made four plaits, then fastened them together on the top of Gracie's head, and let the rest of her hair fall into ringlets behind her ears. The effect was stunning. 'I look so different. Ta, Sheila. I love it.'

'Stay still while I put this fancy pin in. It'll

143

secure the plaits and hide the clips. There, you look lovely, it really suits you off your face.'

Gracie knew this to be a truth and was mesmerised by the difference – she looked ... elegant. That was it. Sophisticated and elegant.

'Come on, we're seeing Rory first. He's meeting his chef at the pier café on Central Pier. I said we'd say hello.'

Gracie felt a tingle of nerves at this prospect. She was used to Rory and loved him very much in a brotherly way, but to meet another young man who had the same leanings was a bit daunting. What if he was an evil person like those nurses at the home, or worse, like Foggie! She hated visiting these memories, and imagining that young uns were still going through what she went through. Her heart longed to help them, but she didn't know what she could do. So far, nothing had happened about her escaping and stealing the money and the keys. At times she wondered if the master had even dared to report it. It was the not knowing that prevented her from even trying to contact Jeannie. But then, Jeannie knew where she was and, if she wanted to, she could come and find her. *How I wished that she would. I so want to know that she is all right.*

Rory's chef was strikingly handsome. And a complete contrast to Rory, whose gypsy looks had become more pronounced as he'd grown into a man. Now, he was even more good-looking and his dark, smouldering eyes gave him a film-star appearance, as did his muscular physique. It was when he talked that his personality seemed

144

alien to his looks, for his voice was soft and his giggle effeminate.

Rory introduced his friend as Sam. Sam was as fair as Rory was dark. His blond, regimental short, back and sides hairstyle, flopped over to the right on the top. His skin was very white against Rory's tanned skin, and his eyes were somewhere between blue and green. They were lovely eyes and twinkled when he smiled, which was often, as he had a jolly disposition. Gracie liked him at once, and felt comfortable in his company.

'So, you're meeting your knights in shining armour tonight then, girls? I know Freddie and Bob, two great guys, and I saw them first, so I don't know whether to scratch your eyes out, or give in gracefully and let you have them.'

'Oh, you fancy them, do you, Sam?' Rory had a mock hurt look as he said this. 'And here's me faithful unto you and you alone. I haven't looked at another man since I met you.'

This conversation embarrassed Gracie, but Sheila laughed an infectious laugh, which made Gracie laugh, too. The moment passed. She'd grown comfortable with the tone of conversation by the time they left the two boys. And though she worried for them, as their attachment to each other, if taken to the extreme, was illegal and punishable by a prison term, she was relieved that the meeting up had gone so well, and that Rory had found happiness.

Freddie was as handsome as she had remembered him to be. He and Bob were waiting across the road from the tower, leaning on the railings and looking out to sea, but as Gracie and Sheila approached, they turned and smiled. Gracie knew in that moment that she loved Freddie. She wanted to run to him, put her arms around him and hold him to her, but it was apparent that her cold treatment of him the last time they were together had affected him. His approach to her wasn't confident and he seemed a little wary. She wasn't sure how to react to him. But the uncertainty left her when he put out his hand. Taking it, she looked up at him.

'You look even more beautiful than I remember you, if that's possible, Gracie,' he said. 'I love your hair, and your frock, and, well ... you look gorgeous.'

'Thank you. You look as handsome as I remember you.'

'Oh? You do remember me then? I thought after the last time that you would block me out of your head and that would be that.'

'I'm sorry, I was very rude. I can't explain. I – I...'

'Hey, no glum faces tonight. All that matters is that you want to know me now. I was jumping through hoops when I heard. Let's forget last time, and have a night to remember. Our first real date.'

The way he said this warmed Gracie, as it sounded as though it would be the first of many, and that filled her with happiness, as did the feel of his hand in hers. It seemed to her that the past drifted away from her at that moment, that something inside her opened once more, and told her that she was ready. Ready to love and be loved by a man. No. Not just any man. Freddie.

The Tower Ballroom was even more magical than she remembered it, and the music swept them along for dance after dance. When they finally returned to their table, Sheila and Bob had left. 'Well, that's a turn up. Oh, wait a minute, they've left a note.'

Needed some fresh air so gone for a walk. See you back at home, Gracie.

Under that, Bob had written. *Meet you at the station for the last train, Freddie. Have a good night.*

'So, it's just us then, Gracie. More dancing after a drink, or would you like to go for a walk, too?'

A nerve tingled in Gracie's stomach. Could she handle being on her own with Freddie?

'Don't be afraid. I'm a gentleman, you'll be safe with me.'

'Oh ... I – I, all right. Yes, I would like a walk.'

It was as they reached the pier, holding hands, not speaking, that Freddie stopped. 'How about we go down on to the beach? The tide's out.'

'Yes, all right.' It was such an unenthusiastic response to how she really felt, but fear still ran through her body, and increased as they went down the slope. To cover this she made a play of taking her shoes off.

Beneath her feet the sand felt soft and squidgy. The sound of the breaking waves and the odd squawking seagull overrode the tinny music of the stallholders, and the salty air vied with the aromas coming from the many food stalls selling fish and chips and hot potatoes.

Freddie took her hand again. 'Shall we go to the water's edge?'

'Aye, that'd be grand, though I'll need to hold me skirt up.'

As Freddie began to run, pulling her along, Gracie laughed out loud, until she slipped. Turning, Freddie caught her, and held her. With his face close to hers, she could feel his breath on her cheek.

He whispered, 'I want to kiss you, Gracie.'

Thrilled, she didn't resist. When his lips brushed hers, a feeling zinged through her, like none she'd ever experienced. Her body begged for more, and her heart thudded in her chest.

Was it Freddie, or her, that deepened the kiss? She didn't know. What was happening to her made her not care, as she drowned in the ecstasy of the love she knew Freddie was giving her.

'Oh, Gracie, Gracie, my love.'

The words were said so close to her lips that she felt the movement of his mouth as he uttered them.

Without knowing she was going to, Gracie whispered, 'I love you, Freddie.'

His arms took her into his body. She could feel every part of him and thrilled at the sensation of knowing that he wanted to make her his own.

How they came to be lying on the sand, she didn't know. Their hands sought and found each other, touching and stroking, and sending quivering feelings through Gracie that had her crying out her joy.

When Freddie's hand pulled her knickers aside and delicately touched her, she didn't resist, but pushed herself towards him. 'Freddie, oh, Freddie, yes, yes...'

It was then that he pulled away and sat up. 'I –
I'm sorry. So sorry. Forgive me. I shouldn't have.'

'But I wanted you to, Freddie, I want–'

'I know, I do too. So very much. But it wouldn't
be right. I love you, Gracie. And I want to make
love to you more than anything I've ever wanted
in my life, but I can't, not like this. I want you to
trust me. For us to get to know one another first.
I feel that you have been through a lot of hurt,
and I don't want to add to that, or for it to return
when you wake up in the light of the day and
realise what we did.'

Gracie couldn't believe what she was hearing.
That someone should care for her that much. She
didn't really understand what had happened, but
she knew that Freddie was right. They shouldn't
go all the way, not on their first date, and not at
all until they were married. *Married! What am I
thinking?* But though the thought had surprised
her, she knew in her heart that that was what she
wanted. To be Freddie's wife.

CHAPTER FOURTEEN

The sun spilled through the curtains the next
morning. Stretching, Gracie knew that she'd slept
better than she had in a long time. Freddie came
to mind, and something stirred in her groin. She
wanted for all the world to put her fingers between
her legs and hold on to the feeling, increase it
even, but she sat up and shook the thought away.

Freddie had walked her home, and had once more kissed her deeply before leaving her. He wasn't sure when his next time off would be, but told her he would contact her very soon. Between little pecks that sent shivers through her, he'd said how he was going to miss her.

They'd talked about what had happened between them, and agreed that they would find it difficult, but that they must keep their loving to kisses and fondling only. Drawing up her knees and hugging them, Gracie wished that it could be more. But then, a sudden picture came to her of the master doing it to her and she cringed. Biting her lip, she was filled with sadness at the thought that she wasn't pure for Freddie. What would he think? Would he know? Should she tell him? But what then? *Oh God. I wished that had never happened to me.* With this thought tears fell from her eyes. Sobs wracked her body.

The door opening made her jump. It was Sheila. 'Hey, sleepyhead... Oh, Gracie, what's the matter? Freddie didn't ... did he?'

'Naw. I... We wanted to, but we held back. Well, Freddie did. I just wished that none of the things that I went through had ever happened to me. What will he do when he knaws? And what about Bertie? How will I tell Freddie that I have had a child? And if he accepts me, how will I leave Bertie behind to go off and marry Freddie? Oh, Sheila, it's all a mess.'

'Poor Gracie. You're so undeserving of all of this. You've had a raw deal and anyone as takes you on has to understand that none of it was your fault.'

'That would take a saint. But it's what it's done

to me an' all. I feel dirty. Used. I was surprised how much I wanted Freddie to make love to me, as I thought I'd never let another man touch me, ever. But when he does, will he knaw?'

'You will have to tell him. And if he is as decent as we think that he is, he will cope with it and not blame you.'

Gracie couldn't think how anyone couldn't blame her. It was always the girl's fault, wasn't it?

'Anyroad, let's not get in the doldrums. It were a smashing night last night. Me and Bob walked and walked, and talked that much that I feel I've known him all me life. I'm falling in love with him, Gracie. And he with me. We were the same, we kissed and then wanted more, but Bob was the perfect gentleman, and nothing happened. He's going to contact me when they can next get time off.'

'Freddie said the same. Oh, I hope it's not too long. I never thought to ever feel like this for a man, but I'm glad I do as it's the best feeling in all the world.'

'It is. Now get dressed. Ma's cooked some bacon; it smells delicious. I'm starving. And we have to meet Rory at eleven.'

Gracie's mood lifted as they made their way down the Central Pier. Rory had several goes at throwing for a coconut, then when he won one, they borrowed the stallholder's hammer to smash it. The milk from it went everywhere, but they dug their teeth into the flesh and enjoyed the bits of it that would come loose. The next stall offered three small bean bags to throw at a range of teddy bears. If you knocked one off the shelf you won it. Gracie had never had a teddy bear, and for some reason at almost twenty years old, she had a longing for one. It was three farthings later that she jumped for joy, holding her prize.

'Eeh, lass, you'd think you'd won the pools. Give over, it's only a mangy old teddy bear.'

'It may be to you, but to me it's a treasure. Now I need to win something for Bertie. Let's have a go at the hoopla.'

Another farthing bought a go on trying to get the small hoops over prizes which stood on pedestals. It was obvious that most of the prizes were too big for the hoops and so could never be won, but Gracie had her eye on a model tram-car. Bertie would love that.

She'd spent tuppence on four goes before she finally won. Clutching her prizes the others laughed at her, but she knew they enjoyed the joy it gave her, even though they teased her.

'Hot dog time, girls. And don't we have sommat to talk over?'

They both agreed with Rory, and a few moments later, biting into the delicious sausage, Gracie winced, 'Eeh, that's really hot. It's burnt me tongue!'

Sheila laughed at her antics. 'It's just come fresh from the brazier, Gracie. Blow on it.'

The steam went up her nose as she blew, bringing with it the aroma of grilled meat, and the scents all around her. On this part of the pier, stall-holders sold all manner of snacks, from cockles and mussels, to doughnuts. A feeling took her of how lucky they were to actually live and work amongst all of this. Those around her would be going home soon, back to their dreary towns and jobs. Her life may not have started well, but now she could have all the excitement she needed and it was all on her doorstep in her lovely Blackpool.

'So, what's your idea of a shop then, Gracie?'

'Well, like I said, Sheila, with premises I can do the cooking in the back, and you sell the rock from the front.'

Their talk was of this for the next half an hour. Some of Rory's ideas were amazing – he had a real flare for how the shop should be decorated, suggesting candy-striped blinds with a matching wall behind the counter. And display baskets that could make use of the floor space and smaller ones that could stand on varying levels of shelves. The picture he painted excited Gracie, but they all came down to earth when they finally got around to realising the cost of this venture, and how difficult it would be to find a shop on the Prom. Blackpool was booming and all available space had been taken.

They fell quiet for a moment, and Gracie watched all the happy holidaymakers milling around. The sand on the beach below where they sat was hardly visible for the amount of folk sitting in deckchairs. The noise they made was a mixture of happy laughter, children screaming with delight and those screaming in temper, as they were forbidden to do whatever it was they wanted to do. Into this came the tinkling bells around the necks of the string of donkeys, who patiently carried young uns up and down the beach, hour after hour.

Today the sea was calm and the horizon so clear that Gracie could see the hills of the Lake District in the distance and the shores of Barrow-in-Furness jutting out. Floating across this she noticed a trawler sailing into Fleetwood, and a shudder went through her as memories were evoked.

'Look, we haven't to give up on this idea,' said Rory. 'I'd like to be a partner, albeit a sleeping one, and like Sheila says, me and Suzy can attract custom to the shop. How about we look further back from the Prom, we might find sommat. I can work on the Prom, but hand out leaflets to me punters. We could maybe give them a discount on their rock with every photo they have taken. Folk'll go further back than the front for a bargain.'

'That's a brilliant idea, Rory.' The suggestion had put hope back into Gracie. 'Once we get known, folk'll come anyways. But how long will it take us to get the capital to start?'

Rory wasn't to be daunted by this. 'Have any of you girls got any savings? I've got a few quid and I'm willing to invest it.'

'I've got some, it ain't much, about twenty quid, but aye, that could go into the pot.'

This from Sheila made Gracie feel a little ashamed, as she had much more, and that shouldn't be so, though Sheila did spend a lot of her earnings on flippant things. Taking a deep breath she told them, 'Aye, and I've got a good bit stashed an' all. Your ma's allus been generous with my share of the profits, Sheila. I've been able to save as much as twenty pounds some years. I've around seventy pounds.'

'Blooming eck, that's a fortune. Depending on what Rory has, we could be halfway there to paying some rent up front for a shop.'

'Mine isn't as much as Gracie's, but I have around thirty.'

'That's one hundred and twenty atween us then, though, you both show me up. I've never been much of a saver. Anyroad, I'd say we've plenty to make a start. Let's go to that agents on Coronation Street and see what he has to let, and what price they're going for. Eeh, I'm that excited, I could do a jig.'

Gracie and Rory laughed out loud as Sheila stood and did a little dance.

Their hopes of their dream beginning were soon dashed as they listened to the agent. 'You'll be lucky. Anything that's half decent has been snapped up. Always is as we approach the lights season. Tradesmen from all walks of life come to Blackpool and take any premises going, but at the end of the lights, you'll have your pick. Not a good time to start a business, but if you pay rent from then, you're assured the premises for the summer season and beyond if you can keep up your payments.'

As they walked away they were a little despondent, until Gracie told the others, 'This could be the proper way to start. Steady like. While we are waiting, we can save more money, and even begin to buy things like the baskets, and you and I can start to line them, Sheila. I reckon as wood baskets, of the type householders use, would be ideal for the floor-standing ones. We can buy some pink and white gingham cloth and make them look fresh and fit for purpose, and wrap ribbon around their handles. And I can start stockpiling the rock, and experimenting with me different flavours and what words I can have running through the middle.'

'Aye, and we could decide on what we're going to call the shop and have some rock with the name of it running through it. That would be a novelty.'

As this forward planning took on a momentum, their excitement and enthusiasm were rekindled. They were so full of ideas that they were all talking at once as they walked back down to the sea front.

When they turned the corner of Foxhall to go back onto the Prom, they met Reggie. Gracie jumped as he staggered towards her. His eyes held anger, his fists were clenched. 'So, you've seen your nancy boy again, have yer?'

Gracie knew that he meant Freddie, but felt embarrassed in case Rory took it that he was referring to him. 'What's it to you, who I see? I told you, Reggie, I'm not your girl. And if this is how you're going to carry on, I don't even want to be friends with you.' With this, she pushed him out of the way.

He landed with his back against the wall. 'I'm telling you, Gracie, you'll regret that, and your rejection of me. You're mine, and naw one else is going to have yer.'

Gracie felt disgust go through her. 'Come on, let's get away from him. I'm sick of him.'

For all his physique, Rory looked like a frightened mouse being challenged by a cat as Reggie turned his attention towards him. He didn't seem able to move out of Reggie's way. Sheila grabbed him, but wasn't able to shield him from Reggie, who lunged at him and landed a punch to his chin. Rory fell to the ground, blood spouting from a cut on his lips.

'You beast!' Gracie threw herself at Reggie, but he caught her wrists and held her fast. His face contorted. His vile-smelling beery and fag-laden breath wafted over her as he leant towards her. His teeth gritted and through them he snarled, 'I'm warning you.'

'Let me go, or I'll scream. There's allus a bobby walking the Prom. I'll scream until one comes, and then they'll arrest you.'

Reggie let go, but the look he gave Gracie sent a fear zinging through her. Somehow, she knew that he would win. Why she knew this, she didn't know, but he had a steel core and he'd never given up on anything he wanted, and had always done all he could until he got it. Gracie shuddered.

The day was ruined after that. Comforting and calming Rory took some time, as did cleaning him, and bathing his lip with their hankies and water that they got from the sink in the public loo.

Gracie was quiet on the way home. They had all been going to make plans for her birthday which was in two days' time, 9 August, but now she didn't feel up to it and just wanted to get home.

Peggy met them when they arrived back at the boarding house. 'Oh, I'm so glad to see you both. I need your help. Aunt Aggie isn't well and the bedrooms haven't been done yet. I can't manage the sheets with these hands of mine.'

Her distress took away any lasting sorrow and fear that lay in Gracie. She would do anything for Peggy. 'Don't worry, Peggy, we'll soon have them done. What's the matter with Aggie?'

'She keeps being sick. I think she must have picked up a bug or something.'

A worry set up in Gracie. She'd thought lately that Aggie looked peaky, but had put it down to the tiredness that beset all those who looked after the demanding guests that came to stay. After months of changeovers and moans and groans, the joy of the beginning of the season began to wear thin, and the busiest time was yet approaching – the switch-on of the Blackpool Illuminations.

The rigour of changing beds and cleaning bathrooms was just what Gracie needed to take her mind off things, but she marvelled at how the dainty Aggie could complete the nine bedrooms on her own. The task of stripping and remaking the beds was back-breaking, and then the carpet sweeper had to be run over the rugs and the dry mop over the linoleum, and the bowl and jug on the washstand had to be cleaned. The jug had to be filled with water, the soap replaced, towels had to be changed and the whole room dusted and polished. It was a mammoth task and wasn't over until they put the bed linen and towels into the wash tub to boil. But even then, they still had to rinse, mangle and hang out the washing.

Sweat poured from Gracie, but she felt better. All thoughts of Reggie and his ways left her as she slumped into the big armchair next to the fire.

Bertie came and sat on her knee. 'Eeh, Gracie, ta for me tram. I love it.' With this, he put his

158

arms around her neck and looked into her eyes. 'Don't tell Sheila, but even though you ain't me sister, I love you more than I do her, and I love her a lot.'

The words dug painfully into Gracie's heart as she knew that one day they would have to part. She couldn't take Bertie with her, if she ever left to marry – it would tear Peggy in two. 'I bet you say the same to Sheila, you little monkey. Give me a cuddle, I'm in need of one.' As his chubby little arms clutched her to him, Gracie felt as though she would burst with her love for him. A tear seeped out of the corner of her eye.

'Did I hurt you, Gracie? I'm sorry, I didn't mean to.'

'Naw, lad. I've sommat in me eye, that's all. You could never hurt me.' And yet the pain he invoked in her was the biggest hurt she'd ever feel, as not being able to acknowledge him as her own hurt her more deeply with every passing year.

'Shall I put the wireless on, Gracie? We never listen to it much now, and I like the music.'

Absent-mindedly saying he could, Gracie immediately regretted it, as the newsreader's voice boomed out more news about what Hitler was up to. She was fed up with it all. And a little frightened by it. Why did he pick on the Jews? He seemed to be taking all rights from them in Germany, and every newspaper was full of warnings about him.

'Turn the dial, Bertie, see if you can find some music.'

The words had hardly left her lips when the door burst open and Sheila's Uncle Ron came through. Just seeing him was surprise enough as he rarely came out of the room he and Aggie occupied when at home, and he spent most of his time at the circus. But to see how grey he looked, in contrast to the rosy-cheeked man she was used to, put a fear into Gracie. 'What is it? Is Aggie all right?'

'Naw, we need the doctor. She's bad. She's got terrible pains.'

'I'll go, as I think Sheila is getting a bath in the cellar.' The cellar housed the copper that they boiled the washing in, and was also used to heat water for a bath. They kept a huge tin bath down there, too. It was somewhere private to have a soak.

'Get your coat, Bertie, you can come with me.'

'Aw, I don't need me coat, Gracie, the sun's shining.'

'I knaw, but its near on six now and there's the sea breeze to contend with. Do as you're told, lad. Hurry!'

'He'll slow you down, lass, and we need the doctor quickly.'

With this, Gracie shouted to Bertie not to bother, grabbed her cardigan and ran through the hall to the front door. The doctor lived on Park Road, just a short sprint up Hornby Road. It took Gracie five minutes from leaving to banging on his door.

A kindly man, he didn't hesitate to grab his bag and follow her, saying, 'Not worth getting the car out, for that short journey. What's happening with Aggie?'

'I only know that she keeps being sick and is in

pain, Doctor. But her husband Ron was distraught, so I think she's badly.'

It seemed the whole house had come to a silence
as they waited for the doctor to emerge from the
top floor room that Aggie and Ron occupied.
Gracie had only been in the room once and had
been amazed at how big it was as it stretched the
length and width of the house, and was filled with
furniture as elegant as Aggie herself was. A bed
stood against one wall, hidden by a beautiful tap-
estry screen. Then, besides a deep mahogany
wardrobe, whose doors were decorated with an
elaborate beaded pattern, the other half of the
room housed an elegant French sofa and matching chairs in pale blue velvet with golden arms and
legs. Occasional tables with glass tops and gilt legs
were placed here and there, and two lovely standard lamps with pale blue lampshades dripping
with gold tassels stood each side of the sofa. The
ornaments adorning the mantelpiece and standing
on tables were of dancing ladies and gentlemen,
and paintings of flowers adorned the walls. It was
altogether a lovely room. Though at the moment,
it had taken on a frightening mask as the moans
coming from within put a fear into everyone.

When the doctor emerged, he had a smile on
his face. 'It's a girl!'

'What!' This was screamed from Peggy, rather
than being a question.

'Yes. There was nothing more wrong with Aggie
than the fact that she was in labour! Oh, and shock
at me telling her that. It's Ron who is the patient
now. He fainted at the news, and I haven't had
time to do any more than throw the water from a

161

flower vase over him. He still hasn't spoken, and looks a case with a stem hanging from his nose.'

The doctor's laugh had them all giggling nervously. *He couldn't have said what he said, could he?*

Peggy moved first. She ran up the flight of stairs. 'You really mean it? A babby? Is Aggie all right? Is the babby all right? Oh God, I can't take this in. Where did she keep it? Well, I mean, she did have a little tummy appear, but she kept saying as it were wind. Some wind, eh?' Peggy began to laugh, a high-pitched sound that was infectious.

Everyone laughed with her. Gracie felt incredulous, but she secretly hoped to see the usually quiet and cool Ron in the pose the doctor had described. That would be a sight!

'Now, now, don't all rush in. This has been a shock to Aggie, let alone Ron. She's had no indication of this being pending, and no preparation. Don't overwhelm her.'

The event was the highlight of the year for the family. The new babby was so tiny that she fitted easily into a drawer. Peggy began to knit frantically, and a hasty shopping spree was done by Gracie and Sheila. Neither could believe that they were hunting down terry nappies, babby powder, little vests and babby dresses. It all seemed surreal.

For Gracie, when she held the babby, it opened up the wounds of the time when she never wanted to hold Bertie. Now she couldn't understand those feelings she'd had. She'd loved him, but hadn't wanted to love him. Somehow this left her feeling deprived of a special time in their lives. She made her mind up to show him more love in the future and to always have time for him.

The babby was christened with a name that none of them could spell, or pronounce properly, but Aggie decided she was to be known by the English version, Alina, which was much easier and, Gracie thought, a prettier name. Aggie and Ron soon got used to her as they were caught up in the routine of her little life. Their adoration for her shone from them.

Alina's arrival lifted the whole household, even Bertram, who had a sad disposition for a clown, especially since he had been worried over his job. It seemed that the rumours of Charlie Cairoli taking over as the lead clown of the circus were gathering pace.

For Gracie, a lot of the family ups and downs were secondary to her excitement when a letter came from Freddie. But, its contents had her falling into a deep despair, as did Bob's for Sheila.

CHAPTER FIFTEEN

It was their second date – and their last for the foreseeable future. Freddie and Bob had been posted to RAF Northolt. They couldn't say much about their posting, except that they would go into training on a fighter aircraft.

Since receiving his letter, Gracie had listened more intently to the news, as worrying as it was, and had heard that a new aircraft, the Hurricane MK II, had been delivered to Northolt. There had been debates as to whether these were more efficient than the Spitfire, and the opinion seemed split. However, Gracie had heard that the Hurricane was cheaper to produce, and assumed that this had been the deciding factor. But whatever the ins and outs, she didn't want her Freddie to go so many miles away from her. It seemed like the end of her world.

There was only one choice for them to spend this time together – the Tower Ballroom. They both loved it there. The music and being close to one another as they danced helped them forget for a while.

The evening was a happy one as they put all thoughts of their coming parting out of their minds. 'You will write to me, won't you, Gracie?'

The words were whispered in her ear as they waltzed – just a little closer to each other than the dance warranted.

'I will, I promise.' Something inside of her wanted to tell him everything about herself. She wanted an open and an honest start to their relationship, but she was afraid.

'Why the face? What's troubling you, Gracie? I always have this feeling that there is a secret side to you.'

Was this her cue? No. She couldn't risk losing him. 'Nothing, just sad you're going that's all.' Changing the subject before she gave in, she distracted him from asking any more questions. 'Hey, I'm hungry, I missed my tea. Shall we go for some fish and chips?'

'Sounds good. The last bus goes at eleven. Do you want to walk along the Prom and eat them?'

'No, I thought we'd get a taxi to Newhouse Rd. There's a chippy there that sells delicious fish and chips. It's a small cottage, and you can sit in and eat your food and have a cup of tea and bread and butter with it. They're the best in Blackpool.'

'That sounds great, somewhere away from the hustle and bustle.'

In the darkness of the back of the taxi, Gracie thrilled to feel Freddie's hand on her knee. She knew that if he wasn't strong like last time, then she would give in to him. *But would that be fair? He deserves to know the truth about me before we go the whole way.*

In the café, Gracie learned a lot about Freddie that had never mattered to her before. His father had been one of the very few pilots in the First World War, and still had a love of flying. Freddie thought that if needed, he'd don his wings again. Since the war, his father had taken up working in the family solicitor's office. 'His heart isn't in it, but it is what he originally trained for and is a qualified lawyer. My mother is a trained nurse, but has been a housewife for a long time now.'

'Are you an only child?'

'Yes. You?'

'Yes. Ma tried to have other children, but she never carried them full time. She died when I was thirteen, as did me da.'

'Oh, that's sad. I'm sorry. Have you lived with Sheila since then?'

'Naw.' Gracie felt her colour rising. 'Anyway, that's enough of our background. We can tell each other all of that in our letters.'

'All right, if you prefer.' For a moment there was

165

a silence between them. Then Freddie put his hand in his pocket. 'I nearly forgot, I've a present for you. I missed your birthday, and in any case, I wanted you to have something to remember me by.'

He brought out a small box. When Gracie opened it, she gasped. A silver locket lay on a bed of royal-blue velvet; her hand went to the one that never left her neck.

'I don't mean to replace that one, it's just that seeing you always wearing it gave me the idea of what you like.'

'Naw, it's beautiful. I – I just, well, this one is the one me da gave to me ma.'

'Oh, I didn't realise. Shall I change this for something else?'

The thought came to Gracie that it was time for her to let go of more of her past. To leave her ma and da's love to them and to take up her own. She unclasped the chain and let her old locket slip from around her neck. 'Naw, I'll allus treasure Ma's, but I'll put it in the box that holds me memories and wear your locket from now on. Thank you.'

Freddie took her ma's locket from her hand. 'May I?'

Gracie nodded.

'Hey, you look just like your mother. She was beautiful, and look how handsome your father was.'

Gracie gave an involuntary shudder.

'I'm sorry, my darling. I didn't mean to upset you.'

'Naw, it's all right. I – I well, it's just...'

166

'Don't say any more, darling, I understand your pain. I should have been more sensitive, or asked Sheila first if a locket would be suitable.'

'It is. It's more than so. It's me own. A symbol of the love we have for each other. I'll never take it off.'

Freddie gazed into her eyes. In the depth of his she found all she ever needed. He leant forward and fastened the locket around her neck. 'A token of our love, darling.'

'Eeh, you've made me cry.'

'You do know that I love you, Gracie, don't you?'

'Aye, and I love you an' all.'

As she gazed into his eyes through a mist of joyful tears, she saw that his welled up, too. 'One day we can have our pictures put inside. Oh, Gracie, I wish we didn't have to part.'

She couldn't speak. They had known each other for such a short time, and yet she knew what they had would last a lifetime.

Freddie held her hand under the table. The moment blocked out all other diners and was one that Gracie wanted to remember as long as she lived. It was as if the locket had sealed their love.

Freddie broke the spell. 'Is it far to the bus station from here?'

'Naw. It's about a mile or so. We can walk it if you like.'

They hadn't gone far before Freddie stopped her. They were on Park Road, the other end to where she lived. He didn't speak, but pulled her to him and kissed her. When they broke apart, he said, 'I'm going to be doing that every few steps, so it's a good job we have plenty of time.'

When they reached Bloomfield Road, Freddie checked his watch. 'How far now?'

'About ten minutes.'

'Let's stop for a while, then.' As he said this he sat down on the wall of a house that was in darkness and pulled Gracie onto his lap. His kisses on her neck sent shivers through her. She clung to him, allowing his deep caressing, and responding by touching him, nervously at first, but then exploring, as he was doing. His moans thrilled her. 'Gracie, oh, Gracie. This is torture. I want you so much.'

'I want you, too. Oh, my darling, I do so want you...'

'No! I'm sorry, Gracie. We can't, it would be so wrong. Forgive me.' With this, he withdrew his hand, and held her in his arms.

Gracie lowered her head. A shame washed over her at how bold she'd been. Freddie's hand lifted her chin. As always, he knew exactly what she was feeling. 'We have nothing to be ashamed of. I have never felt like I did when you touched me. I have such a yearning in me to make you mine, but I must not. We must wait. We'll remember this night. Every time the moon comes up, we'll think of each other. And it won't be too long before I get some leave. I'll come to be with you the minute I am released from duty, I promise.'

After adjusting their clothing, they walked in silence. It was a silence that held their longings and their dreams. For Gracie, it held much more, something sinister that told her their dream would never be realised. She didn't know where the thought came from, but she couldn't shake it.

At the bus depot, they met up with Sheila and Bob. Sheila looked as though she had been crying and Bob had a look of sheepishness. Gracie gave Sheila a quizzical look, but Sheila just looked away.

Waving goodbye was torture. The two girls stood still, their bodies close, trying to get and to give comfort. Once the bus was out of sight, they clung together.

'Are you all right, Sheila? You looked very upset. Oh, I knaw as you are because of seeing Bob off, but more than that.'

'I'll never be all right while I'm not with Bob. How did this happen in such a short time? I feel as though half of me has gone, now that he isn't here. It wasn't so bad before as he was only just up the road, but London! He may as well be on the other side of the world.'

'And is that all that is troubling you? I knaw as that's a lot, but...'

'Naw. We, well ... we did it.'

'Oh, Sheila! All the way?'

'Aye. And it wasn't the magical thing I thought it was going to be. It hurt.'

'It does first time, don't worry about that. But what if you have a babby?'

'I won't. Bob was careful.'

How he was careful Gracie didn't know, or understand that he could be, but Sheila didn't seem worried.

'He held me for ages after, saying how sorry he was, but I didn't want it to be like that. I wanted it to be magical.'

'Oh, Sheila. Maybe next time, eh? Maybe Bob's not very practised at it. Are you sore now?'

'Yes. I'm smarting. And Bob did say that he hadn't ever done it before, but that one of his mates had told him how to make sure that he didn't make a girl pregnant if he did. I trust him. It just seems so horrible parting like that.'

'You'll just have to reassure him in your letters that you're not put off by the experience, and can't wait to practise some more with him.'

Sheila giggled at this. It was a nervous giggle that didn't have much conviction, but it tickled Gracie and she joined in. Somehow the giggle took hold of them and they began to laugh out loud, slapping each other on the shoulder and bending double. 'Hark at the voice of experience!... Oh no! Gracie, I didn't mean that, I – I...'

'I knaw you didn't. But I'm not, anyroad. I've no experience of how to do it, not properly. What happened to me were disgusting. I knaw as it'll never be like that with Freddie. We nearly did it tonight. Would have, if Freddie hadn't been so strong again. I couldn't have pulled back how he did.'

'In some ways, I wish Bob had used that control. He should have done. If Freddie can, then he can. Then I wouldn't be left feeling like this.'

'Don't think like that, love. I think Freddie senses that I've some secrets that hurt me, and that's why he does. I don't think he will go all the way until he's sure that I am all right. But I can't tell him. I'm afraid of losing him.'

'Oh dear, we're a complicated pair. Come on, let's get home, I'm exhausted.'

'Me, too.'

They linked arms and headed home, chatting all the way about their love for Bob and Freddie. When they arrived, it was to find Aggie in tears. 'Alina, she is so upset. I do not know what to do. She cry and cry.'

'Where is she?'

'She is with her daddy. He is trying to get her sleep.'

'I think she may be teething. I remember Bertie at this stage. Where's Peggy? She used to rub a little whisky on Bertie's gums, and then I would walk him in his pram until he went off to sleep. It was the only thing that worked. Bring her down and I'll do the same, and I'll put her in her pram and walk her up and down the street.'

With Alina tucked up and quiet now, Gracie took her towards the front door. 'I'll not be long, she's nearly asleep already. Put the kettle on, Aggie, I could just do with one of your mugs of cocoa when I come in.'

In the street, despite the gas lamps being lit, Gracie regretted making this suggestion. There was an eeriness everywhere, as if a bogeyman lurked in every doorway. But she carried on until she reached the top of Park Road. It was when she turned to go back that she saw the figure of a man coming towards her. Something about his drunken sway alerted her as she walked towards him.

'So, is this another secret babby then?'

'Reggie! What're you doing around here at this time of the night?'

'I've lost me way home.'

'Don't be daft. Get up to Park Road, you might

still get a bus, there's the late one, it goes in about fifteen minutes.'

'Where've you been then? I saw you come in with that Sheila. I were sat on a wall up the road a bit.'

'I've been out. Now, I have to get the babby in, I only walked her until she fell asleep. She's Sheila's cousin, a surprise birth.'

'I bet she was. You keep coming up with surprises, don't you, Gracie?'

'Look, I'm going in. Go for your bus, Reggie. You've had too much to drink and you're not thinking straight.'

'When're you coming to see me ma? She looked after you when you were young, helped hours with your ma, and you can't even find the time to see her. It hurts her, it does. She cried buckets when she knew you'd only lived in Blackpool all them years, when she were worrying about yer.'

'Tell Aunt Massie that I'm sorry, I work hard and don't have a lot of time off. There was a reason I didn't come for a lot of years. One day I'll explain it. I'll come next week, I promise.'

'Yeah, and pigs might fly. You've left the likes of us behind, you like men in uniform and folk who own boarding houses. Well, you remember your roots. I knew you when you were a ragged-arsed, snotty-nosed kid, like the rest of us. You've risen above your station. And it don't suit you. You should be my girl. You allus were and allus will be in my eyes.'

'Reggie, please. I'm no one's girl. Now go and catch your bus. I'll see you next week.'

Turning from him, Gracie tightened her grasp

on the pram as if it would save her. But Reggie caught hold of her arm. 'Kiss me, first. Give me sommat which will make me believe yer.'

'Naw. I don't want to kiss you, let me go!'

Her body slammed into his as he brutally pulled her towards him. The pram left her grasp, but she could do nothing against the strength of Reggie. 'The babby!'

Reggie grabbed the pram with one hand. Gracie tried to release herself but his hold, even with one hand, was too strong. *Oh God, help me.*

The click of the brake on the pram signalled that Reggie would now have two hands free. Gracie lifted her free one to try to defend herself, but he grabbed it in mid-air and twisted it behind her. 'One kiss, that's all. You've given a lot more than that to others, I knaw you have.'

His lips came towards her. Gracie turned her head away. 'Naw! Naw! Let go of me, you're hurting me.' She wanted to scream the words, but was afraid of what folk would think. Especially Peggy. She didn't want Peggy to think badly of her.

Manoeuvring her until her arms were clasped in one of his, Reggie grabbed her face and held with a vice-like grip. His lips came down on hers. His breath stank of beer and stale tobacco. Her stomach heaved. The pressure increased until her lips opened and their teeth clashed. His tongue probed, but she kept her teeth clenched against the intrusion. At last, he let her go.

'That's just a taste of what you're going to get. I'll have you one day, I'm telling yer. One of these days, when you're alone, I'll have yer.'

With this he turned, shoved his hands in his

pockets and stormed away from her.

Gracie sat down on the wall. Her body trembled with shock. She tried to compose herself before taking the babby back, but a light splashed the pavement ahead. Someone had opened the front door. 'Gracie! Gracie, what're you doing?'

'I'm coming, Peggy. Shush now, the babby is asleep.'

Peggy gave her a funny, knowing, kind of a look as she entered the vestibule. So as not to worry her, Gracie smiled. 'It didn't take long for her to drop off. I reckon as that whisky did the trick.'

'Good... Are you all right, Gracie?'

'Aye. I'm fine. I'll leave you with Alina and take me cocoa up with me. I've had a full night of it.'

'Aye, I think you have, lass.'

This, said as Peggy pushed the pram through to the kitchen, sounded strange. It held a little sarcasm, which was not in Peggy's character. *Maybe I'm just tired. It's been a long and eventful night.*

When she reached the bedroom, Sheila was snoring in that gentle way that she had. She always fell asleep the minute her head hit the pillow. Gracie thought it was because she had no troubles, nothing to gnaw away at her in the dark hours of the night, when thoughts couldn't be distracted away. But tonight she'd have thought that Sheila would have been troubled and want to talk. Maybe she had come to a place where she was all right with what had happened to her. Gracie hoped so, she really hoped so, as she wouldn't wish her own troubled mind on anyone.

CHAPTER SIXTEEN

The days dragged. Not even the excitement of the Illuminations could lift Gracie's spirit, and she had always loved this time of year in her beloved Blackpool.

She couldn't make the rock fast enough for Sheila to sell. They seemed to run out every day and more and more batches were needed. Gracie felt her arms would drop off, they ached that much with the pulling and rolling.

But tonight, she and Sheila were going to forget how tired and sad they were and hit the town.

Everything around them as they walked the Prom shone like glittering diamonds. Fairy lights on strings across the Promenade swayed in the wind. Lampposts sparkled from their bases with wrap-around lights, and the twinkling colours of the set pieces stretching from one side of the Prom to the other were magical.

When they came in sight of the tower, they gasped. The whole of it was lit up, defining its graceful shape against the black sky. They stood and stared in wonder. Tradesmen walked up and down with trays hung around their necks, selling everything from a trick mouse that ran up your sleeve to magic cleaning aids for your boots. Side stalls sold candyfloss and toffee apples, and the traffic – there was hardly a thumb space between the nose-to-tail cars and the horse-drawn carriages, a sight unique to Blackpool as the punters took rides in them for a penny – inched their way along. Children hung out of windows calling out in glee, and some open-topped cars had as many as five people standing up and holding on to the roof frame – mostly young men who called out cheeky comments. Everywhere, the air was full of joy and excitement.

Gracie and Sheila were carried along by the wave of happiness and found themselves giggling like they hadn't done for weeks. And this turned into a belly-aching laughter, when Sheila bought a huge stick of pink candyfloss and the wind blew it into her face, leaving her having to peel the sugary mess off.

An imp of a lad came over. He had a bucket of water and a cloth and had been cleaning windscreens. 'I'll wipe it off for you, missus, cost you a three-penny bit, though!'

'You ragged-arsed monkey. Give me your wet cloth, and less of your lippiness.'

The lad laughed and handed Sheila a dripping rag.

'Eeh, Sheila,' said Gracie, 'you're not going to use that, are you.'

'I've no choice. Anyroad, the corner bit's not that bad.' Squeezing the cloth, Sheila wiped her face. It did the trick and, rummaging in her bag, she found a penny for the lad and brought out her powder compact. She soon had her face dusted and used her lipstick to put colour into her cheeks. 'How's that? I can't see much in this bloody little mirror.'

'You look lovely again, just a little lippy on your lips and you'll be back to normal.'

'Ta, love. Eeh, that were funny, we haven't laughed like that for ages.'

'I knaw, not since we last saw Freddie and Bob. Yer know, I still can't get over how two men could have knocked us off our axles like they did. And in such a short space of time an' all. I'm waiting for the postman every day, and if you've a letter and I haven't it can send me into mourning.'

'Aye, Bob writes a lot. Mostly he's full of guilt, and assures me of his love. I keep telling him to forget it, and try to make him laugh by telling him what you said about practising, but, you knaw, he's from a different class to me and doesn't allus get me jokes.'

'Freddie's like that. You don't think we got a bit above ourselves, do you?'

'Naw. Folk are all the same with their clothes off.'

'Ha, that's true. Not that I've seen Freddie with his off, yet.'

'Nor me Bob. It were just a fumble through his flies really. And that's what bothers me, it was a bit sordid when you think of it. More driven by lust than love.'

'Don't think like that, Sheila. If Bob didn't have feelings for you, he wouldn't write. It was unfortunate that you both got carried away, and it didn't work out. Most likely through inexperience. Put it behind you, and try to arrange things a bit different next time. I knaw. Maybe you can borrow Rory's caravan when he's working. That'd be a good place, and private an' all as all of the other

177

caravan dwellers work in the entertainment industry and are out at night.'

'Aye, that'd be good. Shall we call in the tower and see if Rory's finished work? We can catch a tram to North Shore to see the huge tableaux that bring all the scenes to life in lights; they say they're even better this year.'

The three of them stood and gazed in wonder at the animated Swan Lake depiction. The set of the stage was the most beautiful illumination they had ever seen, and the way the model dancers glided around took their breath away.

'I see you're with your new friends again, a gyppo and a floozy, while me ma waits in vain for a visit.'

Rory jumped behind Sheila at the sight of Reggie. Gracie almost laughed out loud at this, but the intrusion of Reggie, and the way he seemed to appear every time she came outside her door, took any humour out of the situation. 'I've been busy. Surely Aunt Massie understands that? This is the first time I've been out of me door since the lights were switched on. I'll come once they're switched off and things get back to normal.'

Sheila, who knew about this latest way that Reggie had of pestering Gracie, spoke up then. 'Tell your ma she's welcome at ours any time. She can talk to Gracie while she's working, can't she, Gracie?'

'Aye, that's a good idea. Pass that message on, she knaws where I live, and I'd love to see her.'

Reggie seemed a bit put out by this. Gracie knew his game – he wanted her at his house on his territory. She didn't mind this, as Aunt Massie would be there to protect her, but it was impossible to make the time for the visit at the moment.

'Some folk should mind their own business. We don't do swanning around others' houses who ain't one of us, and you knaws that, Gracie.'

His stance was menacing as his eye caught Rory's. 'What you staring at? I taught you a lesson last time we met. Want a repeat of that, do yer?'

Rory didn't speak. Gracie had the notion that he wouldn't be able to, even if he had something to say. It still struck her as strange that Rory, with his physique and his fearlessness at going into a cage with four lions, could be so cowardly in the face of another man.

Reggie sneered and turned away from them.

'He's getting to be a blooming nuisance, Gracie, can't you talk to his ma and get her to do sommat to stop him?'

'That'd be naw use, Sheila, she's as afraid of him as we are. He used to rule her, even when he was a kid. I could control him then – he used to hang on me every word – but he scares me now. I didn't tell you, but the night Freddie and Bob were last here...'

Sheila and Rory were shocked as she told them of Reggie forcing a kiss on her.

'Just be careful, Gracie. If you see him, run. It's the only way. Run towards a crowd – we're never short of them in Blackpool. Anyroad, let's forget him. I'm peckish – anyone for a penny banger?'

They sat on the bank behind the tableaux eating their sausage in batter. Gracie bit into hers, only to wince as the hot fat dripping from it burnt her lip. The cold wind whipped around her, lifting her hair and chilling her ears. The waves crashed onto the shore below them, and above them the moon shone and the stars twinkled. If only Reggie hadn't spoiled things, this would have been a night to remember with two friends she loved.

Her thoughts went to Freddie, and she wondered what he was doing tonight and how soon it would be before he was given leave. Her heart longed for him, and her body longed to be held by him. *Aye, and to be caressed by him.* At this thought she screwed up the now-empty piece of newspaper that had been wrapped around her sausage, shoved it in her pocket and wrapped her arms around herself.

'That were a big sigh, lass.' Sheila linked her arm in Gracie's. 'And I don't have to guess what you're thinking about, or should I say, who?'

Gracie laughed. 'Naw, and I reckon as you'd be right first time. Come on, shall we go back?'

As they approached the tram lines, the Lifeboat illuminated tram came along. They jumped aboard, although it was open-topped and would freeze them. This was a real treat. The tram was in the shape of a lifeboat and was swathed in lights. It looked a real sight, and had everyone along the route waving to them.

'Eeh, Gracie, this is grand.'

'It is that, Rory. I've never been on it before, it's allus been packed solid with folk.'

The tram rattled along, giving them a view of the lights overhead, and the sea on their right. All thoughts of Reggie and her fear of him left Gracie as she lost herself in the magic that was the Blackpool Illuminations.

It was November before Gracie could take the time to visit her Aunt Massie. She hoped with all her heart that Reggie was at sea. When she arrived, she found it strange to see a car parked outside Aunt Massie's house. She'd seen nothing of Reggie since the incident on the night of the lights, and didn't want to.

Uncle Percy answered her knock on the door. 'Come away in, lass. Eeh, it's good to see you. You look bonnier than ever. Your ma'll never be gone while you walk the earth.' Turning from her, he shouted, 'Massie! Massie! Lass is here.'

This affectionate greeting increased Gracie's guilt. As did Aunt Massie coming towards her with her arms open when she entered the living-cum-kitchen, which led straight off the street. 'Eeh, lass, it's good to see you. Sit down, I'll have kettle boiling in no time. Where've you been? We missed you.'

This was always a funny saying to Gracie. Aunt Massie knew where she'd been, but it was a saying everyone used when they hadn't seen you for a while. 'I've been busy, Aunt Massie, up to me eyes. I can't make rock fast enough. Me and Sheila, me friend as I live with, and Rory, a circus artist I know, are thinking of opening a shop.'

'A shop! Our little Gracie, owning her own business! Eeh, I never thought to see the day. You landed on your feet when you met them folk, Gracie. But I'm glad. Me and Percy have allus felt the guilt of not offering you a home when you needed it. And then to think you lived in Blackpool all them years and we didn't knaw.'

'I knaw that you've allus felt hurt over that, Aunt Massie, and I'm sorry.'

'Naw, lass, forget it. I don't think about it now.'

'Reggie said that you did, and that you cried a lot over me. I'd like to explain, I hate you thinking that I didn't want to knaw you.'

Though she found it painful, Gracie explained more than she had done previously, telling of the abuse and having to steal money and to keep herself hidden from the police, but still she didn't tell them of Bertie.

'Aw, no, lass. I feel responsible, I should have taken you in.'

'That's why I didn't tell you both. I didn't want that. It's easy to say that you could've had me now, but it wasn't at the time. I came to understand and, in the end, it was for the best. I landed on me feet, and that's what matters.'

'So, when are you and our Reggie going to make an announcement then? I can't believe that he hasn't brought you to tea, and yet he tells us that you're his girl.'

'I'm not! I – I mean, well, I knaw he wants me to be, but I can't think of him in that way. I'm sorry, Aunt Massie, I can't.'

'You'd have a job to find better, lass. He's a hard worker and he's bought himself one of them motors. That's it standing out front.'

'I knaw, Uncle Percy, and of course, I'm fond of him.' Mentally she crossed herself to negate this lie, and then wished she could bite back her next words. 'But I'm in love with somebody else.'

The door banging behind her made her jump. Reggie had come through from outside, without her noticing.

'Now, Reggie, don't–'

'Don't what, Da? She's a two-timing bitch. Who's this somebody else then, that ponce of an airman I've seen you with?'

'I'll have you knaw, Reggie, that he's a gentleman, and kind and he works on keeping aircraft flying. There is nothing about him that warrants you calling him a ponce.'

'Naw, and nowt as warrants you calling lass here a bitch. You mind your tongue in my house, young man. Apologise to Gracie. What's happened to your manners, eh?'

'I'm not knee high to a donkey any longer, Da, and that sort of talk don't wash with me. How I speak to my woman ain't got nowt to do with you, or you, Ma. Gracie has a lesson to learn. She can't keep giving me the run around.'

'I don't knaw what you're talking about, Reggie. Where did this notion that I'm your girl come from? I've said all along that I ain't. You just seemed so thick skulled that you can't, or won't, take it in. Well, I'm telling you now, in front of your ma and da, I ain't your girl, and never will be! Just leave me alone!'

Reggie was by her side in a flash, his hand raised.

'You dare! Go on, you dare hit me, and you'll regret it for the rest of your life, d'yer hear me!' Gracie knew that she was screaming now, but the sound she was making didn't match the screams of Aunt Massie or Uncle Percy. Both were on

183

their feet, Aunt Massie wielding the poker and Uncle Percy with his fists held up in the stance of a boxer. 'Now you see why I haven't been to see you, Aunt Massie? There's the reason. Every time I turn around he's there, pestering me, he even forced me to kiss him on one of the times that he got me alone. I hate you, Reggie, I hate you!'

Reggie turned and stormed out. Within minutes the engine of his car roared into life and the tyres screeched.

A sob had Gracie turning around. 'I – I'm sorry, Aunt Massie. I had to try to get through to him, he's been pestering me for ages.'

To her surprise, her Aunt Massie turned on her, shaking the poker. Her face was not like the kindly aunt she'd always known. She screamed, 'You slut! You must have led him on. You must have made him believe you were his girl! Get out! Get out and don't come back!'

'Massie! Now, none of that, lass. Eeh, I'm ashamed of you. That lad of ours has done wrong. But you can't ever see it, can you? He's not right. He's obsessive. I've seen it before over other things. You should be on Gracie's side, not going for her.'

Aunt Massie crumbled. Her body slumped back in the chair.

'I've to get going, anyroad,' said Gracie. 'I'm sorry. I didn't want this, and I've tried and tried with Reggie.'

Aunt Massie sat with her face in her pinny, sobs wracking her body. Gracie wanted to go to her but thought better of it. She'd leave it to Uncle Percy to sort her out. She'd never realised what a level-headed and kindly man he was.

He followed her to the door and stepped out into the street with her. 'I'm sorry, lass,' he said. 'I think you now knaw the real reason I'd not have you staying with us. Though you'd have fared better than you did. There's sommat not right with our Reggie. If he wants sommat, he never gives up. You be careful, and warn that young man of yours to be an' all. Good luck with that shop you're thinking of. Let me knaw where it is and I'll pop in and see you sometime. Don't worry about your Aunt Massie, she'll come around. The sun shines out of the arse of our Reggie where she's concerned, and yet he treats her like a bit of muck under his boot.'

Everything she'd ever thought about Uncle Percy changed in that moment. She'd thought him stubborn and hard faced, but he wasn't. He was understanding and kindly, and now she knew that he'd foreseen how Reggie would be with her. She leant forward and pecked his cheek. 'See ya, Uncle Percy. Tell Aunt Massie that I love her, and nowt of what's happened today changes that.'

Gracie's legs felt as though they were made of jelly as she walked along Mount Street. Memories tried to visit her of a time when she was a happy child, but happy memories can lead to making the bad ones worse, and they would follow. The bad ones. They'd come into her mind to crowd her if she let the carefree times invade her mind.

Her hand went to her neck and felt for her new locket. Just touching it brought Freddie to her. But better than that, when she arrived home there was a letter waiting for her. Clutching it to herself, she ran up to her bedroom. All thoughts of Reggie, the life that she'd had in Fleetwood and the upset with Aunt Massie, left her. She just wanted to be in Freddie's world. Reading his letter would do that for her.

CHAPTER SEVENTEEN

The letter lifted Gracie's spirits, but gave her a fear, too.

As soon as she opened it, a photo fell out. It was beautiful. Tears ran down her face as she looked at Freddie, standing tall, smartly dressed in his uniform, his cap under his arm, smiling out in that rakish way. And although several shades of brown, the photo didn't take from her imagination the colours of him. His lovely blue eyes, his dark hair, his air force-blue uniform.

And as she read his letter, he was fully in her mind. She could hear his voice, and see the different expressions that would cross his face as he spoke.

The best bit of his news came at the beginning as Freddie told her that he was going to be home for Christmas. He'd been given three weeks' leave. He'd wondered about stopping at Peggy's boarding house for a week of that time, and if she would go to his home for a week. He wanted this to be each side of Christmas week, as he knew he would be away more and more, and felt that he owed it to his parents to have what he thought might be their last Christmas alone with him.

Everyone is talking about the troubles in Europe, and in Japan and China and Russia. Most are more in agreement with Churchill, that we should prepare for war, than Chamberlain, who advocates that there will be peace in our time. There may be, but we all believe that we will have to fight Hitler to get it. He has to be stopped.
At the base, we hardly listen to any music or light radio, but are constantly tuned into the BBC World Service. The news is frightening, and yet we are ready.

Gracie held the letter to her breast. She couldn't imagine what war would be like. Her granny used to sometimes tell her things about the Great War, but none of it had meant much. Not even when she told her of her grandda, who'd lost his life in France. But now, that came to her as the most significant happening. *What was that like for me gran? How would I cope if that happened to Freddie? No! No ... no! I can't bear it, I can't!*
Continuing with the letter, she read the best bit ever, and realised that his saying that this could be his last Christmas alone with his parents wasn't anything sinister:

I know that we haven't known each other long, and in a lot of ways, our lives have been very different, in terms of our upbringing – though I know little of yours. Of what happened to you after your parents died. But despite this, I know that I am deeply in love with you, Gracie, and want to spend my life with you. In the normal run of things, we would have a long courtship and engagement, and would think of marrying in three to four years' time, but, if we do go to war, would you consider marrying me sooner?

Gracie caught her breath. Freddie was asking her to marry him! Her heart raced as she read on.

This isn't how I wanted to propose, and I will go down on one knee when I see you, but if you could indicate to me how you feel about marrying me soon, and it is a 'yes', then it would make the next few weeks away from you so much more bearable. If it is a 'no', then I can prepare myself for having to wait. For, no matter what, I will wait for you, my darling Gracie.

His next words put a trepidation in her.

And I want you to know, that whatever happened to you, to hurt you badly, I can take it. As I know that there is something that you are afraid to tell me. Sheila hinted to Bob, when we first met you both, and you were very cold with me, that it wasn't your fault. That you never felt that you could ever trust any man, and that was due to something that you had suffered, that she could not speak of as it wasn't her place to. This is the reason that I held back from making you mine, when I so wanted to. I didn't want you to think of me in the same light you do of whoever wronged you.

Sheila! *I never thought in a million years that Sheila would betray me. And now, I will be forced to tell, and I can't ... I can't.*

Feeling very cross and thinking that she could

188

throttle Sheila, Gracie stared at the door of the bedroom. A despair entered her, for now she thought she had no choice – she would have to tell Freddie, but would it mean that she would lose him? Oh, Sheila! Why, why?

The last bit of Freddie's letter enlightened her as to how it came about, and she knew that Sheila hadn't meant to put her in this position.

But, my darling, I know how sensitive you are about it all, whatever it is, and I would never have mentioned it, except that I want us to be honest with each other, I don't want you to be forever afraid that I might find out. For this I am so very grateful to Sheila, who couldn't have known on that night that you and I would ever see each other again. Her words, I am sure, were meant as a friend defending you. And something that would be natural to say, as Bob had said that he didn't like you much, that you were unfriendly and cold, and he hoped that I didn't fall for you, as I deserved better. In those circumstances, any friend would stand up for you and give an excuse for you. After all, Sheila knew what Bob and I didn't, that you aren't that cold person we thought you were, but a wonderful, warm, kind and friendly person.

A person that I love very much and want to spend the rest of my life with. Please write again soon, my darling, I will await your answer with bated breath.

Freddie x

Yes. Yes. Yes! Oh, my darling, yes, I will marry you. I will.

Falling back onto her pillow, Gracie hugged herself. Never had she felt happier than she did

189

at this moment. She wanted to shout her answer so loud that he would hear it all the way from Blackpool to London.

But there was the obstacle of having to tell him about her past first. *Oh, Sheila, you have put me in this position and I trusted you!*

But no. Freddie was right, with Bob saying that about her, Gracie knew Sheila would want to defend her, and what she'd said didn't give away what had actually happened to her. Maybe Sheila doing that had made Freddie want to see her again, as it gave him a reason for her behaviour when they first met – it helped him to understand, and had driven his motives of not letting things go too far ever since. This was something she was glad about, as she'd heard that sometimes actually doing it made you think less of the person. She was sure that what happened between Sheila and Bob had tainted Sheila's thinking about Bob for quite some time.

The door opened at that moment. Sheila walked in. 'I have a surprise for you... Oh, is that a letter from Freddie? I haven't had one from Bob for over a week. I thought they were busy, or maybe on training somewhere where they couldn't get mail out. Does Freddie say owt about that?'

'Naw, he's asked me to marry him! Oh, Sheila, I'm so happy, but it does mean that I have to tell him everything, as he knew there was sommat from what you told Bob.'

Sheila sank down on the end of the bed. 'Oh, Gracie, you don't knaw how many times I've regretted that. I'm sorry, it just came out, but I never told him owt more than you had a reason for how you were with men who you didn't knaw, honest.'

'Don't be sorry. Part of me is glad that you did – it has helped Freddie to understand me, and is why he has held back with ... well, you knaw. But now that he realises his true feelings for me, and wants me as his wife, he wants to knaw all about me. I'm afraid, Sheila, it's all so sordid, and sommat as folk in Freddie's class will have no knowledge of. I can't see how he'll want me, once he knaws.'

'Course he will, you daft a'porth. He loves you, anyone can see that. He's proper smitten, lass, and nothing is going to put him off you.'

Gracie wished she felt so confident. 'Anyway, what's this surprise, then?'

'Oh, I forgot. There's someone to see you downstairs. That Jeannie as you told me about.'

'Jeannie! Oh, Sheila, why didn't you say? How wonderful!' Gracie jumped off the bed.

'Hold your horses a mo. You threw me with your news. Jeannie's in trouble, and she ain't a pretty sight. I were afraid of her when she approached me stall. I thought that I'd catch sommat from her. She's scruffy and dirty and has sores around her mouth. Ma ain't too pleased that I brought her home, but her kindly side took over and she's on with filling a bath and asked me to get some clothes for her.'

'Oh, no! No, Sheila. Poor Jeannie. Where is she now?'

'She's in the cellar with Ma, and I reckon for her own dignity, you're best to wait until Ma's got her cleaned up.'

'Oh, poor, poor, Jeannie. Did she tell you what

had happened to her?'

'I didn't ask. Like with you, when you turned up looking like a cross between a lad and a girl, I just brought her here to Ma. I were hoping as you weren't back from your aunt's when we got here, but Ma said as you were in the bedroom. How did it go at your aunt's? Did you have a good time? Did you see that Reggie?'

Gracie told Sheila what had happened while they rummaged for underwear, and a frock and cardigan.

'Eeh, Gracie, he scares me, that Reggie. And it sounds as if his ma is scared of him an' all.'

'She allus has been, bless her. Even when he were a lad, he'd throw tantrums and kick her and all sorts to get his own way. And I thought his da were the same, but as you can tell from what I've told you, I was mistaken in that. Now, what about this long skirt and blouse? Jeannie's taller than me, and so this will look all right on her. Ooh, I can't wait to see her. I've thought about her so much.'

'Well, think on. Jeannie seems like she has the world on her shoulders, and needs help, but you can't bring trouble to me ma's door. She's not the same of late, me ma. Aunt Aggie says it's because she's going through the change of life. She says that hers happened overnight with the birth of Alina, but that some women suffer depression, and become easily aggravated. Ma's like that, and I don't want her upsetting any more than she is.'

'Aye, I've noticed a difference in Peggy meself. What's this change of life then, Sheila? Your ma mentioned it once before, but I didn't take heed of it.'

Listening to Sheila, Gracie had the impression that women had to suffer all their blooming lives! 'It ain't bloody fair! Men don't seem to have owt.'

'Eeh, our Gracie, is that you swearing? Ma'll wash your mouth out with soap if she hears you.'

'It's enough to make anyone swear. I can only imagine what Jeannie's been through because she's a woman, and look at us with the stomach ache and feeling like a wet week every month, and then when you have a babby it near kills you, and what have we to look forward to, eh? More problems when we get too old to have young uns; it all beggars belief.'

'When you get off your soap box, let me knaw, eh?'

They both giggled at this, and then as always happened went into a fit of laughter. 'Come on, let's see how the land lies. I'll sort sommat out for Jeannie, as don't put Peggy out, but first I need to knaw what's happened, and where Jeannie's been all this time.'

Jeannie looked thin and drawn, and not well, as her eyes had sunk into her already hollow cheeks and almost disappeared behind her thick-lensed glasses. Glasses that looked far too small for her face and were held together by a plaster on one side. Her protruding teeth looked huge set in her gaunt face. But above all that, she looked afraid. Terrified, even.

'Awe, Jeannie, it's good to see you, lass, but not like this. What's happened to you?'

Jeannie's eyes darted from Gracie, to Peggy and Sheila.

'You're among friends here, Jeannie, none better, lass. These two were the saving of me. They won't condemn or judge you. Peggy here has been like a ma to me, and Sheila a sister, even though when I came to them I'd only met Sheila a few times. I'll tell you the tale one day of the measures they went to, to protect me.'

Jeannie relaxed. A tear plopped onto her cheek.

'Awe. Come here, lass, let me give you a cuddle.'

As Gracie held Jeannie, she felt the bones and ribs of her, and a deep pity entered her. Jeannie's body shook with sobs. 'Don't cry, lass. You're safe now, I promise.'

'Oh, Gracie, Gracie. I – I, I'm so pleased to see you. Help me, Gracie, help me.'

'I will, lass, I promise, but first, you must tell us what's happened so we knaw what we're up against.'

'I'll put kettle on, Gracie. Ma gave Jeannie a drop of water when she came, but thought to clean her up afore giving her owt else, so I reckon she could do with a cuppa.'

'Are you hungry, Jeannie?'

'Aye. But I don't knaw as I can keep owt down, Gracie, I ain't eaten proper for a long time.'

'I'll make you some of me porridge, Jeannie. That'll lay in you, and won't be too much for your stomach.'

'Ta, Peggy. I can't thank you all enough.'

Once they'd drank their tea and Jeannie had eaten some of the porridge, she seemed to relax a little. 'I can't stay here, Gracie, as there's some men after me. They're ruthless, and would cause trouble for you all. I just didn't knaw where to go, and thought that you might help me find a place.'

'What men?'

Not long after you left, Gracie, the master sold me to a pimp in Manchester. He said as how he'd cover my absence by reporting me as having absconded with you. The pimp took one look at me and said as I'd not bring much in unless they sold me as a freak, or he put a sack over me head. So, he said that I could be his slave in return for me keep.'

A feeling shuddered through Gracie that took her reeling back down the years. She could smell the refuge and see the ugly, pokey-faced master, and a fear set up in her as to whether she was still being sought.

'What happened when I left, Jeannie? Did they have the police out looking for me?'

'Naw. The master told us as you had gone to a more secure home, as you needed more discipline. That you had mental problems, and that we were not to talk about you ever again. Then he told me to go with him. I thought I were in for another rape by him, but he questioned me about you. I didn't tell him owt. Then he put me in solitary until this bloke came. I didn't see any coppers, or hear any more about you.'

A relief entered Gracie. The thought of someone turning up one day had hung over her head, and she'd instinctively kept out of the way of any bobby patrolling the beat. Even the day that Reggie grabbed her and she'd threatened to scream for a copper, she'd known that she wouldn't have.

'That's good, not that it is more important than

you and what has happened to you, but, well, I don't have to be so worried about helping you now, as no one would have followed you to get at me. So, you think this pimp will look for you, then?'

'Aye, he will as I knaws too much. He don't just deal in prostitutes, he has a gang, and they rob, and extort money from businesses. They did that big bank robbery in Manchester last week, and it was that that helped me to escape.'

Everyone was quiet as they absorbed this and the realisation dawned that Jeannie turning up here could mean big trouble.

'Please don't turn me away, Gracie. I've been through hell. For nearly a year, he kept me on a dog lead. I never stood up for all of that time. He taunted me and beat me. He raped me unmercifully, and fed me just a few titbits every now and again. He even made me lap water from a bowl. I – I can't b ... bear to go back, he'll kill me.'

'Oh God! Look, as I see it, you need to go to the police.'

'Naw, Peggy, I daren't, please don't make me.'

'Don't be afraid, Jeannie, we will protect you, but I can't ask Peggy to keep you here. We'll find somewhere. Does this man knaw as you have contacts in Blackpool?'

'Naw.'

'How did you get away? You said it was to do with the robbery?'

'The pimp got a new girlfriend. She were a floozy, but she had some kindness in her. She had a bit of a hold on the pimp an' all. He liked to please her. Well, she demanded that I became her

196

slave. He was bored with me by then, anyway, and so he let me free, and she took over. She gave me a bedroom of me own, but I had to do as she bid. But ... well, she weren't all kindness...'

None of them spoke in the pause that Jeannie took. They waited, letting her tell her horrific tale in her own time.

'This floozy used to like to watch the pimp do things to me. Worse things than he'd ever done. Torture me, and beat me, and sometimes, even rape me while she stood egging him on. It was like a fetish that she had. Then, one day, I heard them planning this robbery. I worked out that at one point there would be no one in the house – which was sommat that never happened, as even if they went out, they would leave one of their henchmen with me and tell him to have a good time with me. But I also worked out that if they left me alone, then they would tie me up, so I began to hide knives around the places that they were likely to leave me. When the night came, I was tied to me bed, and they stuffed a pair of his dirty socks in me mouth. I had a knife under me pillow. I hurt me-self in me effort to wriggle and get hold of the knife, but I managed it. I found some money, and fags and her jewellery. I left and got here by selling stuff, or giving folk stuff if they'd give me a lift.'

'Oh, Jeannie, to think that you have been going through all of that over the last four or five years is heartbreaking. I'm that sorry, lass. I imagined that you'd left the home, found work and were doing all right. I often thought about you. Sometimes I imagined that the cops were still after me and that's why you wouldn't come and look me up. I never dreamt that you were going through all of that.'

'What's the chances that they'll think that you've come to Blackpool, eh, lass?' This from Peggy held a note of worry in her voice.

'I don't think they'll knaw, but I just don't feel safe wherever I am, and I knaw they'll not rest until they find me. They allus talked about everything in front of me, so will be scared that I'll go to the police. But I daren't do that. I've seen coppers in the pimp's house being given money, so I knaw as they turn a blind eye to what the pimp does.'

'Right, well, you can stay here for a couple of days, till you feel a bit better. She can have that single room next to yours and Gracie's, Sheila. I have a job to let that one at the busiest of times. Then, we need to get you to them in the circus that can change your appearance – that's what we did for Gracie. Then we'll have to see.'

At Jeannie's astonished look, Gracie explained. 'This is a circus family. They work in the Tower Circus. These two, selling popcorn, and Bertram, Sheila's da, is a clown.'

'Oh. Well, ta, Peggy. I'll not be any trouble to you. I promise.'

'You're that already, lass, but we don't mind.'

'Ma's allus taken folk in when they're on their uppers. She'll get you sorted. All you have to do is try to eat more, rest and get stronger, then it'll be easier to sort you out.'

'Ta, Sheila. I've never met such kind folk. Would it be all right if I went to me bed now? I just don't think that I can keep awake much longer.'

'I'll take you up, Jeannie, and I'll sit with you until you drop off. When you wake, I'll bring you up to date with all of me news since I left that place.'

Jeannie smiled at Gracie, and at that moment Gracie caught a glimpse of the old Jeannie. It made her want to cry, but instead she helped Jeannie up and took her upstairs.

It didn't take long for Jeannie to fall asleep. Gracie stood looking down at her. To her mind, Jeannie needed checking over by a doctor, but how would they get around that one? Any outside contact could put them in danger, especially as the doctor may want Jeannie to go to the hospital. And then they would involve the police. They'd want to know how she got her injuries and why she was half starved. No, they'd just have to take care of her and hope that she soon recovered. But making this decision didn't lighten Gracie's worries.

CHAPTER EIGHTEEN

Back in the kitchen the talk was of 'what if', and Peggy seemed really afraid.

'Ta for taking Jeannie in, Peggy. You're a wonderful woman.'

'Eeh, what do you want to borrow, eh?'

'Ha, I mean it. Look what you've done for me. And now me mate turns up and you didn't flinch, but have given her somewhere to lay her head.'

'Away with you. It's the circus way. We help each other and others that need it. Now let's talk about how we're going to manage this. I'd like to keep the details from Bertram. He has enough on his plate, with him being about to lose his job.'

'Oh, no! It's official then.'

'Aye, they want a big attraction, and Charlie Cairoli is certainly that. They'll not get rid of Bertram. They've said he can be an understudy, but his main job will be backstage. He's very handy, and I keep telling him it will be regular money. But he's in the doldrums, as he loves being a clown.'

'Poor Bertram. Happen he'll get used to it, and he'll still be around his mates and involved in the life he loves.'

'Aye. But talking about him isn't getting us anywhere. I'm worried about your mate's tale. These folk that she's been with will stop at nothing by the sounds of things.'

'I knaw. I had another go at getting her to go to the police while I helped her to bed, but she says that though no cops here will know of the gang, if her evidence results in them going to jail she'd be dead, anyway. It seems she doesn't knaw all the gang, and those not caught would be after her, and knaw where she is by then.'

'I can see that. There's a few gangs in Blackpool, and we all have to keep on the right side of them, even pay protection money at times, but I'd rather do that than end up at the bottom of the sea.'

This shocked Gracie. She'd had no idea that such things went on. 'I think that our only option is to get Jeannie better, then to see if the artistes at the circus can change her appearance. She can work with me making the rock – I need another hand. I want to get really stocked up so that we can fill the shop we intend to rent with plenty of varieties of rock.'

'Well, that's one way, Gracie, but I'll make me mind up as to whether she can stay here when I see that she isn't recognisable. But I won't see her stuck. I could ask around the travelling community to see where there might be a job going that she could do in the travelling circuses. She'd be safe with them, and with not being in the same place for long, won't be traceable.'

'That's an idea, but I hope she can stay. After a while, if that gang see that she hasn't snitched on them, surely they'll not bother about her anymore.'

'Let's hope not. Anyroad, changing the subject – you just mentioned the shop you intend getting. How's everything going with your plans for that?'

'As soon as the Illuminations end next week, we're going back to that agent. Then, if we find the right place it will be all go to open for Christmas.'

'Sounds good. I miss making the rock and being involved.'

'I knaw. I suppose it was all the years that you did the pulling by hand that affected you, but it would be too painful for you now, even with the machinery that we have. There's still a lot of physical work; no wonder that most sugar boilers are men.'

They were quiet for a moment, and Gracie decided that as they had broached the subject of the shop, now was the time to bring something else up that she needed to discuss. 'Peggy, I ... well, I'm wanting to offer you a price for all the equipment and move it to the shop. What do you think, eh?'

'I thought that's what you had in mind, lass. Well, as far as I'm concerned, you can have it, it's half yours anyway, but my half can be Sheila's contribution.'

Sheila, who'd sat listening without joining in, looked up from the paper she'd been reading. 'Eeh, Ma, that's grand, that'll really help.'

'Well, I'd like to think that you've contributed as much as Gracie, as I knaw you haven't the same amount of money to chip in.'

Gracie stood and went around the table. 'You knaw, Peggy, I've never told you, but I love you like a ma, as that's what you've been to me. If ever you need owt – extra help, or whatever, I'll allus do sommat for you.' With this she put her arms around Peggy and planted a kiss on her head.

Peggy clasped her hand and looked up into her face. There were tears in her eyes.

'I knaw things are not easy for you, Peggy,' Gracie went on, 'so if you want me to cook the breakfasts while you have a lie in any morning, you've only got to say.'

Peggy's hand patted hers. The gesture brought a lump to Gracie's throat.

'And me, Ma. You don't have to carry the load of this place on your own, we're here for you, and I reckon as Jeannie can be a help to us all, she can switch between us, when we need her.' Sheila had risen and come to the other side of Peggy. The three women clung to each other.

It was Peggy who brought it to a halt. 'You girls, you're making me cry, and I can do that as easy as look at you these days. But I'm blessed to have you both. Now, let's talk of sommat cheerful. What was in your letter, Gracie?'

For the next fifteen minutes or so, they talked about Freddie, and what he'd said. Peggy was thrilled at Freddie asking Gracie to marry him. 'You haven't known him long, lass, but I reckon as this Freddie is the one for you. It doesn't take time to knaw that, it can happen as soon as you meet the right one. And I can understand your fear, Gracie, lass, but any man that has you has got to knaw the truth. And if their love is genuine, then they'll find a way of living with the fact that they're not the first.'

Though Gracie knew this, she couldn't see past her telling Freddie, or imagine his reaction.

'Anyroad, now it's got this far, I have a fear of me own. What about Bertie? I don't knaw if I can live without him, or what it will do to him to find out the truth of him being yours and not mine, but the decision is yours, Gracie, lass. And whatever you decide, then I'll live with it.'

'Oh, Peggy. Let's wait and see, eh? But, I promise you that if Bertie does go with me, you will see him as much as you want to, and he'll stay with you often. We'll sort of share him. Though I'm leaning towards letting him be none the wiser. Why should he suffer because I have, bless him? Oh, it's a difficult situation. I just don't knaw, I don't.'

At that moment, Bertie came into the kitchen. And just looking at him made a lie of her last statement. For Gracie did know what she wanted to happen. She knew that she never wanted to live without this son that she adored, and she wanted him to know that she was his ma. But she also knew that for him this might not be for the best.

A few days later there was a drastic change in Jeannie. She came downstairs looking much better, and it was decided to take her to the tower that morning in the hope that the make-up girls could work some magic.

'Afterwards, we'll take you to the clinic and see if we can get your eyes tested and a new pair of glasses, Jeannie.' Gracie kept a kindly tone to her voice, trying to make a joke of Jeannie's need of new glasses. 'Eeh, you look a right one in those. You've long outgrown them, lass. I'd ditch them if I was you.'

'Naw, I can't, everything's a blur. I'd run into lampposts and step in front of a bus and get meself killed. I'm not used to being in the outdoors as it is. When I was coming here, I bumped into a post box and apologised before I could focus and see what it was. I felt that daft.'

They all laughed at this, and Jeannie joined in. It felt good, and Gracie knew that it wouldn't take long for Jeannie to recover her spirits. She was always one for taking things in her stride.

The transformation was amazing. Jeannie emerged from the circus looking so different, that even Gracie had to look again. Her hair, that had been a mousey colour, was now blonde, and her face looked rounder and much more attractive. 'How did they do that? Will you be able to do it for yourself, Jeannie?'

'Aye, I will, Gracie. They did one side, and then let me do the other. It's a false cheek. It isn't very fat, but makes such a difference.' She pulled her hair back. 'Look, it just sticks on and blends right back to my ear, and there's a border around them of very fine rubber that's almost transparent, and that blends the cheek into your surrounding skin. And then I have to cover my whole face evenly with this pan stick make-up. That conceals the joins and gives my face an even complexion. A little rouge completes the transformation. And, I will need to use peroxide on me hair every now and again. Not much, just a rinse through after I shampoo. I love it.'

'And it looks lovely. Even your teeth don't seem to protrude so much now that your face is fuller. They look quite cute, and, not to be rude, but much whiter.'

'Awe, that were the good scrubbing they've had with soot. Ugh, it tasted vile. But they wouldn't let up, they gave them several scrubs, and I've to carry on with that an' all.'

'Well, at least you can finish with a brushing of my peppermint cleaner, that'll take the taste away. I sometimes do mine with soot, to brighten them.' Linking arms with this new Jeannie, Gracie steered her towards the bus. 'Right, now to get your eyes sorted.'

Gracie went in with Jeannie to sit with her through the examination. The optician was appalled at Jeannie's glasses. 'How do you see through them? I can honestly say that I haven't seen the like before. Well, on a kid perhaps, when I was at school. Now, let's begin the examination.'

After half an hour of Jeannie reading this and that, and the optician looking into her eyes with different apparatus, he sat back. A tall, gangly man, with light brown, scruffy-looking hair which he kept running his hands through, he looked to Gracie more like a mad professor type than a medical man. Though there was something about him that made him interesting and not bad looking. His voice was very deep.

'Well, I have good news for you,' he said. 'You will still have to wear glasses, but not thick lenses. You have been wrongly assessed as short-sighted, when the problem is that you have a long-sighted eye and a short-sighted eye, and this is what blurs your vision. Everything is thrown out of focus. I am going to make you a pair of glasses with different lenses in, but neither of the lenses will be thick, like the ones you are wearing now. And they will fit the size of your face, as well as being a lot better looking than those that you have. They will show your lovely hazel eyes off.'

Jeannie looked bashful, and Gracie was sure that if she could see her real cheeks, they would be blushed a pinky shade at this. The comment had made Gracie feel embarrassed and prompted a little giggle from her.

She'd never thought of Jeannie's eyes as being lovely, but then, she'd never seen them properly. She looked now, and yes, she could see what the kindly optician had seen. Jeannie did have lovely eyes. And the colour of them was unusual. Green, but with lots of speckles and flecks in them. A true hazel.

'Your case is fascinating, Miss Roberts. I hope that you will make a few visits here so that I can make a study of you. I would like to monitor the improvement that my lenses make to your sight. I won't charge you for further appointments, as it will be part of my research.'

It came to Gracie that he had more in mind than just monitoring Jeannie's sight, and she felt glad about that. It would do Jeannie good to know that she was attractive to a decent man, and not just the kind that wanted what they could get from her.

Jeannie smiled and nodded, not taking her eyes off the optician. Gracie didn't think that Jeannie had ever felt special in any way in her life before. And as the optician held her hand and helped her down off the stool, the look he gave her confirmed to Gracie the suspicion she had that it wasn't only Jeannie's eyes he was interested in. 'I will work with great speed for you, Miss Roberts. I want you to be able to discard those hideous glasses as soon as possible, but they are at least better than nothing, as I don't want you hurting yourself by bumping into things.'

With the new glasses ready two weeks later, the transformation was complete and Jeannie looked amazingly different, and very attractive. Gracie hugged her. 'Eeh, Jeannie, you're on the up now, lass. And you're putting on weight, your bones are not so pronounced. I reckon you won't have to wear them cheeks for much longer. In any case, you should only wear them when you go out, as I can't see them doing your skin much good. I'm telling you, you've a new life ahead of you, lass, and a handsome optician with his eye on you, an' all.'

Jeannie's playful push of Gracie's shoulder had them both giggling. 'Don't be daft, Gracie, no one could find me attractive. Anyroad, I ain't looking for a man, and probably never will.'

'I said that at first, Jeannie, aye and meant it too, as I suspect you do, but you can heal. I promise you. I have.'

'But, you didn't go through as much as I have, Gracie. I can't see me ever healing. Not deep inside, I can't. I'll be all right though. I'll not be in the doldrums or owt. That'd make yours and everyone's lives a misery, and you don't deserve that.'

'What if I told you that I had a babby, and I can't acknowledge him? That counts as suffering, I can tell you. But I've surmounted it and am ready to live me life and let happiness in, and you can do that an' all.'

'A babby! You mean ... Bertie! Of course, he's the double of you. Oh, Gracie, I'm sorry.'

'You mustn't say owt, as Bertie doesn't knaw. And it may have to stay that way. You see...'

Gracie told Jeannie the story of how Peggy covered for her, just to give her a life. 'So, though I want to, it would be cruel to tell him the truth. He looks on Peggy as his ma, and me as a kind of sister figure.'

'Awe, that must hurt. I'm sorry for you, Gracie.'

'Naw, don't be. Me life's grand. I have me own

business, a man as loves me, a good home with loving, decent folk, and I'm happy, truly happy.'

This wasn't entirely true, because deep down, Gracie was worried. She'd finally written and sent her letter to Freddie a week ago, the longest time she'd taken to answer one of his. But she'd composed it many times, trying to make the contents sound less horrible than they were.

She'd decided that now was as good a time as any, and hadn't accepted his proposal, but told him that she would give him time to think things over to see if he still felt the same after he knew the truth.

The truth had wrung tears from her as she'd written it. It had all sounded so sordid, even to herself, who had lived with it all these years. She couldn't think how it would sound to Freddie. And her worry was compounded by the fact that she'd taken the coward's way out by writing, instead of waiting until he came home to tell him in person. But she hadn't been able to bear the thought of him looking at her in disgust, and turning away from her, maybe even telling her that he couldn't ever associate with someone like her.

She'd told it all, everything, every detail, even about Bertie. In doing so, she'd known a kind of cleansing of herself. The guilt she'd always felt had left her, as she'd come to see that none of it had been her fault. That she had been abused by evil people. Even her own da, who should have loved and respected her, had used her little body – the body of his own child, to gratify himself. She hadn't asked for that. She hadn't asked for any of it. And if Freddie judged her by it, then he wasn't the man she thought him to be.

But, oh, she wanted him to be. She so wanted him to see her as the person that she was now, a victim of horror and evil who'd found help and had grown, not from the evil, but from the love given her, and that she'd taken the hands stretched out to her and changed her life.

Looking back, now that she could see the place where Jeannie was and she had been, she knew that it had taken courage to do what she had done. She only hoped that Freddie could see that, and that he could love her because of that and despite what she'd been put through.

But Gracie hadn't let these thoughts occupy her whole time since the letter dropped into the pillar box. She'd made that visit to the agent with Sheila and Rory, and he'd promised to contact them with some details of suitable rentals as soon as he had them. 'You don't let the grass grow under your feet, I'll give you that,' he'd said. 'By, I've hardly sifted through them as have given their notice in, yet. I'll compile a list and arrange a viewing day, how's that?'

That had suited them well, and the waiting for his call, and their planning, had kept Gracie's mind occupied for some of the time.

They'd wanted to involve Jeannie, but didn't want her to have to don her make-up too often, and especially hadn't wanted her to go out before she had her proper specs.

'You've gone quiet, Gracie. Are you sure you're all right?'

'Aye, sorry, Jeannie. I'm on with planning a

proper Blackpool day out for you, now that you have your glasses. Mind, a lot will be shut, as your timing's not great, arriving at the end of the season, but there's still a good few of the stalls on the Prom, and the piers that open at weekends, so tomorrow, we'll hit the town.'

'Ooh, that sounds fun. Ta, Gracie ... and, well, ta for everything an' all. You've saved me life, you and Sheila and Peggy.'

'You're worth it. You were all that kept me going in that place when we were young uns. Anyroad, we won't talk about that. We'll plan tomorrow instead. There's allus a tomorrow, Jeannie, and there's allus a chance that it'll be better than today.'

CHAPTER NINETEEN

The three girls left the boarding house the next day, wrapped in woolly coats and knitted scarves. Jeannie had borrowed an old coat that Peggy still had from the days when women wore their clothes a lot longer. With Jeannie being tall, this was the only one that reached her calves.

The wind was keen and went straight through you, instead of around you – a saying many Sandgrownians, the name given to those born in Blackpool, used for such a blustery wind as there was today.

'Eeh, Sheila, I reckon we should take Jeannie shopping first, she needs some clothes of her own.'

211

'Naw, don't do that, you both need all the money you have for your new venture. I'll be right. Once I start working with you and earning some money, I'll get a wardrobe together. That's if you don't mind me sharing your clothes until then.'

'Of course we don't, but it's difficult to find them as fit you, you lanky thing!'

'Cheeky. Better like me than down there where you two are. I can see further, especially with me new glasses. Eeh, I'm grateful to you for these, me life's changed with them. And you all did that for me. I don't want you doing owt else. I'll get by.'

'Well, if that's what you want, Jeannie, but it ain't all been one way. You've made our life better an' all. The help you give me ma has made all the difference to her. And to us, hasn't it, Gracie?'

'It has. We've been free to really get going on getting stock ready and sort out a few things we need for our shop. And little Alina has really taken to you, so that's been a big help, you taking her for walks while Aggie gets on with the bedrooms.'

'I love her, and Bertie, I seem to have found sommat in meself that I didn't knaw as I had, when I'm around them. A love of children, and I have a way with them that makes them want to be with me. You knaw, if I'd have had me chances, I'd have liked to be a teacher, or nanny, or sommat.'

'You still can. There's nowt stopping you. Well, I don't knaw about being a teacher, you'd need exams and things for that, but you could apply to one of them big houses to become a nanny. They say as the gentry have a hard job these days getting folk to work for them.'

'Naw. I want to stay with you, Gracie, I feel safe

with you. I'm not ready to branch out on me own.'

With this, Jeannie tightened her pull on Gracie's arm and Gracie laughed as she told her: 'Give over, you nearly had us all in the gutter then, you don't knaw your own strength.'

Jeannie and Sheila joined in the laughter and started to push each other, as if they were youngsters again. This had them squealing out as they tried to dodge each other.

Before they realised it they'd reached the pier café, and finding it open went in for a hot drink.

'I'm having cocoa, what're you both having?'

'You and your cocoa, Gracie, you're like a young un with how you like it. I'll have a cuppa. What about you, Jeannie?'

'I reckon as I'll have a cocoa, there's sommat comforting about it. And I could eat one of them iced buns as well, if you could run to one, Gracie.'

'Eeh, there's no stopping you, you stuff your face at every chance you get.'

Jeannie laughed at Sheila, and Gracie felt a warmth inside her. She was glad that Sheila and Jeannie got on well. It could have been awkward if they didn't.

'Go on then, Gracie, get me a bun an' all. If Jeannie here's going to get fat, I may as well join her.'

Gracie came back to the table near the window with her tray of steaming mugs and three iced buns. 'Phew, I need to take me coat off, it's sweltering in here with the steam from that urn.'

'I could spend the day in here, it smells lovely, and it's warm and welcoming, and safe.'

Jeannie used the word 'safe' a lot, but Gracie

could understand why. She remembered that feeling. It was the most prominent of all the feelings that she'd had once she'd settled in with Peggy and Sheila, and it took a long time for that feeling to become normal so that she didn't mention it as often. She hoped that Jeannie would soon come to that place.

'After this, we'll take you to the back of the circus. You can meet Rory, and see all the animals.'

'As long as there's no reptiles, I can't abide snakes. Gracie, I'd die if I was near one.'

'Ahh, they're lovely, all velvety, and they like to curl around you as if they are cuddling you.'

'Arrgh, naw, naw, please, I couldn't. Just the thought of them sends me all funny.'

'Eeh, lass, you're shaking. Don't worry, we won't take you near to them, they're in a different place to the elephants, lions and tigers.'

'Really! We can see all of them animals? Aren't you scared?'

'Naw, they're all in cages and can't hurt you.' Sheila nudged Gracie and winked, 'mind if they fancy you, Jeannie, then they could break out to get at you.'

Jeannie's eyes widened with terror.

'Stop it, Sheila, you're being cruel, you can see she's afraid. Don't worry, Jeannie, we'll not go there if you don't want to.'

'I think I'll give it a miss, I were scared enough just hearing the roars of the lions and the bellows of the elephants when I were down there having me make-up done. But you can go and see your friend, I've heard you speak of him before, and I knaw you'd like to see him.'

'Naw, we can see him any time, and we'll all be meeting up on Monday to view some shops, so we'll give it a miss an' all. There's plenty of other things to do. We can go along the stalls and have a go on some of them, and we can go into the tower. You'll love the ballroom.'

Jeannie's love and delight of everything made Sheila and Gracie enjoy the outing more than ever. They both loved this side of Blackpool, anyway, but the fresh and exciting approach that Jeannie had brought it even more alive to them.

They were huddled on a bench, two hours later, looking out to sea and eating steaming chips from a newspaper, when an excited Jeannie suddenly changed to a frightened one again. 'Oh God! Oh, Gracie, that's him. He's in the newspaper.'

'Who?'

'The pimp. Eeh, seeing him has made me feel sick.'

Jeannie was pointing at a picture of a man in the newspaper on her knee. 'There, that man there with handcuffs on.'

Carefully pulling the page with the story that had so distressed Jeannie, Gracie managed to get it out and found that the part she was interested in wasn't covered with grease, but had been flapping in the wind, and was the outer layer of the wrapping around her chips. The headline read, ROBBERY GANG ROUNDED UP.

Gracie wrapped her chips back up. 'Here, hold these a mo, Sheila, and don't eat any of them! I want to read what the article says.'

Jeannie had a look of sheer terror on her face as she watched Gracie spread out the crinkled sheet.

Today, Michael Baxter, thought to be the leader of a notorious gang that had reigned terror in the Moss Side area of Manchester, was arrested by police. A spokesman said that Michael had squealed and given the names of every member of the gang, trying to blame them all for what he'd been involved in.

'Bastard! Coward!'

This shocked Gracie, and she could see from Sheila's face that it had stunned her too. She was staring at Jeannie.

'Well, I'm sorry, but he is. Shopping the lot of them like that, hoping to save his own skin. Read on, Gracie, I reckon as this is going to be one story that I'm going to enjoy.'

It turns out that the gang had behaved like amateurs and had left evidence at the scene that linked a number of them to the job. A young detective, who recently joined the Manchester force, has been credited with their capture, and–

'Ha! They hadn't had time to get him into their pockets yet! They would have, but it sounds like he struck first. This is the best news ever, Gracie. What else does it say?'

'Aye, it says here that a number of the police force have been suspended pending enquiries into allegations that they took backhanders to turn a blind eye to the gang's activities. It goes on to say that upwards of twenty arrests were made, and evidence uncovered that links the gang with many sordid activities, including pimping young girls. It is thought that many of the gang, including Baxter, will never see the light of day again. This is going to be a fascinating case to watch unravel, and with the bringing of these men to justice, Manchester will be a much safer place for its citizens to live.'

'Hooray! Hooray!' Jeannie jumped up, put her chips down and did a jig. They were all laughing that much that none of them noticed the seagulls that seemed to be laughing with them, until a crowd of them dived on Jeannie's chips and made off with most of them. Jeannie's face was a picture of astonishment.

Gracie thought that she'd never stop laughing as Jeannie went into a frantic dance of chasing the scavengers that had missed out down the Prom. 'Oh, me sides ache. Oh, Sheila, did you see Jeannie's face? Eeh, help, me, help me.'

But Sheila was bending over herself, with tears running down her face. 'Eeh, I'm going to wet meself. Eeh, stop it, Gracie, make it go away...'

This had the effect of increasing their laughter until Sheila got up and ran to the public loo. Everyone who passed by looked at her as if she were a madwoman, as they did Gracie and Jeannie.

Gracie at last gathered herself enough to call out to Jeannie. 'Oh, Jeannie, lass, come and sit down. You may as well feed the rest of your chips to them, then we'll get you some more. You'll learn a lesson from this, an' all, lass. Allus guard your food. There's more than one scavenger on Blackpool Prom. Look at that mangy dog over there, he's got his eye on you an' all!'

With this, Jeannie gathered the rest of her chips and took them to the dog. 'Where can we get water for him, Gracie? He looks really thirsty.'

'We can't, we haven't owt to put it in, but he'll be fine. There's plenty of puddles, and there's allus food around for him. You don't see many starving strays in Blackpool, if any.'

When Jeannie rejoined them they went in search of more chips for her, then made their way towards the tower. The ballroom was another sight that, much as she already loved it, Gracie saw once more with fresh eyes. Its beauty was stunning. Her heart pounded memories around her of being held by Freddie, and a longing set up in her, nudged gently to one side as pride for her hometown filled her. And when Reginald Dixon appeared from the floor of the stage the effect was magical, as always, but more so with Jeannie calling out her delight.

They were three tired girls that went home that evening. Gracie couldn't wait to get her boots off, her feet were killing her. But nothing could daunt Jeannie.

She ran upstairs and when she reappeared twenty minutes later, the false cheeks were gone from her face and she held them in her hands. 'Here you are, you can take these back to the circus when you go to meet Rory on Monday, girls.' She put the cheeks on the table. Gracie looked at them, feeling glad for Jeannie as she told them, 'I've worn them for the last time. And I'm going to get me hair back to its natural colour an' all.'

Her happiness shone from her.

'Why, what's to do?' Peggy looked from one to the other. Once enlightened, she clapped her hands. 'And you say that they have got them all? None of them will come looking for you, Jeannie?'

'Naw, they'll all knaw that the pimp shopped them, and not many of them knaw of me, and them as does wouldn't care – they have no need to. I'm free, Peggy, free!' The twirl she did ended in front of Peggy, whom she took in her arms and squeezed.

'Eeh, give over, you're taking me breath from me, lass.'

'I don't knaw how to thank you, Peggy. But I will. One day, I will.'

'You thank me enough with the help you give me, and with me seeing that poor soul who stood on me doorstep a few weeks ago looking at death's door grow into the most beautiful of girls. Aye, that's thanks enough, lass. Now, let's put kettle on.'

'I'll do that.' Jeannie rushed to the sink to fill the kettle. The door opened as she did. 'What's all the noise in here, then? A man can't nod off for ten minutes when he's surrounded by cackling women.'

'Sorry, Bertram, it were me. I had some good news.'

After she had explained, Bertram smiled at Jeannie. 'Well, lass, that is good news. And now me household can settle down and not live in fear any more. But I'm warning you, our lass–' he wagged his finger at Sheila '–any more waifs and strays on me doorstep and you'll find yourself out on your arse with them, understood?'

Everyone was silent for a moment, then Bertram put his head back and roared with laughter. 'Eeh, I had you all there. But nice to knaw that a man's word will be listened to. You all looked ready to do me bidding.'

'We weren't, so don't let your head swell. We were just shocked at how brave you were that's all!'

This retort from Peggy had Bertram going to her and lifting her up in the air. 'You allus have sommat to say, but it's why I love you. Give us a kiss.'

'Bertram! Not in front of the girls. Behave yourself. Put me down.'

The room was in uproar, and Gracie felt a happiness that filled her with a feeling of being home. For a fleeting moment, she thought of her own ma, but with a peace as she knew her ma would be happy for her. This was the life she would want for her daughter. Gracie was sure of that.

Monday morning brought a dampener on the household. Sheila received a letter from Bob. After running excitedly to her room with it, the whole house, quiet after the few guests had gone out, was suddenly disrupted by a loud wail.

Gracie, Peggy and Jeannie ran for the stairs, only to find Aggie was already outside Sheila and Gracie's bedroom door. 'What is it? What is matter with our Sheila? The door is locked!'

'We don't knaw yet, love. Sheila, lass, open the door, it's Ma. Let us in. What's to do?'

A wretched sob came from behind the closed door. Gracie moved Peggy out of the way. 'I have me key.' Fumbling in the pocket of her skirt, Gracie found the key and opened the door. The sight that met them was heart-rending. Sheila lay on the floor, face down, her sobs wracking her body, her feet kicking the floorboards. 'Sheila! Oh, lass, lass, what's wrong? What's happened? Is Bob all right? Oh, me love, get up and tell us what's happened.'

'He – he crashed! Bob crashed. He's been in hospital all this time.'

'What? No! When did it happen? Why didn't Freddie let us know?'

Sheila passed the letter to Gracie. Her hands shook as she read:

My dear Sheila. Forgive me for not writing for so many weeks, but I haven't been able to. I crashed my plane in training, and have been badly injured. My life has been in the balance, but I am on the mend – on the mend that is, minus both my legs.

'Oh, dear God, naw!'

Gracie scanned the words for a reason that Freddie hadn't let them know.

You must be wondering why Freddie hasn't informed you, or why he hasn't written to Gracie. But he couldn't as he doesn't yet know, at least, I don't think that he does, as soon after he wrote to Gracie the last time, he was shipped out to Canada. I was to follow on the next ship to leave these shores to complete my training, and Freddie asked me to let Gracie know but then this happened. Please tell Gracie that it is likely that Freddie may stay out there for a long time due to the nature of his work. He was told that it could be a three- to four-year posting. We were told that, initially, we would have no communication with anyone until a postal system was set up and, as it is generally only when ships go there that letters will be delivered, they are few and far between. Only parents and wives were informed that their sons would be out of contact for a few months. Girlfriends are left for parents to inform, but I am not sure how much Freddie has told his parents about Gracie.

This information gave Gracie mixed emotions as she realised that was why she hadn't heard back from Freddie. And that it was likely that Freddie hadn't even received her letter.

Freddie implored me to let Gracie know, and to tell her that he will write as often as he can and will eagerly look forward to her letters.

But back to me, my darling. My flying career is now over, and I do not know what my future holds. I will not hold you to any promises that we made. I will not blame you if you never want to see me again. But I remain holding you in my heart. I love you, my darling Sheila. Bob x

Tears were running down Gracie's face by the time she'd finished reading. For this terrible thing to happen to Bob, and to have Freddie torn away from her so soon, and for years ahead. How was she to bear it? Life was so unfair.

Sheila had calmed a little and now lay still with rebound sobs shaking her body every few moments. 'What am I going to do? My poor Bob.'

Peggy took over. Climbing over Gracie to get to Sheila, she bent down to stroke her daughter's back. 'Lass, if you love him, it makes no difference that he is only half the man he was. We can all take care of him. Invite him here – he will be more than welcome.'

'Oh, Ma, I don't want him to be hurt. I need to see him, I have to.'

'Well, the address of the military hospital where he is staying is in the letter, look.' Gracie held the letter up. 'And a telephone number. You could try ringing to see if it's possible for you to go down to visit him.'

Sheila rose. They all rushed forward to hold her, almost trampling one another to do so.

'Hey, don't squash the poor girl. Come on, all of you out. I'll see to Sheila, and when she's ready she can come down and you can all cuddle her then.' Peggy shooed them all out.

Aggie went towards the stairs that led to her room. 'I come down later, when I have Alina off to sleep. You go down. Our poor Sheila, and this man, her friend. It is terrible.'

Gracie and Jeannie descended the stairs in silence. It wasn't until they were in the kitchen that Jeannie asked more about Bob. 'I knaw as Sheila has been on edge since I got here because she hadn't had a letter, but I didn't realise that she was in love. Poor Sheila. What a terrible thing to happen.'

'She's been a bit down about it all lately, and not mentioned it much. I just don't knaw how all of this is going to affect her and Bob.'

'Well, from the little that I knaw of Sheila, I

223

don't think that she will give up on him, especially with Peggy being so supportive.'

Jeannie had only just said this when the door opened. Gracie rushed at Sheila. 'Oh, Sheila, I'm so sorry. If there's owt that I can do, you only have to say.'

Peggy had hold of Sheila's arm. 'Now, let her get in, Gracie, there's a good un. She's all right. Let her sit by the fire.'

Once Sheila was settled, Gracie squatted in front of her and held her hands.

'Will you come with me, if they let me visit Bob, Gracie?'

'Aye, of course I will.'

'But what about your shop? We were going to look at premises today.'

'Our shop, not mine, yours, mine, and a little bit of Rory's too. Well, that can go on hold. We can carry on as we are for now. Let's get you and Bob settled first.'

'Ta, Gracie. I don't knaw how we are going to manage that, but I do knaw as I won't abandon him. I love him too much for that. And we'll find a way forward, we allus do. We're circus folk. Nowt daunts us. It may knock us off our axle for a while, but nowt beats us altogether.'

'I knaw, love. You're very special folk. I don't knaw what I'd have done without you, and I knaw as Bob's lucky to knaw you, an' all.'

'The letter must have been a bit of a blow to you, an' all, Gracie. Finding out that your Freddie is all those miles away and it's likely as you won't see him for years. Oh, it's all unbearable.'

'Eeh, that's nowt. Don't worry about it, love.

Yes, I'll miss him, but we will write. We'll carry on our relationship by letter.'

But it wasn't nowt, and had been like a kick in the stomach to Gracie. She just wanted to curl up and sob her heart out, but she had to be brave for Sheila, she had to. *Oh, Freddie, my darling, when will I ever see you again?* But then the thought shuddered through her once more, that he may not want to see her after he reads her letter.

CHAPTER TWENTY

The hospital in Millbank, in London, was an imposing building. Both Gracie and Sheila felt out of their depth and amazed that they'd got this far. They had travelled by train, making several changes, which had frightened them, as they worried they'd miss connections or get onto the wrong train. But somehow they had arrived, taking a taxi for the last leg of their journey as both were too daunted by the Underground system.

Asking after Flight Lieutenant Bob Grayson, they were shown along a maze of corridors. When they reached his ward, Gracie stopped. 'You go in, Sheila, and see him on your own. You can fetch me when you're ready. I'll sit on this chair here; I'll be fine.'

Sheila looked grateful, and at the same time fearful. Gracie knew that this was a huge ordeal for her, but saw that as she put her hand on the door knob she took a deep breath and fixed a smile on her face. Bob's familiar voice came to Gracie as he said Sheila's name, and that was it, Sheila was gone behind a closed door. Gracie sat with her head down, praying that all would go well for them both.

She was taken by surprise when the door opened again soon afterwards. And she was even more surprised when the bottom half of a wicker wheelchair came through the door, soon followed by the rest of the chair, carrying Bob. Gracie's reaction was nothing like she truly felt. To say that he was half the man just because he had lost his legs wasn't all the truth of it. Bob was shrunken, in that the little weight he'd had on his body had dropped off, leaving him skeletal. His brown eyes, looked like two lumps of coal in a bed of snow, and his mouth quivered when he attempted to smile.

'Bob! Eeh, you look grand! And look at you, up and about already.'

'Hello, Gracie, it's good to see you. Thank you for helping Sheila to get here.'

'Oh, Bob. I'm so sorry for what has happened. But so happy to see you aren't as bad as I imagined. Where're you taking him, Sheila? Are you helping him to escape, love?'

'Naw, Bob says that there's a nice room where we can sit and have a cuppa. He'll show us where it is.'

Sheila looked as though she was holding herself in check. Her face had lost its colour, and she held her body stiff and tense.

'Well, let's get there then, I'm dying for a cuppa. I'll push, while you walk beside Bob, Sheila.'

The sight of the two of them holding hands was pitiful. Both were like a wound-up coil, and Gracie felt afraid that either one of them would suddenly break. In an effort to cheer them, she made light of the mishaps of hers and Sheila's journey here. Bob did chuckle a little when she told him of how Sheila had run after a bloke thinking that he was a stationmaster, or porter, and would help them, only to find that when he turned around he was a seaman, and was just as astonished to have two girls accost him, as they were embarrassed at their stupidity.

With this little bit of ice chipped, Sheila seemed encouraged. 'It was his uniform. From the back, it looked exactly like the railway staff's.' Her giggle was infectious, and Bob looked up at her and smiled. Gracie could feel his love for Sheila.

The room was the poshest Gracie had ever been in. It was furnished with high-backed, winged chairs of a golden, soft fabric. These stood on a cord carpet of pale blue. Small mahogany tables, piled high with magazines and newspapers, were dotted around the room, and the curtains were beautiful. Draped to the floor, they were of gold colour, with a delicate feather-shaped pattern in blue. There was a little kitchen off to the side of this room with a stove and a sink and a kettle. Next to the stove was a cupboard, which Gracie thought may hold the tea and cups. The feeling it all gave to Gracie was that she wasn't good enough to be here, but she told herself off for this. She was as good as the next one.

'I'll make a cuppa and have one with you, then I'll leave you to yourselves. I can wrap up warm and go for a little walk.'

'Thank you, Gracie. You know, I didn't like you when we first met, but I now know that you are a lovely person. Sheila is cross with me for telling Freddie what she told me, and I'm sorry, I really didn't realise at the time.'

'Naw, don't be sorry, I now knaw that it is the best thing that has happened as I have to be open with Freddie, which is sommat as I have avoided. And then I'll have to leave him to decide if he can live with what I have been through in the past.'

'Oh, he will. Whatever it is, Freddie won't condemn you for it. He isn't like that.'

'D'you reckon as he got me letter afore he went?'

'I don't think he could have, as he came to see me before he was shipped out and told me that he'd just written the most important letter of his life to you, and now wouldn't get your answer for he didn't know how long. He was in the doldrums, I can tell you.'

'Eeh, I'm glad in a way, as the longer he is innocent of the truth about me the better. But it does mean that he will be thousands of miles away when he does read it, and that's sommat as I didn't knaw could happen. And it's left me on pins for a lot longer than I hoped, as to what his reaction will be.' An idea came to her as she said this, and though she felt cheeky asking, she knew she had to. 'Would you do sommat for me, Bob? I – I mean, when you feel up to it? Would you mind if Sheila tells you all about me, and then you can perhaps give me a better judgement of what to expect from Freddie?'

'Of course. If that's what you would like.'

'Awe, ta, it is. This waiting is driving me mad. Oh, I do miss Freddie. And I hope with all me heart that he accepts me.'

'The way he feels about you, I know he will. Try not to worry.'

With this, Bob gave a huge sigh. It was pain filled, and gave Gracie a pang of guilt. She'd hogged his attention for her own need. Poor Sheila had sat there holding Bob's hand, allowing her to rattle on about her own troubles.

'Eeh, I'm sorry, I've intruded on your time together. I'll make that tea.' Not giving them time to answer her, Gracie busied herself finding what she needed and getting the kettle on to the stove. The whistle it made when ready was a demanding sound that made her want to tell it off!

The while she worked, she could hear Bob and Sheila talking in whispered tones but not what they were saying. When she carried the teapot and the delicate china cups over to them – the like of which, she'd never had tea in in her life – they both looked up. The happiness on their faces put her mind at rest.

'You two look like a pair of cats that's managed to topple a bottle of milk off the doorstep. What've you been up to while me back's been turned?'

Bob looked up. His eyes were full of tears. 'My worst fear has been quietened. Sheila hasn't rejected me, sh – she still wants to be my girl.'

'Course, she does, you daft a'porth. Did you doubt her then?'

'I did. I couldn't see anyone wanting me now.'

'More like you thinking you would be a burden.

229

Well, Sheila won't let that happen. She'll have you doing all that you can achieve in naw time!'

'So she has been telling me! But life isn't going to be easy, not for a long time – not ever, but I have dug deep and realised that with Sheila by my side I can cope.'

Gracie wanted to scream out against the injustice of everything. How bad things happen to decent folk, through no fault of their own. Sometimes she wondered just whose side God was on. Didn't he make her ma suffer agony before he took her? And herself and Jeannie, an' all. Just young uns, defenceless and alone in the world. And now Bob – a handsome young man with his future all mapped out, only to have the rug pulled from under him. *Why? Why?*

They were on the last leg of their journey home before Sheila opened up. She'd talked of everything and anything as they'd made it to the train that would take them into Blackpool South station, and Gracie hadn't pressed her.

'I'm not sure how it will all pan out for me and Bob, Gracie, but I'm going to give it me best shot.'

'I knaw you will, lass. And no one could do better than you will. Did Bob make any plans for the future after I left you alone?'

'Aye, it's all we talked about. He says as his mother wants him to live at home with her, and that there's plenty of room for the both of us. But I can't, Gracie. I can't up-sticks and go and live in a posh house in Surrey. I'd be like a football trying to fit into a golf ball hole.'

'Aye, I can see how you're thinking. I've had the

same thoughts. Freddie and Bob are from a different world to us, and it won't be easy for us to step up into theirs, or for them to step down into ours. But, they say as love can surmount all, and we've all got that for each other.'

'I knaw. But saying it and doing it are two different things. We don't speak like them, we haven't had the education they've had, and I, for one, wouldn't knaw how to go on with such things as "going to dinner" that Bob sometimes talks about.'

'We can learn. And we're interesting folk an' all. Look what we do, and what we have around us. Blackpool's the most popular seaside town in Great Britain, and we live there, and we help to run it ... well, we contribute. I'd like to see Bob's ma make rock with lettering running through it, or standing out in all weathers to sell it. And I bet as she's never been inside a circus, let alone knaws how one runs. She don't help to feed elephants, or take them to the beach. Naw, we're different, but we're just as important in the run of things.'

'Ha, Gracie, you have a way of seeing things that brightens every situation. But I'm going to have to stand me ground. I may be as good as her, and their posh friends, but I don't want them in me life on a daily basis.'

'That's sommat as you'll have to thrash out together. But I knaw one thing. The sea air is the best air there can be for folk who are ailing, and it would do Bob the world of good to live in Blackpool, instead of you moving down to Surrey.'

Caught up in the Christmas rush, all plans for

the future had to be put on hold. With no word from Freddie, Gracie's spirit were low. Her thoughts had been full of the time he had spoken of, when they would spend two whole weeks together, but now that wasn't going to happen.

Christmas in the boarding house was a jolly affair. Everyone had done well, and money wasn't an issue. Peggy splashed out on a huge cockerel, and on Christmas Eve they all took turns in plucking it. Golden feathers seemed to be everywhere, even though they tried to contain them in a sack.

Once the body was as bare as they could get it, there was a scorching smell as Peggy singed the bird to clear it of any feathers, or stumps of feathers, that had been missed. Then it was stuffed with crushed chestnuts and breadcrumbs bound together with beaten eggs. All of this labour was accompanied by a glass or two of sherry, and before long they were all singing carols at the tops of their voices and laughing at nothing at all.

It was when the clock struck eleven, that Jeannie said, 'I've not been to midnight mass for ages, we were allus made to at... Well, you knaw. It was one of the highlights of me year, seeing the babby put in the manger in the crib. Does anyone fancy going?'

Gracie stood up. 'Aye, I'll come, but we'll have to be careful not to breathe on the candles, with the alcohol we've drunk we'll be throwing fire, like they do in the circus!'

They all laughed at this.

'I'll not join you, I'm away to me bed to see if Santa comes.'

Peggy declined too, agreeing with Sheila. 'I'm

away to me bed an' all, just as soon as your da comes in. The circus lot have been doing the rounds of the hospitals and children's homes this evening, then they all go to Yates Wine Lodge and have a skinful.'

Outside, snowflakes drifted in the wind. 'Eeh, a white Christmas, that don't happen often.'

'Almost never in Blackpool, Jeannie, as the salty air prevents it from settling, but this looks set to. Look, some of the rooftops are covered already.'

With their heads bent against the wind and biting cold, they made it to St John's church, opposite the Winter Gardens. By now, the trees to the side of the church were covered in snow, which glistened in the light of the gas street lamps. They looked beautiful. Gracie and Jeannie stood a moment, letting the churchgoers walk past them as they took in the sight.

'This is me first Christmas of freedom, Gracie. I can't believe it. Eeh, I'm blessed to have found you, and to have Peggy take me in.'

'Aye, I were an' all. She and Sheila and Bertram are very special people.'

'I'm going to light a candle for them. And for anyone who was ever at Hallford House Children's Refuge too, and those still there today. And I'm going to pray that one day, all of those evil bastards that run it are brought to justice.'

'Oh, Jeannie, fancy swearing just outside church! Come on, we'd better get inside before you're struck by lightning. Not that I don't agree with you. I do, lass. And I'm going to pray for the same thing.'

Inside the church, Gracie was lost in the beauty of the singing, the hundreds of flickering candles and the magical feel of the true meaning of Christmas. She and Jeannie sang their hearts out to all the carols, and prayed as loudly as the next when it came to the Lord's Prayer.

Coming out, Gracie felt lifted to ten feet tall. The world was white. The sparkling snow crunched under their feet. 'Eeh, Jeannie, I feel that happy. Even missing Freddie can't dampen me spirits.'

'It were lovely, weren't it? But, mind, I wish we hadn't to walk such a way home, me toes are freezing.'

'We'll walk briskly, we'll soon toast them up.'

They were just turning into Hornby Road from Coronation Street by the time they spoke again, and that was just a muffled, 'Are you all right?' from Jeannie, through the scarf she had around her face.

Gracie was about to answer when a hand grabbed her. 'What the...!'

'Merry Christmas, Gracie. I've been waiting for you. I've come to collect me Christmas kiss.'

'Get off me, Reggie. Leave me alone!'

Reggie had no time to do anything more as Jeannie swung her bag at him, catching him across the side of his head and sending him reeling backwards. 'Get off her, you oaf, leave her alone!'

'Run, Jeannie. We're nearly home now, we can make it before he recovers.'

Inside the house they stood panting for breath. 'Eeh, ta, Jeannie. You saw him off good and proper.'

'Who was it? Someone you knaw, obviously.'

'I'll tell you about him, but suffice to say, he's the bane of me life, and scares the wits out of me. But forget him. Fancy some cocoa?'

'Aye, that'll warm our lugs.'

As she prepared the cocoa, Gracie made an effort to forget the incident. Surely Reggie would get the message soon? But then she'd thought he'd realised last time that she really didn't want him in her life. Not that she could avoid him, as she wanted to keep in touch with her Aunt Massie and Uncle Percy. A sigh came from her. She didn't know yet if her Aunt Massie wanted her to keep in touch; there'd been no message or anything since the last time she'd visited.

As the steam from the kettle warmed her face, she made her mind up that she would visit them again come the New Year. She'd take her courage in her hands and call around on the off chance. The thought put a dread into her, as every time she went to visit she ran the risk of seeing Reggie and having to fight him off. Life was complicated.

Sipping her cocoa in the dark, in the warmth of her bed, Gracie let herself think about Freddie. What are you doing tonight, me love? Or is it still day where you are? She tried to imagine his arms around her, but the image only brought tears to her eyes, so she brushed it away and snuggled down. One day she would snuggle down with Freddie. She'd cuddle her pillow and pretend. It wasn't long before she had to turn her pillow over, as her tears had soaked it through.

CHAPTER TWENTY-ONE

Two letters dropped through the letterbox on the last day of January 1939. Both Gracie and Sheila squealed with delight when they saw there was one for each of them. Bob had been writing regularly, and Sheila was pining to go to see him, but the weather had been bad and the trains disrupted, and so Peggy had persuaded her to wait.

But for Gracie, this was the first communication that she'd had from Freddie in almost three months.

They were ready to go out as the postman arrived, as at last they felt they could concentrate on finding the shop premises they wanted. Bob had indicated that when he was well enough he would come and live by Sheila until they could be married, and this had given Sheila a settled heart about carrying on with their plans.

Peggy had been put out by talk of marriage when she hadn't even met 'this Bob', as she called him, but had been good natured about it, really. She and Sheila were planning a trip soon to see Bob so that Peggy could meet him before plans got too far under way.

Freddie's letter was all Gracie could wish it to be. He told her that he understood and that his heart hurt to learn what she had been through, and – music to her ears – that none of it would make a difference to how he felt about her.

And then came the part that sealed her happiness and had her whispering, 'Yes, yes, my darling.'

I know that this is very forward of me, but we have spoken of it before, and in your letter, you indicated that you would be willing to marry me. Well, here, there is a base camp being prepared for married couples. It is quite a long way from the air base, and mostly the men have to stay on base, but they do get to go home to be with their wives and children quite often. I don't know if it will happen, or if you have to have been married when you were posted, but if you are in agreement, I would apply for permission for you to come out and for us to be married here and to be allocated a base home. I will pray that your answer will be yes. Write as soon as you can, and often, my darling. It may mean that I get a bunch of letters all at the same time and that you do too, but I want to know everything about you, what you are doing and how your life is, and I want us both to work towards being reunited and becoming man and wife. I love you. F xxx

Gracie was ecstatic. All the worry and the unhappiness she'd felt melted away from her. Life was on the up and up.

For a moment, she wondered about going through with her plans for a shop, but knew she had to for the others' sake. Sheila would most likely need an income if Bob was pensioned out of the RAF. And she would need a job that was flexible, or that Bob could even help with. And Jeannie needed a future too.

Being realistic, Gracie knew that hers and

Freddie's plans could take a couple of years, so she too needed something to occupy her that would take up all her energy and help the time to pass. And then she would leave the shop to them and to Rory to carry on what she hoped by then would be a thriving business, while she sailed away to Canada to be with her darling Freddie.

The first shop they saw was perfect for their needs. 'I can't believe it! It has everything, a large kitchen, and the shopfront is one that we can open up on nice days and spill onto the pavement. When can we have the keys?'

'Don't you want to know the terms of business, miss?'

'Aye, of course, but whatever they are, we will meet them. We only need to be able to fit the kitchen out so that I can make my rock in there, and paint the shop out in the colours we have chosen. Will any of that be a problem?'

'Well, it will depend on the owner approving the use of the premises in that way, but no, there isn't anything specific that would bar you. And you are happy with the rent? This position on New Bonny Street is sought after, and rents are only just lower than those on the Promenade.'

Gracie rethought the rent situation. A year up front, which is what she wanted to pay, would take all that she had, and leave her with just what Rory and Sheila could tip up to do the decorating with. And the season didn't kick off until Easter, which wasn't until the first week of April, but then they would need that time to do everything they had to do. There was no problem with stock – she had stockpiled for a long time now – and they had already bought the baskets they needed. There was a good counter in the shop, so that wasn't a problem, and they could just use a tin for the money to start with. Yes, it was all doable.

'If the others are happy, then I am.'

Rory and Sheila both agreed.

'We have to take it,' said Rory. 'It's the best location that we are going to get for our money. The Promenade is only two hundred yards away. A sign there pointing to our shop will have them popping up in droves, and I can stand on the corner with Suzy and direct the punters up here.'

'I agree with Rory, Gracie, it's worth stretching ourselves for, lass.'

'Right, where do we sign?'

'Ha, it's not that simple, miss. Though it will be after a few days' work that I will have to do. Firstly, I will contact the owner. He may, or may not want to meet you and approve you. Then if all that is in order I will need to draw up a contract, and then you sign and take over. I would say about three weeks in all before I can hand the keys over.'

'That's fine. But no longer than that. We have a lot of work to do, besides having to continue to earn our living, and we want to be ready for Easter.'

'I'll make sure that it isn't any longer than that. Now, you need to pay me a ten-pound fee, which is for the administration and a holding deposit. Five pounds of that will go towards your yearly rent, or be refunded to you if something is amiss and you aren't accepted. And I will need two business references and a bank reference.'

None of these posed any problem to Gracie. She had many business contacts who fully trusted her, and with whom she had a good relationship. She and Peggy had always run their business to the bank's satisfaction. She just couldn't believe that it was all as simple as it was.

Soon afterwards, they sat in the pier café with a pot of tea and a bun, all talking at once, their excitement buzzing their conversation.

'Look, we need a list. All of these ideas need to be scheduled so we knaw what we have to achieve and how much time we can do it in. I'm going to leave that to you two. I'm going to work me fingers to the bone, making sure we have enough stock, as I will have orders coming in around the time we are in the thick of getting ready. I want to make sure that I can fulfil them. We will need the outside business to keep us going, we can't rely solely on the shop.'

They all agreed to this. 'Aye, it's no good us getting all caught up in the excitement; we have to keep our practical heads on. Are you going to manage, Gracie?'

'I will, Rory. Jeannie is a godsend. She has taken to the skills so well, and she will help me increase me output. Not that I want to take her away from Peggy too much, but once the breakfast pots are done and Bertie is off to school, there's not much for her to do other than watching over Alina. But then Alina is a darling and no trouble. She sits in her playpen as happy as Larry until Aggie is finished doing the bedrooms, so she can do that in the shed with us. Aye, I don't see any problems. Then, when the decorating starts in earnest, Bertram and Ron will help us, they said they would. And Peggy said that she and Aggie will make the covers for the baskets and the counter. It'll all be grand. We'll all just have to put all our spare time into it. After all, once it's done and we open, we'll be based there together, Sheila, and you'll be on hand, Rory. By, that'll be sommat, for us all to be working in the same place.'

After supper, during which, plans had been gone over and over, the household fell quiet. Bertram sat reading his paper, Peggy sat at the table folding napkins, Jeannie had her nose in a book, and Gracie and Sheila sat on the opposite side of the table writing letters.

Composing hers to Freddie was an easy task, as Gracie found that she just couldn't stop writing. She told him everything she could remember about what had happened since they last spoke. And then ended by saying:

I am so happy that you still love me despite everything. Since hearing that, it seems to me that a great weight has been lifted off my shoulders. The weight contained my guilt, as I have always felt as though it happened to me because I deserved it. Silly, I know, but it was how it was.

I am wondering how soon you can fix things for us? As though it frightens me to think about the possibility of war, if it does come, then I may not be able to travel to you. Do we have to wait for a base house? Or is there anything near enough to you that we can rent? I feel the need to act quickly, just in case.

My dearest, I cannot say how my life has changed since Sheila and Peggy took me in, and now, knowing you, of all the blessings that I have, you are the very best blessing that I could wish for. I love you. Yours for ever, Gracie x

Finishing the letter had the effect of making her feel bereft. While she was writing to Freddie, she was seeing him and having a conversation with him. There was a deep void inside of her now.

Sighing, she offered to make the cocoa. Four voices spoke at once, saying they would love one, and that she made the best ever. She laughed at them, and threw a cushion at Bertram, who added, 'I thought you'd never ask, you sit there doing nowt, while a man dies of thirst.' He caught the cushion and laughed with her. 'Switch the wireless on as you pass it, lass. Let's hear what's happening in the world.'

That was the last thing Gracie wanted to hear, but she did as she was bid. And as she thought it would be, the crackling news was full of what Adolf Hitler was up to. It seemed his programme to increase his naval fleet was his priority at the moment and that he'd put huge sums of money into it. Gracie shuddered – everything pointed to more unrest. Hitler seemed unstoppable. The German people adored him. As his speech came to an end – or rather, his ranting and raving, as if he were a madman – she wanted to close her ears to the sound of the crowd's chanting: *'Heil Hitler! Heil Hitler!'*

As she turned, she saw Sheila looking at her. Her look held a concern. Gracie knew why. They often talked about what war would be like, how would they cope. What if Hitler invaded their country as he had others?

But he wouldn't, would he? Chamberlain was doing all he could to keep the peace. Please God, let him succeed.

The next day, keeping her head down and working hard to fulfil her commitments, and also to occupy herself and not allow herself to think too much, Gracie was once more in a happy place of anticipation for her future, when the shed door suddenly opened.

'What are you doing back already, Sheila? Please say that's it's because you have sold out of rock.'

'Naw. I've a good bit left. Rory's watching the stall. I have sommat to tell you. Well, warn you of really.'

Gracie gave Sheila her full attention. A trickle of fear clenched her stomach.

'That Reggie came to me stall. He was asking after you, and I told him that he'd better watch out as you had a man now, and he'd sort him out when he came back on leave. He said that *he* was your man, and that anyone interfering with you would knaw about it.' Sheila paused and lowered her head.

'What? What else did he say, Sheila?'

'It wasn't him, it were me. I said, "Well, if that's right, how come that Gracie is organising her wedding then?" He went crazy. He kicked out at me stall, and sent some of the rock flying. Then he threw a punch at me, but I ducked. Rory saw it all from the pier and he ran forwards and set Suzy on to Reggie. You knaw how ferocious that monkey

243

can be if Rory tells her to be. She does everything he says. She clung to Reggie and clawed at his face. There was a lot of blood afore Rory finally called her off. Reggie cursed like I've never heard anyone curse afore. A crowd gathered and they all cheered as they'd seen him go to hit me. But it was what he said as he left that worried me. "You tell Gracie that she has nowhere to hide, that I'll get her, and she'll knaw when I do that she's mine. You tell her."'

'Oh God! Oh, Sheila, why did you tell him?'

'I'm sorry, but you can't keep hiding from him, you can't. He'll get to knaw. And anyways, you intend to go to Canada, so you'll be safe.'

'That might not be for years yet. Oh God, why is he like this? I have never given him any encouragement.'

'He has to be stopped. He's obsessed with you. I'm going to talk to me da. He might knaw someone as can frighten Reggie off. Maybe that strongman at the circus. I've heard tell that he takes on work like that for them gangsters as Ma talked of.'

Gracie knew that Sheila was right. But did she want this settling by violent methods? 'Leave it a while, Sheila, don't tell your ma, or your da, until I see if there's owt that I can do. I'll go and see Aunt Massie. I'll make her see that I haven't ever encouraged Reggie. I'll take me photo of Freddie to show her, and perhaps then she will realise and help Reggie to accept that I'm not his, nor will ever be.'

Sheila walked towards her with her arms open. 'Eeh, Gracie, I'm sorry, lass.'

'I knaw.'

It felt good to be held by Sheila. But the hug turned into something much deeper, and Sheila burst into tears.

'What? What is it, love?'

'I'm worried about the future. Not just mine and Bob's, but yours and Freddie's and, well, the whole world's.'

'We all are, lass. But we have to carry on. It could be that we're worrying for nowt. Come on, cheer up. You get back to your stall, and then tonight we'll go to bed early and talk about our wedding plans. Well, yours in particular as that'll come sooner than mine.'

Sheila brightened up as if someone had switched a light on inside of her. 'Eeh, Gracie, that would be grand. It's been all about the shop lately, and I've so much buzzing around me head.'

'Aye, it will. We have to talk about dresses, and veils, and wedding cake, ooh, all sorts.' Sheila giggled like a young un as she left and Gracie felt glad for her. She didn't let herself fall into the doldrums at it not being her own wedding they would plan, but went back to the task in hand, laying the letters out in strips between white candy, before rolling them into a huge roll.

Then her thoughts went back to Reggie, and she wondered how this obsession of his would all pan out. How was she going to stop him thinking like he did? And what was he capable of? What did he intend doing? The thoughts piled up on top of one another, leaving her trembling.

Putting all her effort into the pulling and rolling of the candy didn't help. Though sweat ran from her, trickling down her back and wetting her

245

body, so did the tears, wetting her face, and she had to admit that she was afraid. Deeply afraid of Reggie.

Not even planning the wedding that evening took the fear away. Several times, Gracie had gone into the front room and looked through the curtains. *Was he in the street now?* A shadow moved on one of the occasions and Gracie jumped back. Her breath came in short pants, her heart pounded, but then she heard the chinking of glass, and looked again. This time she saw that it was a neighbour putting out his empty milk bottles. Sighing, she closed the curtains and went back to the kitchen.

'What is it with you tonight, Gracie?' asked Peggy. 'You're like as if you have all the troubles in the world on your shoulders. What're you doing paying so many visits to the front room?'

'Oh, nothing, Peggy, I'm just a little restless that's all.'

Restless? As she listened to Sheila's excited chatter about dresses and flowers, she had to admit to herself that she was terrified. And that she had a feeling of hopelessness on her, as if something was going to happen and she couldn't stop it.

The feeling was akin to what she'd felt as a youngster. She'd been powerless then. A despair settled in her. *Oh God, help me, help me.*

The next evening, Gracie knew that her prayers were not to be answered.

Taking it on herself to go to see Aunt Massie and Uncle Percy the moment she finished sugar boiling for the day, she'd only just stepped off the tram and was about to cross the road, when a car that she thought she could beat suddenly gained speed and then screeched to a halt just inches from her. Her heart stopped. *Reggie! God, naw, naw.*

The tram trundled away, taking the only safety net she might have had away from her. Frantic, Gracie looked around. The street was deserted. Men wouldn't yet have returned from work and women would be inside cooking tea. Gathering her wits, she took flight, but looking back over her shoulder, she saw Reggie park the car and get out. Panic gripped her. Gasping for breath, as fear clenched her throat, she tried to run faster, calling out for help, but no one came to her aid.

Reggie caught up with her after only a few yards, his grip on her arm causing her deep pain. She opened her mouth to scream but he clamped his free hand over it, twisting her neck so that her body went with it and dragged her to the car. 'Get in!'

'Naw, Reggie, I won't. Let me be. You've naw right to treat me like this.'

The blow he landed on her head sent her into a black world of fog that she couldn't crawl out of. But then she didn't want to, as in this world there was no Reggie, no pain, no memory – just a welcome peace.

CHAPTER TWENTY-TWO

Gracie had the strangest sensation as light came back into her world. She could hear soft, guttural moans, and feel a weight on top of her, crushing her. But more than that. A feeling that was familiar to her was happening between her legs.

This realisation catapulted her back to full consciousness. 'Naw! Get off me. Get off me!'

With a strength that she didn't know she possessed, Gracie arched her body and turned so violently that Reggie lost his grip and fell off her.

Vomit rose in her mouth as the sensation of him coming out from inside her registered with her. Swallowing the stinging liquid, she hit out with all her might. 'How dare you! You beast, you bastard!'

Reggie soon recovered and got onto his knees. Gracie tried to scramble away but the soft sand beneath her hampered her progress. She kicked out at him and sent him reeling backwards.

Trying to get up, but not getting a footing, the realisation came to her that they were alone. From what she could see around her, she knew that they were on Rossall Beach, some three miles from Fleetwood. Reggie must have driven her here and carried her onto the beach.

Her eyes rested on Rossall School, about six hundred yards away, but there was little sign of life there, just a few windows lit up.

The sea crashed onto the shore within feet of them, putting a fear of a different kind into Gracie: *Was the tide coming in? Surely Reggie would know, and not put them in danger of drowning?*

Behind them, the pebble bank was a few feet away, if she could make it to there, she might stand a chance of scrambling on more of a sure footing, up to the path and then across that to run over the field to the school.

Taking her chance, Gracie made another effort to move, but Reggie caught hold of her foot. 'Let go. Please, Reggie, please let me go. Don't do this. I don't want you. Please ... please.'

But nothing stopped him. He had hold of her other foot now, and was forcing her legs apart. Gracie writhed about, but couldn't free herself. Their bodies rolled nearer to the sea. Icy cold water lapped her legs.

Pulling her to him with a force that Gracie was powerless to stop, Reggie got between her legs once more, and grabbed her arms. Held as if in a vice, she felt herself jerk towards him as once more he entered her.

A scream that rasped her throat strangled from her. But no one heard. Only resting seagulls responded, by taking to the air and drowning her screams with their own.

Utter despair entered her as the assault went on and on. Her mouth filled with salt water each time she tried to cry out, but Reggie was oblivious to the rising tide as he pounded her unmercifully.

At last he stiffened, and cried out in a guttural, animal way, that once more sent the gulls into a hideous screaming rage. Then, he slumped down on her, forcing her body below water level. With everything in her, she struggled to release herself. Her effort to hold her breath had her lungs feeling like they would burst.

As the knowledge of her own death crowded her, Gracie thought of Freddie. Beautiful, pure, Freddie. And the realisation came over her that once more she was soiled. She couldn't inflict such filth on him. She wanted to die.

When she came to, choking and vomiting, she thought for a moment that Reggie was taking her again, but he was pumping her chest, and his cries weren't of lust, but of anguish and sorrow. 'I'm sorry, Gracie. Live, my Gracie, come on... Breathe.' Once he realised that she was reacting, he stopped and looked down at her. His tears fell onto her face. 'Oh, Gracie, I love you. I love you. I thought that I had lost you, after at last making you mine.'

Gracie couldn't respond. A hate filled her heart and her feelings turned to stone. She wanted to hit out at him, to claw his face until there was no flesh left on it, but she couldn't, her strength had deserted her.

Nor could she resist when he lifted her into his arms and carried her the few hundred yards to his car. She could only lie limply as he clutched her to him.

After a short drive, she realised that he was taking her to his home. A rush of relief entered her at this, as surely now her Aunt Massie would help her? But when the car drew up outside the cottage it was in darkness. Fear took the place of relief, but she couldn't protest. It was as if all life had gone from her. Her mouth tasted vile, and her throat was too sore to allow her to utter a sound. Even trying to lift her head off the seat was impossible for her, and her body coughed every now and again without any help from her. Each time, salty water came into her mouth.

As Reggie's strong arms lifted her out of the car, Gracie prayed for someone to be in the street, or to come out of one of the cottages, but no one did, and there was no one about. Once inside, the warmth of the room was welcome to her, as was the soft feel of the sofa Reggie laid her on.

She watched, still unable to speak, still coughing intermittently, as Reggie rekindled the fire and swung the hob holding the kettle over the flames. 'I'll get the bath in and get you into some hot water, we've to warm you up, lass.'

The smile he gave her made her want to retch. She shook her head, but he had left her and had made his way out the back. She knew he would go into the yard where the tin bath hung on the wall. And she knew that in the scullery there would be a large pot of water simmering on the stove, something most households had on the go at all times, for washing pots, or clothes, or themselves. Now was her chance. If she could get into the street, she could bang on next door – the house she grew up in – and hope someone there would help her and that house would once more provide her with a sanctuary.

But, try as she might, Gracie couldn't lift herself. It seemed to her that she was weighted down and that all her strength had been taken from her.

'Now, me little darling, I won't be long, I'll have this filled in naw time, and then once I've bathed you, we'll have some cocoa. It'll be like all our future nights together. And don't worry about Ma and Da coming in, they've gone to Manchester to see Ma's sister who's taken badly.'

This news increased Gracie's feeling of trepidation. Her body began to shake uncontrollably.

'Eeh, lass, I'll fetch a blanket, I don't want you catching pneumonia.'

Still, Gracie found that she was unable to speak.

Wrapped in a blanket, some warmth entered her as she watched Reggie come and go, as he filled the tub. He'd discarded his own wet clothes and now had a dressing gown on that was obviously his da's. Boldly striped in drab blacks, reds and purples, it wrapped around him almost twice, even though he had a large muscular frame.

The last kettle full of boiling water went in and Gracie knew that a second ordeal was about to begin for her – one she knew she hadn't the strength to fight against.

The hot water soothed her. Reggie wasn't the Reggie she'd always known, but a caring, gentle being, as he washed her down with a flannel, lingering on her breasts as he cupped each one and stared at them. Gracie wondered if he'd seen or felt any breasts before, and would know that there was something different about hers. Breast feeding had left them sagging a little, whereas previously to having Bertie, they had been perky, and her nipples were a lot bigger and darker. But he didn't seem to notice as he stroked each one. She tried to say no, but only a sound that could have been mistaken for a pleasurable moan, came from her lips.

'That's nice, you like that, don't yer? Oh, Gracie, I've waited so long to make yer mine. You are yer knaw. You're fully mine. We'll marry, and have kids, and it'll be grand.' As he spoke, his hand caressed her, tracing a path nearer and nearer to her thighs. Another moan came from her, when she'd wanted to scream at him to stop. He turned his head and looked at her with a look that held love, mixed with lust.

As his hand touched her between her legs, her body jerked.

'That gave you a thrill, didn't it, Gracie? Aye, well there's a lot more for yer, just relax.'

She could do no other, and endured him exploring her without trying to protest, fearing that any sound that came from her might make him think she was enjoying it.

He even interpreted the sound of her anguish as he stood and took off his gown as her wanting him. 'Take a good look, Gracie, lass. It's all yours, and I'm going to give it to yer, once I have yer dry. You can touch it if yer want.'

He didn't get angry when she didn't. 'That's all right. There's plenty of time. You're bound to be shy at first.'

Bending to his knees, he lifted her out of the water, and wrapped her in a towel. The action increased his ardour, and he held her to him. 'Eeh, Gracie, I've got to have yer again. It might not be the best, as I've already done yer once, but let's get you on the sofa, lass.'

Oh God. Please, please help me. Give me strength

enough to fight him off. Help me to show him that I don't want...

Her back touched the soft cushions, her head flopped back. Reggie opened her legs, and then got on top of her. She felt him enter her. Tears seeped out of her eyes.

Thank God, after one or two thrusts, he cried out as if in agony, and she knew it was over. Reggie rolled off her and slumped on the floor beside her, laying his head on her bare stomach. His thick curls felt soft, which surprised her. She'd thought everything about him would be brittle and horrid.

'Ooh, Gracie, Gracie, you've made me a happy man. But, I'm done for now, lass. I knaw as I didn't give a good show of meself, either times that I had yer, but I will. It's just that I'm so overwhelmed. Me dream's come true. Me Gracie. Me darling Gracie.'

After a moment, he covered her with the blanket and brought his face near to hers. His kiss was gentle on her forehead, and then her nose, and finally resting on her lips. In a stupor, she accepted them all.

Reggie rose then, and busied himself making tea. She watched his naked body, honed to his bones and yet not in any way skinny. Reggie was a handsome man, something she'd never realised before. Many a young woman would enjoy doing with him what he had done to her. He hadn't been rough, not in this second time of taking her, nor had he been repulsive, as he had a fresh smell to him. Even his breath, that normally reeked of drink and fags, had a sweet taste. And he'd been caring and gentle, and yes, loving. Just like her Freddie.

This thought drifted from her, taking her once more into a hazy blackness that she didn't, and couldn't, resist. Into the blackness came Freddie's face, but then it faded away and was replaced by Reggie's dark smooth looks. She tried to kiss him, but he, too, faded. As did the room and everything around her.

How long she stayed in this state, she didn't know. Sometimes she would almost wake and find Reggie was on top of her again, moaning and calling her name. Some nice sensations entered her body when this happened, and she began to have a dream where she called out to him and asked him to make love to her again.

At other times she was conscious of her body shivering, and yet being soaked in sweat. And of Reggie washing her down with a cold wet cloth that soothed her.

Somewhere in the dream there was another man, and she desperately wanted him to do the same to her as Reggie was doing, but she couldn't remember his name, so couldn't call out to him. He wore a uniform and had a rakish grin.

But then came the time that the master appeared. He was naked and repulsive. Desperate to avoid him touching her, she cringed away from him and let out a blood-curdling scream. Her eyes opened. The room came into focus. *Where am I?*

Looking around, Gracie saw a bedroom. She was lying in a bed. She lifted her head, but felt so weak that she flopped back on the pillow. Confusion made her head ache, and her whole body felt stiff and sticky, especially her inner thighs. Memories floated in. With them came the horror of Reggie making love to her, over and over. And in crept the guilt of her having enjoyed him doing so, and not just welcoming him, but begging him for more. But then another memory formed in her head. Freddie!

The door burst open just as she at last focused on Freddie.

'What is it, me little lass? You scared me. What's wrong, do you want your Reggie again? Eeh, you're insatiable, lass.'

'Naw! Naw! What have you done... W – why am I here?' Her throat burned with soreness, and her mouth was so dry, her tongue stuck to the roof of her mouth.

'Now, don't say you don't remember. Naw one could respond like you have done and begged for it like you have, and then try to say they didn't remember doing it. We've been at it for three days. The best three days of me life. Oh, me Gracie, I love you. You're mine, lass, just like you should be.'

'Don't! Don't come near me. I didn't knaw owt, I – I... Three days! Eeh, what will Peggy and Sheila and all of them think, they must ... they must be frantic with worry.'

'The coppers came, but I told them I hadn't see yer. As I knew that's what you'd want of me. You've loved being here. You've loved me, and given me back tenfold what I gave you. You can tell them all that you wanted to be here, and you didn't want to be found. You're an adult, you can go off when you want. We'll get married. I'll take care of yer, and–'

'SHUT UP!'

The effort of screaming this hurt her throat, and took her body into a weak state once more. 'Please, Reggie, fetch Sheila to me. *Please!*'

'Naw. What're yer saying? Why d'yer want to leave me? You love me. You said so.'

'I was delirious ... I must have been. I – I nearly drowned ... I've had a fever. You should have fetched a doctor to me, I – I could have died!' She knew she was talking in broken sentences, but couldn't form a sensible phrase without doing so.

Reggie sat on the end of the bed. 'I wouldn't let you die. I took care of you. I missed a sailing to be with you. Why are you wanting to leave me, eh? Tell me! Don't do this, Gracie.'

A noise from the adjoining house gave Gracie an idea. She turned and thumped on the wall. 'Help me! Help me!'

Reggie grabbed her and pinned her to the bed, trapping her arms beneath her. He covered her mouth with his free hand. 'Don't, d'yer hear me? Look, you've been here willingly. You knaw as you have, and aye, neighbours knaw it an' all. They must have heard us at it every moment we could. I must have had you six times, night and morning, aye and once in the afternoon. You called out for it. They'll be me witness. And, they probably think that you banging on their wall is another of our sex games, so pack it in and think on.'

With a feeling of utter despair, Gracie knew what he said was true. She remembered wanting the nice feeling, over and over. But why? And she remembered feeling so ill, but feeling better when it happened. Now she felt trapped, and dirty, and so poorly. She wanted to go home.

Tears that weakened her further ran down her face. Her body went limp once more. Reggie let her go and became gentle again.

'There, that's better. That's how I need yer to be.' He rose from the bed. 'I'll bring you a hot drink, you've only sipped water for days, and had nowt to eat. D'yer reckon as yer could eat sommat if I brought it up?'

Though she didn't feel like eating, Gracie nodded, realising that she needed to build her strength so that she could help herself out of this situation. 'P – Porridge, does you knaw how to make it?'

'Aye, I'm a dab hand in the kitchen. I often make me ma and da a meal.'

This shocked and surprised Gracie, and she realised that there was a side to Reggie that she'd never known. 'When is your ma back?'

'She said that she'd be a week at least. Now me da's retired, they do go off now and again. I take them to the station, and they get on a train. Never knew they had an adventurist streak in their bones, but they have, and love their little trips away.'

When Reggie returned with the porridge, he had to wake Gracie. She hadn't meant to drift off, but sleep seemed to claim her most of the time. She'd meant to plot what to do. But it was as if her brain only had a few clear moments; mostly she was shrouded in a fog that she couldn't penetrate. And yet she had the strange feeling of knowing what was happening and either not being able to stop it or not wanting to. Which left her confused, out of control and afraid.

'Yer knaw, Gracie, I'm proper tenant of this cottage now, me ma and da only stay because I want them to, but when we're wed, they'll move out. I bet you'd like to come back here to live, wouldn't yer? Be like when we were young uns again, having you back as part of the fishing community.'

Gracie wanted to scream out that it would never happen, but she kept quiet. She had to be very clever over her actions. She had to trick Reggie into feeling that she was willing, and then he may drop his guard. The thought shuddered through her that she may even have to let him make love to her and show willing then, too, but if that's what it took to get out of here, then she'd do it. She had to.

The porridge was delicious, smooth and creamy, and Gracie was surprised by how hungry she felt and that eating it didn't make her feel sick.

Reggie sat on the end of the bed the while she ate. 'I want to make sure it goes down all right, lass. I don't want you on your own in case you vomit again. I've cleaned up some of that over these last days, I can tell yer. You must have swallowed a bucket load of sea.'

At this, she'd wanted to rant at him that it was his fault, that he'd nearly drowned her. And aye, that many a time since, in her short lucid moments, she'd wished he had.

'I – I need to wash, Reggie.'

'Aye, I've done that for yer an' all. I've given you cold and warm bed baths, I've taken care of you, good and proper. The copper's been boiling almost night and day, as I've had to wash your sheets, and me ma's nighties that I've dressed you in. The scullery is dripping with wet washing hanging on the airer, as it's not been the weather for drying.'

Would she ever stop being surprised at this Reggie whom she knew nothing about? The Reggie she'd always known was surly and wanting his own way, not the gentle person he'd shown himself to be, nor the domesticated person either. It was a strange trait for a man to have, as men of the North were a proud bunch who left women's work to women, and thought of their work as men's work, and men's work only, and never should one cross over to the other. She wondered how Reggie managed this side of himself and kept it from his mates.

'Right, love, I'll fetch a bowl of hot water for yer, and I reckon as one of me ma's nighties is dry now, I'll run the iron over it. I've kept the iron on the side of the stove constantly, so that it's hot enough for me to have kept ironing the bed linen and your nighties.

Gracie shook her head. Mixed feelings went through her. She could like this Reggie. She could like him very much. But then she came to her senses and told herself that she must remember that he was also a violent, possessive man who thought it all right to rape a woman just because he wanted her.

With her head clear once more, her plight hit her, as did the horror of what had happened to her. She hardly dared to let her Freddie into her mind. Her body had betrayed him, because even though she had been only semi-conscious, and not fully aware of what was happening, she could remember wanting what Reggie had done to her. And to her deep shame, she had also been aware that it was Reggie.

Oh, Freddie, Freddie. My love, my only love, what now? What now? Weak sobs wracked her body. Her despair deepened. She coiled up into a ball.

'Hey, sleepyhead, I was only gone for a mo. I have everything you need for a wash.'

Stretching, Gracie took a moment to register what was going on. 'Oh, ta. I'll call you when I'm done.'

Reggie put the enamel bowl of water on top of the dresser. 'Naw, I'll stay. I want to make sure that you manage, and I want to watch you.'

Gracie knew it was no use wasting her energy in arguing with him, so didn't protest. In her mind, an idea formed. She'd get to the bowl, then lift it and swing it at him, taking him by surprise. He was sitting on the end of the bed, under the window, so he wouldn't be between her and the door. If she was quick, she'd have time to lock the door, as she'd seen that the key was left in the lock on the outside.

Standing took a lot from her. Reggie went to help her, but she refused him. 'I want to manage, thanks. It's the only way that I am going to get stronger.' Her heart sank as she made her way towards the bowl and found her legs were like jelly. She'd never beat him to the door. But when she reached the bowl, she took a deep breath, lifted it, and swung her arms in a movement that surprised her. Reggie fell back on the bed in an attempt to shield himself, and knocked his head on the wall. Not stopping to see if he was all right or not, Gracie made for the door. Sheer will-power took her forward. At last she reached it. Behind her she heard a movement which spurred her on. The door shut behind her. The key turned. *I'm free! Free! Oh, thank God!*

CHAPTER TWENTY-THREE

Outside, the icy cold March wind whipped through her thin cotton nightie. Her frozen feet stuck to the iced-covered path. 'Help me! Someone, help me!'

The door of the cottage on the left opened and Mrs Wincelet looked at her in astonishment. 'Gracie! What are you doing? You'll catch your death. Get back inside. Have you been at the drink?'

'Help me, please help me, Mrs Wincelet. Reggie has held me a prisoner.'

'What? I've never heard the like. Wait there.'

Mrs Wincelet pulled her cardigan around her and ran to Mrs Parsons's house. 'Jenny, Jenny, are you there?'

'What's the emergency? I thought you'd knock me bloomin' door down! Gracie. Eeh, lass, what're you doing outside in just a nightie? Eeh, me little darling, let's get you inside. Bring her in, Gertie. That's right, now get by the fire. Oh, dear, you're shaking.'

'H – he, kept me prisoner. Re – Reggie.'

262

'Eeh, naw. By, I've allus thought that there's sommat not right with that one.'

'Can you g – get me friend for me? Sh – she'll come and get me.'

'Let's warm you up first, lass, and then you can tell us all about it. The cops were here asking after you, but none of us had seen you. Ain't that right, Gertie?'

'Aye, it is. How long have you been there then?'

Mrs Wincelet looked suspicious. Gracie wondered if she had heard things. The walls to these cottages were like paper – you almost lived with your neighbour. But then the bedroom was on the other side of Aunt Massie's cottage, adjoining the one Gracie had been brought up in, so it was unlikely that she had.

Before Gracie could answer, Mrs Parsons came back with a knitted rug she'd fetched and wrapped it around Gracie.

'L – lock the door. H – he'll get in, he'll come after me.'

'Just let him try. I'll floor him with me poker. Mr Parsons has had to duck it a few times, but once I caught him with it when he were after his games, and I knocked him to the ground. He didn't come after me again for a long time after that.'

Gracie wanted to smile but she hadn't any huour in her. The Parsons had been well known for their fights, even when she was a girl. And it was always said amongst the women that it happened when Mr Parsons tried to get randy. It was said as it was Mrs Parsons's own family planning method.

Thinking of it did make Gracie feel safer, as she

didn't think that Reggie would be a match for Mrs Parsons. After all, her husband wasn't and he was a bigger bloke than Reggie. With this thought, Gracie felt calmer and able to tell them what happened. She didn't leave out the rape on the beach, but didn't say about the sexual activity that had taken place since.

'I – I've been really ill for days, drifting in and out of consciousness.'

'Aye, and you look proper poorly now. Hold on. I'll get our Ted. He's in his shed. He can go to the telephone box. Does your friend have a phone number?'

'She does, but I can't remember it. I knaw it, but it won't come to me, me head's like a fog.'

'Right, well, I reckon that you need an ambulance, lass. You could be concussed. Did you have a blow to your head at all?'

'I think so. I think I banged me head when Reggie hit me, when we were on the beach, and I nearly drowned an' all.'

'He's a wicked man. You stay away from him.'

Gracie wanted to say that she had tried. She'd tried so hard, but nothing she did helped, and now she had a feeling that it was going to get worse.

Ted hadn't been gone five minutes when another woman came to the door. She was a stranger to Gracie, so she imagined that she was the one that now lived in her old home.

'What's going on? There's a lot of banging and clanging coming from next door. Eeh, the noises from there these last few days! It's been like living next door to an orgy.'

Gracie felt her face redden. Both Mrs Parsons and Mrs Wincelet looked at her with knowing expressions.

Not able to answer the knowing nods, Gracie lowered her head.

'It'll be Reggie. This one's locked him in the bedroom.'

'Aye, well, I'd do the same if he'd been at me like he has her.' There was a pause, and then the woman said: 'Like bloody rabbits they were, and both bloody enjoying it by the sounds. What's up, love, Reggie worn you out, eh? You look like death.'

Gracie wanted to tell this crude woman to shut her mouth, but instead, she leant back and closed her eyes.

'Leave her, Shirley, she ain't well. It seems Reggie forced himself on her.'

'Humph! That ain't what it sounded like, Jenny. She were begging him for it. She'll land up with her belly up, I shouldn't wonder.'

'Had your ear to the wall, did you, Shirley? Well, listeners hear no good. We knaw Gracie, she used to live in your house. And we knaw Reggie an' all, and we're more likely to believe her than him!'

'Well, you haven't the evidence that I have. Crying rape is she? Well, just let the police ask me, I'll tell them.'

'Get out! Get out of me house. Everyone knaws as you've had Reggie a few times, you old hag. You make me sick, he's a good fifteen years younger than you, and you have a man of your own an' all. I think when they knaw that, the cops won't want to knaw your story.'

'At least I ain't a cold fish like you, Jenny. If everyone knaws that about me, then they all knaw as how you beat your man rather than let him have his way. I'd have offered meself to him if he were half decent, but folk say as from what their menfolk have seen, he's only got one like a penny whistle.'

Gracie gasped in disbelief at this exchange, and then cringed as Mrs Parsons went for the poker. Looking towards the door she saw that the woman called Shirley had gone.

'Don't waste your time on her, Jenny. You'll only get the cops doing you for assault. She ain't worth it.'

'I'd swing for her. I'll tell you, Gertie, I'd bloody swing for her.'

Gertie looked through the door. 'Hey-up, she's gone in Reggie's house. She'll let him free. Eeh, Jenny, lock your door, hurry, lass.'

Gracie held her breath. Mrs Parsons flew across the room and turned the key. 'And don't anyone open it until either our Ted gets back or the cops get here.'

To see Mrs Parsons shaking deepened Gracie's fear. If a woman as formidable as she was felt afraid of Reggie, then they must have known what he was capable of.

Leaning back once more, Gracie stared into the fire. It seemed to her that the life she had planned for herself was over. The horrific thought came to her that she would surely be having Reggie's babby. No one could do it the many times that they had and not be pregnant. As this despair hit the pit of her stomach, Gracie knew a defiance in her that no matter what, she wouldn't marry Reggie. She'd rather be classed as a hussy, an un-married mother, or go into one of those convents and give the babby away. But then a picture of Bertie came to her and what her life would have been like without him in it, and she knew that she wouldn't do that.

A sob came from her as her mind gave her an image of Freddie – good, clean, Freddie. He wouldn't want her now, of that she was certain.

'Eeh, lass. God knaws as you've sommat to cry over, but it don't help matters. The copper will be here soon, he'll sort it out. But don't be telling him any lies, stick to the truth, no matter what that is, as they find out and then it's worse for you.'

'I ain't done nowt wrong, Mrs Parsons, I've told the truth.'

'But what about what that Shirley said about hearing you? Is there any truth in that, lass?'

'Aye, some. I don't knaw how it happened. It was as if I were another person, and in and out of consciousness. Reggie wasn't Reggie most of the time to me. But sometimes he was. I can't explain it. I couldn't call out, when I did it came out like a moan.' Saying this much exhausted Gracie. She put her head back. The fog she'd fought through came over her to blot everything out once more. The room faded away from her. Her hand dropped off the wooden arm of the chair.

The voices of the other two seemed as if they were a long way away from her, and spoken through water. Nothing they said was clear, except one sentence: 'Eeh, it sounds like she asked for it, all right.'

'Ahh, you're awake. How do you feel?'

Gracie moved her eyes in the direction of the voice, and saw a face framed by a nurse's veil. A feeling of being safe came over her, and yet she couldn't remember why she had felt unsafe.

'Can you sit up, Gracie? Here, let me give you a hand. That's it, now, hold onto my arm while I get some pillows behind you.'

'My head hurts.'

'It will, you have concussion, and have had for a while. You've been very ill.'

Confusion crowded Gracie. *Ill? What made me ill?*

'You're in Blackpool Victoria Hospital, love. You were brought in four days ago. The doctors have kept you asleep, whereas before you came here you probably drifted in and out of consciousness, I expect. But you needed to let your brain rest. Let it heal from the knock you must have taken that cracked your skull.'

As Gracie absorbed this, pockets of memory opened and scenes came back to her. Tears ran down her face. She wanted it all to have been a dream, but she knew it wasn't.

'Now, I know you feel like crying, but it won't do you any good. You need to try to keep your spirits up. Think of something really good in your life, not what brought you to this. There'll be plenty of time for that as the police are waiting to talk to you. But we need you stronger first.'

As she talked, the nurse had busied herself

straightening the bed. With this done, she asked if Gracie was comfortable. Gracie nodded, not trusting that she could speak without crying.

'Good. Your visitors will be glad to see you awake. They've been here every hour that we've let them. Your friends – Sheila, Jeannie and Rory, they told us their names were. And then a Peggy and Bertram and Aggie came, too. So, that's something good in your life. Something for you to hold on to.'

Gracie felt even more like crying now. No. Not just crying, but wailing like a babby. For every person the nurse had named was a good person in her life, and she loved them all dearly. And now she so wanted to hug them and be hugged by them. But none of them could make her better. Nothing could do that. She'd visited a strange place in herself. One that she didn't understand, where she'd allowed things to happen to her, and by the man she most hated in all the world. But then, it hadn't been that man. Not the Reggie who was aggressive, and wanting his own way, but a gentle person she hadn't recognised. A loving man who had been everything she'd ever wanted in life. *Oh God, how was that so? Help me … help me.*

A doctor came to her within a few moments, followed by the nurse. A middle-aged man with a bald crown and spiky hair around the edge that was a little too long, and spectacles on the end of his nose, giving him the appearance of a mad professor, he had a kindly voice. 'Well, you're a good sight. How do you feel?'

'I have a headache, and I don't seem able to sort me thoughts out.'

'All normal. The drugs we gave you will have caused most of the pain in your head. I'm afraid that you will have to bear with it until they completely wear off – I can't give you anything to help that for now. And as for the confused thoughts, they will become clearer too as the effects of the drugs wear off. Have you any pain anywhere else?'

Gracie indicated her side.

'What about when you breathe in? Is it worse?'

'No.'

'Good. You had some fluid on your lungs that we had to drain. The soreness of your side is where we put the tube in. That will get better in a few days. You have been lucky. The woman who came in with you said that you told her that you had your head under water for a while and that the man with you saved you from drowning. But you should have had medical attention then. He didn't get all the fluid off your lungs and you may have lasting damage from that. You also have traces of pneumonia, which we think has been a lot worse, and again, whatever that man did for you saved your life. And, on top of all that, you have concussion. Which accounts for the rest of your story that the woman told us, of you drifting in and out of consciousness. We are treating you with penicillin for the traces of pneumonia, and that is improving daily. You need to stay with us a few more days so that we can monitor you, and then you can go home, where we are confident that your friends will take care of you. Do you have any questions?'

'I – I do. When I was... I – I mean, would I have been able to stop things happening to me?'

'I understand what you're asking, we have been given the full picture as you told it. And, no. In my opinion, you cannot be responsible for all that happened to you. You told the woman that came with you that you knew what was happening at times, and you confirmed what another woman, who claimed to have overheard what was happening, said – that you were willing. Well, your mind wouldn't have been really registering anything as it truly was. It's not possible for it to, as you were concussed, and your body was dealing with a killer infection, which in itself would have made you confused. Any reality would have been fed into you by another person, making himself and you believe what they wanted the truth to be. I'm very sorry for all that you have been through. The woman told us about your past, too, losing your loved ones, and having to go away to a refuge. And now this. It is all too much for one person to have to bear, but I hope what I have told you helps you, just a little. Whatever went on over the last weeks or so is not your fault.'

'Will they believe me?'

'The police, you mean? Well, I will give them my assessment of your state of mind as I have just given to you. I think they will understand that. And I hope that whoever did this to you will get their just deserts. Now I'll examine you, and if I am happy with what I find I'll allow you to have visitors later today, and then let the police talk to you tomorrow.'

After the doctor had left telling her, that yes, he would let her visitors come to see her, Gracie relaxed. All that he had said had helped her.

271

There was still some confusion as she tried to sort out the times that she remembered liking what Reggie was doing, and how she knew that it was him. This made her feel the guilt of it all, but when she tried to put what the doctor had said into the picture, she wasn't sure if the times that she knew it was Reggie were the same times that he was making love to her or not. It now felt as though it wasn't, and that she only knew it was him when she came around for short periods of time. Otherwise, why was she so desperate to escape? And she did remember Reggie telling her that she was liking what he was doing, and that she was willing and asked for more. Did it really happen that she did, or was it as the doctor had said, that this had been suggested to her and had become real to her? *Oh, I don't knaw. I don't knaw. Everything is so confusing.*

Looking up at the ceiling, Gracie wished that her head would clear, and that she would remember the truth of it all. Her eyes began to feel heavy, and closed of their own accord. Images came to her. She could hear herself moaning, *Naw, naw, don't do this, Reggie, please.*

Then his voice: *You want it, you asked me to, you called out to me.*

Naw, I didn't want this, I wanted to go home.

You're liking it, you're moaning with pleasure. Look, when I touch you there, you gasp with the feel of it. Ask me, Gracie, ask me to do it.

I want... I want to–

Yes, yes, I knaw, you want me to do it again. Oh, me Gracie, I'm here, I'm your Reggie. Then the feel of him climbing on to her, and then... *Naw!*

272

Her eyes opened. Sweat ran down her face. Looking around, there was no one about. It registered with her for the first time that she was in a room on her own. Gasping with the horror of the dream, Gracie forced herself to relax back. The protest that had woken her was against knowing that she'd then enjoyed what Reggie had done. How could that be? She hadn't wanted him to do it, and yet she had to admit to herself that once he started, she'd liked it. It was this that was causing her so much anguish.

For the first time since waking, Freddie came to her, and it was then that she knew. In her confusion, she'd thought that it was him. She had! But Reggie had blocked that out from her too. He'd constantly told her that it was him, *It's your Reggie, you love me, you like me doing this.* Did that override in her mind what she truly felt was happening? That Freddie was making love to her? It had to be that. It had to be.

When she next woke it was to find her bed surrounded by loving faces. A deep sob wracked her body.

'Eeh, me lass. You cry it out. Eeh, Gracie, Gracie.' Peggy's voice soothed her, as did her hand stroking her hair. 'Poor Gracie. We're so sorry.'

'I knew he had sommat to do with it, Gracie,' said Sheila. 'I told the police, but they said they called there and he didn't look suspicious to them, and that he told them he hadn't seen you and that he was just going to go to Manchester to join his parents who'd gone there. I begged them not to believe him. Then someone came forward after an appeal in the *Gazette* and said they'd seen a couple on the beach at Rossall, and that, though he couldn't see them clearly, the woman did have long curly hair. He thought that they were lovers, so he didn't pay much attention, other than to think that they were cutting it fine not leaving the beach as the tide was coming in. Then he said that when he walked by again, some ten minutes later, the couple were gone. The police found your scarf, and they said that it was likely that you and whoever you were with could have been caught out by the tide, and that they would have to wait a few days to see if your bodies were washed up. We begged them, but they said that there wasn't a lot that they could do, that you were an adult, and if you were still alive, you could have chosen to go off. That they could only really get involved if they suspected a crime had been committed, and there was no evidence of that. They said that there was witnesses to you getting on the tram and getting off in Fleetwood, but after that, nothing. We just couldn't reason with them. We tried, Gracie, we really tried.'

'I knaw, Sheila, don't distress yourself, lass.'

'Me and Sheila went to Fleetwood, and walked along the cottages as we didn't knaw which one it was,' said Jeannie, 'and all those who answered their doors said they'd not seen nowt of you. They all said as they knew you, and would have known if you'd been in the area.'

Gracie realised they couldn't have knocked on Reggie's door, nor her old house, but then if they'd started at the top of the row and had nothing but folk saying they hadn't seen her, they'd probably have given up before reaching them. 'I knaw that you all would have done your best to find me. Don't worry, none of this is your fault.'

'We've been told what's been happening to you, Gracie.'

Though she'd known this was likely, the shame of them knowing washed over her. 'I didn't want... I didn't...'

'Shush, we knaw. We knaw that he would have forced himself on you. We're here now, lass. You're safe now.'

Peggy had tears running down her face as she said this. Sheila sobbed, and Jeannie stood like a statue as if she was warding off any hurt that might come her way. All of this was too close for her. Horrific memories must have been evoked.

Seeing these beloved friends suffering so much made Gracie realise that she had to be strong. 'Eeh, come on all of you. You're meant to be cheering me up. I'm not dead yet, and you're acting like you're at me wake. Eeh, I'm that glad to see you all.'

Peggy looked astonished, and then gave a nervous giggle. Sheila lifted her head and stared, and Jeannie let out a loud laugh.

'Oh, Gracie,' she said. 'Trust you. Here we are thinking as your life's over and mourning you, and you give us all what for. Eeh, I love you, lass.' Jeannie bent over her and hugged her. The gesture caused Gracie pain, but she didn't care, it was what she needed. When Jeannie let go, Gracie put her arms out to Peggy, and then to Sheila.

'Eeh, I can't tell you how good it feels to have you all with me. I'll be right. I couldn't be owt else now that I'm back with you.'

They all smiled teary smiles.

'How's Bertie? Has he missed me?'

'He has. We told him that when you got to Fleetwood you found that your friend was poorly and so you sent a message to say that you would be staying a few days. I think he knew sommat was going on, but he didn't ask any more questions.'

'That's not right, Ma. Every day, he asked when you were coming back, Gracie. And if he could go to visit you. He was pining for you.'

Gracie noticed that Peggy lowered her head as Sheila said this, so to make her feel better, she made light of it. 'Ha, he'd be the same if any of us went off for a while. He likes things to be normal around him – all young uns do.'

Peggy smiled at this, and the chatter took on a less strained character once more, but in her heart Gracie had been lifted by the thought of her son pining for her, and wished as she had a thousand times that she could acknowledge him as her own.

Her mind revisited her earlier fear, and she knew that if she was having another babby she'd never give it up. No matter what it meant for her, she couldn't do that again.

PART THREE

1939–1941

A CHANGING WORLD

CHAPTER TWENTY-FOUR

Throwing herself into getting the shop ready didn't help Gracie to come to terms with all that had happened. Not inside it didn't, although to the world she pretended that what to them was a seven-day wonder was the same for her.

But it wasn't. Her heart was seared with the pain of remembering, as the nightmare of it visited her day and night and she fought with trying to make it all clear in her mind.

She lived in fear of the consequences too, as her monthly bleeding hadn't happened for the second month in a row, and because Reggie's case was soon to come to court and she was the chief witness. She'd known the date since the police arrested him and he'd been brought up before the magistrates, as then his case had been sent to Crown Court. But she'd also known from the interview that she'd had with a solicitor for the prosecution that the chances of him getting off were very good as the evidence of the neighbour was in his favour, and her own was very weak due to her confused memory of it all.

The shop had been open for over a month now, and business was brisk. The shutters were down after yet another busy day and Gracie and Sheila were tidying and counting the day's takings.

'Eeh, Gracie, you've gone into your head again. I'll be glad for you when that beast is locked away and you can put it all behind you.'

Gracie fixed a smile on her face when she answered. 'Aye, we've only a week to go now. May sixteenth, but I'm nervous. What if he gets off?'

'He won't. I knaw as you think that woman next door has a lot to say against you, but the neighbour on the other side is willing to discredit her by saying that she has seen her going into Reggie's when his ma and da were out and heard what they got up to.'

'I knaw, but does that really make her a liar? And if it does, how does it? Oh, I wish it was all over.'

'Gracie, why don't you write to Freddie? He is out of his mind with worry, and it's unfair to have sworn me and Bob to secrecy. It's hanging over us like a cloud and spoiling our wedding plans. Freddie begged us in the letter that he sent to talk to you and to find out the reason that you have broken off with him. Bob feels that he is betraying his best friend.'

'I want him to come to terms with it. If he knaws the reason then he will be all noble and want to marry me anyway, but that can't happen, it can't. That would be more than unfair to him – it would ruin his life.'

'Why? If he is willing to live with it, how can it ruin his life? And if he rejects you, then you will be no different to what you are now, facing a life without the one you love.'

'It all sounds so logical, I knaw. Maybe I'm afraid of that rejection. I don't knaw, but why put us both through it all? It is breaking me heart. Maybe if the case is proven it will make it easier.

I'll be vindicated. But if it's not, then I'll always be that woman who cried rape but was willing. How's that going to sit with Freddie? He'll allus have a doubt in his mind.'

'So we can tell him after the case, then?'

'I – I don't knaw. Oh, Sheila, it's all so sordid.'

Jeannie, who had been cleaning down in the kitchen and must have heard the conversation, came through to the shop. 'You can tell me as it's none of me business, Gracie, but I think as you'd feel better if you wrote to Freddie and explained, and I think that he deserves that explanation an' all. Imagine how he is feeling, thousands of miles away, looking forward to the love of his life coming out to marry him and to being with him, and then he gets a letter saying it is all off, and with no proper explanation. I reckon as that's cruel.'

Feeling cornered, and knowing they were right, and yet unable to do as they said, snapped Gracie's temper. 'Oh, so you think he would be all forgiving of me, do you? After receiving a letter telling him the sordid details of me past, and how I have a son, you think he'd take kindly to being told that I was in another man's house for days being subjected to a rape that I can't remember the details of, and that a witness says I was a willing party to, and now I am having another bastard child?'

'What!' Jeannie's face was aghast.

'Aw, naw. Naw, Gracie, Gracie, are you sure?'

'Aye, I am, Sheila, I'm as sure as missing me bleeding twice and me breasts swelling and hurting can tell me. And from what I can remember, Reggie never took any precautions. In fact, it

281

seemed his aim. He wanted me pregnant. He–'

A banging on the shutter stopped what Gracie was going to say. The noise was a frantic hammering. Gracie looked from Sheila to Jeannie. She couldn't speak. Her mind screamed at her that this was Reggie, that he'd broken the police instructions not to make contact with her.

Sheila recovered first. 'I'll go around the back and sneak to the front and see who it is. Don't answer it, just stay quiet. If it's him, I won't let him see me, and I'll nip to the phone box and call the police.'

But before Sheila had even got to the kitchen door, a wailing told them who it was. 'Gracie ... Gracie, please, please talk to me. Please don't do this to our Reggie and to me and your uncle Percy.'

'Aunt Massie! Oh, naw, I were dreading this happening. Oh, Sheila, how am I to face her?'

'You can't. I'll go and calm her and tell her that she must leave you alone.'

'Naw. I have to talk to her. There was nowt said about me not doing so. I've dreaded this moment, and thought that it'd come a lot sooner, but now that it's here, I have to face it. Go and let her in, Sheila, then you and Jeannie get off home. I'll come later. I'll be all right, me Aunt Massie would never hurt me.'

Aunt Massie's distraught tears as she begged tore at Gracie's resolve. 'We're dying little by little, Gracie. Our son, our only son is in bits. He can't work, he won't leave his bed. He cries a lot with the pain of it all. He thought that you loved him, Gracie. He truly believes that you wanted it

282

all to happen. And Shirley next door is adamant that she was subjected to hearing you calling out to Reggie, to come to you again and again. How can you do this, Gracie? How can you behave in such a way? Your ma would turn in her grave. She loved our Reggie, and we often talked about one day you two being a match for each other, and she said that would make her the happiest person in the world. As then she would knaw as I were your ma by law, and you'd be safe, and looked after by us.'

Gracie wanted to scream out that they hadn't tried to make her safe when she'd most needed them to. Hadn't they betrayed her ma's trust then? How come they suddenly wanted to fulfil it now? But she didn't. She stayed quiet while Aunt Massie ranted on.

'You can't see him go to prison, you can't, it would kill me and Uncle Percy. We've gone through enough with the court case looming and the pointing fingers, though most say that they think that you are lying, that there's naw such thing as rape, and that you could have got to the window or sommat and called for help, or even just screamed out for help and the neighbours would have heard you. Why, Gracie? Why tell these lies, just because you changed your mind?'

It shocked Gracie to hear the truth of what folk in Fleetwood were saying. She stared at her Aunt Massie. To see her so distraught was heartbreaking, as was the knowing that she could stop all of this now. She'd no need to go through with going to court and facing the ordeal of being publicly disgraced if Reggie was found not guilty. And

283

surely he would be with the way opinion was against her.

'Please, Gracie. You need never see us again, you can carry on with your fancy life, owning a shop and living with them as have money, and you can leave your roots behind, as you have for a long time. And we can lift our head once more and knaw as our son ain't going to face going to prison.'

This nastiness brought Gracie out from feeling sorry for her aunt and almost giving in. 'You want me to say that I've been lying? That I was willing, and you think that will be the end of it, Aunt Massie? I'm not lying. Reggie did grab me when I got off the tram. He did hit me so hard that I was unconscious. He did take me to the beach and raped and near drowned me, and he did take me back to yours and keep me there for days. I had concussion, I had pneumonia, and yes, he did save me life, but I could have died! And through it all, he did have sex with me, and confused me, and made me believe as I was willing. But I weren't. Through the fog I was in, I knew that. I just couldn't express it, or sort out what was happening. And you think those actions by your son can be justified, eh? You think that they can be put squarely on my shoulders, and Reggie has to shoulder naw blame whatsoever?'

'What does it matter, eh? If you think you can come out of this with your halo intact, then you have another thought coming to you, you hussy.'

Never before had Gracie thought of her Aunt Massie as ugly, but now as she snarled these words she saw it – an ugliness that came from deep within her and showed her true colours.

'I knaw as they'll all be saying that there's naw smoke without fire, but I don't care. *I'll* knaw the truth.' Tapping herself on her chest, Gracie leaned forward. 'In here, that's where I'll knaw the truth, and that's where it matters.'

'And what if you lose? What then? Will you knaw the truth then, when the whole world knaws you as a liar and a whore, eh? What then? Do you reckon as this fancy shop will still do all right then? What when it's in the nationals that you, the owner of a fancy shop, and gives the address of it, have cried rape and been found guilty of lying? That you ruined the life of the woman who cared for you when you were a child? And that you were now vilified by all who you grew up with? And all so as you could have your cake and eat it. By, I never thought I'd see the day. To say as your ma is turning in her grave don't give meaning to how she must be writhing in constant unrest because of you and your behaviour. You're nowt but a whore. A floozy, who's out for her own gain, and thinks nowt of them as she's left behind.'

This was too much for Gracie. She backed onto the only chair in the kitchen and slumped down onto it. Never did she think to hear her Aunt Massie talking to her in such a way. 'Please go, Aunt Massie. Just–'

'Aunt Massie! You dare to still call me that! After what you've put me through, eh? I'm naw aunt to you, and wished I'd never set eyes on yer. I'll go all right. I'll go back to me husband and me son, and breathe the decent air that they breathe, because here, there's nowt but foul air breathed

285

by a liar.'

When the door shut behind the woman she'd once loved with all her heart, Gracie felt a grief enter her. It was as if she had lost the last thread to her former life. But how was she going to face the new life ahead of her with no Freddie to love her and the stigma of being an unmarried mother to face?

When Gracie reached home, Peggy called to her the moment she opened the front door, 'Gracie! Eeh, Gracie, come on through, lass. We have to talk.'

'I'm tired, Peggy. I need a bath and me bed.'

'I knaw as you do, and you'll get that, but Sheila's told me of what's happening, and I have to have me say. I deserve that, don't I?'

There was something in the way this was said that sent a trickle of apprehension through Gracie. Sheila must have told her ma about her thinking she was expecting a babby – it could be about nothing else, as nothing got everyone roused like it. All were condemning of a woman having a babby out of wedlock. Even those who loved you most would be against having to be associated with that stigma.

Gracie followed Peggy into the kitchen. Sheila was there, but not Jeannie. 'I've asked Jeannie to give us some privacy. I've to say what I have to say, Gracie, and though it will hurt me, I've to stand by what I think is right in this instance. You having another babby out of wedlock ain't sommat as I can cover up again. I'm too old, and doing it the first time is costing me. I live in daily fear of you taking Bertie back from me.'

'Oh, Peggy, I wouldn't. I promised you.'

'Oh? And were you planning to go off to Canada and leave him behind, then? I can't see that meself. I can see how it tears you apart not being able to acknowledge him, but I knaw as long as you're with him then that will stop you doing that, but away from him? Naw. Anyroad, I couldn't go through losing him, or having him learning the truth. I stood by you, lass, even though you were a stranger to me and I changed your life around. Now it's your turn to make sacrifices.'

Gracie couldn't speak. She dreaded what was coming, but knew she'd have very little choice in the matter.

'As I see it, you have one of two choices. You go to Canada and see that Freddie, and tell him of what's happened, and take your chance, because you can't wait for letters to go back and forward, that would take too long and your belly will be well up, and you'd not be able to travel, and will have already brought shame down on this house. Or you can stop this court case and go to the man who put you with child and give the child his father's name.'

Gracie couldn't believe what she was hearing, and yet she knew that everyone changed when it came to situations like she was in. At all costs, names had to be protected, and Peggy would see it as shameful to house an unmarried mother-to-be when there was nothing that she could do to hide the fact.

'Look, Gracie. You don't dislike this Reggie fella, I saw you kissing him that night when you took Alina for a walk to soothe her. I thought then it was strange for you to offer, and I watched you go up the road. He met you, and then I saw you kissing.'

This finally loosened Gracie's tongue, which had felt as though it had stuck to the roof of her mouth. 'I didn't, Peggy. I didn't. He forced himself on me.'

'Oh, Gracie. I don't knaw what fascination it is that you have for the lad, especially when you have a bloke like Freddie willing to take you on, but you can't keep crying rape when your actions go wrong. I didn't see you struggle, lass. You looked willing to me. And that woman who lives next door to Reggie is saying the same. I just don't knaw what the truth is any more.'

Gracie felt her world crashing around her. Not even Peggy believed her. She looked over towards Sheila. Sheila put her head down without uttering a word in her defence. 'Sheila! Sheila, you knaw. You've seen how he is with me. You've seen me fight him off.'

'I knaw, but you didn't knaw as me ma were watching you. You didn't think anyone could see you. Ma wouldn't lie, Gracie. She saw what she saw. You, making an excuse to get out of the house and meeting up with Reggie. And him kissing you, and you seeming to be willing. You said nowt to her when you came in about having been attacked by him. You just took your cocoa to bed with you. You didn't even wake me to seek comfort from me.'

'Oh, Sheila, Peggy, don't. Please don't lose faith in me. I'm nowt without you both. Don't desert me when I most need you by me side.' Tears streamed down her face as a sense of desolation took her into its depths. But Peggy stood resolute.

'We ain't doing that. We just want you to do the right thing by us. We don't deserve to be lied to, nor to have to shoulder the burden of supporting you in your unwed state. We'll allus be here for you, but only if you do the right thing, Gracie. It's up to you.'

With these words, not only had Gracie's world collapsed, but she felt cornered. Yes, there were two choices, but she could only take one of them. She loved Freddie too much to put him through years of having to father a child that wasn't his, and to come to terms with this not having happened once, but twice. Nor could she leave Bertie and go to Canada without him. She had to go to Reggie. *No, oh no. Dear God, why is such a thing asked of me?*

But in her despair, Gracie knew that it was the only solution. With it would come forgiveness from all those she loved. It would be bittersweet as she had not sinned, nor did she deserve their disdain, but she couldn't live without them in her life.

Not in an emotional way she couldn't, as they had become her props, the family she didn't have any more, and not in a practical way, as she had to admit there was only one other option for her without their support – to seek refuge in a convent for wayward women. But then they would take her babby from her, and she knew she couldn't live without it.

Even though it had been planted inside her by the man she most hated in all the world, she could not put her heart through the torment of her child not knowing that she was its ma.

What had happened with Bertie was bad enough, but at least she saw him on a daily basis and that needn't change. He would come to the shop to see her when he was on his way home from school. And that would be enough. For one thing that she was going to insist on was that she and Reggie lived above the shop, not in Fleetwood. She was a Blackpool lass now, and would always be, and she had to hang onto the one thing that she had built up and was her pride and joy, the Little Bit of Blackpool Rock shop. Oh yes, Sheila and Rory had played their part and were her partners, but they couldn't have done it without her and she wasn't about to give it up now.

Gracie looked up at the expectant faces of those she loved. And though her voice shook, she was determined to say what she had to.

'I'll do it. I'll go to Reggie. But that ain't an admission of me guilt because I ain't guilty of owt. I knaw how it looks, and I'm heart-sore that me word ain't enough for me closest and dearest friends. I'll do it to save you all your pride, and to save the man I love from years of torment. And because I can't bear to go into a convent and give another child up. You say that it's my turn to make a sacrifice. Huh, my whole life has been that, so one more won't hurt. But, I'm telling you, I'll not give up the shop. Nowt will make me do that.'

The door opened and Jeannie came through. 'You don't have to do this, Gracie, you don't. I'm sorry as I listened in, but I won't abandon you. I believe you. I knaw as it ain't easy for you and Sheila to believe her, Peggy, but you ain't been in the helpless positions that me and Gracie have been in. You can't begin to imagine how it can happen, but it does, and I knaw without doubt that Gracie hasn't deserved this. We could find a place together, Gracie, away from here. We could go to Manchester, and I could get a job.'

'Oh, Jeannie, you don't knaw how much that means to me, but naw. It wouldn't work. I'd drag you down, as folk'd soon cotton on that I didn't have a man.'

'We could say as he were killed, or sommat.'

'But then I wouldn't be accepted back here. How could Peggy and Sheila have me back knawing that everyone around here would knaw the truth, that I weren't wed? And me little Bertie. I'd have to walk away from him, and I can't do that. I can't wipe them as I look on as me family out of me life. I've been with them since I were a lass of fourteen. They've been everything to me.'

'Oh, Gracie, lass, I'm sorry. But you have to look at it from where we're standing. Even if we say we believe you, where does that leave us, eh? What do you expect of us? That we let you live here for the world to see you have a babby out of wedlock? I helped you all I could over the years, but I can't do that. Bertram wouldn't allow – nor does he deserve – that.'

Suddenly Gracie felt very selfish to expect this. She knew the stigma of such a situation. And for her babby to be a bastard, too. What had she been thinking of? She couldn't do that to her child.

All at once, her mind was made up. She would

291

go to Reggie. *May God help me. Not that he does often, but maybe if I do the right thing by everyone that loves me, then just maybe, he will.*

CHAPTER TWENTY-FIVE

Jeannie and Sheila offered to go with Gracie, but she still felt sore at Sheila for not believing her, so refused them both.

'Does it have to be tonight that you go, Gracie?'

'It does, Peggy. If I don't I may change me mind through cold feet and take a path that would be even worse. It's a nice evening, so I'll be fine.'

'But you haven't eaten.'

'I'll get some chips. I just want this over with. I'll just get changed out of me uniform and then I'll go.'

When she came back downstairs, all three were still in the kitchen. 'Right, I'm off.'

'Gracie, I'm sorry, lass. I truly am, but–'

'Don't, whatever you do, say that I brought this on meself, Peggy. That insinuation that you made hurt me more than owt has done for a long time. Not to be trusted by you and Sheila, of all folk, I never thought I'd see the day. I can accept how it looked to you that night, but for you not to take me word is too much for me to bear. But, anyroad, it's of no consequence now. I'm doing this for me babby, not anyone else. And because it's the only course that's left for me to take. I'll see you later.'

With this she walked out of the door, through the hall and out into the street. Once there she wanted to scream, *please don't make me do this, please help me,* but instead she lifted her head and walked determinedly towards the Prom to catch the tram.

'And what d'yer think that you're doing here, madam, after the way you spoke to me earlier?'

'I'm pregnant, Aunt Massie.'

Aunt Massie's face registered many expressions as this news sank in. After a moment, she opened the door wider. 'You'd better come in then.'

Uncle Percy lowered his paper, 'Eeh, lass. What's thee come here for? You shouldn't be doing that.'

'She's got her belly up, Percy.'

'Oh, I see. Well, you'd better fetch lad down, he has to face this.'

'Not before you tell me, Gracie, what it is that you intend. Because if you're looking to go through with the case but want money off Reggie to see to getting rid then you can leave the house now.'

'Massie! Good God, woman, what's got into you?' Uncle Percy's voice held anger. 'Owt as affects lad and you're like a vixen. Well, I'm the man of this house, and I say that you're to fetch our Reggie down. NOW!'

Aunt Massie jumped out of her skin, but she did Percy's bidding without another word.

'I don't knaw what to make of this lot, Gracie, but I'm inclined to believe you rather than what me lad says. So, tell me, what have you come for?'

'To see if Reggie will take me on. I can't have

the babby out of wedlock, and I can't ask me fiancé, as was, to take me on with me carrying another man's child, and so I've two choices – go into a convent and give me babby away, or ask the father of me child to marry me. I can't bear either, but getting married is the lesser of the two.'

'Eeh, I say one thing for you, you speak your mind, lass.'

The door opened and Aunt Massie and Reggie came through. Reggie had a wary look about him.

'I've not said owt, so you can tell him now, yourself.'

Taking a deep breath, Gracie announced: 'I'm having your babby, Reggie, and I'm here to ask you if you'll take me on. If you don't then I'll–'

'Take yer on? Marry you, yer mean?'

'Aye, I do.'

'Eeh, me lass, of course I will. Come here.'

'Naw. Leave me be.'

'Well, there'll be none of that. If you become me wife, it's got to be proper, like we were for them few days as we had on our own.'

'That wasn't proper, Reggie, and you knaws it. But I am willing to be a proper wife once we're wed. But I have some conditions.'

'I reckon as that's for me to lay down, not you.'

His tone had Gracie's stomach knotting. She knew what he was capable of.

'Now, lad. You want to think yourself lucky that this is the outcome, and you're getting a second chance.'

'Well, I ain't having naw woman rule me, Da. If she's to be me wife, it's to be on my terms.'

Gracie lifted her head in an attempt to show her pride and determination that this would go her way, or no way. 'And what are your terms then, Reggie?'

'That we'll live in this house, with me ma and da, until they get settled elsewhere, and that you give up your ways – that shop and them friends, and that you knaw as I wear the trousers.'

'Then I'll not be your wife, it's as simple as that. I'd rather take the option of the convent. I'll see you in court as planned.' Gracie went to turn towards the door, but Reggie was across the room and grabbed her arm before she could move.

'You think yourself somebody, missie. Well, you're not. You're a lass without a man and with your belly up and that ain't a good position to be in.'

'Let go of me.'

'You heard her, Reggie. Let go of her arm, or you'll have me to contend with. Now, sit down the pair of you. Massie, put kettle on.'

They all did as Uncle Percy commanded.

'Now. As I see it, Reggie, what lass is asking of you is to marry her. It's what you've wanted all along, so I'd take the offer, and if there's a few things that she needs in return, well listen to them, don't make your mind up before you've even heard. Marriage is give and take. If you get a good un, they do a lot of giving, and yes, you have to keep a hand on the reins, but you don't knaw that you can't live with what she asks until you've heard Gracie out. Give her a chance, and don't ruin the best one that you've ever been given.'

Gracie didn't know what to make of this speech. On the one hand Uncle Percy was saying that she had to do what Reggie decided and on the other that he should let her have her say!

'I don't want to live here is one stipulation. I'm a Blackpool lass now and me work's there, and I've no intention of giving it up. There's a flat above the shop and I want to live there.'

'Naw. It ain't right that me wife works. I'll bring the money in, you stay at home and look after the house, that's how it's allus been done, and I don't want owt different.'

'I'm not moving on this, Reggie. I keep me shop, or I go into a convent, give me babby away, and then come back to me shop.'

Reggie was quiet for a long moment. The kettle whistled in the background, a sound that Gracie had heard so often over the days that she was held here. Memory flooded in. Her cheeks flushed as the gentleness Reggie had shown her visited her, and yes, the skill he had at lovemaking, which lived with her every day. That was part of what had made this, coming to him, just bearable, as she knew that he wasn't repulsive to her.

'Reggie, can I say sommat?'

'What is it, Ma?'

'Well, the only family to ever get on from this row were the Philips. And that was because Mrs Philips worked. She wouldn't stay at home, and with her bringing in a wage, they soon got enough to buy their own place and have never looked back. They go on fancy holidays, and she's allus got nice clothes. I'd take Gracie's offer and have a chance at a better life for the pair of you and your young uns.'

'But it ain't how things are done. Other crew members'll laugh at me.' Reggie looked towards his da. Gracie could see he expected support from him, but what Uncle Percy said must have surprised him, as much as it did her.

'I agree. In my day, it weren't, but things are changing. Besides, as sure as there's night and day, there's a war coming, and in the last lot the women had to work, so you may not have a choice in the matter.'

'But, Da, you knaw how it is. I'll not be able to hold me head up.'

'I do, and it wouldn't do for me, but lass seems pretty determined, and so I don't think as you've much choice. If you want her and you want your young un, then I'd say yes, and let's get on with cancelling this court appearance that's hanging over you. Besides, you'll have the last laugh when, as your ma says, you have a better car than you have now, and family holidays, and them as smirk at you don't have them things.'

'Well, I'm not happy about it, but I'll give it a try, and if me home ain't run right, or me needs seen to, then I'll be putting me foot down.'

'You can try, Reggie, but I'll tell you now, I'll fight you every step of the way. I've made it clear what my future plans are and that should be good enough for you.'

Suddenly, Reggie's other side came to the fore. 'Eeh, me lass, I allus knew you had a determined streak, but I loved you anyways, despite it, so I can't say as this stance is a surprise, can I?' With this, he opened his arms. His expression was one of tenderness and love, and something in Gracie responded as she went to him. She couldn't deny that it felt good to be held in his strong arms. A cuddle is what she had dearly needed, and if that was only forthcoming from Reggie, well so be it. Maybe, just maybe, it boded well for their future together.

'Eeh, Gracie, you've made your Aunt Massie a very happy woman, and I'm sorry about how I spoke to you, lass, I were so afraid as to what would happen to our Reggie, but you've made that right now, and we'll put it behind us, eh?'

Gracie wanted to yell at this woman who'd betrayed her trust as a child, that no, she would never put everything behind her, and that she'd be just as wary of her as she was of Reggie. But she just smiled.

'And I for one, am a happy man. It's good to think of our Reggie getting married, and to the best girl he could, and your news is welcome an' all, lass. The other side of the blanket it may be, but I look forward to having a grandchild.'

This Gracie could answer, because out of them all she'd found her Uncle Percy to be the most genuine, speaking from his heart and not as suits the occasion. 'Ta, Uncle Percy, and I look forward to calling you Da, as I could have none better.'

To this Uncle Percy got out his hanky and blew his nose loudly. 'Thank you, lass, and you've allus been like a daughter, though I failed you once, but as Massie says, let's have a fresh start with all the bad bits about the past forgotten. Now then, Massie, haven't you a drop of that sherry left from Christmas?'

'Aye, I have, Percy. I'll get it now, as there's never been a better day to finish it off.'

The sherry warmed most of Gracie as she took a sip and it traced a path into her stomach. And although that warmth didn't extend to her painful heart, she knew she'd to get on with it now, and accept how everything was. There was nothing else for her.

'Massie, give us a tune. Go on, me lass. You haven't played the piano for this good while.'

At this from Uncle Percy, Aunt Massie went gleefully over to the piano, lifted the lid and ran her fingers over the keyboard. Never having had any training, she played by ear, and soon filled the room with music. Uncle Percy sang along to the honky-tonk sound of 'I'm Leaning on a Lamp-post'. His gaze and gestures as he sang were aimed at Gracie, and this made her blush.

'Play "I'm in the Mood for Love". I like to hear our Reggie sing that, he's done a few good renditions of it in the pub.'

Reggie didn't let go of Gracie, but took her with him to stand at the side of the piano. When the music started, his hand tightened on her waist and he looked down at her. His body began to sway to the music. Gracie's cheeks burned as she saw his eyes smoulder with a look she remembered seeing many times over the days he had kept her captive. Something lit inside her, a feeling that she wanted to welcome, and the thought came to her that, yes, there were times when she'd been willing over the course of those days, and so had mapped out her own future. And it came to her, too, that she'd been wrong to have sought justice the way she had, as just being willing once was enough to make her allegations a lie.

Something of an acceptance entered her, and she smiled up at Reggie. His voice soothed and caressed her, his firm hold on her waist made her feel safe and that everything would turn out all right. Before she knew it, she was dancing with him, his body pressed into hers, his breath tickling her cheek as he sang on, and then, on the chorus, he bent her backwards, and leaned over her. 'I'm in the mood for love.' This was whispered, and sent a feeling zinging through Gracie that she couldn't deny.

'Hey, that's enough, that's for when you are on your own, lad, not in company.'

'Sorry, Da, I got carried away.'

Gracie flushed crimson, and also apologised.

'Well, I for one, don't want you to be sorry. You're an old fuddy-duddy, Percy. It's good to see the love they have for one another. Aye, and that Gracie has at last realised that is what she feels for our Reggie.'

Gracie didn't deny this. Something in her had objected, and made her want to say that she would never love Reggie as her heart was taken, but she knew that wasn't altogether true. Yes, the bit about her heart being taken, that was the truth and would always be so, but about not ever finding some love for Reggie, she didn't know. She did know that she was attracted to him, and wanted to be doing what they had done many times before.

A little shame entered her at these thoughts. How can it be that I feel this way? *How can it be possible after all that has happened?* But then she had to admit to being glad that she did as a lifetime was a very long time to be tied to someone that you couldn't find some love for.

Looking at the clock as a way of distracting herself, Gracie was surprised to see how late it was. 'Well, I must go, the last tram goes from here soon, and I don't want to miss it.'

'I'll take you, Gracie. I'll just get me jumper. It may be June, but that wind is whipping up outside.'

In contradiction to how she'd felt a few moments ago, Gracie recoiled at this suggestion from Reggie. But she didn't protest. It would have been silly to, and would set the atmosphere back to being tense once more.

'Come here, lass. Let me give you a hug,' Gracie went willingly into Aunt Massie's arms, and welcomed them being on a good footing, as they always used to be.

'Oh, me little lass, this is a happy day for me, and I knaw as your ma is smiling in heaven and feeling more at peace, now she knaws as you're going to be an official part of our family. Let's make the wedding soon, eh?'

Holding on tightly to Aunt Massie, Gracie nodded. 'Yes, I'd like that. If it's all right with you, I could come here on Sunday when I'm not working, and we can talk it all over and make arrangements.'

As Aunt Massie let her go, Uncle Percy told them, 'Well, the banns have to be posted for three weeks, so maybe our Reggie had better go to see the vicar tomorrow, as he hasn't a sailing till later in the week.'

'Oh, does that mean that he won't be here on Sunday?'

'Aye, it's likely, Gracie, but if banns are posted by him, then it won't be of any concern, as he most likely won't want to be involved in the talk about the dress and the catering and so forth. He'll be happy to leave all that to you and Massie.'

'Leave all what to me ma and Gracie?' Reggie had come back into the room.

'Oh, we were just saying while you were upstairs, Reggie, that if Gracie comes on Sunday to talk everything over and get the wedding settled, that you'd be happy to leave all of that to them.'

'Aye, I would, and be glad to, that's woman's work.'

Reggie had a clear knowledge of what he thought of as 'woman's work' and Gracie could see them clashing in the future, as she had other ideas. She'd read many magazines, and knew that some things were very different down in the south of England. The men down there didn't seem to make these divisions so apparent. But then, this is the north, and how Reggie thought and acted was very different to the modern way. But that was northern men for you – stuck in their ways, and Gracie didn't see a time that they would change.

CHAPTER TWENTY-SIX

Reggie fussed over getting her into the car, making sure she was comfortable and leaning over her and kissing her when he thought that she was settled.

Once he'd cranked the engine and got into the car himself, he looked at her and smiled. 'Eeh, me lass, you've made me a happy man. I love you, Gracie, and I'll take care of you, like a husband should.'

He didn't speak again until they reached Rossall Way. 'I've a mind to take you to the beach again, and to have you willing to take me this time.'

'You admit that I wasn't willing then?'

'Eeh, don't go down that road, Gracie. I knaw what I did the first time were wrong, but you liked it after that, you knaw as you did.'

'Oh, what's the use? I suppose you admitting the one rape of me is all you're ever going to do, and I take it that by doing so you're sorry. You're right, we can't keep going over it. But I'd like to go home, Reggie. I think we can make things better between us by not making love again until after we are wed.'

'How can that make owt right? I'll not be able to wait that long, Gracie. I want you now, this minute. It's dark, and there'll not be anyone on that stretch of beach. It ain't as if the holidaymakers come down there often, they like the bright lights, and the locals'll be all indoors by now. Come on, lass. I've a blanket in the back of the car.'

Before she could protest, Reggie swung the car into Westway. Once in the lane, his hand found her knee. 'Eeh, me lass, I can't wait.'

His voice gravelled as he spoke, giving Gracie the realisation that she had to go along with this. Her heart didn't want it, but her body betrayed her as Reggie's hand travelled further up her skirt and found her thigh. Unwittingly, she drew in a deep breath of pleasure as the thrills he evoked zinged through her.

When he stopped the car, he didn't get out, but turned to her and replaced his hand where it had been, and squeezed the flesh of her thigh above the line of her stocking. 'You do want me, Gracie, don't you?'

Her whispered 'yes' sounded alien to her. Didn't she want to say, 'No'? But she knew that she didn't and that she couldn't stop the progress of Reggie's hand. Rather, she arched her back a little to help him reach where she so wanted him to touch her.

Leaning over her, he brought his lips down onto hers. His kiss was gentle at first, but then deepened until she yielded and opened her mouth to him. The probing of his tongue felt strange – tingly. She couldn't remember this sensation happening to her before. If she'd thought about it happening, she'd have been repulsed. Instead, her whole body reacted to the pleasure of it and she wanted to beg Reggie to take her, and to do so now.

As he came out of the kiss, he let out a deep sigh. 'I've to have you, Gracie, and I knaw as you feel the same. Let's go on to the beach and wipe the memory of that first time. We need to do that.'

She couldn't say so, but knew that she agreed. But she also knew that if she did have any doubts, she wouldn't be able to resist. This new her was a stranger to herself, though some memory trickled in at having felt this way before, and of having known a sating of the feeling.

Once they reached the beach, Reggie held her to him as he whispered, 'Let's take our clouts off before we lie down, lass.'

Again, that trickle of uncertainty came, but it wasn't strong enough to urge her to stop as she unclipped her stockings from her suspender and slipped her knickers off.

When she lowered herself, Reggie accepted her into his arms, and then rolled her over till he was above her. His passion was evident, but he remained gentle, something that Gracie was grateful for, as the uncertainty remained with her.

But all doubts left her as Reggie kissed her gently, the while prising open her legs, then finding the heart of her and probing her gently with his fingers, giving her feelings that dispelled all doubt.

Her moans of acceptance went into the wind, but encouraged Reggie. He responded by deepening his kiss, as he had done in the car. His darting tongue built a frenzy of longings into her till she tried to cry out to ask him to take her – a cry that came out as a deep throaty moan.

Reggie lifted his head and looked down at her, before kissing her on the nose, and then adjusting himself between her legs. 'Oh, me Gracie, me Gracie.'

Not even her memory gave Gracie the feelings that she experienced as her body surrendered to his. Feelings that built and built until she could hardly bear the intensity of them and cried out the joy of her own release.

Her action triggered something in Reggie as his moans joined hers and he stiffened, and then slumped down on her. 'Oh, Gracie, me Gracie, I love you, lass.'

Gracie couldn't say the words. She knew that love – deep love – wasn't happening for her. She had a strong attraction for Reggie, and loved what he did to her and had to admit that his skill at lovemaking had her melting into him, but she couldn't call that love. She could never feel for him what she felt for Freddie.

At this thought, tears trickled down her cheeks, for she knew beyond doubt now that Freddie was lost to her for ever.

'Hey, why the tears?'

'I don't knaw. I just felt like crying.'

'Well, I don't think that's a bad thing. I were told once that if a man did it right to a woman, and she reached a climax, then she did cry after with the emotion of it.'

Yes, Gracie could see that, as the feelings she'd experienced had undone her emotions.

'Tell me that you love me, Gracie. I need to hear it. I don't want to think that you've just come to me so that you didn't have me babby out of wedlock.'

There was a silence for a moment, but then Gracie realised that she owed Reggie that much, didn't she? Besides, was it possible to yield to a man, as she had done, if you didn't love him? And anyway, she and Reggie had known each other since birth, so that counted for sommat, didn't it?

'I do love you, Reggie, and will as long as you treat me right and don't allus want your own way. And as long as you don't impose on me your daft ideas about how a man ain't a man if his wife works.'

It was Reggie's turn to be quiet. He sat up and looked out to sea. His action brought her surroundings into focus, and a shudder went through her as the spot where Reggie had raped her came into her view.

'Are you cold, me lass?'

Glad that the moment had passed, though annoyed that Reggie hadn't affirmed that he wouldn't pursue his ways, Gracie sighed. 'Aye, a little. Pass me me things, Reggie.'

'Only if I can watch you put them on.'

His look made her laugh and settled her some. 'You're incorrigible, Reggie. You'll only want to have me again. Look the other way, like a gentleman would.'

'Is that how your gentleman friend treats you then?'

The tone of his voice sent a fear through Gracie. She tried to make light of it. 'Don't be daft, I don't have a gentleman friend, he went off a long time ago.'

'Aye, but he meant a lot to you at one time. Did he have you? Did he do what I've done to you?'

'Naw, he didn't.' Before she could stop herself, she added, 'He were too much of a gentleman for that.'

Reggie pulled his trousers on and stood up. 'Well somebody's had you, as you were no virgin when I took you.'

Gracie lowered her head. As she had told Freddie, so she must tell Reggie, but though she knew and had expected Freddie's reaction, she couldn't predict Reggie's.

'Sit down, Reggie. There's sommat that you should knaw. You may not want me after me telling, but I have to be straight with you. I told your ma and da some of it, but it seems that they haven't told you.'

'What? What have you to tell me, Gracie? Because I can't take it yer knaw. I can't take another man having been there afore me.'

'You knaw as they have.'

'Christ! Get up. I'm going to the car. I've gone all cold.'

A terror entered Gracie, but whatever Reggie did about it once he knew, she had to tell him the truth.

Dressing as quickly as she could, she ran after him. He was already sitting in the car and had the engine running. He didn't speak.

'Reggie, how I come not to be a virgin is through me first rape that happened when I was just fourteen, it was–'

'Your first! How many times have yer been raped then?'

'A few times by you, and once by the master of the refuge home that they took me to when me granny died.'

The sound of Reggie hitting the steering wheel

with palm of his hand made Gracie jump. He hung his head.

'And that's not all. There's sommat else, but it's for your ears only. I want you to swear that you won't tell anyone.'

'There can't be more. I can't take it, thou knaws.'

'You have to, as you have to knaw the truth of me past if we're to be wed. There's to be naw secrets atween us. After I've told you, you can tell me about that Shirley as now lives in the house that I grew up in.'

'There's nowt to knaw.'

'There is. I was told as you are having an affair with her. I want that to stop.'

'Well, there might have been a couple of times, but nowt like what we have. She showed that she wanted me so I took me chance for a quick release. But I allus felt disgusted afterwards.'

'Well, mine's a lot worse than that. Because of what the master did to me, I had a babby.'

'Christ! The ginger-head at that boarding house where yer live! Naw, naw, Gracie, you can't expect me to accept that, I'll not have your bastard under me roof.'

'I'm not asking you to do that. Bertie believes that Peggy is his ma, and it's going to stay that way, but I want him to be able to visit me whenever he likes. He may not knaw as I'm his ma, but he has strong feelings for me, and I couldn't hurt him by shutting him out. Besides, I have a need in me to be with him as much as I can.'

'Naw. I don't even want to clap eyes on him.'

'Then we don't wed.'

'What? Look, this is all your fault, you tempt men. And I dare say as you did the same to that bloke as you call the master.'

'I didn't. How could you say such a thing? I were fourteen, I knew nowt of what men did to make you have a babby – well, only what your ma told me, but as for wanting the master to do it to me, he were repulsive, disgusting and he raped all the lasses in turn, not just me – Aye, and the lads an' all – all the kids in there were sexually abused, and probably still are.' Taking a breath, but not wanting to let him off the hook, Gracie told him, 'If anyone's to blame, it's your ma and da. They turned me away. They could have taken me in, but they shunned me and sent me off to me fate!'

Reggie was quiet for a long time. 'I didn't knaw as such folk existed.'

Still angry at him, Gracie came back at him, 'Oh, they do. And I'm sitting next to one right now. Don't forget as you raped me, an' all, Reggie. And worse, you hurt me, you made me ill and kept me captive.'

'Aw, shut up, Gracie! You brought all of that on yourself, you knaw you did.'

'I don't knaw that, and will never accept that I did. But I am willing to put it all behind me for the sake of not having to give our child up.'

'Ours? How do I knaw as you're telling the truth on that? It's more than likely that bloke's as you were seeing, and you see me as an easy target to take responsibility for it. Does he knaw? Is that it? He ran out on you, didn't he?'

'I never had sex with him. And, Reggie, I'm telling you this much. If I wanted to, I could

310

write and tell him what has happened to me at your hands, and I knaw as he'll take me on, babby an' all. But I won't do that, as it's not fair to him. This is your babby, and you either wed me and take care of us, or I go to a convent, like I keep telling you.'

Reggie put the car into gear, screeched it around on two wheels, and roared up the road. He didn't speak again until he drew up a little way down the street from the boarding house.

'Right, as I see it, we're to wed, and you've made all the rules. Where we live, you carrying on with your work, me having to accept others have had you before me, and your bastard visiting us. Well, I have a few rules an' all. You're to let me have you whenever I want, and you show willing, like you did earlier. And I have to be master in me own home, my decisions are final.'

Gracie opened the door, got out and slammed it behind her. She jumped as she heard Reggie do the same. His hand caught hers, his grip painful.

'Let go of me, Reggie. I've had enough. I thought earlier that we could go along together, give and take, and we'd enjoy ... well ... you knaw, being together like we were earlier, but you're de-termined to have the last say, and you bring the only thing that's good between us down to the level of sommat you have a right to, and I have no say in.'

'Don't go, Gracie. I just don't understand yer. Life's allus been like that, the woman allus obeys the man, and I want it to carry on for us. I don't want you saying, "Naw, not tonight, Reggie, I don't feel like it," and me having to force meself on to yer.'

'It won't be like that, Reggie, if you're like you were tonight. You awaken feelings in me that make me want you.'

'I do, don't I?

'Aye. So think on. Treat me right, and things'll be right between us. Now, I'm going in. I'll see you when you come back on shore, and I'll see your ma and da on Sunday, as we said.'

'Kiss me, before you go, Gracie.'

Lifting her lips, the thought came to Gracie that she wished with all her heart that this was Freddie she was kissing.

Reggie's hand cupped her breast. 'Eeh, me lass.'

Gently pulling from him, Gracie looked up at him. 'I've to go.'

'I'll watch you till you're inside.'

Tears flowed down Gracie's cheeks. She was made for loving, she must be, to enjoy all that Reggie did, even though he was the wrong man doing it. She'd have to hang on to that. She'd have to let the feelings Reggie gave her be enough. And she'd have to try to forget Freddie.

Going through to the kitchen, she was met by three questioning faces.

'It's done, you needn't worry.'

'Eeh, Gracie, you're crying.'

'Aye. I'm entitled to, Jeannie. Me life's taken a turn that I didn't ask for and not one that I want.'

'Don't be bitter, lass, you've to make the best of things.'

Gracie wanted to shout at Peggy that she had every right to be bitter. That she – her friend, had betrayed her. That she'd taken away all the options that she had and left her with the only one that she didn't want. But then, as she saw the hurt in Peggy's face and the fear in Sheila's, she knew they didn't deserve that. Gracie had taken away one of her own options when she'd finished with Freddie and refused to go to him – the option that she most wanted, and these women she loved, were unable to give her any other alternatives. She couldn't expect them to. But it tore at her heart that deep down they didn't believe her, and that it was this fact that had driven them. This, she knew, she would never get over – or forgive.

Suddenly, Gracie's legs would hold her no more. She slumped into a chair and folded her arms on the table. Her head rested on them as she allowed her body to cry.

'Gracie. Gracie. I'm sorry. I were wrong to side with me ma. I do believe what you said happened, and I've given me ma what for for making me doubt you.'

'Sheila!'

'Well, you did, Ma.'

Peggy stormed out of the room.

'Naw, Sheila. This ain't what I want. I don't want you falling out and hurting each other. Go after your ma and say as you're sorry. I knaw you never really believed as she did. But I don't blame her for believing it. She saw sommat as didn't happen, but it looked to her that it did. Anyone of us would take seeing me kissing Reggie, and looking as though I wanted to, as me fancying him... Oh, I don't knaw, it's all a mess.'

Sheila's hug didn't help. Something inside of

Gracie had been changed for ever and the sadness of that prevented her feeling what she had felt for Sheila since they'd first met. This added to her desolation, making her feel bereft.

As Sheila left the room, Jeannie came over to sit beside Gracie. 'Eeh, Gracie, I don't knaw what to say. I've offered to go away with you and I will. You don't have to go through with this. I've thought on, an' all. Freddie need never knaw. We could say as the babby were mine, and–'

'Naw! I'm not giving another child up. I can't, Jeannie. That's a pain that feels like a sore being rubbed with sandpaper. And it never ceases. Day after day, to watch your child growing and for him not to knaw as you're his ma. I can't, I can't. But, lass, I appreciate you trying to help me and love you for it.'

The door opened and Peggy came back in with Sheila. They both looked wary.

'Eeh, come here, you two. It's all right.' Gracie stood and held her arms open. 'I'm being silly. Me and Reggie have talked.' She told them what the arrangements were so far. 'And so not a lot will change for me. I've made me mind up to make the most of it. It were just coming back in here, it triggered me emotions. But you have to remember, I have me belly up, so I'm bound to be hard to handle.'

'That's two of you, then. Me ma on her menopause is bad enough. I reckon as you and me'll emigrate, Jeannie.'

They all giggled at this. The mood lightened and Gracie was able to tell them that the final arrangements were going to be made on Sunday. 'I'll be wed in three weeks! But I haven't forgotten your wedding, Sheila. We've to get on with all of them arrangements, an' all.'

For the next half an hour, over cocoa and a special treat of chocolate biscuits, they talked weddings and Gracie came to a place of forgiveness for her friends and a real sense of family. For that's what they were – a real family of women who faced together whatever life threw at them. And she knew, in that moment, they always would be.

CHAPTER TWENTY-SEVEN

'You're getting fat, Gracie.'

'Ha, cheeky. You should never say such things to a lady, Bertie. You're going on six now, and you should knaw better.'

'It's hard to knaw what I can say and can't. Sometimes I say sommat and everyone laughs, and says that I'm a one, and then another time I can say the same and get told off!'

His indignant face made Gracie laugh. 'That's part of growing up, learning when sommat can be said and when it can't. You'll get the hang of it. Anyroad, there's a reason that my tummy is getting big. I have a babby growing inside me.'

This time Bertie's expression made Gracie double over. But she wasn't ready for his next question. 'How did it get there?'

'That's for me to knaw and you to wonder about. You'll find out when you're older.'

315

'Everyone says that about everything, but I want to knaw now.'

Gracie looked at this son of hers, and thought for the umpteenth time that he was much cleverer than his years. He was never accepting of simple explanations, but always suspected that there was more to know, and went in search of the knowledge. He'd been able to read at the age of three. She'd put it down to having so many eager teachers in herself, Sheila and Peggy, but now realised that it was much more than that.

Distracting him, she told him to go into the shop and ask Jeannie to come and collect the basket of rock that she'd been making into a display. It was a new line she'd done with the Union Jack running through it.

All talk was of war, and of standing together and getting through it. Of being victorious and, if it came, being over before it started. But Gracie detected that, like herself, everyone was afraid. And as they got further into August, that fear deepened, with all the preparations taking place. One of these – blacking out signposts – made them all laugh. One look at the Blackpool Tower soaring into the sky and even an Eskimo would know they were in Blackpool, let alone a German!

But behind the laughter was the knowledge that with two airports geared up to take major roles in defence and training – Squires Gate Lane and Stanley Park aerodromes, as well as Vickers Armstrong Aircraft factory, Warton Air Base and Naval training centres – Blackpool would be a prime target and an easy one with its many landmarks easily seen from the air.

The season had been the worst ever, as this fear was nationwide, and many folk chose to stay away. Yet Blackpool buzzed with servicemen and many venues were busier than ever after dark as these men took their recreation as seriously as they did their training for war.

Trying to come up with something different to sell to the few holidaymakers who did come, and to appeal to the servicemen and her few outside outlets, took a lot of Gracie's time. There was so much competition, and with their shop being just off the Prom they weren't the first port of call and had to build themselves a name.

Amidst it all Gracie, Sheila, Jeannie and Peggy were busy making the final preparations for Sheila's wedding that was to take place the following week on Saturday 2 September.

Gracie's own wedding had gone without a hitch and she and Reggie were muddling along – helped by the intense fishing that was taking place to stockpile in the event of war, which meant that Reggie was away for two to three weeks at a time. His short homecomings were taken up with their lovemaking, leaving no time for any discord to rise between them.

The trawlers were going as far as Iceland to make sure of a good catch. Danger lurked on the seas as U-boats and aircraft raids were a constant danger to the boats, even though war hadn't been declared.

'Ma's having some lads to stay, thou knaws, Gracie.'

This statement from Bertie as he came through the door with Jeannie threw Gracie. She looked at Jeannie, but before she could ask, Jeannie said, 'Evacuees.'

'Oh? Where from?'

'Manchester. They reckon as the cities will be the ones to take the bombing raids, as if we aren't in as much danger with all that we've got around us.'

'Aye, well, let's hope that it all fizzles out and Chamberlain gets a peace agreement signed. He's still hopeful.'

'I'd rather listen to Churchill, he tells it as it is. He doesn't bury his head in the sand. If it were left to some of the government, we wouldn't even have the preparations that we do have in place.'

'Eeh, it's a funny lot. Blackpool don't seem like Blackpool anymore.'

'Naw, but I like it. I get asked out every day, and that never happened before. And, before you say it, it ain't because the soldiers are desperate, either!'

'Jeannie! I'd never say that, lass. That's you, with your constant need for reassurance. And you've no need of it. You're beautiful in a cute kind of way, and the sooner you realise it the more confidence you'll have to start accepting the odd date. You need to do some fishing to make a good catch.'

'Hark at the voice of experience!'

'Aye, well, it didn't happen like that for me.'

'Are you all right, Gracie? I mean, really, all right? Are you happy, or do you still pine for–'

'Don't! Don't go down that road. I can't let meself think about it all, let alone talk about it. Reggie's never going to be the love of me life, but he ain't a bad bloke. I've to accept me lot and get on with it. I daren't let meself think on what might have been.'

'Oh, and what's that then? And who is going to be the love of your life then?'

The effect of these words had Gracie, Jeannie and little Bertie stand still and stare, as if they'd been turned to stone.

'Not so much of your chatter now, is there? Get out you, you ugly sod. And you, you bastard lad, can scarper, an' all.'

'Reggie!'

'Aye, me, the bloke as took you on, with me thinking that you loved me. Well, I knaw now, don't I? I knaw the truth as your mates here seem to have known all along.'

'Reggie, I can explain. It wasn't what you thought. You caught the tail end of a conversation.'

The door closed on Bertie and Jeannie, and as it did, fear clutched Gracie as she looked into the face of evil.

Not speaking to her, Reggie opened the connecting door to the shop and shouted. 'Shut the bloody shop and get gone. Me and me wife have sommat to say to each other.'

Sheila came back at him. 'Naw. I for one ain't leaving you with Gracie whilst you're in that mood. I don't trust you.'

The door opened and Jeannie reappeared. 'Naw, nor me. You touch her, Reggie, and you'll have to take on all three of us.'

Gracie's fear deepened. This was getting out of hand. 'I'll be all right, me lasses. Honest. I just need to clear this up with Reggie. It's near on four, so we can shut a bit early. Get Bertie home, go on. He doesn't need to hear this.'

Sheila got her coat, but as she went to go out of the door she stopped. 'I'm warning you, Reggie, if you harm a hair on her head, you'll live to regret it.'

'Bugger off. She's me wife and I have the right. I'm not taking what she said lying down. Naw man would.'

'Well, I don't knaw what she said, but I don't see you listening to her side, so I'm staying. You can have your talk in front of me.'

Reggie swung round, his fist raised.

'Reggie, naw. Naw!' The rolling pin that Gracie had picked up smashed across Reggie's back. He sank to his knees.

Hardly able to breathe, he looked round at Gracie. His face held shock.

'I warned you – I said I'd not stand for your violence, and that meant against me friends, an' all.'

Reggie regained his breath and stood up. Without a word, he crossed the room and went through the door that led to the stairs to their flat above the shop.

'Eeh, Gracie, I fear for you.'

'You should have gone, Sheila. His pride was hurt, that's all. I can handle him. But ta, anyroad. You're a real friend. You both are. Though I have to face it and you can't allus get involved. Look at poor Bertie, he's scared out of his wits.' Making light of it all, Gracie put her arms out to her son. 'Come and give Gracie a hug, afore you go, lad.' Holding Bertie close to her, Gracie's hands trembled as she stroked his hair. 'Eeh, lad, us redheads are the ones who are supposed to have tempers, but I reckon as those with black hair can beat us. Don't worry about your Uncle Reggie. He mistook sommat he heard and blew up. He'll be as right as ninepence when I go up to him and make his tea.'

Her heart soared, despite it all, as Bertie clung on to her and told her that he loved her and didn't want her to be hurt.

Gently pushing him from her and holding him at arm's length, she looked into his face. 'Naw, lad. Uncle Reggie won't hurt me. He might shout a bit. Most men do when they're angry. You've heard your Uncle Ron a few times. He's allus on a short fuse, and even your da can have a go when things ain't how he wants them to be. That's all it is. Nowt more. There'll be a bit of shouting, and I can do me share of that, and then we'll have a cuddle and make up. I promise. Now, go with Jeannie and Sheila. I'll see you in a couple of days.'

Gracie's heart clanged her fear around her body as she climbed the stairs. Reggie came to the landing and looked down at her. 'Get up here, you. You rotten cow!'

'I – I told you, I can explain, Reggie. At least give me a chance to do that.'

'A chance! A chance to explain? A chance to lie, yer mean. I heard what I heard. You said that I weren't the love of your life, and you couldn't think on what might have been. That hurt me, Gracie. It hurt me here.' His hand tapped his chest.

'I – I... Oh, Reggie, I'm sorry. It was girls' talk.

You knaw how it was between us, when we married. We were forced into it, but thought we could make a good job of it, and we have. And I am growing to love you more and more. Let me get upstairs and we can sit and talk.'

'Talk?'

Reggie didn't seem capable of doing anything other than repeating what she said. His whole demeanour spoke of shock and disbelief. Had he really believed that he was her one and only true love?

'Yes, talk. It's what grown-ups do when they have a dispute. Shouting and raising your fist won't get you anywhere. You frightened the life out of Bertie.'

'Your bastard, you mean, eh? Your bastard!'

Reaching the top of the stairs, Gracie's legs seemed to turn to jelly. For all her bravado, inside she dreaded what Reggie might do. His face, red with temper, his eyes glaring and his fists clenched until his knuckles were white told her that she wasn't going to get off lightly. His hand shot out and grabbed her hair before she could step back. Her head burned with the agony of him pulling her into their bedroom that led off to the right of the landing. Throwing her on the bed, Reggie made as if to undo his belt. The thought went through her that he intended to take her, to assert his masculinity that way and with it came a relief. She could play up to this, and calm him.

'Eeh, Reggie, don't be rough. There's no need–'

'I ain't going to shag you, you dirty cow, I'm going to beat yer. You're going to knaw once and for all that I'm yer man, and you do as I say. You don't go dreaming about what might have been without me and without me babby in your belly. That's if it is mine. Any man would do for you, I just happened to be the daft sod that wanted you. You bitch!'

Horror filled Gracie as Reggie unleashed his belt and snapped it in the air. 'Naw, Reggie. Naw. I didn't mean it. I told yer, it were girls' talk. Naw!'

Her body rolled away in an attempt to escape the striking belt. She caught her breath deep in her lungs as it sliced across her back. Tears stung her eyes, saliva dripped from her gaping mouth, but she made an extreme effort and rolled even further away from him and swung her legs off the side of the bed. In one movement, she was standing facing Reggie.

'You swine! I hate you! I'll never love you now, never!' Her tears rained down her face, and mingled with her snot, but she didn't attempt to wipe them, such was the feeling in her that her only quest was to vilify this man.

Reggie sank as if someone had taken his stuffing from him. His body slumped on to the bed. 'I'm sorry, Gracie. Don't say as yer hate me, don't.'

'Well, I do. You vicious swine!'

With no more defensive action to take, the realisation and the pain of what he'd done seeped into her. She sat down and winced against the severity of it.

'If I'm a vicious swine, then you are an' all. Me back's killing me. I reckon as you've cracked me ribs with that rolling pin.'

'I had to stop you hitting Sheila. You would have done. You went for her with your fist raised. And aye, if I had the strength now, I'd fetch that rolling pin and beat you to death with it.'

Lying back on the bed, Gracie felt the soreness of her back. She rolled on to her side. Her sobs increased. They tore her heart with the knowledge that this was to be her life. And that if this could happen in the first few months of marriage to Reggie, God knew what was in store for her in the future.

'I'm sorry, Gracie, but you did ask for it. You've to learn as you can't treat your man like that and not have to face the consequences.'

With her sobs near strangling her, Gracie couldn't answer, but she knew that if she could she'd tell him that she would never bow to his wishes. That she wanted a marriage that was a partnership, not a dictatorship. And one where they talked through their grievances, not beat the hell out of each other, but she doubted if Reggie could ever understand that concept.

'Can I come and help yer, Gracie? I can bathe your back, and you can bathe mine, and we can call it quits, eh?'

Wanting to scream 'no!' but knowing that they had to go forward from here, and hoping that a lesson had been learned, Gracie agreed.

'Aw, Gracie. Look what I've done to yer. Oh, me little lass. You shouldn't have made me so mad. You're to think on.'

Gracie gritted her teeth.

'It ain't cut yer, but it has left a massive welt. Have a look at mine.'

With this Reggie removed his shirt. Gracie grimaced with pain as she sat up, but then felt the shame of what she'd been capable of as she saw the bruise across Reggie's back.

It came to her to tell him the same. That he had to think on before he threatened violent action against her friends, but she didn't – her sorrow that it had all happened was too much. She ran her hand over his bruise. Reggie winced.

'I'm sorry, Reggie. I shouldn't have said what I did. It were only banter; of the kind as you'll have with your mates when talking of me. And if I thought as you would hear me, I'd have never had said it. I'll get a bowl and we can see to each other's wounds.'

The cold water stung, but Gracie lay on her stomach as best she could and allowed the gentle patting that Reggie administered to her wound.

'I love your freckly skin, Gracie.' His voice, low and husky, repulsed her. This was something she'd not felt since the night he'd raped her. Not even through her ordeal of being held prisoner by him did she feel what she did now.

His hands traced a path around to her side, and under her until he was holding her breasts, his body closed in on her, his lips sought her neck. Everything in her screamed against this, but what was the use? They were married. She had her duty as a wife to give him his marital rights. That much she had complied with, and aye, enjoyed, but would she ever again?

'Come on, Gracie, yer knaw as yer like it. Better that we make love than fight.'

'I'm sore, Reggie.'

325

'I'll be gentle. You knaw as I allus am when we do it.'

She could give him that much. He was a gentle lover, and a considerate one and something in her responded just a little as he ran his hand down her back, and reached her bottom, then dug through her skirt to feel her. Though disgusted with herself, she allowed the feeling to rule her. A sigh left her, leaving her relaxed and wanting.

Reggie stood and undid the buttons of his trousers. His need was showing in the bulge of them, and came into full view as he slipped his trousers down. Gracie was lost. There was no more resistance in her. Still she didn't understand how this was, but a hunger she couldn't deny flared in her every time Reggie approached her to make love to her. She'd even instigated it on a couple of occasions when she should have been sated but wanted more.

'Just lay there, me little lass, and I'll take your knickers off for you. There. Eeh, me Gracie. Me lovely Gracie.'

He was on top of her and entering her. Nothing in her was repulsed now as she arched towards him. Accepting him gave her extreme pleasure. Her cry told him of the intensity of the feeling that took her whole body.

At moments like this, she did love Reggie, and the cry of her love resounded around them as she reached her climax. 'Oh, Reggie, Reggie, my love.'

Reggie shuddered, then his cries joined hers, before he slumped down on her. She only allowed this for a few seconds as she felt afraid for their unborn. 'Eeh, get off me belly, Reggie, you're squashing me.'

'That's not what you said a moment ago.' Reggie laughed as he rolled off her. Then he did something he'd never done before, he ran his hand over the mound of her stomach. 'I wonder if it's a lad or a lass? Which would you prefer, eh?'

'I don't care as long as it's healthy. A lass would be nice.'

'That's because you already have a lad. But I wished that you didn't, Gracie. I wished with all me heart that you'd fought that man off yer and not let him take yer. But there's sommat in you as needs it. You love it, and I reckon as any man'd do.'

Rolling to the other side of the bed, Gracie got up, went through the door and slammed it as hard as she could. Its hinges rattled.

On the landing, she held on to the small part of banister that curved around the top of the stairs. Her body shook with temper and frustration. She'd thought that Reggie understood. Oh, aye, he couldn't stand the sight of Bertie, and that was to be expected from him. He saw everything in one way and one way only, and that was that if it was what he wanted and fitted into his way of things, then it was acceptable. But anything else he took an intense dislike to. Bertie wasn't what he wanted. Reggie could only really be happy if she'd have come to him as a virgin. *Why? Why can't he accept how it happened?* But then she knew why. It was her fault. It was her need of sex, her utter enjoyment of it. Her acceptance of it, no matter when he wanted it, even after he'd taken his belt to her. The fault was in her. To Reggie,

327

she couldn't and wouldn't ever refuse the chance to have a man take her. How am I to convince him that he is wrong? Somehow, I must. Because if I don't it will eat away at him. And God knows what that will make him do.

CHAPTER TWENTY-EIGHT

After washing herself down, Gracie was in the kitchen before Reggie came out of the bedroom. He didn't mention the incident, but came up behind her and put his arms around her waist. Gracie wanted to shrug him off, but she knew that she had to manage Reggie and his temper, not provoke him. There was no apology forthcoming, as there never was.

He still hadn't put his shirt on, and she could feel his muscles against her. *If only he was the right man.* If only the past hadn't happened. How often she'd wished that.

'That was a sigh and a half. I thought as what I gave you had sorted everything.'

'It did, Reggie. It's just that me back is sore and you're rubbing against it. I can hardly bear me blouse against it, let alone owt else.'

'Ha, yer didn't say that when you lay on it and I was on top of yer.'

She laughed with him and felt better for it. 'Tea's nearly ready. I've a stew on the hob that's been simmering all day, so meat'll drop off the bone. I'll lay the table and cut the bread up into the doorsteps that you like. It'll be ready in a few minutes.'

'Good, you've made me ravenous, and not just with the smell of the food. Shagging yer took it out of me. I couldn't even run after you when you stormed out.'

'Aye, well that's passed now, don't drag it up again.'

'It'll never pass, Gracie. It gnaws away at me. And it's right what I said – I can't imagine you, with how you are, not wanting it done to yer.'

Gracie stiffened. Her teeth clenched. Her hand tightened on the knife that she was chopping the boiled tatties with in readiness to mash them with a fork, the way Reggie liked them. 'You're only going on how I am with you, Reggie. You awoke sommat in me when you held me prisoner in your bedroom. Before that, I'd have said as no man were ever going to touch me in that way again. I were sick when it happened. I vomited all over the master. He hurt me. It was vile. Please, please, Reggie, get the notion out of your head that I wanted to be raped by him.'

Reggie walked away from her. Frustration boiled her temper. But she kept it in check. She knew Reggie. She knew him well enough to realise that whatever she said, she wouldn't convince him. This frightened her, but she was to live with it, and to manage him as she knew she must. Somehow she would get through it all.

Sheila looked lovely. Her cream silk gown flowed to the floor. She wore her hair up and had a pearl clip holding her long veil in place. Her face shone with happiness, especially when she entered St John's church and saw her Bob sitting at the altar. As she approached, his best man, his elder brother, Graham, helped him onto crutches, and he managed to stand.

Everyone cheered.

Graham continued to support Bob throughout the exchange of vows. Gracie joined so many in wiping away a tear. But for her, the tears weren't just at the moving moment, but for her own loss. She should have stood at this altar with her Freddie. *Oh Freddie, Freddie.*

Forcing herself to concentrate on what was going on and to be happy for Sheila, Gracie let her eyes wander to Jeannie. She'd never seen a prettier bridesmaid. Wearing a pale blue silk dress that was cut in the Empire line – fitted to below the bust and then flowing to the floor – and with her usually frizzy hair tamed into ringlets held in place by a blue band, it was hard to imagine Jeannie as the same tall, lanky girl with spots, buck teeth and thick-rimmed glasses whom she'd first met.

Outside, the sun shone as the small party came out of the church. Standing by the gate, Gracie saw a familiar figure. Not looking quite so mad-professor-ish and smiling all over his face, David, as they now knew Jeannie's optician was called, gave a little wave. Gracie walked over to him. 'I didn't see you in the church, I thought you hadn't made it.'

'I had an appointment that I couldn't get out of. A fascinating case of a child whose eyes have been affected by her having measles. And–'

'David, it may be fascinating to you, but it'll

take you ages to tell me about it and I think a certain lady is waiting for you to say hello.'

'Oh, yes, yes of course.'

As he walked over to where the wedding party was gathering for a photo, Gracie wondered how Jeannie ever had the patience to listen to him. A nice man, but oh, so boring. At least to her he was. But Jeannie loved him, Gracie knew that now, and that's all that mattered. It did Gracie's heart good to see Jeannie's face light up as David approached her.

Jeannie never said if she'd told David about her past, but if she had, Gracie hoped he'd understand and not let it have an impact on him. A loner, with no friends, just a couple of acquaintances from his university days, David had lost both his parents in the bombing of London in 1917. He'd been seven years old at the time, and had been staying with his grandparents in the countryside. They had since died, leaving him with no family. For Jeannie, this boded well, as she wouldn't have the fear that Sheila had had of not being good enough for Bob's parents – something that had proved to be true as they'd looked down their noses at her and didn't make her at all welcome when Bob took her home.

Something flashing caught Gracie's eye at that moment. The window of a taxi had reflected the sun as the driver closed the door on Bob's parents. It seemed they had booked a train to go back to Surrey the moment the service was over. Gracie knew a sadness as Bob sat in his wheelchair, on the pavement and waved them off. But then his brother came over to him and patted him on the shoulder, and Bob looked up and smiled. And she realised that the brothers knew their parents well, and conspired together, as they exchanged a look that said 'typical' and then laughed out loud.

Sheila stayed by the church door, not even looking in the direction of her departing parents-in-law, but not able to hide her hurt from Gracie, who knew her so well. Frustration took Gracie. *This is 1939! Any minute now we could hear that we are at war with Germany, and yet folk display that kind of behaviour! It all beggars belief.*

The guests crowded Peggy's large front room, all chatting happily, but a thread of tension trickled through the atmosphere of joviality, as no one could forget that a deadline was in place for Germany to pull out of Poland which, if not met, would mean war would be declared. So far, the whispers were of there being no response to Chamberlain's demand.

Gracie had a dread in the bottom of her stomach that not even two glasses of sherry could lift. She looked around the room and spotted Rory. 'Eeh, there you are. Are you having a good time?'

Rory didn't answer but put his hand in his pocket and handed Gracie a brown envelope. Her heart sank as she guessed what it was. 'When?'

'I've to report to Devonport in Plymouth as I've elected to join the Navy.' A grin spread over Rory's face. 'I thought I might meet like-minded men in there – you knaw what they say about a sailor!'

Gracie giggled.

'Where's bullyboy, Gracie?'

'He's at sea. And don't call him that, Rory,

332

Reggie's all right most of the time.'

'Oh? The girls told me about your back. You only have to say the word and I can have him seen to. I'm well in with one of the top gang leaders. He's one of us, though no one knows it.'

'A homosexual gang leader! Really?'

'Aye. But you'd never guess it. Just give me the word and Reggie'll never walk again.'

'Naw, Rory. I'd never do that. Anyroad, don't let's talk about it.'

'I reckon as that's just what you need to do, Gracie. Today can't have been easy. I can feel the tension in you. Let's take our sherries outside and sit on the bench at the front.'

Talking was the last thing Gracie felt like doing, but she followed Rory.

'I didn't say, but you look lovely, Gracie. I recognised that frock, but it looks different.'

'It's had an adjustment. I added this overskirt to even out my shape.'

The frock was pale green, with a slimline cut, reaching to her calves. Large pleats at the front had given it a balloon style and were perfect for fitting around her expanding tummy, but Gracie hadn't liked how she'd looked in it. 'I found this chiffon in the Abingdon Street market. I thought that the darker green colour would complement the colour of the frock, so, I just gather stitched in around the waist and then made this wrap to put around my shoulders out of the same material. I was pleased with the result.'

'So you should be. Eeh, lass, it suits you, being pregnant. More than it did the last time, but you were just a bairn then. I feel for you, Gracie. Life seems to kick you in the pants. It must be horrible being wed to the wrong man.'

'We get by, Rory. I have to work at it, but we manage. It helps that I really knaw him well. We grew up next door, so I knaw his moods and what triggers his temper; though I can't allus help matters. He's insanely jealous, and can't come to terms with me having had a babby with another man, and he knaws, deep down that I love someone else, so it can't be easy for him.' Gracie told Rory what brought on the fight between herself and Reggie.

'Don't even try to justify his action, Gracie. Do that and you're on your way to accepting that as the normal way of things. It's not. Awe, I knaw as you hit him, but though I hate violence, that was a necessary action, or he'd have hurt Sheila, but taking his belt to you? Naw. That ain't right.'

'There's not many as think like you, Rory. You knaw what folk say: "A man has a right to keep his missus in check." And most would say that Reggie had good cause to beat me, if he told of his grievances.'

'Wouldn't the police help you?'

'Naw, they'd say that it's a domestic matter. I just have to manage things as best I can. Give in to his needs, take care that he doesn't suffer through me work, and not cross him.'

'Be his bed slave and pander to his every whim, you mean. Is he good at it?'

'Rory!' But far from being offended, Gracie laughed. Rory was like the best type of girlfriend that anyone could have. He'd talk about anything and allow you to, too. With this thought, Gracie asked something that she wouldn't ask of anyone else in the world. 'Seriously, Rory, is it possible to enjoy sex with someone you don't love? I mean, does that make you some kind of a harlot, or sommat?'

'Naw, it makes you a lovely, warm, human being. Sex isn't sommat as there should be so many rules about. Bloody hell, they criminalise folk for doing sommat as they enjoy and find natural to them. I take it that the bullyboy is good at it, and satisfies you in that way?'

Gracie nodded.

'Good. At least you got sommat out of the bloody deal. But don't start thinking that you're a bad person because of it. I've thought meself in love many a time because of what I've felt when having sex with a bloke, but they say that when it is done with someone you love, it is enhanced. I don't see how, but I can see the way that you're thinking. Look, darling, sex has more to do with your body than your heart, and with the skill and care of who you do it with, whether you love them or not. And it seems that bullyboy has the right skills, and he's a handsome brute with it. But that don't make up for him not being Freddie, does it?'

'Naw. Nowt will ever make up for that. And nor will I ever get over him. I've hurt him badly, but I had naw choice, Rory. You do believe me, don't you? Even though I've told you what I have, you believe me when I say as I weren't willing when Reggie raped me and kept me prisoner?'

'I never doubted you. Eeh, Gracie. I love you, lass, and it hurts me to see everything you go

335

through. No one least deserves it.' He paused. 'Gracie, can I tell you sommat?'

'Aye, of course you can. Haven't I just told you me most deepest secrets?'

'Well, I – I, look, when I say as I love you, I mean it. I've never loved a woman more, or in this way. Since meeting you, I've even had feelings that are alien to me. Can you understand that, Gracie?'

Shocked at the intensity with which Rory had meant this, Gracie couldn't speak for a moment. Her eyes held his deep coal-black ones, and in them she saw the love he held for her, and knew that it was just as painful to him as her love for Freddie was to her. 'I understand. Oh, Rory. It's another one of those "if onlys" that you've given me, because I knaw as I could feel the same for you. Have done, before I met Freddie, but I knew it was hopeless, so didn't give it me attention.'

Rory took her hand. 'Eeh, Gracie, me Gracie. To be able to take that with me is going to help. I have a picture of you near to me heart, where I allus carry it. Look.' Rory pulled out a picture of her with Suzy. Suzy was curling her ringlets around her finger, just as she herself had done to her ma's. It was a beautiful picture, with the sun glistening on her and the adorable monkey. And laughter, carefree laughter, lit her face, because this picture was taken after she'd had her Bertie, and had come to terms with everything and was looking towards a bright future.

Tears welled up in her eyes. 'Oh, Rory...'

'I knaw, lass. I'll miss you.'

His kiss on her cheek was gentle, and yet held a

deep love that warmed her.

There was a long moment of silence. Gracie broke it. 'Poor Suzy. How will she cope without you? She'll pine for you.'

'She already is. She's not well at all. She's even off her food, when I usually have a job to stop her stealing everything that she can. Me da'll take care of her, though it'll break me heart to leave her. She's old now.'

'Life's going to change again, Rory. God knaws what's in store for us all. I'm going to miss you, me lovely Rory. You'll write, won't you?'

'Aye, I will. I'll write to Sheila, and put a sealed one in for you. That'll be me best letter, because I'll be able to tell you lots more than I can Sheila. I daren't send it to your address in case bullyboy sees it. I don't want you getting in any more trouble than you do already.'

'I'll look forward to that. But be careful. Don't talk of your ... well, you knaw, your tendencies.' They both giggled. 'Naw, seriously, though. What if someone sees what you've written? You'd get into serious trouble.'

'You're right. I knaw. I'll tell you stuff, but put a girl's name and say she and her. So, if I say, "I met this lass. Her name's Pat, and as the song goes, we made whoopee," you will knaw as I mean Patrick and that I had great sex with him. How does that sound, eh?'

Again, they laughed. They doubled over, and Gracie thought that it was a laughter that restored them to the place that they had always been comfortable with each other, before Rory's declaration.

'I take it that you're not going to miss your chef, then?'

'Oh, he was old news a long time ago, darling. It's been weeks since I gave him the elbow.'

'Oh, I didn't knaw. Anyroad, Rory, me darling, I wish you all the luck in the world. Don't be a hero. And, Rory ... take me love with you.'

Rory looked once more into her eyes. 'Aye, and I leave mine with you, an' all.'

Sheila appeared at their side. 'Hey, what are you two doing out here? You look like you're conspiring over a secret.'

'Nothing, beautiful bride. We're just saying what a lovely day it's been. Everything's perfect and we've wanted for nowt.'

As Rory said this, Gracie realised that he hadn't yet told Sheila about his call up, so she took the same line and kept the banter light. 'Eeh, Mrs Robert Hanley. Very posh, our Sheila. I'm so happy for you.'

Sheila's hug at this told Gracie that she knew her pain. But did she? Could she ever know what it was like to watch the ceremony today while longing for it to be her at the altar with Freddie standing by her side?

Rory took the thought from her with his next question. 'Tell us again about your new bungalow.'

With this Sheila surprised them by plonking herself next to Gracie with an expression on her face that didn't speak of happiness. 'I'm likely to be there on me own, if war's declared.'

'What do you mean, lass?' Rory sounded as surprised as Gracie felt.

'Bob's been in talks with the RAF. It seems that

far from discharging him, they think they can find a vital job for him. He won't say what it is. Well, he says that he can't, but he'll be stationed at a place called Bletchley, somewhere down south. He goes in two weeks. He has to go on a training course first, though, and that'll take around four to six weeks. I don't think he's well enough to go, but it appears that there'll be doctors and a physiotherapist on hand to take care of him. In fact, he's been told that he'll be billeted with a doctor and his family.'

'Naw! Eeh, lass, I didn't think in a million years that would happen.' Gracie put her arm around Sheila and pulled her close. 'Can't you go down there and be with him?'

'Not yet. I may be able to, if Bob can find a place. But ... well, it ain't how I thought as things'd be. Everything's changing.'

'It is. And seeing as though you have that news, then my news won't come as such a shock.' Rory pulled out the brown envelope from his pocket. 'I've been called up, Sheila. I'm going in the Navy.'

'Awe, naw, Rory. I can't stand it. That bloody Hitler. He's spoiling everything.'

'I'll still be here for you, Sheila, and I'm sure that it won't be long before Bob gets a place for you. Let's look on the bright side, it's your wedding day. You're going to Southport for your honeymoon, and besides, Hitler may yet pull out of Poland and it'll all fizzle out.'

At eleven o'clock the next morning, they all learnt that it wasn't all to fizzle out. Britain was at war with Germany.

CHAPTER TWENTY-NINE

Sugar rationing wasn't the only problem that Gracie had to contend with as the first day of spring of 1940 burst in with a ray of sunshine. Not that it gave any cheer or warmth as the March wind cut through her as she pushed the heavily loaded pram.

Little Rita had arrived two days before Christmas. Now almost three months old, she was the apple of her da's eye and no trouble at all. A sleepyhead, it was difficult to wake her for her feed, and yet she was thriving well.

A ray of sunshine in Gracie's crumbling world.

Reggie had become more and more obsessed with her past, and taunted her at every opportunity, relentlessly so towards the end of her pregnancy when she'd been unable to give herself to him. His frustration had him abusing her in far worse ways than anyone had ever done in the past. Some nights she'd been in so much pain from his intrusion into her that she had had to sit up all night on two cushions, with one cheek on each so as not to put any pressure on her bottom.

Things had eased six weeks after the birth, when she was able to take Reggie to her once more, but his temper still flared more often than not.

And now, here she was, making the journey that she'd fought against.

Unable to keep up with the full rent of the shop

premises, she'd changed the lease to rent the shop only and was making her way to Fleetwood. There was no other way to get the pram there than to walk, and there was so many things that she needed for Rita that she'd filled the hollow in the bottom of the pram, as well as the top of the rainproof cover, fixed so tightly over Rita's blankets that it didn't sag with the weight.

Jeannie had rented the flat from the agent and was to move in the following week. David was still courting her, after his own fashion, though there seemed very little romance between them. It was more a kind of companionship, where David used Jeannie as someone to listen to his theories and fascinations.

Jeannie was now doing a job that Gracie had never in a million years thought to see – she drove a tram. The shortage of men after the massive call up meant that women were doing many jobs that they would have never been considered for before the war. Jeannie was in her element. But without hers and Sheila's help, now that Sheila had gone to live in Kent to be near to Bob, and with Rory somewhere out at sea, Gracie hadn't been able to keep the shop open for many hours a day.

In the morning she made what rock she could from what ingredients she had – often a little more than she was supposed to have, as Peggy had so much sugar rationed to her on account of the soldiers billeted with her that she sold a little of it to Gracie. More often now, Gracie made novelties rather than the usual sticks – rock made into fruit shapes, and the popular dummies with ribbons tied to them. They were easier to make and she could produce larger quantities. In the afternoon, she opened the shop for a few hours. Surprisingly, business was brisk, and selling in the shop much more involved as she had the added task of marking folk's ration cards with the points they had used towards their purchase.

Blackpool was crowded. War hadn't put the punters off. It seemed they all looked for a release from the fear and austerity. But they didn't find it on the beaches. These were taken over by the men in service, who were being put through their paces as they trained for war, and by workmen building tanks to hold water, in case of a shortage, and others building pill boxes as lookouts. The Blackpool Gracie knew and loved was being swallowed up into the fight to defend its shores against the enemy.

Most of those seeking a bit of fun came for a short break rather than the usual fortnight. That's if they could find accommodation, as most boarding houses had been conscripted to house troops and evacuees.

Peggy never had a moment, what with looking after four evacuee boys, besides Bertie, and having her vacant rooms full of soldiers. At night, these men, away from their families, took solace in drinking and most venues were doing a roaring trade.

Aunt Massie and Uncle Percy had given up their cottage to Reggie, as usually happened when the father retired and the son worked at the Fisheries and took himself a wife. The cottage had been in Reggie's name for some time, and Massie and Percy were glad to be finally moving out. They had moved into a rented bungalow in Fleetwood, and were the happiest that Gracie had ever known them.

A happiness that Gracie envied.

Her back ached as she reached Cleveleys, and yet she still had nearly three miles to trudge. All her furniture had been taken on a horse and cart by a local farmer, who often did removals as a part-time job. He had grumbled away as he loaded his cart, saying that with having to dig for Britain he was to lose this valuable extra income and work at turning all of his land over to arable farming. Even his resting fields had to be cultivated.

The sound of the key unlocking the front door of what she'd always think of as Aunt Massie's house echoed around the empty rooms inside. Gracie entered the front room and looked around. Her feet squeaked on the linoleum as she walked across to the scullery door. A warmth hit her. Uncle Percy had been in, as he'd said he would, and had lit the copper so that she'd have hot water for a bath later.

'There you go, Rita, me little lass, your pram just fits in the scullery, so at least you'll be warm while I get on.' Inwardly, Gracie hoped that Rita would stay asleep for a while, as though her breasts were heavy with milk, there was so much to do. Boxes were piled high at the bottom of the stairs, and the furniture should be here at any moment.

It was when Gracie bent over to begin opening the second box marked 'Kitchen' that the sickness came over her. Running out into the back yard, she just made it to the lav in time to throw up the contents of her stomach.

'You got your belly up again, then? Your Reggie don't hang about, does he?'

The dreaded Shirley.

Wiping her mouth on her pinny, Gracie backed out of the loo and turned to see Shirley looking over the wall. A fag hung from the side of her mouth. The smoke made her squint. Her bleached blonde hair was caught up in a bunch at the back, but strands of it hung around her over-made-up face. She was the kind of woman whom men drooled over, with most of her large breasts on show, squeezed into a too-tight blouse, and her ample hips waddling in straight skirts that were meant for a much slimmer figure.

'Naw. It's sommat as I've ate. I'll be right.' With this, Gracie hurried back inside, closed the door and leaned on it. Shirley had spoken her worst fear. After her initial bleeding following the birth, Gracie hadn't seen another. *Dear God, no! I don't see a way as I can cope.*

A knock on her front door brought her out of these thoughts. The cart was in the street, and Joe Pike stood on her step. 'Me and me ma are coming to give yer a hand, Gracie. We knaw as your man's at sea, and yer can't manage on yer own.'

Gracie could have burst into tears. 'Ta, Joe. You're a welcome sight. How've you been?'

'I'm all right. I failed call up. Not sure why, so I'm going to join the local defence group. I'm just about the only male tram driver left, except a few as were ready to retire and have stayed on. Me ma's bringing a pot of tea with her. Have you got any mugs unpacked?' This rambling from one subject to another was typical of the lovely Joe.

'Aye, they're all hanging on the dresser there. Aunt Massie left the dresser behind for me as it was too big for her new place. I'll see to getting them down. If you could help the farmer unload, it'll be quicker that way, and I can tell you where everything is to go.'

The three of them – Joe, Mrs Pike and herself – were on their second cup of tea, having polished the first one off in haste so that they could get on, and though tired to the bones, Gracie knew a sense of relief at how much they had achieved. The room looked lovely now, with Gracie's sofas in place, and Reggie's rocking chair next to the fireplace, something Gracie had picked up at an auction she'd attended when looking for a cot. Reggie had been over the moon with it, and loved to sit in it, rocking away, smoking a fag.

Already, the rest of Gracie's china was displayed on the dresser, and a fire crackled away in the grate.

'Eeh, you've some nice bits, Gracie.'

'Ta. I've been lucky. Me work, making and selling rock, brought me a good income until now and I browsed auctions and markets to get what I liked.'

'D'yer reckon as you'll be able to carry on in the shop much longer, lass?'

'I don't knaw. It's not going to be easy.'

'Awe, well. We've all to make sacrifices.'

'Aye.' There wasn't much to say to this. It was a statement uttered by everyone, as if they were convincing themselves that they could.

'Right, our Joe. Get up them stairs and put the

bed and the cot together. Then me and Gracie can get them made.' As Joe got up, Mrs Pike leant forward. 'He's handy is Joe. He can do most things, but I tell yer, I've never been more glad of him being a little short of a shilling. As it means as at least one of me lads is safe.'

'Have the others joined up?'

'Naw, but fishing is more dangerous than ever, and a lot more intense. We've already lost men when that U-boat sunk the *Davara,* and then three others have come under fire and the men taken prisoner. I thought it'd be them as had joined up as we'd be losing, not our fishermen. I expect you're worried about your Reggie.'

'I am. But he don't seem worried. He just takes it all in his stride, though he's away a lot more that he used to be, as all the men are.'

'You knaw, I believed yer, lass, when you said as Reggie held you against your will that time. I knaw him, and what he's capable of, and so do most of the women around here. Most wished that you'd carried through with the court case, even though you found yourself with your belly up, but we don't blame you, and you've got on with it, as your ma would have expected of you.'

This show of trust and understanding undid Gracie. Her body heaved in a huge sob.

'Eeh, lass. You've shouldered more than most, but you'll be welcome back amongst us, so don't you worry.'

'Ta, Mrs Pike. I thought as most would give me the cold shoulder.'

'Naw, lass. And don't let her next door get you down. Nobody likes her. She's allus been after

346

Reggie. He visited a few times when you got near to your time. He'd come to see his ma, but we all saw him slip in next door when her man were away.'

This shocked Gracie, and yes, if she was truthful, hurt and embarrassed her. Mrs Pike didn't seem to notice, or if she did, she chose to ignore it. 'Well, shall we get on? I'll help you make your bed, as that's important.'

Rita chose that moment to yell out.

'Uh-uh,' said Mrs Pike. 'Little one has her own ideas about what you're to do next. Well, no matter, tell me which box your bedding is in and I'll sort it.'

As Gracie sat with Rita suckling at her breast, her mind went over and over the possibility of her being pregnant again, and she knew that the chances were strong. Reggie had taken her every time he'd made it home, so much so that she couldn't imagine him being able, or needing, to go to Shirley next door. But then, Mrs Pike had said that was before the babby was born.

Making love had lost the appeal that it had held for her. It was as if the pain and disrespect that Reggie had shown her in his quest to gratify himself at all costs had deadened the hunger that had once had her craving for him to do it to her.

Leaning back, tiredness made her ache, but as Rita lifted a hand and Gracie took her tiny fingers in hers, a peace came to her. There were worse things than having babbies. Much worse. At least they gave unconditional love, and though demanding at times, she knew that she had it in her to see to all of their needs and to give all of

347

the love she possibly could.

Her thoughts went to Bertie. She would see less of him now, although, if she did manage to keep the shop open, then he might pop in most days.

A dread settled in her that her days at the shop were numbered. *Maybe I should warn Jeannie?* It would be awful to have her settle in only to find that she was living over an empty shop – or worse, the new tenants, if any were found, wanted the accommodation. Jeannie would have nowhere to go. She wouldn't be able to go back to Peggy's. Peggy needed every room she had for letting out.

It was three days later that Reggie turned up. There was no advance warning now, as few messages could be sent for fear of being intercepted, but then Reggie liked it that way as he had always tried to surprise her – or rather, thought he would catch her out.

'Eeh, me lass, it's good to be back here. This is where we should have been from the beginning.'

Gracie didn't answer this. It wasn't something she could agree with, and it never did to disagree with Reggie. She wriggled out of his embrace, avoiding the kiss he tried to give her.

'You smell of fish, and oil, Reggie. I'll get your bath on the go. How long are you likely to be on shore?'

'Wanting rid of me already, are yer?'

'Naw. Don't be daft.'

'Aye, well, it's sommat as we don't knaw. They could come for me tonight if there's a problem with one of the boats. Some part of the fleet has to be out at sea at all times.'

With the bath pulled in front of the fire, Gracie set about filling it from the hot water in the copper. Once Reggie was in the bath, she filled her dolly tub with the rest of the water, before topping the copper up once more. In no time, she had his clothes on the line.

Reggie was sitting in his rocking chair when she came back in. He'd donned a clean winceyette vest and long underpants but hadn't bothered to put any trousers on. Nor had he attempted to empty the bath and didn't speak while she went backwards and forwards with the bucket.

With the bath hanging in the scullery once more, Gracie knew the dread that had settled in her to deepen. Reggie was bound to start his games, and it was the last thing she wanted to do. 'Right, I'll make you a cuppa now, I have the kettle on the boil.

As she went to pass him the steaming mug he didn't take it. Instead, he told her to put it on the table and come and sit on his knee. 'It's not tea as I want, lass.'

'The babby will wake in a mo, Reggie. We'll do it after, eh?'

'What is it with you? Before you had our Rita you were gagging for it the moment I walked in the door. I'll not wait on your whim. You're me wife, and you'll open your legs for me whenever I want yer to.'

'It's that kind of talk that puts me off. You using me like I'm goods and chattel, not a woman. You're the one who's changed! You demand, rather than romance me.'

'Oh, don't start. Look at me, I've got to have it,

whether you want it or not.'

Gracie could see the bulge in his underpants.

'Just watching yer walk around seeing to me needs did this to me. Now come and sit on me knee and let me get yer ready.'

Everything in Gracie cried out against going to him, but the nasty tone of his voice when she'd gone back at him had made her afraid. Sighing, she went to him.

Nothing he did raised in her a need of him. Not his hands seeking and finding her breasts, nor when he lifted her skirt and fingered inside her knickers. It was as if that part of her had died.

'Christ, Gracie, you're as cold as a lump of ice. Why? Why? I just don't understand it.'

'Maybe you should have been more caring of me just before and just after I gave birth. You hurt me badly, and sommat in me died.'

'Don't blame me. Other women love taking it that way.'

'Oh, so you knaw, do you? No doubt, you mean that whore, Shirley, next door.'

Reggie stood, sending Gracie tumbling to the floor. He stared down at her. 'Either you open up for me, or I go around there now, and make her squeal that loud with the pleasure of me that you'll hear it. Then you'll be sorry.'

'It's true, then? You've been unfaithful to me, as well as abused me?'

'Abused you? You're me wife. Me wife! A man can't abuse his own wife!' His hand grasped hers. Her shoulder socket burned as he pulled her up in one movement. Her head wobbled on her neck under the violence of the slap he gave her. 'Get up them stairs. Go on. I'm having yer, if I have to force meself on yer.'

Gracie scrambled up the stairs. In the bedroom, she took off her knickers, the while looking at him with defiance. Lying on the bed she opened her legs. 'There, I'm ready. Do what you have to do.'

Reggie sank onto the end of the bed and covered his face in his hands. *Was that a sob?* Reggie? Reggie?'

'What's happened, to you, Gracie? I was the happiest man alive when we married. And for months after. You loved doing it with me, and I loved doing it and looked forward to it every time I came home. Then you started refusing me. I knaw as it was probable uncomfortable, but other men have told me that their wives happily turned on their side for them. They say that happens when they have their monthly bleeding an' all. But not you. You wanted nothing to do with me.'

'I tried, but it hurt too much, Reggie. And you wouldn't listen to me. You kept saying that it would get better, but it didn't, and then you forced me to do it. That's naw way to go on. I told yer, sommat died in me after that.'

'I repulsed yer, I could tell. But you made me angry. I don't knaw what I'm doing when I'm angry. Aye, I went next door a few times, before I came home to you, but only because I wanted to get satisfaction without fighting you for it and making you cry. Shirley's nowt to me, once I've shagged her.'

This was getting them nowhere, and Gracie wanted an end to it. She knew there was only one way. She had to give into him and show the enthusiasm that she always had done. 'Come here, Reggie. Help me to like it again. Start gently, kissing me, like. And touching me. Let's see how we go, eh?'

Reggie knelt on the bed. Tears flowed down his cheeks. 'Eeh, me little lass. I love yer. I do. You've got to stop making me angry. If you're more willing, we'll get back to where we were before.'

Gracie left it at that. She accepted his kisses, and moaned when he touched her, but inside she was dead. Nothing he did lit the fire in her as he had once done. And she couldn't say that she loved him like she used to make herself say, because she knew that she hated him – more than she ever had done now that she knew he visited next door.

She could forgive most things, but the humiliation of that she couldn't forgive.

CHAPTER THIRTY

'Eeh, Gracie, lass, I feel sorry for yer, I do. Little Rita's not yet one year old and here you are about to drop another. How're you going to manage?'

'I'm not, Jeannie. Well, not as I am now. Like I warned you months ago, I'm going to have to give me notice in on the shop. It's hardly making enough to cover the rent these days. Is Rita all right?'

'Aye, she's having a nap, so I thought I'd come down and have a chat with you.'

'It's good of you to look after her for me, lass.'

'I love having her. She's adorable, and so good. Anyroad, while I'm here there's no point in her being under your feet.'

Gracie renewed her effort in rolling the lump, as the huge mound of candy was called. She was on with making some sticks of rock with lettering in them for an order that had come in – one of the rare orders that she received nowadays. This one had come to her because the shop's usual suppliers hadn't enough sugar to meet demand. Most manufacturers were now using fondant instead of sugar. It was a mixture of sugar and fat, but it had to be imported and that meant running the gauntlet of the U-boats, and so came at a price that Gracie couldn't afford. But, she still had her extra supply of sugar from Peggy.

'Oh, Gracie, I'm sorry. I wish that I could've carried on helping you, but with all the talk of women having to go into the munitions, or to help on farms, I panicked. I didn't want to leave Blackpool and start a new life again. And then I heard as they needed women to become tram drivers, and that seemed me best option.'

'Naw, lass, it ain't your fault. I were having a job to find your wages, anyroad. And as for leaving Blackpool, don't you mean not leaving David?'

Jeannie smiled. 'I have news on that front. We were going nowhere. We were just like good friends, then I started to get attention from a soldier as regularly took me tram, and I told David about him. Well, you'd think that I was his wife and had been unfaithful to him, the way that he reacted. He begged me not to leave him. I asked him

353

why he was so worried, and told him that I'd still be his friend. Well, he suddenly grabbed me and kissed me for the first time. It weren't much of a kiss as I weren't ready and me teeth knocked on his.'

Jeannie laughed at this point, and Gracie laughed with her. 'Go on, tell me the rest of it, then.'

'It was a revelation, I can tell yer. We were upstairs in the flat – David had taken to coming for a cup of tea when he'd finished work, as he said that it helped him to unwind – and he was telling me all that had happened during his day.'

'Jeannie, you've the patience of Job. Don't you find all that stuff boring?'

Jeannie looked hurt, and Gracie wished she could take her words back.

'Naw. I don't. I feel honoured that someone thinks me worthy of hearing all about such things, and of understanding the pressure that such a job can give. I've never been used to that from a man. It makes me feel valued.'

'Eeh, I'm sorry, lass. I didn't mean owt ... anyroad. Carry on with your tale.'

'Well, David only does no more than tells me that he loves me and wants to spend the rest of his life with me! I was so shocked that I blurted out to him that he doesn't knaw me, and when he hears what happened to me, he'd hate me. Eeh, Gracie, he was the kindest of men as he persuaded me to tell him.'

'Oh, Jeannie, bless you. What did he do when he heard it all?' Gracie held her breath. She'd have crossed her fingers as well if she could have.

But then the answer had her even more shocked than at what she'd heard so far.

'He held me and cried with me, and then said as he'd like to make love to me the way that I should be made love to, but that he'd never make me, and would wait for ever if it took me that time to accept him doing so.'

Gracie couldn't believe what she was hearing. She'd wondered at times if David had any feelings other than those he gave to his work.

'I don't knaw why, Gracie, as I'd sort of vowed that I wouldn't ever do it again, and was settled with David not bothering with all that, but when that soldier started calling me beautiful and asking me out, sommat awoke in me. And I never thought it would do so for David. But it did. I wanted him to ... and well, you knaw...'

'I'm glad for you, Jeannie. Who'd have thought, eh? David, a romantic at heart.'

'Aye, he is an' all. It were good, really good. Like nowt I've ever known or thought to knaw. And he was careful an' all, to make sure as I weren't caught with a babby. But he wants to have babbies, and so do I, so we're going to get wed, and soon.'

'Oh, Jeannie!' Without warning, Gracie realised that she was going to cry. Her legs went to jelly. Backing towards the chair that stood against the wall of the kitchen, she sat down and buried her head in her hands.

'Naw, naw, lass. Don't take on. I didn't mean to upset you. I thought as you'd be happy for me.'

'I am. Oh, Jeannie, lass, I'm happier than I can tell you. It's just, oh I don't knaw. I'm like this these days. It's me condition, don't take any notice of me.'

'Look as you knaw, Gracie, I'm not on shift until this evening. I was going to go and see Peggy once you got your shop open. But how about I help you get this batch finished, and then we can deliver it to the shop that's ordered it, and you come with me, eh? It won't hurt not to open the shop and Peggy would love to see you, and so would little Bertie. I didn't tell you, with all you have on your plate, but he's not been so well, he's got mumps. Ron got on me tram the other day and he told me. And little Alina is coming down with sommat an' all.'

'Naw! Not me little Bertie?' This news opened the floodgates further, and Gracie thought that she would collapse. That her son should be ill and she didn't even know. Why hadn't Peggy sent a message? But then she could understand why. She'd not want to add to the burden already on Gracie's shoulders.

'Don't take on. He's all right. It's best for lads to get mumps when they're young uns. And he's over the worst, anyroad.'

Using her pinny, Gracie wiped her face. 'Aye, you're right. It's just the thought of him being mine, and yet, not. I have as much love for him as I have for Rita, and me little unborn, but I have to keep me distance. I ain't seen him for over a week, but I just thought as he had stuff to do and he'd come when he was ready. Though that didn't stop me keeping me eye out for him when it got to homecoming time for the schools. And as for Peggy, it must be two months since I saw her. Bertram has been delivering me sugar to me, on his way to the tower, but I haven't had any for over a week.'

'Well then, it'll do you good. And me an' all. I've not been to see her for a couple of weeks and I can't wait to tell her me news.'

'Don't go telling her what you got up to, she'll have a fit.'

'Ha, I won't, I only tell you stuff like that. But don't expect a running commentary. You've heard all you're going to on that front.'

This made Gracie laugh, and when Jeannie joined in with her and gave a little snort as she drew in her breath, they both doubled over in a fit of giggles they couldn't control.

'Eeh, Gracie, you're a one. One minute you're crying your eyes out and the next you're helpless with laughter. I've allus loved the strength of you. You've been an inspiration to me ever since I met you.'

Somehow, they found they were in each other's arms, holding each other tightly. Gracie was the one to make the move to come out of the clinch. 'We've been through the mill all right, Jeannie.'

'Aye, and you're still going through it. It ain't fair.'

'I've a way to go to catch up with what you went through, lass.'

'And you helped me with all of that an' all.'

'Me?'

'Aye, I used to think of your courage. Of how you escaped, and though I wondered how you'd fared, I hung on to it being a possibility. There were times without number that I wished that I'd have gone with you. You gave me the chance, but I was too scared.'

'I landed on me feet, that's for sure, but I was soon knocked down into the gutter again.'

'But that's it. You just seem to accept your lot now, Gracie. You don't fight to get out of it.'

'I've had the fight knocked out of me.'

'I thought you winced when I held you. Has he been at you again?'

Gracie turned and lifted her blouse at the back.

Jeannie's gasp was full of pity. 'I'll bloody swing for him one of these days, if he don't stop beating you. Oh, me Gracie, you don't deserve what comes to you. What riled him this time?'

'The usual. He don't seem to realise that I can't see to his need. Not like this I can't. Anyroad, he's took to going next door this last week, so I've had some peace from his advances, but then I get mad as I feel humiliated, and that starts a fight. But he ain't home much, so it's getting less and less that I have to face the ordeal.'

Peggy welcomed them with open arms. 'Eeh, me lasses, I miss your company. It's nowt but work, work and more work these days. Feeding the men and boys is like trying to keep a furnace alight when you've only got newspaper to stoke it with.'

Gracie laughed. 'Well, I hear as you're doing a good job. No sooner does a young soldier ship out than you have another one billeted with you.'

'I find it hard, I can tell you. I have a pan of stew on the go from morning till night. They come in at all hours. And the evacuee lads from Manchester, they're a handful. City kids have a lot more side to them than our lads. But bless them, it ain't easy being away from their mams. Anyroad, where's me lovely little Rita?'

'She's outside in the pram, fast asleep as usual. By, she could sleep for the Olympics that one. We used her pram for the rock that I had to deliver, and as soon as we put her in it she nodded off.'

'Awe, bless her. Let's have a cuppa, afore she wakes, eh?'

As Peggy busied herself, Gracie carried on the conversation about the evacuees. 'I heard as some of the mothers who had to send their kids away have fetched them back.'

'Aye, I had one here, but I persuaded her to leave him with me. I told her that she could visit when she wants, and I'll try to accommodate her. Anyroad, how are you both? Your time's near, ain't it, Gracie?'

'Another two weeks by my reckoning.'

'And you're still working?'

'Well, not for much longer.' Gracie told Peggy about the shop closing.

'I thought it would come to that, and I'm sorry for you. You've put your heart into that place, Gracie.' Peggy's face showed her concern. 'Look, the shed's still not in use. Have all the equipment and your stock brought back here, then you can start up again in the future. I'm sure Bertram'll find an outlet for your stock. Rock's in big demand still.'

'You mean them black market lot? It's them as have put me out of business. God knaws where they get their supplies.'

'Well then, you may as well profit back from

them. They ain't a bad crowd; they get me many a side of beef, now and again. And I even had some eggs off them the other day.'

'Eggs! Eeh, Peggy, you shouldn't encourage them. If you get caught you could go to prison.'

'You're as bad – you've been buying me excess sugar. We've to keep going as best that we can, and keep our noses to the ground for what we can get. As long as it ain't out of the mouths of babbies, I don't care what comes my way, I'm having some of it.'

Gracie laughed at this. Peggy was right. What they had been doing with the sugar was illegal.

'Talking of me excess sugar, let me knaw if you need any at any time, but mostly, I'll be selling it on the black market meself.'

'Walls have ears, Peggy.'

With this statement from Jeannie, they all laughed. But though she laughed just as loudly, Peggy went to the kitchen door and looked into the hall. 'There's no one about. But you're right. Walls do have ears, and the young lads that are here have some bigger than any. I worry what they might say.'

'Do they give you trouble, Peggy?'

'Naw. I can handle them, and they keep Bertie happy.'

At last Gracie saw her chance. She was always wary of seeming too eager to see Bertie as that upset Peggy. She'd once said: 'Can't you let go yet, lass? Not even though you've got little Rita now?'

'How's Bertie doing? Jeannie told me he wasn't well.'

'You can go up and see him if you like. The lad called Alec is sitting with him. You knaw, it's funny, but none of the evacuee lads have caught it, and I wanted them to. It gets it out of the road for them.'

'Aye, Jeannie were saying that it's not good for them to get it when they're older. I wonder why they haven't caught it?'

'They seem immune to owt. Must be sommat about living in a big industrial city. It hardens them up.'

Gracie was already going through the door to the hall. As she closed the door, she heard Peggy say to Jeannie: 'Lass has still got it bad for Bertie. She don't fool me by not mentioning him. It breaks me heart to see her pining, but I can't give him up. I can't.'

Gracie stood a moment as this had taken the wind out of her sails. But then, Jeannie's answer surprised her: 'You do right, Peggy. You have to keep the lad's best interest at heart, and it won't be in his interest to go to Gracie. Not to live in the atmosphere that she endures. I feel for little Rita when she's older, and for the new babby. What's their lives going to be like living under the same roof as that Reggie? He's a swine. I wish as she'd leave him. I knaw I would.'

Gracie climbed the stairs. *If only it were that simple! Where would I go? How would I fend for me babbies? It's all right for Jeannie, as it was for Sheila, marrying decent men. What choice did I have? What choice do I have now?*

Her stash came to mind. It wasn't much, but over the last months, particularly in the busy

361

times of the early part of the year, she'd kept back all she could. She'd many a time thought to use it to keep the shop going, but then she'd have had no hope for the future, as the writing had been on the wall for the shop closing, in any case. Her fifty pounds wouldn't have saved it – would have been swallowed up in no time. No, it was better that she kept hold of it. Now, it gave her a feeling that she had sommat that might one day help her. *Aye, and the first opportunity that I get, I'll take me chance. I will escape.* Because, like Jeannie had said, she couldn't see her babbies growing up with Reggie as their da.

Bertie looked very pale, but the swelling around his neck wasn't near as bad as she thought it would be. His smile put the sunshine back into her life as he greeted her. His little arms clung to her neck.

'Eeh let me go, lad. You're strangling me.'

'I've missed you, Gracie. I thought you'd come every day, but you didn't.'

'I didn't knaw as you were poorly, or I would have. I found out after Uncle Ron told Jeannie.'

'I'm going to have a ride on Jeannie's tram, Gracie. And I'm taking Alec, and Simon, and Andy and Phil with me.'

'Oh, that'll be good for you all. This is Alec, ain't it?'

'Aye, he stopped off school to look after me as me ma has so much to do. She's allus busy these days.'

'Well, nice to meet you, Alec. Have you settled in all right?'

'I have, but I miss me mam and me sister. Are

you Bertie's sister? You really look like him.'

Gracie's cheeks reddened. 'Naw. I used to live here before I was married. And it's just the colour of his hair that's all. It makes him look like me, when we're not even related. Anyroad, what about your da? You never said that you missed your da.'

'He were killed at Dunkirk, missus. And I do miss him, but I can't let me mind think about him.'

'Oh, I'm sorry. Nobody told me, or I wouldn't have mentioned it.'

'Your man went over to try to save some of the soldiers, didn't he?'

'He did. A lot of fishermen did, as the trawlers were ideal for getting in close to the beach.'

'He's very brave; I'd like to meet him. After all, he may have seen me da.'

Gracie didn't know what to say to this. She'd never thought of Reggie as being brave, but she supposed that he was. He, and all fishermen, took their lives in their hands every time they sailed, what with the threat of U-boat attacks and the real possibility of hitting one of the mines that float around in the sea. Already there had been fifty or so fishing vessels destroyed by these means, and the men lost totalled almost six hundred from ports all around the coast of Britain.

'Yes, he is brave. But I doubt that he saw your da. He said there were hundreds of soldiers to be rescued. And anyroad, if he'd have seen your da, he would have saved him above them all. Your da's a hero, Alec. A hero to be proud of. And when they get around to giving out the medals for them who were on the beaches of Dunkirk, you should wear his with pride.'

'I will. You knaw, I should be looking after me mam for him, an' all. Me dad would expect that of me. She needs me, but the government makes me stay here, and I've naw idea where me sister is, 'cause they won't let her stay at home, either.'

Gracie's heart was heavy for the lad. Her own troubles seemed to pale in comparison to his. He couldn't be more than thirteen years old, and yet he was talking like a man. She only hoped that the war didn't go on long enough for him to become one, and to have to go and fight like his da did.

Bertie became petulant then, something that was out of character for him, but feeling as he was, Gracie didn't tell him off when he chirped in. 'Stop talking to Gracie, Alec. She's come to see me.'

'Ha, you cheeky monkey, you. I look after you all day and now you chuck me out.' Alec rose from the chair he'd been sitting on and moved the puzzle that he and Bertie had been doing together. 'There you go, missus. I expect you could do with a seat. I never thought.'

'Naw. Don't worry. I didn't give you chance to offer. Ta, anyroad. You're right, I could do with a sit down.'

Alec went to say something, which Gracie suspected might be about her condition, but Bertie took her attention. His little hand took hold of hers and he gazed into her eyes. 'I wish you were me sister, Gracie. I love our Sheila, but I allus love you the most.'

Tears prickled Gracie's eyes, but she fought

them back. *How can I ever leave and go as far away as I'd have to to escape Reggie finding me? I could never be away from my dear son. Just to see him occasionally makes up a lot for what I suffer.*

CHAPTER THIRTY-ONE

Bending over the bed to kiss Bertie, Gracie experienced a sudden pain in her back.

'Are you all right, Gracie? Have you wet yourself?'

'Naw, Alec. Me babby's coming. Me waters have broken. I've naw time to explain. Run and fetch Peggy and Jeannie.'

In the early hours of the next morning, delivered on a spare bed in Aggie's flat, little Donna made her appearance, with the intent of waking the household, which, during the long and painful labour, Gracie had tried not to do.

'Eeh, she's a good pair of lungs on her.' Peggy straightened her back. Gracie wanted to tell her to sit down, but knew there was more to be done that Peggy would have to do. 'And she's big an' all, Gracie. I reckon around eight to nine pounds or more. You never looked that big while carrying her, lass.'

Although exhausted, Gracie sat up to try to peep at her babby. 'What colour's her hair?'

'Blooming heck, that's the first question you asked when... I – I mean, well, let me get her

365

cleaned up and then you can see for yourself. Cut the cord, Jeannie, that's right, just there, leave enough for me to tie in a knot. And you get on with pushing the afterbirth out, Gracie, lass, we don't want that inside you for long.'

What seemed like an age later, Gracie finally held her second daughter and saw what they hadn't told her, that little Donna, as she'd long since decided to call her babby if a girl, had bright red hair. 'Eeh, me little bairn, you're beautiful, but I wish you'd stop with your wailing. Here, let's put you to me breast, that might soothe you. It's hungry work coming out of Mummy's tummy, ain't it?'

Donna gave a gurgle that sounded very grumpy, and then latched on to Gracie with a tug that made her wince.

'She's hungry for life that one. Look at her sucking. Eeh, but she's bonny, just like her ma. Well done, lass. You did a good job there.' Gracie smiled up at Peggy, but then cringed as she added: 'Now, you see as you make sure there's no more. You have to learn to not give into them yearnings that take you, and if you do, then be sensible about it. Aggie will tell you how. She's helped many of her trapeze artists to have fun but not to get pregnant. Managed it herself for years, and she's no idea how it did happen when it did, or so she maintains.'

Aggie's advice consisted of a round rubber cap, which Gracie was to insert inside herself before she and Reggie had sex. 'Where can I buy it from, Aggie? I daren't go to the chemist to get one, I'd die of embarrassment.'

'I get you one. I have man who supplies me and has been doing for years. As long as you insert this way, it is as safe as houses.'

Aggie gave a demonstration, which in itself embarrassed Gracie, though she had long known that nothing fazed Aggie. 'Now, is it that you think that you can do that?'

'Aye. I won't let Reggie near me until it's in place. Thanks, Aggie. I wish that you'd told me about it before, I wouldn't be in this mess... Oh, I mean ... not that I would be without me babbies, bless them.'

Jeannie, who'd been in and out of the bedroom as she cleaned up after the birth, came in at that moment. 'That's good, as I have little Rita here. It seems that she had too much sleep during the day. She's had a restless night, and now won't stop crying till she sees you.'

'Awe, come here, little one. Come and meet your sister. There. This is Donna. Isn't she beautiful? That's right, hold her hand, but gently, now.'

Peggy leaned over and helped Rita to take hold of Donna's little hand. 'I'll tell you sommat, Gracie, Donna'll soon catch up in size with Rita. There's only ten months between them, they'll be like twins. Eeh, lass, you're going to have your hands full. You make sure that you take Aggie's advice from now on.'

'What advice is that, then?' asked Jeannie.

'Oh, you missed sommat there, Jeannie.' Gracie giggled, her embarrassment forgotten. 'It's a cap that goes inside you and stops you having babbies.'

'I've heard of them. Will you show me, Aggie,

367

and tell me where to get one?'

'Enough of that, lass. You wait until you're wed. We don't want another one like Gracie – going up the altar with her belly up.'

This, from Peggy, hurt Gracie, bringing to her mind how Peggy had never believed that she was taken down against her will. But a little giggle from Rita took her attention. Looking down she saw that Rita had her arms around Donna and her head laid on her shoulder. It was a picture that Gracie wanted to keep in her head for ever. Her two little girls. And as the love she had for them filled her, she resolved that nothing was ever going to happen to them. *I'll protect you, me little ones. I'll make sure that your life is better than mine. No matter what it takes, I promise you both that.*

Donna's hand broke free from the shawl that Aggie had given her to wrap around her, and reached up towards Gracie. Taking it, Gracie knew that from this moment she'd work towards the pledge that she made her daughters with everything that she had in her. Cradling them both, she laid her head back on the pillow and prayed that God would help her in her quest.

Reggie came to see her on the third day. 'Another girl, eh? I were hoping for a lad. You had a bastard one, why can't you give me a son, an' all?'

'Reggie! Mind what you say. You knaw as Bertie doesn't knaw he's me son. Anyroad, what does it matter, as long as she's healthy?'

'I suppose so. Let me see her then.'

'She's in a drawer on the floor. There were no room in here to put the crib that Alina had when she were little. But she's got all of Alina's babby clothes on. Aggie had kept them all. And all of her nappies, thank goodness. There's been a boiling every day, what with Donna and Rita using them.'

'Donna? I thought we were going to call a girl after me ma?'

'I thought that could be her second name. I did mention to you that I liked the name of Donna, and Rita's got my ma's name for her second name, so I thought we'd do the same.'

Reggie took this in without comment.

'Eeh, she's just like you. Ahh, look at her, she's opened one eye as if she's winking at me. Do yer reckon as she'll wake so as I can hold her?'

This side of Reggie always baffled Gracie. How can a man who could be so violent and so demanding in a sexual way have such tenderness inside him? Because he had and she'd experienced it herself a few times. She smiled at Reggie. 'Pick her up anyway, but be warned, if she ain't wanting you to, she'll yell the place down. She's got your nature, she likes to have her own way.'

As she said the words, Gracie regretted them. Reggie's softness left him. 'Well, good for her, because with a ma like you, she's going to need to stand her ground.'

'Reggie, I didn't mean–'

'I knaw, but that's it with you, ain't it? You don't mean a lot of things, but you can hurt folk with that tongue of yours. Anyroad, how long are you staying here? You should be in our bed at home, where you can look after me needs. You don't realise what it's like for me at sea for three weeks at a time without it.'

369

'Me tongue may run away with itself, but it ain't wrong, is it? Hark at you, you're already thinking of making your demands. Well, I won't ever come home unless you promise to leave me be for a few weeks. I need to recover.'

'Well, if that's how it's going to be, I knaw where to go. Shirley's been very accommodating, and she'll carry on being. She knaws a few tricks an' all. She knaws how to please a man. You seem to have forgotten the basics of how it's done.'

'I don't care, Reggie. You can go and live with Shirley for all I care, and she's welcome to you.'

At this, Reggie sat down on the bottom of the bed. Gracie could see he was close to tears. If she lived to be a hundred, she doubted that she'd ever understand him. 'I'm sorry, Reggie, I didn't mean that. It does bother me that you have Shirley as your mistress, but I'll put up with it, as long as you are discreet about it, and you leave me alone.'

'Will you ever want me like you used to, Gracie? I miss that. I do. We were good. Better than I ever have with Shirley, and I felt loved by you.'

It was no use telling him again that he'd caused the rift between them. He had no understanding of how, and didn't see anything wrong with his actions. To him it was all her fault. But she'd rather have him as he was now than upset him again, so she played along.

'Aye. Maybe after I'm recovered. We'll try. I've sommat to tell you of. I reckon as it will help me be more relaxed.'

His reaction to the birth control surprised her. 'It ain't right to interfere with nature, Gracie. I'd rather you didn't use it.'

'But, we can't keep having a babby every year, Reggie. I don't want to get so that we're living hand to mouth.'

'You're not natural like other women. You don't want to stop being the businesswoman to stay at home and see to your man and your family.'

'I've lost me shop, Reggie. It failed. I couldn't compete with the big boys, not under the conditions of rationing. I lost me orders from me out-sales, and we're down to just making novelties with the little sugar that I could get. The bigger factories can afford to use fondant from abroad, but I can't.'

'I can't say as I'm sorry. I'm glad to hear it. I should never have agreed to let you carry on. And as for living in that flat, it near killed me. We're in our rightful place now, among our own. And you can get it out of your head that you're a Blackpool lass, because you're not, Gracie, you're a fisherman's daughter from Fleetwood. And now, you're a fisherman's wife – at least, one as keeps the fisherman's trawler going. And the sooner you start to behave like one the better me and you will fare.'

Gracie wanted to scream at him that she had nothing but bad memories of being a Fleetwood fisherman's daughter, and that she didn't want the same for her daughters. But what was the use? 'Pick your daughter up then, Reggie. Say a proper hello to her. She's about ready for her feed anyroad.'

Once more Reggie returned to the gentle person that she knew he could be. His tenderness as he picked up Donna warmed her heart. Donna had no such tenderness to give back. She immediately screamed out with such force that she passed wind loudly at the same time. Reggie put his head back and laughed out loud. Gracie couldn't help but join him, and in some way, as it always was, their laughter was a healing for them.

It was when Donna was noisily sucking away that a small tension crept into Gracie once more.

'Eeh, she's a lucky lass. I wish it were me sucking your nipples, Gracie.'

'Not in front of your daughter, Reggie.' Gracie said this with a little giggle, and Reggie took it well, though his hand did reach out and stroke her breast, and his eyes misted over. Gracie allowed it, fearing his temper flaring once more. She wished she could feel as she used to when he was tender like this, but inside was a cold knot that she couldn't undo. 'Stop now, Reggie, someone might come in.'

'Stop? I want to lay beside you and have you see to me with your hand. Will you do that, Gracie?'

'Naw, Reggie. Not here, I can't. I...' The sound of over loud footsteps and an exaggerated cough had him sitting up and moving away from her, back to the bottom of the bed. Jeannie came in carrying Rita. 'She knaws as you're here, Reggie, she must have sensed it, as she was playing quite happily and then became fractious pointing to the door.'

Reggie looked panicky. Gracie guessed that he daren't stand up as the bulge in his trousers would show.

'Awe, come and sit on the bed, me little Rita,' she said. 'Only don't think as you can feed an' all.

I'm too sore.'

Reggie's voice sounded normal again as he asked, 'Is that what she's been trying to do, then?'

'Aye, she's not forgotten that this was her watering hole until very recently. She's a little minx. But she doesn't object to Donna, she just tries to get my other one out.'

'Ha! Come here, Rita, me little darlin'. Come and give Daddy a cuddle.'

With these words from Reggie, memory reared up in Gracie, and though she knew that it was unfair of her to think it, she knew a moment when she wanted to grab Rita from Reggie, but she stopped herself. Her stomach turned over and she thought she was going to be sick. Swallowing hard, she controlled the feeling.

'I'll bring you both a cup of tea, the pot's on the go as usual. Then I've to go to work. When Alec ran to the tram depot last night, they only agreed to me having one night off.'

'Are you taking a tram to Fleetwood, Jeannie?'

'Aye, Reggie, me first run's out of the depot at six.'

'I'll be on it, then. I've to get back in case I'm called out.'

After Jeannie had left the room, Reggie played with Rita, making her giggle and keeping her attention until Donna had taken her fill. The feeling that had visited Gracie came back. Taking Donna from her, Reggie held her a moment. This upset Rita like Gracie had never seen her. Her reaction was out of character, as she screamed, 'Da-da ... Da!'

Reggie lay Donna down and took Rita in his

arms. 'Hey, you'll allus be me special little girl, darlin'. You're Daddy's little girl and allus will be, me little Rita.'

Rita stopped crying immediately and giggled at him as he rubbed her hand along his stubbly chin. 'There, you like that, don't yer?'

The bile came up into Gracie's throat. Swallowing the acid liquid stung her throat and made her cough. Jeannie came in at that moment with a mug of tea for each of them.

'Eeh, lass, are you choking? Have a sip of this tea. That's right. What happened?'

Gracie couldn't speak, but shook her head. Her eyes were full of tears, and the movement had them running down her face. They weren't crying tears, though she felt like sobbing her heart out, for hadn't she been catapulted back to a past that she'd didn't want to remember? And something deep in her told her that her past could be Rita's future. *Naw! Naw! I'll never let that happen.*

With this thought, a determination came into her that somehow she would get away from Reggie. Somehow, she would protect her daughters. Even if it cost her her life.

When Reggie had gone, Gracie tried to get the thoughts out of her head. Not all men interfered with children. Reggie hadn't shown any of those inclinations. Women were his forte, and she guessed that he'd go to Shirley the minute he got home.

Thinking of him going home, she wondered why he had to catch the tram, but then, he was probably short of petrol. Everything was difficult to come by these days. Life itself was difficult.

Everyone was feeling the pinch, and it looked set to get worse. *I wish that I could help in some way. So many women are doing their bit.* A guilt entered Gracie, as she thought of the extra sugar she'd used to help her make a profit. *I'm no better than the black market lads. Well, I'll look for ways as I can help folk from now on. It'll help me to have sommat to focus on.*

Her bedroom door burst open as she lay back, bringing Gracie to a sitting-up position. She stared at Peggy as she told her in an anguished voice, 'Eeh, Gracie, Gracie, they've gone and done it. The bloody Germans have set London alight.'

'What? How?'

'Air raids, hundreds and hundreds of bombs have been dropped. The news on the wireless is full of it.'

'Aw, naw. Awe, Peggy, it feels like the end of the world. Them poor Londoners. I wish we could help them.'

'The Red Cross have put an appeal out over the radio. They need food, clothes, blankets, well, owt as anyone can spare. We've to do all we can, but don't be worrying, lass. We're safe here.'

'I do worry, though, Peggy. How can we think of ourselves as safe? They've already dropped one bomb that landed in North Shore, all be it didn't do any damage, but surely they'll target us, and look at what damage they could do. We've got hundreds of servicemen here, and Vickers factory where they make fighter planes, two airfields ... it beggars belief that they haven't flattened us by now.'

'That's scaremongering talk, Gracie, and we

mustn't give in to it. We've to think of them Londoners and to keep our chins up. No bloody Hitler's going to ruin our Blackpool. He'll have me to contend with if he tries.'

Four days later, Peggy was to eat her words. A bomb, targeting North Shore railway station, killed eight nearby residents in Seed Street.

With it happening within her rest period of fourteen days after the birth of Donna, that was the normal practice but frustrated Gracie, she was unable to do anything to help the stricken, but the incident reaffirmed her resolve to do something to help those affected by this horrible war.

CHAPTER THIRTY-TWO

The shed in Gracie's back yard, which, till now, they'd never used, had in the eight weeks since Donna had been born become a store for everything and anything that Gracie could collect as a result of her numerous appeals, made through the *Gazette* and by word of mouth.

Blankets were stacked high, as were tins of Spam, and old kettles and pots and pans, crockery and clothes. The latter were sorted into female and male and babbies and children.

Some of the stockpile spilled into the attic as Rita's and Donna's cots didn't take up too much of the space.

The women of the row, even Shirley, came around whenever they were needed to help sort what should be sent where and to parcel it all up. Most went to London. The railway companies shipped it to the Red Cross free of charge. This operation usually happened when Reggie was in dock as they would get hold of what petrol they could and he would take the parcels to the station.

'It's a grand job that you're doing, Gracie. You have such a head for organising everything.'

'Ta, Mrs Parsons.'

'Jenny, call me Jenny, love. You're all grown up, and a mother yourself, you shouldn't be calling us all Mrs, not now.'

Mrs Wincelet chirped in: 'Aye, and call me Gertie. Everyone else calls me that, and you're one of us once more, Gracie. And I join Jenny here in singing your praises. You've made us all feel that we are doing sommat to help the war effort, lass.'

With this, Mrs Pike, the last person Gracie would ever think of calling by anything other than her proper name, said, 'Aye, and I'm Dot, only don't ever be calling me Dotty – one woman did and had her lugs boxed.'

Gracie laughed, as they all did.

'I'll never call you that, and it'll be a bit difficult for me to use all of your Christian names at first as I've known you by your married names all me life. But I'd like to and'll get used to it.'

'Right, that's settled, so, what are we up to today, Gracie?'

'Well, Mrs ... Dot, I thought I might talk to you all about us having roles. You've allus been the one to organise this kind of thing when we've had disasters in this town, and I reckon that although we've not done too badly up to now with this

377

operation, we need some sort of structure, rather than everyone wondering what they will be needed to do.'

Dot's smile showed how grateful she was to be asked to play a major role and be back in the driving seat, so to speak. 'Well, lass, I didn't want to interfere, but I do have experience as you say, and this has become a lot bigger than you, or any of us first thought. I think that, yes, whilst them down in London do need our help, and we'll allus give it, that there are a lot on our own doorstep – the fishing community – that need help an' all. There's been boats lost at sea and hundreds of fishermen's lives lost all around the coastline of Britain, and most of the boats have at some time been in and out of our port. We need to find a way of getting aid to them.'

'That would be wonderful, but a massive task. Could we really do both? And how would we reach them, or, even gather enough of everything to distribute?'

Dot didn't seem concerned about distribution. 'Reaching them wouldn't be a problem. The Red Cross works all over the country, not just in London. As soon as we hear of a disaster, we could send aid to that area.'

'Aye, and I read sommat the other day, Gracie, where the local Red Cross will pick up from anyone who has owt.'

'Really?' said Dot. 'Eeh, Gertie, I didn't knaw that. That'd be grand. It would save us such a lot of work.'

Gracie agreed. What a blessing just to get everything ready and have it collected. 'If we're to expand in this way, I reckon as we need somewhere as a storage depot, and as I've mentioned before, we will need to increase our stock levels.'

'Well, I think that you're all thinking too big. We're only a few women in a fishing port as is as busy as it's ever been, and we have to support our men. I reckon as we should choose. Support for them going through the Blitz, or support for our own – the fishermen around the coast.' This from Ethel, another volunteer who hadn't spoken before, but had been quietly carrying on with sorting bags of clothes, had them all falling silent.

Gracie realised that Ethel was right. 'I agree. It's a wonderful idea, but we could be setting ourselves up to fail. I think that we've done all that can be expected of us for the poor folk of London, and now it's time to look to our own.'

Shirley, who always kept her head down, doing what was asked of her, but not joining in with the banter, surprised them as she spoke up, 'I vote to look after our own an' all. I were only a nipper when me da were drowned at sea. We lived in Grimsby at the time. And it were only the help that we received that got me and me ma through. And that was from our own. Communities like this one. It enabled us to seek a new life in Black-pool and we never looked back.'

No one spoke for a moment, most ignored Shirley, not liking the way she carried on around their menfolk. Gertie broke the awkward silence, 'Aye, and it's a pity that you didn't keep looking forward, Shirley, instead of up at the bloody ceiling, then we could all have a bit of peace from your antics.'

379

The tension in the room gave an atmosphere that Gracie didn't know how to cope with, but suddenly Shirley put her head back and laughed out loud. This set them all off, but though Gracie joined in, the comment had been a bit too close to home for her, and she couldn't dispel the embarrassment it had caused her. She covered up by bringing the conversation back to the business in hand. 'Right, is everyone in agreement?'

All said, 'Aye.'

'Well, then,' Gracie told them, 'that's our new mission. And I reckon as our first batch should go to Shirley's home town. To Grimsby – they've had more than their fair share of losses.'

Shirley smiled. Gracie couldn't smile back.

'And I'll contact the Red Cross and see if taking our stock to where we want it to go is sommat they can do for us.'

'Ta, Gertie.'

Dot spoke up again. Having been given the lead, she seemed bent on keeping it. Gracie didn't mind – she had a lot on her plate with her babbies to care for. 'Well, that's settled then. And I reckon as we carry on as we have been, but if the load gets too much, then we look for somewhere to store all of the stuff and to work out of. And I've a few ideas of how we can raise the money for that, though we might find a businessman who'd let us have some space for free. I'll look into all of that.'

'And I've got a good contact an' all.' Shirley, who seemed emboldened now that she was accepted, told of a man she knew who had a printing press. 'I'll get him to make us some posters. We can get the lads to take them around all the village shops and into Blackpool an' all. Most have got bikes, so it won't harm them. We can ask for donations of owt anyone can spare.'

'And how will we knaw when they have owt for us, or even be able to collect them?'

'I hadn't thought of that, Gracie.'

'I reckon we could get George Digby to help.' Dot seemed to be able to work most things out and now told them of her idea. 'He's got a van. And he allus does owt for the fishermen's charities. We'll have to be precise with our posters. For instance, we do an area at a time, and put a poster in the best place, where we think it will be seen. So, if we're going to do Poulton, we put it in a shop there, and it says that the van will be parked on a certain pub car park between such and such hours for folk to bring what they can spare.'

'That's grand.' Gracie felt a smile coming from the bottom of her heart. 'Eeh, ladies, I reckon as we'll have a good, workable operation, and one that we can keep going for as long as it's needed. Ta, all. I'll put the kettle on.'

'It's all down to you, Gracie. You started all of this. And in doing so, you've given us all a purpose, a sense of us helping others in these terrible times.'

'Ta, Dot, but I couldn't have done it without you all.' Gracie had already put the kettle on the grate, and now reached down for their communal tin of tea. From the beginning, they'd all agreed that they would contribute to the supply of tea, saccharin and milk so that she wouldn't be out of pocket, or use up her rations on them.

'And I've brought a treat along, I've baked some jam tartlets. Made with me own jam, and it's been in me stock cupboard from before the war, so it were made using real sugar!'

There was a collective, 'ooh, ta Gertie', accompanied by a determined yelling from Donna. Rita had played happily in her playpen, gurgling away, and practising the tentative steps that she'd begun to take. Donna was outside in the pram where Gracie had hoped she would sleep for a while. But an hour is all she'd managed.

'I'll get her.'

Gracie wanted to tell Shirley no. She didn't want the woman touching her children, but it would have been petty to refuse her, and might even highlight to the others the humiliation she felt at the part the woman played in her marriage. She'd found that the best way to handle the situation was to carry on as if she was oblivious to it. Secretly she was glad that Reggie could go to Shirley. With him being away such a lot since Donna's birth, there hadn't been many times that she'd had to fight him off. When she had, he'd gone next door and she'd had to cover her ears to the sounds of the pleasure her husband found there.

This was all something she knew she couldn't do if she loved Reggie. But with her hate of him growing, it was only her pride that hurt.

On many long, lonely evenings and nights, Freddie would come to Gracie's mind. She'd had letters from Sheila, telling her that he still pined for her and begged of them to tell him what had gone wrong. Sheila begged in turn to be allowed to tell him, but Gracie always refused. She was caught between the need for him to know that she hadn't just abandoned him and her even greater need to protect him. Letting him find out she'd been sullied once more would be the ultimate pain she could inflict on him. She had to leave him to think that she'd just not wanted to join him in Canada and had chosen to end their relationship instead. That way, he had a chance of getting over her and finding someone else.

When Shirley came in carrying Donna, Jenny Parsons embarrassed them all once more. She was a woman who spoke her mind, no matter what. 'You've never had young uns of your own, Shirley. How've managed that then, with your antics?'

'I – I lost three to miscarriage, and then I were told as I'd never have any. It broke me heart. Look, I knaw as you all knaw me ways, but you'd all have a lot more trouble from your men if I weren't here, I can tell yer.'

Gracie froze. *Did Shirley go with all of their men? Even the older ones amongst us?*

After a moment, Shirley laughed. 'Ha, that shut you up, didn't it, Jenny, and I reckon as what I get up to is none of your business, so you should shut up and stop spoiling this gathering for everyone. This is sommat as has brought us all together, and no one else objects to me being here, so why should you keep sniping at me, eh? And you can all stop catching flies. She just riled me. I didn't mean as I've been with all your men.'

Naw, only mine. Gracie sighed. She had to tackle this. 'I think that all of us either make Shirley welcome despite undercurrents, or we ask her not to join us, but to keep sniping at her and embarrassing us all has to stop. I for one want her to carry on helping us and for her private life to stay just that.'

'Well, that's rich coming from you, Gracie.'

'Jenny! We'll have none of that.' This from Dot shut Jenny up. 'And I'm for her staying. There's a war on, and if Gracie can take her being here, then we all should.'

Gracie wished the floor would open up and swallow her. She didn't want this woman in her house, she wanted to hate her, but couldn't. Yes, she wanted to keep her at arm's length, but she'd chosen to deal with this as if she was innocent of the goings on, and now she had to stick by it.

'Let's all enjoy me cakes, eh? We've a grand set-up here, and nowt should spoil it.'

'I agree, Gertie. I for one am looking forward to having a treat. But, if none of you mind, I'll have to feed our Donna. She's quiet at the mo, but she'll yell the place down if I keep her waiting.'

With this, Gracie put the teapot amongst the cups laid out on her table and took Donna from Shirley. A look passed between them that Gracie knew was an acknowledgement of each other's role with Reggie, but she didn't care. Her position was as it was, and she had the more important task of feeding her child to think of.

Sitting in Reggie's rocking chair, she adjusted herself and fed Donna. Her noisy sucking had them all laughing and eased the tension.

The postman was late that day, and when Gracie

384

saw the letters that had come for her, she was glad for it. The ladies had washed up the teacups and plates, and left everything tidy before they'd left. Donna slept happily in her pram and Rita was curled up on the sofa, sucking her thumb and drifting off for her afternoon nap. The house had a peace about it that Gracie welcomed.

Gracie ripped open the letter, disappointed at how thin the one from Sheila was, but she would read it before Rory's that was inside the envelope, too.

After the usual greeting and asking after her health, Sheila had written:

I'm missing you, and Jeannie, and it goes without saying – me ma, da and everyone. But I am so happy. I have news that might surprise you, but then again, you don't need legs to make babbies. Aye, I'm pregnant. Five months gone. Bob is over the moon. And, guess what, his ma came to visit, and left to ourselves, we broke the barriers down between us and got on like a house on fire. Bob's that happy about it.

And he loves being of use to the war effort, it's made all the difference to him.

Well, that's us.

Me other news ain't going to help you none, but I have to tell you. It breaks me heart to do so, but Freddie is getting engaged. I'm so sorry. He met this Canadian girl, and strangely, she looks a lot like you by the photo he took of them together.

Gracie dropped the letter on to her lap. Pain pierced her heart with an unbearable agony that took her breath from her. *Naw, Naw ...* but then, what had she expected? That he'd remain single and never pick up with another woman?

Standing up, she paced the floor. *Freddie, my Freddie. You're lost to me for ever now.* And as the thought came to her, she realised that a small part of her had always hoped that somehow it would all come right. She'd always been happy that Freddie was safe. That he wasn't in the firing line. And relieved that he was thousands of miles away so that there was no chance that he could look her up.

Slumping back in the chair, Gracie tried to control her anguish. She picked up the letter once more.

I know that you won't wish him anything but a happy life, and as he can't have you, then we hope that this lass brings him that happiness.

Gracie's heart wouldn't let her be that generous, not yet. She wanted the girl to not exist at all. She wanted her Freddie free, just in case.

Bob and I hope that you can find it in yourself, me lovely friend, to give us sommat to tell Freddie. He has been desolate over the break up with you, and he least deserves that. And we'd like him to go forward and know that it wasn't his fault.

Gracie suddenly realised with these words how selfish she had been. She had never thought that Freddie would take the blame on to his shoulders, or even thought of him being desolate.

Try to find it in your heart to let us tell him sommat of what happened to you, please, Gracie.

Well, to change the subject. We were so happy that the birth of your babby went well, and hope that your little Donna is thriving, and that Rita too is doing well.

Write soon. All my love, your friend, Sheila.

Wishing that she'd read Rory's first, she laid the letter on her lap and opened the one from him.

It seemed that he was enjoying his war. He was now part of the crew of a hospital ship, and so felt that he was a lot safer than when he was when training on a freight line.

Hospital ships are protected by the Geneva Convention, not that that means owt to the Germans, so we are always on our guard.

I had the sad news that Suzy died. It broke me heart, Gracie, but led to me making a special friend. One of the nurses on board. She was having a cigarette on deck when she heard me sobs and came over to offer me some comfort. Her name's Pat. How funny is that after us making a joke about this possibility?

Anyroad, love, write soon, I haven't had a letter for a long time. Nowt from Sheila, or Jeannie, but it especially hurts me with nowt coming from you. You know what a special place you have in me heart. I need to know that you are all right.

My love always, darling Gracie.

Rory x

Though her heart still hurt, Gracie smiled. It was good to know that Rory had made a new

387

friend, and she was glad that he hadn't revealed the true nature of the friendship in writing. She always worried about him being caught, he was so flamboyant, and would raise suspicion easily. And who knew who read these letters from him? They never looked freshly folded, but as if others had handled them first. *Oh, Rory, keep safe. Don't take any chances. I can't bear for owt to happen to you.* But then her smile returned as she remembered how Rory had said he would disguise any man friend by using a female name in his letters. And the very example he'd made had been Pat, for Patrick!

CHAPTER THIRTY-THREE

With the warmth from the fire and the peacefulness of the house, Gracie found herself drifting off to sleep. She always felt tired these days, but then Donna kept her awake most of the night.

An anguished, 'What the – bloody hell? I knew it! You, cow!' shocked her awake. Reggie stood staring down at her. In his hand he had her letter from Sheila.

Fear clenched her heart.

'So, you still get news of that RAF bloke then? You told me it was over.'

Trying to clear her brain of the fog that sleep had left on it, Gracie couldn't think what to say.

'Well? How long have you been getting news of what he's up to, then? And what does Sheila want to tell him? There's nowt that's his business about me wife. Nowt!'

'Oh, Reggie, don't take on so. The letter confirms that I've had nowt to do with Freddie since we got together. I can't help that he is still pining. Sheila wants to tell him why I gave him up. Well, you can see that from the letter, but I don't think that I should. I broke off our relationship and that's that.'

'And what about this poncy bloke? That Rory, what's he doing telling you such sloppy stuff, eh?'

'He don't mean nowt by it, it's the way he talks.'

'Blokes like him make me feel sick. I don't like you around them. They can get into trouble, and rightly so. I've a good mind to report him.'

'Naw, Reggie. Don't do that. He's never done you any harm. He's a seaman, like you, doing his bit for the country.'

'Aye, well, I bet he has a better welcome home than I get.'

'He hasn't made it home, yet. And what d'yer expect when you attack me the moment you walk in the door?'

Reggie sat down at the foot of the sofa next to Rita's legs. 'I'm tired, that's all. Tired of the lot of it. I never knaw how you're going to be with me, and it drives me crazy when I'm not here.'

'You've no need to worry, what with the kids to look after, and me work for charity, I'm kept too busy to get into mischief. Now let me get you your bath. I'll not be a mo.'

When she rose, Reggie got to his feet. Before she could move away, he clutched her arm and pulled her close to him. 'You looked lovely sitting there with your eyes closed. All I could hear when I came in was the clock ticking, and little Rita snoring. It gave me a good feeling, to look at you all – me family, safe and cared for.'

Gracie wasn't sure what this was about. Or whether something was about to boil his temper, so she stayed quiet.

'That's how I want me life to be. I want to come home, to find you all like that. But then I read sommat about your past, and it all starts up again.'

'Reggie, that's what it is. Me past. It's gone, it's over.'

'Oh, Gracie. I've wanted you since we were nippers. I want it all to be right between us.' His lips came close to hers. She could smell that he'd been drinking, and he reeked of stale cigarette smoke. But above these was the smell of fish that always hung around him when he came in from a trip. She turned her head from the odour.

'Don't turn from me. I'll not do owt as yer don't want. I've been thinking about everything, and you're right. I'm to blame. I've not treated yer right. Well, I want to make a fresh start. I want to put everything right.'

This shocked Gracie. She didn't know how to handle it. Was it a trick? A new tactic, just to get her to let him do as he pleased with her?

'I mean it, love.' He bent forward and kissed her cheek. His hand tapped her bottom. 'Go on, then, get me bath ready. I don't feel fit to touch you while I'm in this state. I'll get cleaned up first.'

This was a new Reggie, one she hadn't known for a long time, but even then, different to before. Gracie didn't know how to cope. Her nerves

390

jangled as she went about the task of getting his bath ready for him.

Once bathed, he dressed without approaching her. His conversation was all about his experiences on the boat. What this man had said and what that one had. He'd been to Iceland and back without encountering a single U-boat or having to negotiate a mine, and he was relieved about that. He asked after the children, and when Rita woke he played with her, before nursing the screaming Donna for a while, until Gracie had their dinner on the go. As always, he'd brought some fish home with him, and Gracie had some tatties to boil and mash to go with it.

While these were cooking she sat and fed Donna. Reggie fed Rita with the rusk that Gracie had mashed into hot milk. Every now and then Reggie glanced at her, but didn't make any lewd remarks about wishing it was him sucking her breasts. The while, Reggie had a gentle smile on his face.

Gracie was at a loss to explain this change, and began to relax and enjoy being with him and the children. At last, it felt as though they were a proper family.

'I've only got the night, Gracie. I've to report again in the morning. There's naw let up. But then, most of our number joined up, either the merchants or the Royal Navy, and a lot of the trawlers were requisitioned, so that puts a lot on our shoulders. I've been helping with hauling the fish in so that we can make haste out of the waters. We daren't linger too long anywhere.'

From the relaxed state they were in, Gracie

tensed when Reggie suggested an early night. As she followed him upstairs, she wondered if she should put her protection in place. She'd fought with him about it the last time, but he'd given in. Bringing the subject up left her open to him thinking that she wanted him, but not bringing it up meant she risked making him mad if he started his games and she stopped him to mess with the contraption.

Unsure, she began to undress. In the corner of the room there was a screen, behind which sat the goes-under. It was another thing that Aunt Massie had left her, as she told her that a woman should keep a little privacy around such matters as having a pee at night.

Going behind it, Gracie began the process of inserting the cap.

'What're you up to, Gracie? I can't hear you having a pee. You're not putting that thing in, are you?'

'I won't be a minute, Reggie. Don't worry about it.'

'I do worry. I want you to leave it out.'

She heard him get off the bed. Afraid of upsetting him, she shoved the cap under the pile of clothes at her feet. As she stood, her breast came free from her shift. 'Eeh, lass. You're beautiful. Come here.'

'Reggie, let me—'

'Naw, don't ask that of me. I want you as you should be. You're me wife, and I want you to obey me in this, lass.'

Still his tone was gentle. At this moment, she'd rather he was aggressive so that she could fight her corner.

His hand came out to her. This Reggie confused her. She took his hand. Without resisting, she went with him to the bed and accepted him lying her down and getting in beside her. 'Get the covers over us, Gracie, it's freezing in here. That's right, snuggle up to me. By, your toes are cold.'

His leg came over her. His lips came down on hers. Something stirred inside of her, something that had been dead for a long time. She didn't resist as he explored her body. Instead she arched towards him. Feelings that she welcomed flowed through her, warming the whole of her, and giving her a sense of wanting what Reggie was doing.

'Eeh, me lass, me lass.'

The deep tone to his voice thrilled her. Without her bidding, a moan escaped her. Her breath came in short pants, her throat felt tight. Sensations zinged through her. Her hands seemed to have a mind of their own as they caressed him, finding his manhood and thrilling at the feel of him.

When he at last climbed on top of her and entered her, a forgotten explosion of feelings had her crying out the joy of them as they built to an unbearable level, and she begged of Reggie to stop and to just hold her. He couldn't. His own climax was on him, and he thrust harder until she thought that she would die. Together, they rode the wave of ecstasy. Then together, they sobbed as they clung to one another.

In the silence that followed, Gracie had a moment's fear that she'd allowed this without protecting herself, but then a feeling of not caring came over her. If this was how it could be in the future, maybe she could grow to like Reggie again and, who knows, love could follow. She hoped so. She was trapped now, and a lifetime of hate and fighting wasn't what she wanted.

Reggie cradled her to him. 'We can make things better, can't we, eh, Gracie? Like it used to be. Eeh, lass, I love you. I do. I'd never bother with her next door if we could be like this.'

Gracie wished that he hadn't mentioned Shirley, but she had to accept that his affair with her had been in the open, and yes, with her consent. 'I'd like us to be like this all of the time, Reggie. We can try. We can.'

'I'll go tomorrow with a happy heart, me Gracie. But, eeh, you've drained me, so I'll have to turn over and go to sleep now. I'll try not to wake you in the morning as I've to leave at three.'

'Ha, I'll most likely be awake with Donna. She never gives me a full night's sleep.' With this, Gracie turned over herself and snuggled down. She didn't let her mind go over the news that she'd had today. That would spoil her enjoying the after feelings still giving her pleasure. Instead, she yawned a contented yawn and fell into a deep sleep.

When Gracie woke the next morning, a feeling of disorientation cloaked her. She couldn't remember waking since... *Oh God! What time is it? I didn't hear Reggie go. Donna! Why hasn't she woken?*

Scrambling out of bed, Gracie dashed to Donna's cot. Relief filled her as she saw her daughter sleeping soundly. A smile developed into a little giggle. *Eeh, little lass has gone through her first night. And about time, too!*

Memory gave her what had happened the night before, and her heart filled with hope. If she had to live with Reggie, then how much better it would be to have him as he was last night. And it could happen. Now that he'd awoken her feelings again, it could happen.

Something of a happiness warmed Gracie through. It was tentative, and she wondered if it would last, but the future looked much brighter than the past had. That is until she got back into bed and the awful truth of Freddie being engaged to someone else hit her. It was as if a huge gulf of emptiness opened up inside her, and she crumbled.

If only Reggie hadn't had to go away. Maybe he could have kept her from this dreadful mourning. But then, maybe she had to go through it to heal from it. With this thought, Gracie let her whole body weep her despair.

It was six o'clock the next evening that the news came in. The *Appleton*, the trawler that Reggie had gone out on, had been destroyed by a mine earlier that day, and all crew had been lost.

Gracie stood in the street with the other women, shivering from cold, fear and shock. Where she could, she gave comfort, but there was no consoling Dot. Two of her brood of seven had been on the boat. Joe was distraught, walking around his mother as Gracie held her.

For herself, she couldn't cry. Everything inside her felt as though it had closed down. Only the night before, she'd rediscovered the old Reggie, and now he was gone. The cruelty of that mingled with the shock of finding herself a widow. A single woman, once more. She couldn't comprehend it.

A sudden wail, louder than any the women were making had her turning. 'Aunt Massie. Oh, Ma.' Letting go of Dot, Gracie ran to Massie. Massie clung to her. 'Naw, naw, Gracie, don't let it be true. Don't let it.'

This triggered Gracie's tears, and she felt glad of the release. 'Come inside, Ma.' It came so easy to call her Aunt Massie this. 'Come on. It's freezing out here.'

'Naw,' said Gertie. 'All come to mine. Let's stay together. I haven't lost anyone, but I feel your pain. I've some of me homemade elderberry wine – that'll help you all.'

'Ta, Gertie. Go with Gertie, Ma. I'll fetch the babbies.'

Gertie's small front room was crowded with crying women. The men stayed outside, their breath vaporising in the cold air. The crate of beer with which they sought to drown their sorrows caused a swishing noise as they clipped the tops off the bottles. Gracie looked around at these folk as she'd grown up with, and their expressions of grief were familiar to her. They'd all shouldered loss over the years, as she herself had. And this was how they coped. Grouping together, drinking away their sorrows and stopping each other from falling.

Gradually, couples left, huddled together, to take their grief into their own homes. Massie and Percy had said that they would stay the night. They wouldn't leave Gracie on her own. But they might as well have, as their grief, and the drink they'd consumed, had them going out like a light, snuggled up in her bed. Gracie made a makeshift up on the sofa, and kept Rita with her, and Donna in her pram beside her. Her body hadn't stopped shaking since the news, but she hadn't let herself think it all through. Now in the dark, she did.

Reggie was gone. He was really and truly gone. Just a couple of days ago she would have welcomed this news. Now she couldn't take it in and had a knot of sadness inside her for what might have been.

Then the worry started to set in. They'd want her out of the cottage. Where would she go? How would she manage to feed and look after the babbies? No answers would come to her. Yet again, a promise of a new life had been snatched from her. What would the future hold now?

At last, she fell into a fitful sleep, only to wake a few hours later, feeling a heavy weight on her shoulders. Her mind began to plot over and over. *Maybe I could use the shed again to make rock?* Funnily enough, the rock business was still booming. Folk couldn't get enough of Blackpool Rock. *It must be the sweetness that folk are missing. Well, I can pander to that. I could contact the black market boys and sell through them.*

The last time she had visited Peggy, there was talk of the evacuees being allowed home. *Perhaps I could move back into mine and Sheila's old room – it's big enough for me and two cots.* With these thoughts a trickle of hope entered her and she began to plan out a life without Reggie. And as bad as it seemed, she knew a big part of her to be relieved.

She'd always remember how he was the night before he lost his life and try to forget the horror of her past years with him. He deserved that much. Anyone deserved that much.

CHAPTER THIRTY-FOUR

The letter from Rory made her smile, though she sought to put him right in her reply.

Eeh, Gracie, I was that glad to receive your letter – so the bullyboy is no more, three cheers! At least Hitler got something right. And so, now you can marry me! We'll be so happy. I can do the housework, while you make the money. Life will be full of fun and laughter.

I don't know how I'll do in the bedroom department, I've not had much experience, as you know, but I know that I could learn and could do so with you as my feelings are so deep for you – I pine for you. Anyroad, you can teach me where all the important bits are. It'll be fun!

Gracie dropped her hands into her lap and laughed out loud.

'Well, that's a good sound, lass. What's so funny?'

Peggy joined her in the laughter when she read out what Rory had said. 'Eeh, he's a one. He wouldn't knaw one end of a woman's body from the other.'

'Oh, Peggy, don't! I feel irreverent laughing like

398

this when me man's only been gone a few weeks.'

'Well, it's good to see. And you've nowt to feel guilty about. I have though, Gracie. Can you ever forgive me? I haven't said, but I put you in that position of having to marry that brute of a man.'

'Naw. There were nowt else as you could do. It happened and that was that. All I ever wanted was for you to believe me. I've naw need now to say that Reggie took me against me will, unless it were true. But that's what did happen, Peggy. I swear.'

'Aw, me Gracie. I don't knaw what got into me. I can only blame the menopause. I just didn't seem to think straight when it were at its peak. All that sweating drained me, me nerves felt on edge. I just sought the easy way out for me, and didn't have the energy to think about others.'

'Oh, Peggy, as long as you truly believe me now, that will make up for it all.'

'I do ... I did, I – I...'

'Let's put it behind us then, eh?'

'You've more than made up for it by having me and me babbies back here and giving us a chance at making a new life.'

It felt good to hold Peggy. Really hold her with all the love that flowed between them – a love that had been caged by untruths and lack of trust.

'I've got another letter for you, lass.' Peggy came out of the embrace, wiping her tears away with her sleeve. 'It's from Sheila, and was inside mine. Eeh, I miss her. And I so want to be with her for the birth of me little grandbabby.'

'Well, then, you must. I can take over here with Aggie to help me. You and Bertram take yourselves down to Kent and be with Sheila, it's only right that you should be.'

'Really? You'd do that for me? Eeh, Gracie, it were a good day when you walked through that door. We've had a blip, but we're back on track now, ain't we?'

'We have been for a long time, Peggy. I never stopped loving you, you knaw that. And, yes, I'd love to pay you back all the kindness that you've shown me by helping you to be with Sheila. It'd put me mind at rest an' all to knaw as she had you with her. By, I wished that I could have it for her. She don't knaw what she's in for.'

'Oh, I don't knaw. You weren't quiet about it all. She heard you screaming like a banshee, so she must have a good idea.'

'Ha! I did, didn't I? Eeh, I've brought some trouble to your door, Peggy, it's a wonder you opened it to me again. But I'll not get into owt like that again, I promise. I'll hardly venture from here, but for taking me babbies for a walk. Oh, and I can do the queueing for the supplies an' all, I don't want you out in all weathers.'

'We're going to rub along all right, lass. We allus did and we will again. And, as soon as I can, I'll allocate the room as Jeannie used to have to you, and you can start to get the girls in there so you can have a room to yourself.'

'When do the lads go home then?'

'The mothers will start to come for them any day now. They're just waiting for railway passes. Though, Alec, poor lad, will have to go home on his own. His ma ain't been well since she lost her man. He has to be the man of the house when he gets home.'

'Bless him. Did he ever find out where his sister went?'

'Aye, she's in the Norfolk countryside. He wants her home, but I reckon as she should stay there; it's still not safe in the big cities. Alec is old enough to bear it now, but she's only a nipper of around five or six.'

'We're lucky here in Blackpool. Despite all that would be achieved by wiping us out, Hitler don't send owt our way.'

'Well, let's hope as they don't win, because rumour has it that he's keeping Blackpool intact as he wants it to be the Germans' playground once he invades.'

'He'll never do that, not with how our boys fight him off, he won't.'

'And women. Don't forget what role the women are taking. They've stepped up, and doing a grand job. I'm proud of them all. And you, with your charity work.'

'I enjoyed that. It made me feel that I was doing my bit. Dot's taken it over now. Best thing for her, throwing herself into organising sommat. She's got a barn for all the stock, and at naw cost an' all. A farmer as used to do removals on his cart let her have it. I said as I would try to help when I can, but they all understood that I had to make a life for me and me bairns.'

'Right. I'm to get this laundry up to Aggie, she's changing beds on the top floor today. I'll leave you to your letter. Lads'll be in soon from school. I just don't knaw where the day goes. Before I knaw it, I'll have them rowdy soldiers back here wanting their dinner!'

When Peggy had left the kitchen, Gracie sat down next to the fire. Rita and Donna were having an afternoon nap, a time she loved as it gave her space for others and for herself. Donna had settled well now, and was much easier to get into a routine. Rita hadn't yet missed her da. She was used to him being away. She did occasionally say 'da-da' in a questioning way as if he had suddenly come into her mind. Two months was a long time for her not to have seen Reggie, but she was soon quietened when Gracie took her attention to something else. She was into everything now that she was walking, and looked more and more like Reggie with her dark hair and eyes. Neither of the girls had Reggie's demanding, must-have nature, and Gracie was glad of that. And they had doting grandparents in Massie and Percy, who collected them every week and took them out, or to their home for the day. Percy had taken to driving Reggie's old car, and that had given them more freedom.

Sheila's letter was full of her condolences for Gracie.

Oh, Gracie. I wish I was there to hold you. You are like a sister to me, and I cannot tell you how much I miss you. Part of me is glad that you are released from that bully, but I couldn't say so in my last letter. All I could do was to try to offer you comfort. Even now, my sadness for you is so deep as I think of your life ahead, a widow with two children, and I feel the pain of your situation.

But, Gracie, it's not too late.

I have done something that you're going to be very cross about. I took it on meself to tell Freddie what had happened to you and why you rejected him, despite you saying that I shouldn't. Forgive me. Please, please forgive me, but I felt really bad knowing and not telling him. His letters were heart wrenching. I have kept them all, and will send them to you, if you want me to.

Gracie broke off from reading. A realisation came to her that her face was wet with tears. She wasn't crying, not consciously – her heart was bleeding tears for her.

If Freddie still loves me, now that he knaws, can I go to him? Will he accept my babbies? Will he accept me, now that he knaws all about me? My past? My marriage, my children? No! It is too much for any man to live with. And, can I do it again? Can I commit to another man? How do I know that all men aren't like me da, the master and Reggie? Naw. Never, never again. I'm going to be me own woman. I don't need a man in me life!

Turning her attention back to the letter, Gracie read on with a clearer head. She was cross with Sheila for telling Freddie, but only because she may have spoiled what Freddie and his fiancée had together.

Freddie said that his heart was breaking at the way you and he had been torn apart, but that now that he knew it was really and truly over, and that you had married, he would go forward with his life.

I wrote to him the moment I heard of Reggie's passing. I haven't heard yet, and delayed writing to you, in the hope that I would receive a letter and have some hope to give to you.

Reading how much Sheila loved her didn't help with how cross Gracie felt at her. *How dare she? Her meddling has opened up sores for me, and will have unsettled Freddie. He had a chance of getting over me with him thinking that I just didn't want him. That I had changed my mind and wasn't prepared to go halfway across the world to be with him. Now, he must think that my love for him didn't die – what am I thinking? It didn't! Oh God, I love him now, just as much as I did, more even, as joined to my love is the ache of missing him. I do miss him so very much.*

Banishing these thoughts, Gracie stood up. *No! Stop this! From now on, I will be a mother to my children, and more than a sister to my darling Bertie. And these roles will fulfil me, and sustain me.*

Going through to the front room, Gracie found paper and pen in the bureau. Sitting at the desk, made by the pull-down lid of the bureau, she penned a letter to Sheila.

Sheila, I am very cross that you told Freddie. Please write to him at once and tell him that my feelings for him, or for any man, are dead. Tell him that I wish him every happiness in the future, and I hope that he will remember me, and us, as we were, and not taint his memory by what has happened. Tell him never to try to contact me, that my life is going to be devoted to my children and their futures.

I forgive you, Sheila, but am relying on you to put this right for me and for Freddie, so that we can both carve out a future for ourselves.

Love you very much (you interfering old busy-body)

Gracie x

The sigh released when she stood gave a finality to it all. It was over – well and truly over. Straightening her shoulders, Gracie walked through to the hall and up the stairs to check on her little girls.

Before Gracie knew it, Christmas was on them. The queue at the butcher's, on the day before Christmas Eve, stretched all along South King Street and spilled into Church Street. Gracie could see that there were at least twenty in front of her and was worried as to what would be left for her to take back home to the boarding house. There was to be about as many to feed there as there was in the queue. But that would be helped by the rations provided for the soldiers. Still, though, they needed something extra for the family, and for Jeannie and David, and Peggy and Bertram. Sadly, Sheila couldn't make it as not only was she near her time, but Bob would be working for most of the Christmas period.

Stamping her feet to keep warm, and pulling her scarf around her ears, Gracie wished that, just for once, there would not be this need to queue, but she had to admire the Brits. They knew how to do it, and kept cheerful while they did.

Suddenly, the air filled with the sound of 'Silent Night'. The Sally Army band, made up of very old men and a few old ladies, had struck up.

The lady in front of Gracie began to sing. And soon everyone was joining in with the lovely carol. There were more than a few tears shed during the rendition, and yet an uplifting feeling could be detected at the end of it as all cheered to the sound of the collection tins being rattled. No one refused to part with a coin or two.

The dining room looked lovely. Holly draped with tinsel hung from every wall lamp and the mirror over the fire. A tree sparkled in the corner near to the window, laden with baubles and more tinsel.

Dinner was a lively affair, with plenty to eat for everyone. Gracie had managed to buy a leg of lamb – not from the butcher, but from a black market tout who had beckoned to her from the queue. A small amount of guilt had entered her at doing so, but now, as she watched her family and the young soldiers tucking in, it left her completely.

After dinner, they tuned the crackling wireless into the King's speech. His hesitant tones always moved everyone. Far from ridiculing him, they all loved him the more for his impediment, and the way that he bravely spoke to them:

War brings, among other sorrows, the sadness of separation. There are many in the Forces away from their homes today because they must stand ready and alert to resist the invader should he dare to come, or because they are guarding the dark seas or pursuing the beaten foe in the Libyan Desert.
Many family circles are broken…

His words drew more than a few tears from everyone, including the soldiers, whose usual manner was one of bravado and joviality. A rousing cheer went up at the end of the speech, and a toast to King and country, made with glasses of sherry, gave a patriotic feel.

Everyone helped with the clearing away, and tables and chairs were put around the walls, leaving the floor clear in the middle. The room settled into groups, cosily chatting. Gracie took this time to catch up with Jeannie. She was so happy to have her there. Life and all they had to contend with had kept them apart for too long.

David was a much more relaxed chap these days, different altogether, in fact. He no longer spouted optical facts to all and sundry, something that Jeannie said had been due to his nerves, and being out of his depth around women. He'd stuck to talking about what he knew and hadn't realised how boring it was to others. Today he even tried the odd joke, though most fell flat. Gracie found herself warming to him and no longer wanting to ridicule him. Bertie loved him, and hung on his every word.

Bertie was coping well without Alec, his special pal. Having Gracie back with him had helped him. She smiled as she looked over at him playing with the skeleton that David had bought for him. David was showing him all the parts of the body. Apparently, the skeleton was a male, though it had no bits to show that.

The room just happened to go quiet at the wrong moment. David's voice sounded loud and clear. 'Now, you know, Bertie, what extra parts a man has, as you have them yourself. Now, a woman…'

Three of the soldiers cheered. 'Go on, David, what's a woman got, then?' It was said as if they didn't believe he knew.

David rose to the challenge. 'Something we all hanker after!'

This brought uproar and a male guffawing that even Bertie joined in with.

'David!' Jeannie looked mortified. 'Not in front of the children!'

'Sorry, darling.'

Jeannie gave an impish smile that changed her face. David's relief that she wasn't really cross with him showed in his expression, but David being David, he went back to his lesson, oblivious to the embarrassment he might cause.

Peggy saved the day. She had been winding the gramophone up, and now Glenn Miller's uplifting song, 'Pennsylvania 6-5000' blared out. The soldiers began to dance. One caught hold of Gracie and swung her around. Excitement filled her as she went into a boogie with him as if she'd danced it all her life. All stopped when the chorus blared out, and as one they shouted, 'PENNSYLVANIA 6-5000!', then laughed and clapped as if they were all children.

Even Jeannie and David danced, and David showed that he was no novice, to the point where everyone stood around him and clapped him as he took centre stage. Gracie was amazed. It came to her that the old saying of 'don't judge a book by its cover' was so true where he was concerned.

In no time, it all seemed like a distant memory as the winter bit deep and the shortages worsened, and Peggy and Bertram set off in February to be with Sheila.

'I can hardly make a stew to go around them all, Aggie,' said Gracie. 'I've doctored it with lentils, and baked some loaves of crusty bread, but I couldn't get any tatties or swede at the market this morning. I don't seem to have owt of substance to feed everyone with.'

'Well, it is simple. Peggy just placed an order with the chippy on such days. Then Ron went to collect them just before tea. The soldiers love them and it is that they go well with anything, even stew.'

'Oh, I never thought of that. I'll see what money I've got in that purse that Peggy left.'

'And I go and queue early in morning,' said Aggie. 'I see what I can get. Make sure you keep plenty of stew for Rita and for yourself. You need strength. Though you will have to give up breast-feeding soon. Donna is five months old now, she take all of goodness out of you.'

'Yes, I'm not producing much at all now, but I have my milk coupons and give her a milk powder substitute. I even put some rusk in her bottle, though I knaw as it's a bit soon for her, she's such a hungry little thing.'

'Alina was like that, then went through time when she did not want to eat. I think she lived off baby fat. They are all different, even sisters.'

'Eeh, you can say that again.'

When the news came through that Sheila had given birth to a healthy baby boy, Gracie felt the pain of not being able to acknowledge her own son. It was a physical pain and sent her running for the loo.

Wiping her mouth of the nasty-tasting vomit, a dread set up inside her. *Naw, Naw, don't let Reggie have left me with me belly up. I can't take it. I can't. Please let this just be a stomach upset.*

By the time Peggy came home, Gracie knew for certain, as the scant bleeding that she had experienced didn't appear again. *But why should I have lost any blood at all? That can't be right. I shouldn't have seen owt, not even a spotting.*

Telling Peggy proved something that Gracie couldn't face. Afraid of her condemnation, she decided to keep her pregnancy secret for as long as she could. *I can't bear having Peggy upset with me after all she has done.* Neither could she bear to face the future with yet another babby to feed and care for, but somehow, she would. Somehow, she'd get through this as she had done with everything that had been thrown at her.

CHAPTER THIRTY-FIVE

By May, Gracie couldn't hide her pregnancy any longer.

Peggy stood with her arms crossed over her chest, leaning against the sink. 'When were you going to tell me, then?'

'Oh, Peggy, I'm sorry. Please don't be cross. I used the protection, I did. But Reggie was dead against it, and the night before he – he died, I – I had no choice.'

'Well, we all knaw what he were like...'

'Naw, it weren't like that. If it had been, I could have fought, but he was different, loving and gentle, and I just couldn't go against his wishes. I didn't want to upset him. I'm glad an' all. Not about having another babby, but that his last night but one on earth was the best that it could be, despite what he put me through for the years before that.'

'Aye, well, men try all different tactics. But the fact is as this has left you in the cart again. Eeh, Gracie. You least deserved all of this. Why it keeps happening to you, I'll never knaw. Well, we've to get on with it.'

'I have, and me business is going to be the last thing that suffers. I'm doing well.'

'But you take a risk, lass. Can't you find some legit customers? They say as the bobbies are determined to break the black market gang. You could go to prison.'

'I knaw. As it happens, I'm seeing a bloke today. He has a chain of shops across Morecambe and Southport, and even in Wales. It were his Welsh one that put him onto me. That was what that letter was that went to me old shop, the one that Jeannie brought round for me. He's taken over one of the shops which I used to supply and found an old invoice with me name on it. He wants to talk to see if I can supply him as he says that the big boys are pricing him out.'

'Well, fingers crossed on that, then. Are you thinking that you'd take another shop?'

411

'Naw. If owt, it would be premises where I could produce more and more rock as I can see a boom happening once the war is over. Folk are going to want to get back to how things were.'

Gracie could have jumped through hoops when she left Mr Starkey. A gentleman, and an astute businessman, he had found her fascinating and hung on her every word as she told him how she produced the rock. So much so, that he told her he was looking for a number of small businesses to invest in as he saw them as the ones set to grow, when peace finally came. Costs and trying to keep a labour force who were constantly being taken to war was hampering the larger manufacturers.

'You do a good job for me, miss, and I'll be looking to invest in you. That factory that you told me that you're interested in obtaining in the future could come to fruition with my money behind you. In the meantime, I'm going to give you an order, and if you fulfil it and on time, and the quality is as I ask for, then I'll be having talks with you about your expansion.'

His order was huge and Gracie was glad that the touts hadn't called on her lately, as this meant that she had a stockpile. But with just three weeks to have the order ready, she had to work her socks off. Getting the sugar was going to be the problem, and would mean finding a supply, black market or not. She would get it somehow.

Using the touts to get supplies of sugar served a purpose, as it kept them off her back. As she pointed out to them, she was now giving *them* business, rather than the other way round. She felt safer doing this, for as much as buying from touts was frowned upon, prosecuting buyers was more difficult unless they were caught red handed, and it would mean that all the gentry in the land would have to come up in front of the magistrates, as they were the tout's biggest customers. Whereas supplying the black market was a much more serious offence.

Everything went well, and more orders came in. So much so that by June, Gracie was able to take on help. She found a gem in Pete. An experienced sugar boiler, he'd retired but wanted to keep his hand in and do a few hours work a week. Pete was a tonic, and could turn out far more than she could, and in less time.

Twice today, he'd had to help her with a task that she could usually do on her own. This time it was lifting the lump onto the machine to pull it.

'Why don't you leave this to me, lass, and go and put your feet up? You look all in.'

'I'm feeling it, an' all, Pete. Babby's due any time, and I'm struggling with me own lump, let alone a lump of toffee.'

In the kitchen, Gracie felt as though she was going to pass out. The heat in the shed was enough to bake you, but in here Peggy had been baking bread and had her two ovens on to prove them. Gracie just made it to the chair as her heavy body sagged.

At the same moment, her pants soaked and she knew her waters had broken. 'Peggy! Peggy!'

'What is it? Oh, Gracie, what is happening?'

'I think babby's on the way, Aggie. Fetch Peggy. Hurry!'

Peggy's exclamation of 'Oh, dear God!' held a fear Gracie had never heard her express at a babby about to come into the world. Gracie looked down. A pool of blood had formed at her feet. 'Oh, Peggy, what's happening to me? Me babby. Naw! Don't let me lose me babby.'

'All right, me lass, don't take on as that won't help matters. Aggie, get Bertie to run for the doctor, and tell him to be quick. Lock the kitchen door so that he can't come barging in, and keep the key with you so you can determine who does come in.'

Aggie didn't question any of this and was gone in a flash.

'Now, Gracie, are you having pains, lass?'

'Naw ... oooh, yes! Oooh, Peggy, Peggy, I need to push!'

'Naw, lass. Naw.'

But Gracie couldn't stop the urge. She sidled forwards and pushed with all her might. Her babby shot out and down the leg of her knickers. Peggy moved like a football player and caught the child before the floor did.

Gracie waited. The silence was broken only by Peggy's urgent pleas. 'Breathe little man, breathe.' Gracie watched in horror as Peggy slapped and shook the limp form, to no avail. Her prayers tumbled over each other as she begged and begged God to let her child live. But despite everything Peggy tried, he didn't respond.

Gracie's cry of agony was wrenched from her. 'Naw! NAW!'

The door bursting open stopped her as seeing the doctor gave her hope. 'Help him, Doctor, please, please help him!'

The doctor knelt down to where Peggy had laid the babby while she tried to revive it. Gracie could see his head shaking. 'Do sommat!' she shouted. 'Do sommat, Doctor, please, do sommat.'

The doctor rose. 'I'm sorry, lass. The poor little mite was born dead. He must have died in the womb. He has signs that his development stopped some time ago. I'm truly sorry, but now we must concentrate on you. You have to be cleaned out or you could get peritonitis. I'm going to need you on the table.' Turning to Peggy and Aggie, he barked out instructions to scrub the table down, and then to cover it with a clean sheet. On top of that he wanted layers of newspaper and then clean towels. 'And have boiling water to hand quickly, I need plenty of boiling water!'

Once Gracie was lying on the table the doctor examined her, before telling her that he was going to put her to sleep. 'Then, I'm going to do all that I can to stop you getting an infection from anything that might be left inside of you.'

When Gracie came around, she was in a hospital bed. A sea of faces surrounded her – loved faces, Ma- and Da-in-law, Peggy, and Bertram, and Jeannie.

'Me babby? What happened to me babby?'

Ma's face told it wasn't good news, on a sob, she said, 'Eeh, me lass, his body is in the morgue here. But, Gracie, lass, you have to remember that he never lived, so...'

'What? What are you saying, Ma?'

Massie looked down. A tear plopped onto her

nose and ran down to the end before it dripped off.

'Ma?'

Peggy stepped forward. 'Little lad cannot be registered as a birth. He was stillborn and therefore he cannot be buried. I'm so sorry, lass.'

'Oh God, Peggy, what will happen to him?'

'I don't knaw, lass, but they told us that his body won't be released to you. I'm sorry, me darlin'.'

'They can't do that! They can't. He's mine, he's mine!'

'Now, now, what's all this?'

A huge nurse came over. She wasn't fat, but just big in every way. Her head was big and her shoulders were broad. Her bosom stuck out almost a foot in front of her, and she must have been six foot tall.

'My babby. They're saying that I can't have me babby. I want to bury him, proper, but–'

'Honey, you can't do that. Not with your baby's body you can't, but you can do something that will help doctors in the future to help other babbies. You see, there can be no burial as there hasn't been a person. I know it is difficult to understand. But your darling child can be of use to the medical researchers to find out what went wrong, and how they can prevent this occurring for another poor child and mother. Now, I know it is a lot to ask of you, but if you agree, your child won't have been in vain. He will have given a great service to future babies, do you understand?'

Gracie was quiet for a moment, but then an understanding did come to her. 'Aye. I does.'

'Good girl. And, if you give your permission, then you can say that you had a little saint, a pioneer. But you know, even if you can't bury him, you can name him. You can find a nice spot in your garden, or in a park, and put something there in memory of him.'

All of this made sense to Gracie. She had to accept that the law was the law, and a child who hadn't taken a breath, even though he'd lived in the womb for months, wasn't a human being in the eyes of the law. But she would name him, and she would find somewhere to honour the life he'd had inside of her. 'I'm going to name him Reginald Percy, and hope that his soul has gone to be with his da.'

For this last bit, Gracie crossed her fingers against the lie that it was, as she was sure that Reggie would have gone to hell, and her babby's soul wouldn't join him there. But it was for Massie and Percy that she'd said it. They both smiled at her now.

'Ta, lass.' Percy wiped away a tear. 'That means a lot. We could do a little patch of our garden for him; how would that be? I can keep it tended and we could have one of those angel statues there, and it's somewhere that you can come whenever you want to.'

'That'll be grand, Da. And you're good at carving, so we could get a nice bit of wood and carve his name into it, eh? And I can have another one done, and place it on me Ma and Da's grave, in memory of him, as I reckon me ma will be holding him, an all.'

'We can, lass. We can that. And, for me, I'd like

to think as his body is going to help others. It gives him a purpose.'

'Aye. You're right, Da. I'll sign the papers, nurse.'

The sniffles and snuffles told of everyone's heartache, but Gracie suddenly felt strong, and as if she hadn't been through almost nine months of carrying her child for nothing, but had given something for the future.

Going home was more painful than she had imagined it would be. Sheila had stayed on for a while after visiting her in hospital, to help her to settle, but that meant meeting her little boy for the first time, when everything was still so very raw for her.

Little Stuart was the image of his dad. Sandy haired and brown eyed, he had the same mischievousness about him. Gracie adored him from the moment she picked him up and he chuckled at her, raising his hand as if in a gesture of comfort.

'He's gorgeous, Sheila. How did you manage that!'

'Ha! Cheeky.'

They had fallen into being sisters again, and any awkwardness had gone. Without warning, Sheila put her arms around Gracie and her child. 'Eeh, me happy world's complete having you both together like this, me best friend – well, sister, really, and me babby. I never knew that anyone could feel so happy.'

As they sat at the kitchen table, which she'd been assured had been scrubbed fifty times or more since she'd been laid on it, they fell into an easy banter. 'Seriously though, how is life down in the south? Are you looked on as some sort of freak from the north, or sommat?'

'Naw, not at all. There's a war on don't forget, and folk from all over are finding themselves in places they never thought they would. In the countryside we've got land girls from every corner of Britain. And girls working at Bletchley billeted with families in our street that are also from far and wide. Everyone accepts everyone, and there's an attitude of, "We're all in this together." But, oh, Gracie, when Bob took me to London, I cried me eyes out. It's near flattened, and folk are in a poor way. Homeless are everywhere, some are living in the Underground stations, others camping out on the side of the road. Soup kitchens are everywhere, an' all. It's devastating to see. You've all been so lucky up here.'

'Aye, we have. But we've done our bit.' Gracie told Sheila about the charity she had started.

'Eeh, that's grand. I'm proud of you. And now you have a right good little business going again. I helped Pete yesterday. He's a grand fellow. He was worried about finishing a batch so that it could be shipped to Morecambe, so I did the wrapping and packing. It felt like old times.'

'We'll never have them times back now, lass. They were good days, weren't they?'

'Aye, they were. But we can have better times, thou knaws... Gracie, I've sommat to tell you. I – I heard from Freddie. He broke off with his girl just as soon as he heard about Reggie. He wants to write to you, Gracie.'

Gracie felt her heart lurch. 'You mean, after all he knaws about me, he still wants to knaw me?'

'Aye, he does. He begged me to beg you to let

419

him write. He said to tell you that there'll be no strings attached and he won't push you into owt you don't want, but well, he just wants to write, that's all.'

Gracie wanted to scream out that, yes! Yes! Yes! He could write and that she would write back, an' all. But she just said, 'All right. Aye, if he wants to write that would be nice.'

'Oh, Gracie ... Gracie! That's wonderful, wonderful. I'm a happy, happy bunny!'

Little Stuart's face spread out into a wide grin. 'Ha, he looks like you asked him to persuade me an' all. He looks like a cat with cream as if he's won a victory, or sommat.'

'We have. We've won a victory on behalf of a smashing bloke, who didn't deserve to be treated how you've treated him, Gracie. He's been ill with pining for you. He suffers ulcers, and may be medically discharged in the near future.'

'Oh ... I – I ... I mean, there was nowt I could do. Nowt. I couldn't land him with a babby that wasn't his, it wouldn't have been fair.'

'You should have let him be the judge of that. He's man enough to have coped with that. He didn't deserve you just dropping him like a ton of bricks with naw explanation. You broke his heart.'

Gracie felt the shame of her action deep in her heart. Sheila was right, she should have been honest with Freddie. She should have given him the chance. But she'd been so hurt. So damaged by most men that she'd come into contact with, that she'd been unable to think straight.

'Does he knaw as I now have two babbies, besides the one I told him about?' Under her

420

breath, Gracie mouthed Bertie's name.

'Aye, he does, but he don't care. He said if only you would just write to him and give him some hope, then his world would fit back together again.'

'Oh, Freddie, Freddie. Oh God. I've been a fool, Sheila. A bloody fool, but I'll make it up to him, if he'll have me, Sheila, I will.'

'Oh, he'll have you all right.'

Gracie's heart soared. Could it be true? Really, really true? Could she at last find happiness with her Freddie?

EPILOGUE

PICKING UP THE PIECES

1945

Gracie added the latest letter to the bundle tied with a pink ribbon. Freddie was coming home. At last! Four years after they had begun to write to each other.

The letters had been friendly at first. Catching up with one another, helping hurts to heal. Freddie's health had gradually improved and he was able to give of his all to his job once more.

Gracie had thrown herself into her work and was now a partner in Rimmer's Rock Company of Blackpool, and a majority shareholder. Mr Starkey had kept his promise, and it was he who had attained the building in Coronation Street, Blackpool, and set it all up. They employed ten sugar boilers and four packers. Pete was still with Gracie, and worked as a manager and advisor. Business was booming, and set to do even better as the war finally ended in victory.

Life would be wonderful, if it wasn't for Peggy's illness. Peggy had cancer of the stomach, and it was breaking the hearts of the family to see her fading, slowly and painfully.

Locking her bundle of letters into the office safe, it was to Pete that Gracie now turned more and more. 'I have to go early again, Pete. Jeannie can only stay with Peggy for the morning, and Aggie can't take over as she has to fetch the children from school. They all have to go to the clinic for treatment for the head lice they picked up. There's an epidemic amongst young uns.'

'It's not a problem. My Margaret expects me to be late home these days, she says it's as bad now as before I retired! I laughed at that one. "When did I retire then, darling?" I asked her, and—'

'Sorry, Pete, I've got to go. Lock up for me, won't you? And I'll make it up to you and to Margaret one of these days. I will.'

With this, Gracie dashed out to her car. She loved her Austin Healey, and felt like a princess when she drove it, though she tried to avoid doing so as much as possible as petrol was still in short supply, even though the war was won.

Back at the boarding house, a silence that was deeper than usual put a fear into Gracie. Bertram met her. Tears ran down his cheeks. 'She's going, lass. Me Peggy's going.'

'Awe, naw. Dear God!'

Taking the stairs two at a time, Gracie rushed into Peggy's bedroom. Peggy lay with her eyes closed. The little flesh left on her face sank around her cheekbones. Her mouth had flopped open. 'Peggy, Peggy, lass, I'm here. Gracie's here.'

'G – Gra...'

'Don't try to talk, me darling. Rest. I'll get sommat to wet your lips with.'

Coming back from the bathroom with a sponge, Gracie dampened Peggy's blackened lips. 'There you go, me darling, Peggy.'

'Bertie... T – e – ll him. Ta – ke him.'

'Awe, Peggy, I'll take care of him, I promise. He's a fine twelve-year-old, and you've made him what he is, me lass. He's a credit to you. Thank you, Peggy. Thank you, for looking after me son.'

Peggy smiled. 'Bert ... me Bert.'

'I'm here, me darling girl. Your Bertram's here.' Bertram stepped forward. He sat on the side of the bed, and then swung his legs over and lay beside Peggy. 'D'yer remember song as I used to sing to you, Peggy?'

In soft tones, Bertram began to sing. His voice was beautiful as he changed the words of 'Daisy, Daisy' to 'Peggy, Peggy, give me your answer do...'

He'd just finished 'all for the love of you' when Peggy sighed heavily, and didn't take another breath back in. Reggie carried on singing. His tears ran into his mouth, but he kept the tune and the words in perfect accord. When he came to the end, he held Peggy's body to him and sobbed.

Going to him, Gracie gently guided him off the

bed. 'We have to lay her flat, Bertram. We have to do things right for her.'

'Aye, lass. As far as she could, she did everything right for everybody. We have to do the same for her, as you say.'

After the undertakers had taken Peggy's body away, Bertram said he needed to go for a walk. He never came back. His body was washed up on Southport Beach four days later.

They stood as a family around the double grave and watched as Bertram was lowered in first, and Peggy's coffin was placed on top of his. At this point Gracie felt a hand come into hers, and she looked down into the face of her son. His was awash with tears and Gracie pulled him to her.

When she looked up she could see Sheila with Bob by her side. Her heart was broken, and that agony showed on her face. Next to her stood Jeannie and David, now man and wife of two years, but as yet with no children. Both of them were crying. Aggie was next with Ron – a distant, strange fellow, not a bit like his sister, but who now had lost all his stiffness and was leant on his tiny wife, his grief evident.

Gracie couldn't cry. It was all too sad for her to cry. She had done – she'd cried buckets into her pillow when alone at night. But today they all needed her to be strong, and she was.

The handfuls of earth hitting Peggy's coffin resounded around Gracie. Her mind went back over the years to when she'd taken a handful and dropped it on to her ma's coffin. She hadn't wanted to do it, but her Aunt Massie had said she must, that it was a way of showing your last respects and helping to make the last resting place for the body.

So much sadness, so much.

As one by one the mourners left the grave, Gracie stayed. She held on to Bertie's hand. Sheila looked over and nodded, as did Jeannie. When at last they were alone, Gracie said Bertie's name.

He looked up at her. The sun shone onto his red hair, as she imagined it did on hers. But at that moment, she couldn't tell him who he really was, as they'd all said she should. She'd let him get over his grief a while, first. 'Bertie, you will allus have a home with me, lad. You're not to worry. We'll stay on at the boarding house for the time being, but Aggie and Ron are going to run that business. They'll take the lease over. Then, when my Freddie gets home, we will be married, and have a home of our own, and that will be your home an' all.'

Bertie reacted by hugging her waist. His sobs undid him, and at that moment, Gracie knew she'd done the right thing in not telling him yet.

'Come on, me lad. Let's get home and start the wake. We have that to do. It's a better time than you've been through here. Everyone will eat and be jolly and we'll all feel better.'

'Are you sure as Freddie will want me, Gracie?'

'I am, lad. He knaws as we come as a package, me and you and me girls. We're a family that he is joining, and we're to make him feel that we want him. It's not going to be easy for him to take us all on, thou knaws.'

'Naw, it would be difficult. But I'll make a

friend of him. I'm going to need to, living with all you lasses. Me and him'll be mates, and stand against you all.'

'Ha! Cheek of you. But I'm glad as you feel like that, Bertie. And I'm glad as you want to stay with me.'

'I'll allus want to stay with you, Gracie. I've told you before, only never tell Sheila, but I feel more close to you than I do her. I love her and miss her when she ain't home, but I feel sommat's different about us two.'

They had reached the cemetery gate. Gracie stood still. Was now her time? Would there be a better time? *Naw. I'll wait.* Instead, she hugged her son to her, and allowed herself the happiness she felt at his expression of his love for her.

Life began to slowly get back to a routine – different one to the one they had known, but one within which they all functioned. There was very little merriment; mostly the boarding house wasn't a home, as it had been, but somewhere to be that they were familiar with.

But at last the day came when Freddie was arriving. Gracie was a bag of nerves as she prepared to leave her girls with Massie and Percy.

'Eeh, give over, Gracie. You've combed poor Rita's hair a dozen times now, and that ribbon in Donna's hair has been tied and untied I don't knaw how many times.'

Gracie laughed at Massie. 'I knaw, Ma, I'm just nervous. Suppose I look different to me photo that I sent him. What if he finds that he doesn't love me after all?'

426

Massie was quiet for a moment. Then what she said shocked Gracie. 'Did you never love me lad, Gracie?'

'Eeh, Ma, what's brought that on?'

'Well, I knaw as you were going with this chap before Reggie. And it seems to me that you loved him then and have never stopped.'

'I – I, oh, Ma, what happened, happened. Let's let it lie where it should, eh?'

'I don't blame you, you knaw. I knaw what our Reggie was. I just tried to shield him, that's all. We all did wrong by you, Gracie. And yet you still offer us love. I want to say that I'm sorry. I knaw Percy is an' all. What you've been through has been as much our fault as anyone's.'

'Ta, Ma, that means a lot to me. To have people I love believe me, and you in particular, is all the world to me. I never asked for any of it, never!'

'Eeh, lass. How can you ever forgive us?'

'I did a long time ago. Now, give over, you're making the children worry.' Bending down and kissing first Rita and then Donna, Gracie went to leave the house.

Massie followed her. 'Have you told Bertie, yet?'

Gracie was taken aback. 'You knaw?'

'Aye, I've known for years. Peggy told me.'

'Oh?'

'Knawing adds to me burden, that such a thing should have happened to you, and all because me and Percy wouldn't take you in.'

'Please, Ma, it's in the past. I told you afore, there were reasons that you didn't, and I understood. Now, let's put it behind us. And yes, I have told Bertie.'

'How did he take it?'

'He's still coming to terms with it. He says that he's happy about it and allus knew we were more connected than everyone said, but it's all new to him, so I'm unsure.'

'Will he be in later?'

'Aye, I reckon. Now, I must go. I'll be back in a couple of days. You'll be all right with the girls, won't you? Bertie will stay with Aggie at the boarding house, but I'm sure he'll call in to see the girls on his way from school.'

Massie stood at the door with Rita and Donna, and they all waved Gracie off. Gracie wished that she could have seen Bertie. He'd been strange since she'd told him that she was his real ma. Happy at first, but then very quiet.

Arriving at North Shore station, Gracie looked up at the clock. There was still half an hour till her train, which would take her to Preston. From there she would catch a train to Liverpool, where Freddie would be waiting for her. He'd docked there over a week ago and was now, at last, on leave. They had booked into a hotel and were to spend two days and three nights together. Gracie felt her stomach clench at the thought.

'Ma!'

The voice sounded familiar, but Gracie didn't think that it was addressed to her.

'Gracie! Ma!'

Turning, Gracie saw Bertie coming towards her. His face was lit with the smile she adored. 'I thought I'd try out your new name, but you didn't answer to it.'

Bertie grinned, and Gracie laughed out loud at

him. 'Eeh, lad. Come here.' They were in each other's arms, hugging like they had never hugged before. 'Me lad, me son. Eeh, I love you, me Bertie.'

'Eeh, Ma, gerroff, you're making me all soppy and embarrassing me.'

Gracie laughed again at this, and before they knew it they were giggling together like a pair of nippers.

'I don't want to leave you now, son.'

'I knaw. I feel the same, but you've to go and to find your man.'

'That's grown-up talk for a young man.'

'Aunt Aggie told me your story, Ma. She told it me all as she thought it would help me, and it did. I never want you to be unhappy again, and Aunt Aggie said that if you thought that I was upset, or didn't want you to go to your Freddie, then your happiness wouldn't be complete. I want you to be happy, Ma. I want Freddie to make you the happiest you've ever been.'

'He will, Bertie, he will. I'll see you when I get back, and then we'll begin our new life, and live it the way we should allus have, as mother and son.'

Tears welled in Bertie's eyes. He hugged her once more, then turned abruptly and left.

Freddie stood on the platform of Liverpool Lime Street station with his arms open, as she emerged from the train. He looked beautiful. And she knew that he was. A beautiful man that she loved with all her heart.

In his arms, Gracie found her peace – found

herself, and a completion of who she was. They had a long road to travel, but they would do that together. Freddie's strength and love would help her.

A Letter from Maggie

Dear Reader

I hope you have enjoyed *Blackpool Lass.*

I live in Blackpool and have done for the most part of thirty-three years. It is a lovely place to live.

Peopled by a cosmopolitan population, who all bring something to Britain's most popular seaside resort, Blackpool is both lively, exciting, and has the best lights show on earth as well as being steeped in history. Oh, and the best neighbours, as a community spirit still exists on its many housing estates.

In my novel, I have tried to bring all of Blackpool's many sides alive. Especially as it was during the war.

Blackpool had a good war. Which was very surprising given that the town had much going on, and, if targeted, could have greatly affected the outcome of the conflict. But, as it has now been documented, Hitler intended to invade Blackpool on his victory; and make the town a playground for the German hierarchy, so he didn't want it destroyed.

If your journey with Gracie, Sheila and Jeannie touched your heart, and had you turning the pages, would you be kind enough to please leave me a review? A review is like a hug to an author. It doesn't have to be a long, detailed insight to the book, just a short 'I enjoyed this book', or 'It kept me turning the pages'. Something like this is so much appreciated.

I also want to invite you to interact with me. I would love to hear from you. You can write to me by email: marywood@authornmarywood.com; join me on Facebook: www.facebook.com/HistoricalNovels; tweet me: @Authormary or visit my website www.authormarywood.com where you can read first chapters of all my novels, and much more, and, if you wish, subscribe to my newsletter. You can also friend and follow me on Goodreads https://wwwgoodreads.com/author/list/ 4336970.Mary_Wood. I hold many competitions for my followers to win personally signed books and other prizes.

I would love to get to know you. To hear your own stories, and to generally chat about everything and anything.

For the connection between Maggie and Mary, please read my bio in the front of the book.

Much love to all,

Maggie x

ACKNOWLEDGEMENTS

Thank you to my agent Judith Murdoch, for your encouragement, and much, much more. You work very hard for your authors, and I am proud to be two of them – Maggie Mason and Mary Wood. With you by my side, I know I will succeed.

No author is anything without her editor(s). And I am blessed to be looked after at Sphere by the lovely Maddie West and her team. I love that you 'get' my work, and are sensitive to my voice when carrying out edits. Thank you for your faith in me. I am encouraged and grateful.

In my career, I have many who have taken various roles to help me and who contributed in my self-publishing days – cover designs, and edits – you helped to make me the author I am today: Christine Martin, James Wood, Julie Hitchen, the late and much missed Stan Livingston, Patrick Fox, and Rebecca Keys deserve a special mention. Thank you. But this list can never be exhaustive as there are many family and friends who have helped me along the way. Thank you all.

Special mention and thanks to James Wood, who has read umpteen versions of this book and gave me very valuable advice and help with his special editing skills.

And lastly, but most importantly, I would like to

thank my family. My darling husband Roy, who takes care of me and has, bless him, taken over all the household chores, and cooks delicious meals for me, so that I can dedicate my time to my writing. This year we celebrate our Emerald Wedding Anniversary. Happy Anniversary, Sweetheart. Our love is eternal.

My daughters, Christine, Julie, and Rachel, and my son James, and all my grandchildren and great grandchildren. You are all a source of love, support and encouragement, and put up with my crazy ways. I love you all dearly.

And thank you to my lovely Olley and Wood families, all of you encourage me on and I am blessed to have you all in my life. You help me to climb my mountain.

Research for *Blackpool Lass*

I am grateful to the following for writing such interesting and detailed books that guided me in the history of Blackpool:
The Story of Blackpool Rock by Margaret Race
Blackpool at War by John Ellis
Blackpool's Trams by J. Joyce
Blackpool – History Tour by Allan W. Wood & Ted Lightbown
Blackpool's Seaside Heritage by Allan Brodie and Mathew Whitfield

The publishers hope that this book has given you enjoyable reading. Large Print Books are especially designed to be as easy to see and hold as possible. If you wish a catalogue please ask at your local library or write directly to:

Magna Large Print Books
Cawood House,
Asquith Industrial Estate,
Gargrave,
Nr Skipton, North Yorkshire.
BD23 3SE